THE ORPHAN
THE KRAFTEN TRILOGY

TALLBERGS FÖRLAG

TALLBERGS FÖRLAG

First published by Tallbergs Förlag, a publishing house in Sweden.
Sverkersvägen 10, 17754 Järfälla, Sweden

www.tallbergsforlag.se

The Orphan

© Marcus Tallberg
© Elin Frykholm

Original title: Kraften
Cover and interior design by Tallbergs Förlag
"The Kraften Trilogy" logo by rock_0407
Edited by S.V. Teague

ISBN: 978-91-986547-4-5

THIS BOOK IS DEDICATED TO EVERYONE WHO HAS
EXPERIENCED BEING DIFFERENT AND NOT BELONGING

WE ALL HAVE OUR SPECIAL POWERS

PROLOGUE

Thunder crashes in the distance. Apsel sits at his desk and listens to the raindrops hitting the window. Every now and then, the dark skies are illuminated by quick, angry flashes that light up the cornfields outside. It's been a long time since they had a storm like this; the rain will be good for the dry soil. Apsel stops for a moment and tries to remember whether they set up the rain-barrels or not, out on the farm. After thinking about it carefully, he concludes that they did.

A low beep draws Apsel's attention back to what he really should be doing: taking care of the bills. He stares at the screen that emitted the beep. At the bottom right corner of the screen, there are over a dozen reminders that Apsel has been putting off: fix the roof over the front porch, trim Freda's wool, replace some pipes in the kitchen, and so on. It's not easy, maintaining this place all alone. A stack of notifications on his screen all bear the word *BILLS* in glaring red capital letters at the top. Apsel has always made sure to pay them on time, but in the last month it's been challenging to keep up because four of the kids had been sick and all of his energy had gone into taking care of them. He also hadn't gotten a chance to take many trips into Ithmah to sell crops. The monthly stipend and rations from the Authority would be gone soon, and Apsel was forced to take money out of his small pension to keep things running.

Apsel's room isn't big, despite its high ceilings, like most of the other rooms in the house. Just like the others, this room has large beams overhead that double as storage space. There's a ladder that Apsel uses to access various books and boxes that are suspended there, below the roof. This particular room serves as both a study and a bedroom. Along the cracked walls are bookshelves, filing cabinets, a dresser, and two beds. The majority of the room is taken up by odds and ends that don't fit in the office on the other side of the wall that Apsel's bed is pushed up against. He loves the dark, musty scent and the feeling of the cool wall against his forehead, which is especially appreciated on the days when he gets headaches. The room is a little crowded but still fully functional.

Apsel closes his eyes for a moment and draws in a long sigh. When he opens them again, he sees his reflection in the window. His face is illuminated by the wax candles on the desk. He sees the dark shadows under his eyes, the dark hair that's not so dark anymore because of all the gray. The reflection is too blurry to see the wrinkles beginning to form. If he squints and pushes the chair back a little, the image becomes so blurry that he can almost imagine that he's young again. Maybe he should shave so he could at least *feel* young again. Outside the window, the sky suddenly lights up and Apsel can see a flash strike down on the other side of the field.

"That was close!" he bursts out, anxious that the storm will damage the corn. It's a constant worry.

A whimper comes from behind him, and Apsel gets up and walks over to the smaller of the two beds.

"Did the thunder wake you up, little one?" He says softly to the little girl looking up at him from the bed. "Yeah, I can understand that."

He lifts the girl up in his arms. Her curly red hair sticks up wildly in all directions. She is sobbing, but soon calms down and leans her head on Apsel's shoulder. Embla sneaks herself into Apsel's shirt and breathes in the smell of his moth-eaten coat. That scent has always calmed her down, throughout all the years that he has taken care of her. He had adopted her when she was only an infant—after that horrible event.

"Are you scared, Embla?" whispers Apsel. "Nothing's going to hurt you."

Apsel sits down at the desk again with Embla in his arms, but he quickly realizes that he's far too tired to think about numbers and finances anymore tonight. He brings Embla with him while he makes the rounds, checking on the kids in the other rooms, though everyone else seems to be sleeping peacefully. Apsel returns to his room and lays Embla back down in her bed. He's just about to take off his work clothes and go to sleep when he hears a noise. The raindrops are still hitting the window pane and the wind whips around the knotted walls of the house, but he'd heard something else entirely. *Or was it?* An old house like this makes all sorts of noises and sometimes it even seems to have a life of its own. He steps out into the corridor to see if it was one of the children and he hears the sound again, clearer this time.

No one in their right mind would be out in this weather, he thinks. Apsel hesitates, but when he hears a third knock, he goes out into the hall. When he opens the door, he is greeted by the cold wind and stinging rain. But there's someone out there too, someone in a dark coat with the hood raised over their head.

"Can I come in?"

The woman has to make an effort to be heard over the howling wind. Apsel steps aside to let her in. When he closes the door again, he turns to look at the woman. He has a hard time seeing her face under the hood, but her breathing sounds strained.

"Do you want to take off your coat?" he asks her.

The woman looks around as if she's searching for something, then shudders:

"No... No, I'll be leaving soon."

Apsel stands there puzzled for a while. What can this woman possibly want, showing up in the middle of the night like this? Not to mention the storm still raging outside. It's freezing out there and she's clearly soaked to the bone, how is she not hypothermic by now?

"Would you like something to drink then?" he asks her. "A little hot tea before you head out there again?"

"Yes..." says the woman thoughtfully. "Yes, that would be nice."

Apsel shows her into the kitchen, which is next to his room. He checks on Embla and leaves the door open as he lights some candles and boils water in the kettle. The woman stands near the table but doesn't sit down. Water drips from her cloak down to the stone floor.

"Are you sure you don't want to hang up your coat?" Apsel tries again.

The woman looks up at him quickly.

"Sorry ... But this is an orphanage, right?"

"Yes."

"Sethunya Home for Wayward Children?"

"Exactly."

"And you're Apsel Faas, the director?"

"That's right."

The woman lets out a sigh of relief and finally takes a seat on one of the empty chairs at the table. The water is already boiling and Apsel knows that he should just ask her what kind of tea she wants, but instead he sits across from her and clasps his hands in front of him on the table. The boiling water is forgotten. She's about to say something, but then she opens her coat to reveal what she's been hiding in her arms ever since she came in. As the director of an orphanage, Apsel is used to people bringing him children, but it's not often that anyone brings such a young child and this one must be almost new-born.

"Hello, little friend," he hums, caressing the baby's syrupy brown cheek. The child has a luster only a new-born can have, and it smells of wet grass and forest. Its little hand clings desperately to the blanket wrapped around it.

When he looks up again, the woman has taken off her hood. Her lemon-blonde hair sits half up in a tight ball that somehow looks completely untouched, despite the hood and the stormy weather. On her straight, pointed nose rests a pair of rectangular glasses. The bags under her eyes are subtle, barely visible in the dim light of the kitchen, but she has a hard face and is very pale.

"It's a girl," the woman says before Apsel has a chance to say anything else. "Her mother is dead." Suddenly the woman gets up and starts pacing back and forth in the small kitchen. "I've already taken too long…" she mumbles quietly. She stops and turns towards Apsel. "Listen. This baby's mother fled a couple of weeks ago. I helped her escape. Me and… She was already pregnant then, and tonight she gave birth. But her body just couldn't handle it… So much blood…" The woman shakes her head. "Her husband is highly regarded by the President. No one can ever know that this is his daughter. Do you understand?"

Apsel sits there stunned, barely able to take in what the woman is saying as she steps forward and leans across the table towards him.

"This child… She's special."

It's like the whole world is holding its breath. Apsel no longer hears the wind, or the rain, or the gurgling sounds of the baby he holds in his arms. The woman's blue eyes bore into him like sharp needles.

"Special?" Apsel gets up. "You mean... *special?*"

The woman nods and repeats it:

"Special. You know what I mean. I thought this orphanage would be good for her. Your own mother was... Yes, I thought you would be a good person to leave her with."

Apsel doesn't know where to begin. How can this woman, this stranger, know anything about his mother?

"But the baby..." is what he manages to get out, "... she's only a new-born. How can you be so sure...?"

The woman holds up a hand to interrupt him.

"Don't ask me how I know. Just trust me. She must be protected."

Apsel can't find the words to answer, so he just nods in silent agreement. The woman steps back and looks around the room as if she's sizing it up. Her gaze fixes on two paintings hanging on one of the walls. They're portraits of two of Ela's former Presidents. The woman walks over to the pictures, reading the names below them. She nods.

"She'll do well here," the woman says after a moment, more to convince herself than Apsel. She glances over the kitchen one last time. "Here, she can grow up to be anyone."

She walks up to Apsel, leans towards the girl, and gently strokes her cheek. It's as smooth as a freshly picked peach. As the woman comes close, Apsel can smell her wet clothes, soil, and something else ... Blood?

"I have to go now," the woman says as she moves out into the hall.

Apsel hurries after her.

"Wait," he says quickly, and the woman stops herself with one hand already on the doorknob. "Does she have a name?"

In the dim light of the hallway, Apsel thinks he can see the woman wiping away a tear.

"Freija. Her name is Freija. Promise you'll take good care of her. And remember," she takes a step towards Apsel so that her face is very close to his, "I was never here."

He nods. The woman casts one last glance at the child in Apsel's arms before disappearing into the darkness of the raging storm. Apsel returns to the kitchen and sits down at the table again. He is very confused. Sure, people have come knocking, wanting to leave children with him before, but not under these circumstances and certainly not...He lifts up the girl, who opens her dark eyes and stares up at him.

"Well, Freija, is there really something special about you? Don't worry, no one will find you here."

Apsel falls silent and looks around. Suddenly he gets the feeling that someone is watching him, that someone has been listening to his conversation with the woman. Of course not. No one is here, and not a soul is awake except him and little Freija. But you can never know who's listening. Whether it turns out that Freija is special or not, Apsel decides never to mention it again, not to anyone. It will be safer that way.

Somewhere deep in a kitchen drawer, Apsel searches for baby formula to feed Freija. After she's had her fill, he finds a small crib and sets it up in his bedroom between Embla's bed and his own.

"Em-em, when you wake up tomorrow you'll get to meet your new sister," Apsel whispers to Embla and kisses her red curls.

By the time Apsel gets to bed, he realizes that there isn't much time left before the sun rises. It's not every day that he has to take care of a brand-new baby. The last time had been four years ago when Embla came into his life, under the terrible circumstances of what had happened at the oasis. He had decided to raise Embla as his own to protect her from others. It's been tough, but somehow he's managed to make it work. Apsel looks at the two sleeping girls, feeling confident that they'll grow up to become good friends. They already have a few things in common.

He's not worried about Freija being "special." He's used to taking risks. Apsel understands why the woman had to flee with the child. He would have done the same thing if he'd been in her shoes. Especially considering what had happened in the capital, Adali, where several of *them* had lost their lives during a riot last year. It had been all over the news. He's hanging on to the hope that he can protect her from the outside world, but also from herself.

Apsel has already decided to do his best to take care of Freija, but it's essential to think through a decision like this, considering that this is no ordinary child. He has a lot to lose by doing this, but to Apsel—a life is a life. Everyone is equal regardless of their differences.

Eventually, Apsel falls asleep and he dreams of the little girl who has become the latest addition to the orphanage. In his dream, she looks at him and he feels a light shining from within her. By the end, it shines so brightly that he becomes blinded by it. The next morning, Apsel thinks about the strange dream for a while, but soon his hands are full with making sure that all the children wake up, wash, get dressed, and have breakfast.

The dream is quickly forgotten.

1

Hello?

Can you hear me?

I hope so.

Depending on where you're from, maybe you believe that there are endless opportunities in life. That anyone can be anything. And for you, maybe it's true. Maybe you were born into a world where you have everything you need to succeed, to achieve your dreams.

But not me. That's never been the case for me.

Where I grew up, our lives are predetermined for us. Everything is calculated by algorithms starting when we're six years old. For me, there have only ever been a few paths I could take – usually only one – but that doesn't mean that I don't value my life. I've played by the rules of the game set out by the Authority. *The few choices I've made for myself have been based on what I believed was right.*

If I don't play – and win – it will all have been for nothing. Our country will experience another Disaster, and our population will die out or worse: become homeless Wanderers with only a single goal, to find food where there isn't any and protection that doesn't exist. This isn't an exaggeration; it's a reality. No matter how much I wish things were different, the truth is that only I can control how this ends.

No pressure.

What was it you told me, Embla? "Freija, it's not about whether you want to or not, it's about taking action."

I'm not here because fate has chosen me, I'm here because I've chosen to be. Sometimes you have to force yourself to do things even though it's hard. If we don't — who will? I have to do this, even though it seems impossible and scary.

There's a dream that haunts me. A vision of pain, war, and fire. I can never see the details clearly, but it always leaves me with a sense of emptiness and fear. Fear that I'll lose everything I hold dear. I wish I could be like Onni, who was always smiling and spreading laughter and warmth wherever he went. No matter how hard I try, I can't shake the feeling that this dream is important. That it's trying to tell me something. I saw something else in the dream as well: a white ship that breaks through the darkness and leads me out of it.

There's complete silence. Being under for this long makes your lungs burn, but I've grown used to the feeling. The visibility is excellent, and despite the blue that tinges everything, a vibrant orange or red sometimes breaks through it and then disappears as quickly as it came. Below me, everything is gray and white. I reach down to touch the bottom. The silt is smooth and flows through my fingers like smoke. This is a good place for diving because the boat traffic here isn't as lively and there isn't much trash to speak of, aside from the odd tin can or woodchips. The pressure in my chest is getting heavier, so I decide to go back up to the surface to take a quick breath before diving again. I love the water. It makes me feel as immortal as the sea.

Something glints at the bottom. After a few strokes, I can see that there's a bracelet half-buried in the sand. I grab it with one hand and swim back up to the surface.

Once I've broken through the waves, into the fresh air again, I realize that I've swum out much farther than I usually do. The short pier on the beach looks even smaller from where I'm floating — and a little out of place among the greenery. The palms grow tall there and cover most of the pier in their shade. There's also a fruit tree that's rumored to bear papayas, but I've never seen any fruit on it, so I don't know for sure. Along both sides of the pier, large bushes are growing, generously clothed in orange flowers with big petals. That's one of the reasons I love this place, it stands out from the desert-like steppe that makes up most of the land surrounding Ithmah's high walls. Here at the water, life thrives.

I swim back over to the pier and – before I pull myself up onto it – I wade in close to the reeds, looking around carefully to make sure none of the city kids are close enough to see me. When the coast is clear, I haul myself up onto the pier, accidentally cutting myself on one of the sharp reeds. They're like knives at this time of year.

I walk over to my school bag, which is hidden in a palm bush, and pull out a pair of clean socks to press hard against my wound. It must be pretty deep, because it takes a good while for it to stop bleeding before I can focus on the treasure I just found.

The bracelet is made up of twenty-eight small, black beads that surround a larger turquoise one, which glitters in the high sun.

It probably isn't worth more than a plate of corn, but I think it's beautiful. Two of the beads have words engraved on them – "Fdokr" and "Matåv" – but I have no idea what they mean. I've never seen words like these before.

A perfect birthday present, I think to myself as I slip it on. I let out a deep sigh as I'm reminded of what today is. My sixteenth birthday. Judgement Day. A pit begins to form in my stomach and, instead of letting it grow into even more anxiety, I get up to head down to the seabed again. I'm stopped in my tracks by the sound of a familiar voice.

"Freija Falinn, what have you done this time?"

I turn around to see a smiling Embla walking towards me. As always, she has a sly grin on her face, and her freckles and wavy red hair are sparkling in the sunlight.

"What makes you think I've done something?" I reply, gratefully accepting a hug from my sister. She's a little shorter than me, so I always have to take the upper part of the embrace. We have the best hugs. She must have just come from the market because her clothes smell strongly of spices.

Embla rolls her eyes. "Because you always come here when you need to get something off your mind. Spill it!"

"Am I that easy to read?" I giggle. "Nothing's happened today, other than the usual, I just didn't feel like going home right now. I'm not ready to see everyone and make it official, at least not yet. I really just wanted to stay here as long as possible. It's silly, I know."

"What do you think the Leaders are going to assign you?" wonders Embla. She understands exactly what I mean. We lie down in the yellow-green grass, which – despite it being a sweltering spring day – is nice to rest on. It tickles a little now and then as an ant crawls across my calf or a blade of grass dances against my skin in the breeze.

As everyone knows, you finish school when you're sixteen. Those who pass are assigned a job in a profession that's carefully selected for each person.

"I don't want to say goodbye," I whisper, feeling tears begin to form. They don't show as clearly below the surface and I find myself wishing I was back in the water.

"You might not have to leave Ithmah. I mean, I got to stay at the orphanage, right?"

I know Embla's trying to cheer me up, but we both know that she was a special case. Apsel paid to hire her so that she could stay and work as his assistant. I doubt I'll have the same luck.

I breathe in the scent of seaweed and stare out across the water, over the bay of the city. Ruins from a bygone era. The rusty city has looked the same for as long as I can remember. From here, it looks like the city is burning, with the orangey-red houses gleaming in the sunlight and the smoke from thousands of vehicles driving through the city. The sounds of the city's activities can be heard over the lapping of the waves and the screaming of gulls overhead, and I swear I can smell the iron and rust from here.

What did Ithmah look like before all the melting – *the Disaster* – happened? Had the houses been this rusty back then? Would it have been just as crowded to live here? Did people build things this high even then? It probably wasn't as decayed and overcrowded as it is now, anyway. Actually, I've always felt like I don't belong here. There's something inside me that feels incomplete, like there's something else out there that can fill this pit in me, but it won't be easy to find the answer.

"Sometimes, I hate that our lives are so predetermined."

"*Sometimes*? Try 'always,'" sighs Embla.

"I wish I could get out of here and live my life the way I want, not based on what anyone else determines from tests and surveys."

"I know. But there's nothing we can do about it as things are. You know what Marcell would say if he were here?"

Embla stands up. Her sandals slap against the planks of the pier as she paces back and forth on it with her arms firmly crossed.

"The system works, Freija, there's a reason why the Leaders decide things for us. Or do you want a repeat of the Disaster? Or for some new kind of horror to befall us?" Embla says, imitating Marcell's dialect and his dark voice. I burst out laughing.

"You sound just like him!"

Actually, I think Marcell should be more against the system than anyone. He was torn from his family and sent to the orphanage when he was only six years old, after failing the Six-Year Trial. Just because he had failed to score enough points, it had been decided that he wouldn't be allowed to finish school. He came to Ithmah and was put to work in the harbor.

I shudder at the thought that this is one of the possibilities before me – port work – and shake myself.

"Where are you going?" Embla exclaims as I get up. "Shouldn't we be getting back?"

Embla knows the answer before she even finishes the question, probably because I have that look in my eye that tells her I'm about to jump back in the water. Embla points it out every time. She takes off her sandals and sits down on the pier, dipping her feet in the water as she watches me dive under the surface. Had it been a typical day, she might have made me hurry before it gets dark, but since it's my birthday she probably figures it doesn't matter if I take a few more dives. Embla's thick, red hair glows in the sunshine and as she stares out at the horizon, her freckled, button nose curves into a little ball. She doesn't notice me come up to the pier until I give her a cold hug.

"Ugh, no hug! You're completely soaked!" Embla cries out and laughs. She grabs my hand instead and squeezes twice. I squeeze back – twice – and smile. It's our way of saying, "I love you."

I walk over to my bag and start getting dressed. I don't like the feeling of wet fabric under dry clothes, so I hang on to the t-shirt and let my bikini dry as much as possible in the setting sun. I inspect my clothes while I'm waiting and am amazed at how nice they are, considering I had to sew them myself.

Apsel taught us very early how to sew clothes for ourselves and the other kids from the fabrics that were occasionally donated to the orphanage. That way, we could save money for other things. Like food.

It's then that I see something flying through the air towards us. It's a bird, but not any kind of bird I've seen before. It's completely yellow. No, not yellow, but golden. As the rays of twilight hit it, it's almost dazzling. The bird floats farther and farther down until it eventually lands on one of the posts of the pier — right next to Embla, who's still sitting there completely unfazed. I can't find words, and I don't want to scream for fear of scaring the bird away. The bird is quite large, like a swan maybe, and it seems to be looking right at me. I'm completely mesmerized by it. I've never seen anything like it. I want to get a closer look, but it suddenly stretches out its glittering wings and lets out a shriek. A shriek like nothing I've ever heard. It sounds scary, like it came from someone in danger. At the same time, the noise stirs something in me. I feel like it's something important, but I don't know what. It's as if the bird's scream was some kind of battle cry. The bird continues to soar ever higher until it disappears out over the sea.

Embla doesn't seem to have noticed anything.

"Should we go then?" she says, turning her gaze to me. When she sees my apparently shocked face, she immediately becomes worried. "What is it? Is it the Guardians?" I shake my head. "Well, what is it then? Hello? *Cuckoo!*"

"Are you seriously telling me you didn't just hear that? Or see it?"

"See what?"

I thought about it quickly. Was the bird really there? I decided to keep it to myself. A secret. *The two of us have never kept secrets from each other.*

That was the first, and now, after all this time, there are even more.

"See *what*?" repeats Embla.

"Nothing. Should we head home? The sun is on its way down, and I don't want to be out when it gets cold."

"Maybe you shouldn't stay in the water so long, Sister Little," Embla teases as she throws an arm around me and walks us away from the bay, out onto a large field.

The city kids often come out to this field to play with a ball or other games. I used to come here sometimes after school to hang out with my classmates, but usually I only got to watch. Or I'd go down to the pier to take a dip in the sea. I just had to watch out for other kids so they wouldn't snatch my clothes and hide them high up in a palm tree.

Along one side of the field, a long wall stretches out, concealing Ithmah. I've always wondered why the wall faces this way because it seemed to me that it was the sea that the city needed to be protected from. It's not much to brag about either, since it's so rusty and it's covered with ivy in several places. Then it hits me that it's because of the heavy sandstorms, of course.

Soon, sunflower fields are spreading across both sides of the small dirt road that leads from the field near the pier to the orphanage. I love sunflowers. Deep in the fields, herons and flamingos take shelter in their shade when they're not down by the water.

When I was a kid, I used to run straight out into the fields. I saw thousands of birds take to the sky, painting it pink with their bright feathers. I wish I could be that free. A feeling I'll probably never experience.

The sun has already set, and the evening is unforgivingly dark. The cold is already starting to feel intrusive. Embla and I pick up the pace. The road is familiar, and although the visibility is terrible, we know exactly where to go.

"I knew we should have left earlier," Embla mumbles to herself. It wouldn't be clear to anyone else, but I understand exactly what she means by every word, and I feel a little guilty for taking that extra dip. I know all too well what kinds of dangers can lurk in the dark. We've heard them so many times: stories of cat-like mutants kidnapping children, or nasty animals waking up in the evening to hunt fresh meat for their breakfasts.

They're just fairy tales, I try to convince myself, but it's difficult. My heart beats faster and faster, and finally my hand finds Embla's and we hold on to each other until we see light a little farther ahead. It's the orphanage. If we can just make it a few more yards, we'll be safe. We've just taken the first step into the orphanage's front yard when we hear it.

A scream.

2

"Onni!" exclaims Embla.

"It sounded like it came from inside the orphanage," I whisper, my eyes wide. "You go first!"

Embla gives me a meaningful look and we, with our hands still clasped tightly, walk towards the orphanage's main building. Embla opens the door gently and peers into the hallway. It's completely silent. Eerily silent. The orphanage is always full of life: children running, laughing, teasing each other. Even at this time of day.

"Dad?" whispers Embla. No answer. She dares to call out a little louder this time: "Hello?" Still no answer.

"That's strange," says Embla as she walks into the hall with me following close behind. I ease the door closed and sneak forward as we look in each direction. We take off our sandals so that we won't make too much noise as we walk. The cold stone floor feels uncomfortable under my feet.

"What could have happened?" I wonder, but Embla just shrugs her shoulders. It doesn't look like things have been violent here. Whatever happened must have happened under calm circumstances. But how could anyone have robbed an entire orphanage of two dozen children and the director? I don't understand.

"Check in the kitchen," Embla tells me, "I'll go check in Dad's room."

I can barely bring myself to do as Embla asks, but I muster up the courage and walk towards the kitchen. The door to the kitchen creaks horribly as I step into the room, and I'm greeted with such a shock that I nearly faint on the spot.

"CONGRATULATIONS!" echoes through the kitchen as the lights come on, and the children are shouting so loud that I have to grab the door frame to keep myself from falling backward. It takes me a few seconds to realize that everyone is smiling at me.

"Haha! You fell for it!" Embla laughs wickedly and pats me on the back.

"But wait, someone was screaming," I say.

"Guilty." The voice comes from a giggling little boy with black hair hanging so low over his eyes that he has to push it out of the way with his hand to see anything. It's Onni.

Oh, Onni ... Little guy. Big smile. I miss you so much.

"Are you hurt?"

"No, it was all part of the plan. So you wouldn't suspect anything. Come on, let's eat," Apsel suddenly comes flying in and herds all the children into the dining room. Then he walks up to me, gives me a kiss on the forehead, and says, "Happy Birthday."

"Thanks," I answer, though I still don't really understand what just happened.

"Don't you have anything to say, Marcell?" Embla asks, referring to the big guy with mousy brown hair sitting quietly at the table. He nods and congratulates me, but he doesn't expend any more energy than that.

A giggling Embla leads me over to the long table in the dining hall, which, in honor of the evening, has been turned into a fabulous buffet of pancakes, potato dumplings, sugared figs, cream, jam, and bread that I know has been baked by hand. The food is interspersed with long wax candles that light up the echoing room.

It's not until I'm in the middle of eating some fluffy pancakes that I realize what's happened. This is my birthday party. A surprise party. Embla had been scaring me on purpose when we were out in the sunflower field.

I pick up a bun and pitch it at Embla, shooting her a meaningful look. Embla mouths the words, "you're welcome," and smiles as slyly as ever.

"Ahem," Apsel clears his throat and clinks his glass of milk. He stands up and looks over the table. The light of the candles allows me to see how old he's gotten. The gray, wild hair and the scraggly beard. Somewhere in that hairy mass were a pair of the kindest eyes I've ever seen. They're tired, absolutely, but always full of love and understanding. "My children. Every one of you has a special place in my heart, as you know. Although I would love to keep you all here until you're as old as me, my greatest wish for each of you is for you to find a home where you will be loved and respected for who you are. Most often, my wish is granted too quickly, but in some special cases, it hasn't happened yet." Apsel looks specifically at Marcell and I, "but I'm glad for that. Without the help of my own daughter, Em-em, and you long-term children here at the orphanage, I don't know what I would have done. Your presence here is invaluable. But today, we get to toast and sing for a special miss."

Apsel raises his glass and everyone else in the room, large and small, imitates him.

"You came here sixteen years ago today. I've been following you since your first steps, your first word — which was 'sea' by the way," I giggle and see that Embla is already getting teary-eyed as the memories come flooding back, "Until you started school, and now in recent years, as you've completed the various trials that prepare you for your assigned career. Before I say too much, I just want to tell you that all of it has been special to me. You are *special*, Freija, and that is what I would like us to toast tonight."

"Cheers!" echoes through the room and I have to wipe away a tear. Onni takes notice and begins to sing the birthday song as the others join in, and they sing until the very last note.

After dinner, I'm presented with drawings and other crafts that the kids made during the day. I'm delighted by every piece of art I get. Then they show off a dance they've been rehearsing, and even though I've seen the exact same dance on everyone else's birthdays, I can't help feeling like it was created just for me. The children are incredibly talented as they sing and dance and, despite a few small mistakes here and there, the performance ends with laughter that lifts the ceiling.

There are many children in the orphanage, and everyone demands their share of attention, but on your birthday you get to be the center of everyone's attention. I remember how happy I used to be on my birthdays with all of that light shining on me. That day, however, I had a bitter-sweet feeling about the fact that I had turned sixteen and officially become an adult. The summer was approaching, when school would be done and my new life would begin. In the following days, I would walk around in an uncertain, dark cloud of constant worry. If only I had known then what I know now. I could have changed everything.

Everyone was so tired that no one had to read bedtime stories to the kids. Even Embla and I were out the second we crawled into our beds in our shared bedroom, and each of us only managed a half-enthusiastic, "Good night." I've slept anxiously ever since that night. My sleep has been invaded by dreams. Dreams that would prove to contain vital information.

When I wake up in the morning, I have a knot in my stomach. Even though the sun came up a while ago, I haven't wanted to get out of bed because of my turmoil. It's my first day being sixteen, and even though I know that nothing will be decided until after the final exams, I can't stop myself from imagining the worst-case scenarios for my work assignment. If I stay in Ithmah, it could mean having to work in the harbor, like Marcell, or breeding dromedaries and horses on the Ranch, or at one of the large olive orchards or vineyards, picking grapes or olives from dawn to dusk. I make a pained face when I realize how many burns I would get from the sun if that happened. I guess it's probably better than freezing to death in a cold storage facility or cleaning down in the sewers, which are crawling with dangerous reptiles. Those kinds of jobs aren't found in Ithmah, but I'm not bound to the city just because I grew up here. I know that where I end up will be decided by the Leaders after careful analysis of my achievements in life.

"Come on, lazybones," teases Embla. I hadn't even noticed that she had come back after breakfast. "Just because there's no school today, that doesn't mean that you can stay in bed all day! There's still food left for you if you're hungry. Leftovers from last night. Yum!"

I groan loudly and pull the covers over my head.

"Are you sick?" Embla walks over to me and puts her hand under the blanket so she can feel my forehead.

"No," I sigh. "Yeah, yeah, I'm coming."

"Good! Because I have to do something today and I need your help!"

"And here I thought you cared if I was sick or not," I grin.

"Me? Care? Forget it, sister little!"

Embla laughs and gives me a kiss on the cheek. Once I get down to the kitchen, I get another kiss, this time a forehead kiss from Apsel.

"Good morning, Freija," he says, hugging me. "Sleep well?"

I shrug my shoulders and serve myself some of the leftovers from yesterday's party. Apsel, or one of the kids, has gone out and picked kale from the garden, which I happily add to my pancakes along with some jam made from carissaberries.

I miss that kitchen. It was big and airy and didn't match Ithmah's rusty aesthetic at all. Like the rest of the orphanage, the walls were earthy colors and the ceiling was supported by thick wooden pillars and beams. The large, open window above the sink let in sunlight and the fresh smell of the harvest fields outside. It's been a long time since I was able to enjoy a view like that. All I see now is water. An endless sea. Before all of this, I loved the sea more than anything else. Now I'm not so sure.

"When you're done eating, can you come out and help me with something?" asks Embla. She's standing in the kitchen doorway wearing her usual work clothes: a pair of worn trousers that were once light gray but are now stained a sandy brown, and a sweater that's at least as worn in a slightly darker shade. The sweater is torn in some places. Her red hair is pulled back into a bulky ponytail.

"Before you go out and start your chores, can we talk a little? Just you and me?" asks Apsel. "I'll be waiting in my office."

I nod. Time to start the day.

There's something special about Apsel's room, I think. Actually, his room consists of two adjacent rooms. He usually keeps the door between them open to make the space feel bigger than it is. These two rooms, according to Apsel, used to be the only rooms in the house. Long before it became an orphanage, it had been a small cottage. The other rooms were built later. I remember living in the smaller house with Embla and Apsel when we were very small. It was crowded but cozy. The room is darker now because Apsel has so many things lined up along the walls that it's hardly possible to look out the windows through all of the books. Leaning up against one of the walls is the mandatory hologram portrait of our current President: Didrik Daegal. It should actually be hanging out in the foyer, but Apsel would rather have the other two portraits there. Portraits of Presidents he looked up to. Despite this, the portrait of President Daegal is carefully maintained, with a well-polished gold frame and projectors that play the portrait in the highest quality. On the floor next to the frame, there's a box containing a special cloth that can only be used to clean the portrait. The books that Apsel has stacked around the room aren't even available at school, and the teachers always act like they've never heard of them.

There's something unique about the feel of physical books and being able to breathe in the earthy scent. I could stay there smelling the pages for days on end. Apsel's collection is unique. Books like these ones hardly even exist anymore. These days, all stories, novels, non-fiction books, maps, and things like that are only found in the databases of advanced technological devices.

Like the one I'm recording my voice on right now.

I notice Apsel sitting in front of the screen at the desk, but I walk up to one of the bookshelves and pull down a dusty tome with a worn green cover and yellowed pages: "*Animals of Another Age, Volume 1.*" It was my favorite book when I was a kid, and maybe it still is. It's full of pictures and descriptions of ancient animals. I've searched through the database at school, but I haven't been able to find any of the animals shown in the book, which I find strange, but somehow it fascinates me even more. I open it to a random page and read: *The Emperor penguin can grow to over 3 feet tall and weigh just over 60 lbs.*

I look at the picture of a black and white animal that's unlike anything I've ever seen outside of this particular book. I continue reading about how the Emperor penguins live in Antarctica, but I've never understood what place they're talking about. There's nowhere called Antarctica in Ela.

I put the book back on the shelf and sit down at the desk next to Apsel. My gaze falls on the two world maps that hang on the wall above his bed. One is the ordinary world map that we study in school when we learn about all of the cities and provinces, the one that shows the country of Ela. Ithmah is located in Efricia. The other map shows the old world. It's so old and worn that several of the names have faded away. As always, when I look at the map of the old world my eyes are drawn mainly to the northern and southern parts of the map where great white fields reign.

Snow. It's a word I learned in school. I know what it means in theory, but I've never seen real snow for myself. Only in pictures. The climate Ela has now makes it impossible for me to believe that in the past, before the Disaster, there were vast areas covered with snow and ice. The closest thing to ice we get is at night, after the sun goes down, when frost can form if it gets really cold. There's also the popsicles and ice cubes I've seen at restaurants in Ithmah. I shake my head. I'm pulled

29

out of my thoughts when Apsel clears his throat. He leans back in his chair at the desk.

"How are you feeling today?" he asks.

I let out a deep sigh.

"I see," Apsel smiles and scratches his gray beard. "Yeah, I don't really know where to start."

I'm getting worried. The fact that Apsel doesn't want to meet my gaze isn't making me feel any better.

"You know I want nothing more than for you to stay at the orphanage and work for me with Embla. Even though it's not official, I've always seen you as a daughter."

I nod, I feel the same way. Apsel has always been a father to me, and Embla is my sister. Nobody can take that away from me.

"Unfortunately, that decision isn't up to me."

I nod again. I know this all too well.

"I've sent applications to the Authority for more money to be able to hire you here at the orphanage, but I haven't received an answer yet."

"It's okay. I didn't expect to be able to stay."

I feel a surge of joy, but I don't dare to hope for the best. I know it was hard for Apsel to get through the process the first time — when he hired Embla. Would the Authority really give him approval for two assistants? I doubt it.

"They'll probably wait until after the final exams to tell us, I'm sorry that I can't give you a better answer."

I know I can't expect anything better than this. Once the Leaders have made their decision, it's not something you can challenge.

"If it's not approved, then I just hope I don't get sent too far away," I say.

"Me too. I care about you, and I'll do everything in the little power I have to keep you here. I won't be around forever, you know, and somebody has to keep Embla in line when I'm gone," Apsel says, trying to make me smile. I give him the satisfaction of a small smile.

"I don't want to seem ungrateful, but was that all?" I ask, remembering that Embla needed my help. Apsel nods and lets me go.

What had they said at school the day before? When they were talking about the final exams and work assignments? "The Authority is never wrong."

I'm living proof that they've been wrong at least once.

I still regret that I didn't stay in the room with you that day. I would do anything to be back there with you now.

I'm sorry, Dad. I really tried.

One of the reasons I love Sethunya is because it's so different from the dirty city an hour's walk away. Here, there are only three buildings instead of the thousands that are crammed inside Ithmah's city walls. The houses there are built so tall that they seem to reach the clouds. I probably wouldn't dare to stay in one of those apartments, in case an emergency situation arose and I needed to get out quickly. You can't just jump out the window. That's why I like Sethunya's single-story house, which certainly has high ceilings. The farm consists of three buildings plus a shed and a storage room. There's an L-shaped main house, with the dorms in the longer section and the kitchen, dining room, and Apsel's rooms in the shorter section. There's also a circular building with two toilets, a shower room, and a laundry room. The third building is a stable where Freda, the goat, lives with the chickens. The youngest children all sleep in the same large dorm room, while the slightly older kids share rooms in pairs. I remember that we used to have a donkey a long time ago, but we eventually had to slaughter it because of a drought that caused famine. Looking back, it had made for a good dinner despite its age.

But the best thing about the farm is the large fields where we grow genetically modified vegetables and grains. Since southern Efricia has an arid climate, and the orphanage rarely has water to give the crops and fields, the genetically modified seeds are vital. Farms all over Ela receive genetically modified seeds from Pari, Uropi's largest city. About fifty years ago, they developed a way to grow food despite the harsh climate of the earth, and they spread that knowledge around the world. Every weekend I walk with the other older kids to Ithmah to sell food from the harvest or honey from the hives. Sometimes we also sell wax candles that we make ourselves.

I find Embla near the carrot patch, where she's showing some of the kids how to clear weeds. In the glaring sunlight, it's hard to see which kids they are from far away but as I approach I see that it's Disa, a five-year-old girl with straw-colored hair, and Kali, who's the same age as Disa but she has black hair and chestnut brown skin like mine.

"Are you finally awake now?"

Embla teases when she sees me.

"What did you need help with?" Just like Embla has, I put my hair up in a ponytail. It's so thick that I have to have a strong band to hold all the black strands in place.

"Well, that's enough for now. You can sit in the shade and rest a little," Embla says to the girls. They go and sit in the shade of a hedge, where they soon start playing with some palm leaves. Embla wipes the sweat from her brow and pulls off her dirty gloves.

"I thought we could take a box of tools out of the storage room," Embla says, explaining that the pipes in the shower room need to be repaired. "The box is so high on a shelf that I didn't want to do it by myself, but we can try it together."

We walk over to the storage room where a worn black raven is staring at us. It must be used to people, because it doesn't move from its spot as we approach. We ignore it and head into the storage room. The contrast from the sunlight outside leaves us unable to see anything in the dark at first, but Embla soon finds a small chest to stand on.

"If you stand on the chest, you should be able to pull the box down from up there." Embla points to a dusty wooden box that sits on a shelf near the roof. "You pull it out carefully, and I'll stand here and try to receive it."

Right under the shelf is a workbench laden with pieces of wood, jars, and a few other things. Embla stands next to the bench and readies herself.

"Apsel said he's applied to hire me as an assistant," I tell her.

"I know," says Embla. "He told me already. I don't dare to hope for too much."

"Mm."

"Do you see the box?" asks Embla, and I reply that I do, but it's difficult to reach. "Did you know that the Authority reduces our rations every year because they think that we could actually be self-sufficient?"

"Yeah, but we still have enough to get by, right?"

"Hardly. Dad negotiates with them every year, but every year our food rations are less and less, so we have to find other ways to put food on the table."

"I didn't know that."

The box is stuck between some things on the shelf, so I have to move them before I can get to it. I feel guilty for worrying about myself without thinking about the sacrifices Apsel makes.

"We've actually reached our limit on how many children we can take care of, but the Authority doesn't seem to take that into account. It just means higher electricity costs, more water consumption, and more mouths for us to feed," continues Embla.

"Isn't there anything we can do?" I ask. I stretch as much as I can and feel the box moving around here and there as I try to grab hold of it.

"Work harder, sell more, I don't know. I've suggested that we hide some of what we harvest to feed ourselves. But it's against the law, and if we got caught, fines would be the least of our worries."

"We definitely don't need anything else to worry about," I agree.

The box finally comes loose with such speed that Embla and I are both caught by surprise. It's much heavier than either of us expected, and I can't stop it when it comes flying straight towards Embla, who falls into the workbench with the toolbox on top of her. I let out a scream. Embla's arm is pinned at an odd angle between the box and the bench.

It looks broken.

"Help me get it off!"

I quickly jump down from the chest and manage to lift the box, which seems to weigh a ton, off of Embla's arm.

"Sorry, it was too heavy! Are you okay?"

We go out into the light again while Embla bends her elbow and flexes her fingers. There's not even a scratch on her freckled skin.

"But..." I gasp.

"It's fine," she says. "It doesn't hurt at all."

"I thought you broke your arm," I say as my heart beats hard in my chest.

The kids, who heard my scream, come running over to see what's happened.

"There's nothing wrong," Embla assures them. "We dropped a box and Freija thought it had hit me. Now you can help me go through the stuff in the box to see if anything got broken. But we'll leave the box on the bench inside, it's too heavy to move."

Embla and the kids go into the storage room. I'm still in shock, and I start to go through the incident again in my head. I lost control of the box and it fell straight onto Embla. Somehow, it must have looked worse than it actually was. If her arm had been broken, Embla wouldn't have been so calm. Since no one else seems to be making a big deal out of it, I decide not to either and we all continue with our chores as if nothing happened.

Is it weird that I miss our days at the orphanage? I have to make an effort to really see it, but when I succeed, I can still see them there: Embla in the vegetable garden, Marcell and Onni taking turns driving that rusty tractor and planting by hand so that they can get the harvest ready by summer. I was taught in school that it was an outdated method, but since we weren't as privileged as the farmers in Pari, for example, where machines do the job, we had to put our trust in the tractor. It was too expensive to buy the newer farming equipment, so we had to rely on ancient technology. It was probably the only tractor of its kind. I can even see myself with Apsel as we prepare lunches with turnips, tomatoes, and garlic vinegar.

The afternoon sun makes the crops smell lovely. I stretch myself out and take in the fantastic air. Not even the dust that's continuously surrounding us can ruin the moment. Well, maybe the thousands of insects that occasionally sweep past with the wind could. They often get caught in the wide nets slung over the garden beds to provide shelter for the crops. The trapped insects make for a lovely buffet for the many birds and rodents that live here, which helps to deter the hungry scavengers from going after the crops.

Then I'm reminded of what today is, and I immediately feel less enthusiastic. It's a weekend, so we have to go to Ithmah to sell crops and grain. I sigh and head over to the shed to retrieve the wagon.

I place the wagon in the middle of the yard and I'm joined by Embla, Marcell, and Onni, who are each carrying a heavy bag. The wagon is soon covered by a dozen sacks.

After walking for a bit on the country road, I start to regret not wearing something with long sleeves. The sun is burning hot, and it's still only spring. If you're not careful, the sun can be really harmful. A little farther on, two dromedary riders come from the opposite direction. It would've been nice to ride back and forth on one of those. Or horses. Of course, it would've been best if we had a car so that we could get some protection from the sun. But transportation, no matter what kind, is something the orphanage has never been able to afford — unless you count the donkey that was too old to ride.

When we reach Ithmah, we walk gratefully into the shady alleyways. We board the tram at the station closest to the city wall. It's a rusty orange except for a green stripe right below the windows. We ride it straight to the city center without having to make any detours. It's the middle of the day, but there are a lot of sketchy neighborhoods in Ithmah and Apsel has made us promise never to leave the center or get off the tram anywhere else. Luckily, the wagon carrying our crops can fit with no problems. We still have plenty of space around us for people to pass by.

I sit next to Onni, looking out the window and wondering if all the cities are as brown and rusty as Ithmah. I've only ever seen pictures of Adali, Pari, and Takai, but they look so much whiter and cleaner. There don't seem to be any poor or dirty people in the pictures, but in Ithmah they're everywhere.

Over the broadcasts, we probably only get to see a fraction of what the cities actually look like, and the same is likely true for you. Many aren't shown at all, but everyone knows that Pari is the big agricultural city with the thousands of artificial islands that they grow crops on. The contrast between the sea, the white island sands, and the green grain is wonderful. The buildings have round, elegant shapes, and the one that stands out the most to me has to be the Opera House. It's in the center of Pari on its own island with the rest of Pari enclosing the Opera House in a perfect circle. The Opera House itself looks like three huge mussels in the front and three smaller mussels behind them. Palm trees surround the island, and at night the whole sky glows in pink and orange. I only got to see it once in person, and it was probably the last time.

Our capital is fascinating as well, though I'd never be able to live there. The city is bigger than five Ithmahs put together, but I know that won't help much since you probably have no idea how big Ithmah is. It's huge. Adali consists of hundreds of high-rise buildings in the middle of the sea, whose walls are all made of windows. It looks like they go all the way up into the clouds. Between the high-rise buildings, there are like fifty lanes for public transportation and even more for pedestrians. The trains look like trams; they hang below the tracks, instead of driving on top like they do in Ithmah. Calling Adali a tech city isn't an exaggeration. Everything there is high-tech. From the streetlights to the windows that double as screens to the drones flying through the air. Every person has their own personal screen that they never take their eyes off. They take them everywhere, but somehow they never run into each other. Everything is synchronized in a system that works efficiently, as long as you know it. What's fascinating about our capital, though, isn't this. It's what's under the city. The high-rise buildings continue far below the water. Before the Disaster, this was one of the old cities that have since been built on top of. In large spaces between the houses, they've built glass walkways, where it looks like you're walking on water. It's scary, because you can really see just how far down the high-rises go. It's a forgotten, sunken world down there.

We're just pulling into a station when Onni bursts out, "Check it out!" as he presses both hands against the windowpane. We have just enough time to see Guardians hitting some people with their whips before the tram rattles past. We're going pretty fast, but it's not hard to tell that they're Guardians, given their burgundy uniforms and golden helmets.

"No, don't look," I say, but he still turns his head to see.

"What do you think they did?" wonders Onni. He tucks his black hair behind his ear.

"I don't know," I lie.

I had seen exactly what was scrawled boldly on the metal wall, but I have no idea what it means. I've seen it a few times before but never connected it to anything. It's the symbol of an animal that sort of looks like a cross between a rat and a cat. It was chewing on a scorpion's venomous tail. My stomach knots up. I'll never get used to the Guardians' violence.

We get off at the station in The Plaza at the city's center, which is the closest one to the marketplace. There are TV screens everywhere, along with Ela's flag, which bears the same colors as the Guardian's uniforms. The flag has a burgundy background with a gold motif in the middle. The motif represents the New World — the silhouette of modern-day Ela. The TV screens display informational text interspersed with advertisements for the military school, Bionbyr. It's the school that trains EMES soldiers to fight for the President and the country of Ela.

"I would do anything to get out of working in the harbor and go to Bionbyr instead," Marcell says when he sees an advertisement for the school with the words "*Together for Ela — a country worth fighting for.*"

"Never in my life would I hold a weapon," Embla snorts loudly. "Why do you even want to be a soldier?"

"Anything is better than this rotten city. Besides, the money alone makes it worth all that," Marcell responds. "When you graduate, you get a hefty sum for your family and then you get one of Ela's highest-paying jobs. Depending on how good your exam results are, the salary varies of course, but I bet I'd be the best in my class."

Embla rolls her eyes.

"What good is money if you're dead?"

"I don't really feel alive here anyway," Marcell answers.

Marcell's words cause me to realize something. Even though military school has never been something I've aspired to, I can't shake the feeling of being stuck. I want to get out of Ithmah too. To find my family. I think of the ships in the harbor, dreaming of how one day I'd board one of them and sail into the sunset. Maybe even on my own boat. Free to go wherever I want. So I can understand Marcell, who's in the orphanage even though he has a family. He must have wondered why they didn't come for him. And since he's underage, he has to stay at the orphanage — because he has no one to take care of him. He has Apsel there for him now instead, just like the rest of us at home.

There are a lot of apartments crowded around The Plaza and the buildings are tall. In Ithmah, we're good at using the sun for energy and you can see solar panels everywhere, busily transforming the rays into clean energy. At least there's no shortage of sunlight. The townspeople use every nook and cranny to grow things. If you pay attention, you'll spot the tufts of green and smell the fantastic scents of herbs, vegetables, fruits, and anything you can think of growing nearby. They hang baskets from ceilings and grow things on balconies and even on the walls. Ithmah is a balancing act of hope and despair.

As we move through the dense crowd, we walk along each side of the wagon to make sure no one steals the food. Marcell (who is the strongest of the four of us) pulls the trolley and Onni (who's the smallest) takes the back. Traffic is the worst. It's always nerve-wracking when we have to stand still amidst all the cars that seem to be driving without a rulebook. Fortunately, some other pedestrians are getting tired of the traffic and they waltz right out into the road. This forces traffic to come to a stop and we get a chance to cross to the other side. The cars hum and honk, people are talking everywhere, and music is playing in all the shops, and I'm already longing to go back to Sethunya.

The marketplace emits the distinctive smells of spices, stews, and sweat under the large swathes of fabric that are suspended between the houses. The heat is relentless for the merchants who have to spend long days standing in one place with only short bathroom breaks. The shade barely helps. I feel most sorry for the ones that have to stand near boiling pots for hours at a time, where they sell steaming vegetable stews. The scents blend in with the sounds of vendors shouting about fresh fish, dates, and rice.

Embla decides that we should split up to work more efficiently. Onni and I can take some of the smaller bags and head in one direction while Embla and Marcell take the wagon and the bigger bags. It's great when Marcell helps because he's so big and strong. The long days in the harbor have certainly done him good.

Onni and I have barely made it a few meters before I see two of my classmates walking towards us. They each have a bread roll in their hand, eating them as they walk. I sigh inwardly and begin to pull Onni in another direction, but it's too late.

"Look, Eskild," says one of them, pointing at us. They laugh and saunter over in our direction.

"Not only did their parents not want them, but that old man doesn't want them at home either," says Eskild. He's a roundish boy with a big nose. He laughs at his own cruelty. I know he's talking about Apsel, and deep down, I know that Eskild is wrong. We have to do this to help out the farm.

"They think they're so special, but they're really just slaves. I don't understand why the Authority bothers sending them to school. They're nothing," says the other one, called Brutus. I'd say he's not very exceptional either, and if he doesn't shape up, he's not going to get a good job after graduation. He struggles with a lot of subjects.

We've always been different, us orphans. We're always picked last when we split into groups. Even the teachers treat us differently. It wouldn't have mattered if a teacher had been here to see this. They would've thought the same thing. It's never felt right to me, but after so many years, I'm used to it. I've learned to ignore it, and so far, that's worked best. In the end, Eskild and Brutus get bored. They leave with their bread rolls, and Onni and I continue on our way.

Embla really pulled the short stick today, I think when Onni and I sell our lot in almost record time.

"Do you want to do something else before we head back home?"

"What would that be?" asks Onni.

I dig in my pockets.

"I have a little money…" I count out the coins in my hand. "It should be enough for each of us to get a popsicle."

Onni's eyes widen.

We look for the nearest food stall and I buy us each a popsicle that tastes like figs and lime. Then we start walking back to the station where we're supposed to meet Embla and Marcell. We stop near a backyard that functions as a dump, with trash cans and recycling bins lined up along the walls of the surrounding buildings. The only kind of life that's likely to show up around here is the sugar gliders — the small flying squirrels that are attracted by the trash and leftovers. They originally came to Ithmah as stowaways on ships coming into the harbor. They had survived the journey by feasting on sugary cargo, and that's how they got the name "sugar glider," because of their famous sweet-tooth. These days, the townspeople sometimes put out poison to keep them away.

"It's not very nice here," notes Onni, throwing his popsicle stick into one of the garbage cans.

He starts to head back towards the station, but then I get an idea.

"Follow me!" I smile, but Onni looks skeptical.

I walk up to one of the bins next to the wall of a house.

"Come over here."

I help Onni up onto the bin and then climb up myself.

"Check this out," I tell him. "You can climb up the drainpipe."

"You're crazy!" Onni exclaims, but I've already started climbing.

The drainpipe is a little rusty, but it still seems pretty sturdy. I keep climbing and almost burst out laughing. This was something Embla taught me a few years ago. I had reacted the same way as Onni, but I'd followed Embla, just like Onni is following me now. It's been a long time since she and I were in town together without a goal or errand to run, and even longer since we climbed up on a roof. I feel the adrenaline pumping through my body, but I know better than to look down.

"Don't look down!" I shout to Onni, just to be safe.

When I get to the top, I pull myself over the edge and give Onni a hand when he catches up to me. We've climbed up four stories, and now we have a pretty good view of the neighborhood's rooftops. Closer to the city center, the buildings are taller, but towards the outskirts of town we can see pretty far.

"Wow, it's like a whole other world," Onni says as he holds up his hand to shield his eyes from the sun, staring out over the rooftops. Beyond the city, the sea stretches out like a blanket, creating the illusion that Ithmah is just a tiny island dotting the vast blue expanse. Ithmah's architecture rises up like a collection of rusty pipes, morphing from clean white to the bright red-orange of cheap metal. It's all connected by walkways in the air above, cables, and overgrown vegetation. The city is crowded, and people often live with several others all crammed into one room. Far below is the harbor that houses all the ships that come into the city. On the other side, you can look out over the high city wall, over the sprawling fields leading back to the orphanage. It all looks so small from up here. Beyond the orphanage and the fields is the dry savanna that eventually turns into a desert, stretching as far as the eye can see.

We sit down and let our legs dangle over the edge.

"Apsel wouldn't like this," Onni says after a while.

"Then it's best that we don't tell him," I reply with a smile.

Onni looks a little skeptical, but then he seems to conclude that it's probably a good idea to keep this between us. We sit for a while, talking and enjoying the view. Even though it's already afternoon, neither of us wants to leave the roof just yet.

"This sounds really cheesy, but I wish we could freeze this moment and stay here forever," I say. I think about this morning and the anxiety I feel now that I'm sixteen. I don't want to grow up. I really wish I didn't have to.

"It's not cheesy. I'd like that too," Onni smiles and grabs my hand.

There's this thing that sometimes happens when I touch people. Pictures go through my head, often so fast that I can barely make them out, and afterwards I get all sweaty and need a few minutes to myself. This has happened several times in recent years, but a little more often in the last few months. The images tend to be blurry, like I'm spinning around in a hurricane, and I can't focus on anything. Now, for the first time, I see something more clearly.

At first, it's not so much a picture as a feeling, a feeling of warmth and security—the feeling of another person's closeness and love. It's like being in a place you never want to leave because nowhere else could ever feel this safe. But then the feeling disappears, and it's replaced by an image: a man with dark hair, as black and straight as Onni's, but with a few gray streaks. He sits bent over a table in a dark room, and there are bottles on the table. There's a murmur, and it sounds like someone is talking in another room. Then the man disappears from focus and I hear screaming. It's a woman screaming. It gets quiet, but then there's a loud bang and someone is crying.

It all goes through my head in a single moment and I quickly let go of Onni's hand.

"What is it?" Onni asks worriedly, pushing his hair out of the way with his hand. "You look like you've seen a ghost."

I swallow.

I'm dizzy and need a few moments to regain my focus. If I tried to stand right now, I'd definitely fall—and since we're on a rooftop that's not an option for me. My mouth is dry, so I swallow again before attempting to form words.

"Hey, Onni, do you remember anything about what it was like before... I mean, before you came to the orphanage?"

"Well..." Onni says slowly, looking like he's wondering what I'm getting at. "Not very much. That was six years ago."

I remember that Apsel had taken extra care with Onni right after he came to the orphanage. The worst thing about the older kids, Apsel had once said, is that they have memories. And those memories are often not good.

I hesitate. I know Onni doesn't like to talk about his past. No matter how small the question, he always brushes it off, smiles, and says that it doesn't matter now. As if I can read Onni's thoughts, that's precisely what he answers.

"It's not worth thinking about. What's done is done."

What kind of images had I seen? Were they memories from my childhood? But that can't be right because I was a baby when I came to the orphanage. Also, the man had looked like an older version of Onni, but it couldn't have been one of his memories. That's impossible. Isn't it? Maybe it was something he'd told me before. No, that can't be right either since he never opens up like that.

"Did something happen with your dad?" I ask gently.

Onni meets my gaze for a moment. He stares down at the harbor as if he's remembering something.

"He wasn't doing well, was he?" I pry even more. Why am I doing this? I know he doesn't want to talk about the past, but I can't let go of the short film that was just playing in my mind.

"How do you know...?" asks Onni. "No. I don't know. No, I don't think so."

Onni falls silent again. I feel like I'm in deep water and I know I shouldn't ask my next question, but I still do:

"He died, right?"

I can see Onni trying to hide the tears running down his cheek from under his dark hair, but the sunlight is reflecting them too well. They make his cheeks sparkle. He nods.

"Mom shot him."

Just then, a familiar signal echoes throughout Ithmah. You can't miss it, and everyone knows exactly what it means: a TV broadcast from Adali. Even though I want to know more about Onni's past, I also know that it's mandatory to go to the nearest screen to see what the Authority has to say. The second signal sounds to let everyone know that the transmission is about to begin.

Down in The Plaza, we find Embla and Marcell, who are also finished with today's trading. The massive screen in the square is probably as wide as the big dormitory at the orphanage. MANDATORY TRANSMISSION, it says in burgundy letters in the middle of the screen. Ithmah's residents are lined up along the square and all of the traffic has stopped.

The screen goes from black to footage of a middle-aged woman in light, pastel orange clothes walking around in a sterile hospital setting. Behind her, you can see some people who are all dressed in the same uniforms, only these ones are a cool gray. They're being helped by people who are dressed like the woman.

"In our Tabian sanctuaries, Tabians live good lives where they are not a danger to the public. Here we can study their abilities to find out how ordinary people can be born with special abilities, or Kraften, which may be devastating in some cases. Even two ordinary people who don't have the Tabian gene in their families can have a child who possesses a power," narrates the woman. Her voice plays over clips of happy children in a Tabian sanctuary. "Do you know someone with a special ability? Perhaps someone at your workplace has a secret? Has your teenager started behaving strangely? Remember, anyone could be a Tabia. You can't tell just by looking at them. Maybe you already know a Tabia who begged you not to tell anyone? Remember that Tabians are dangerous. Their powers can have terrible consequences. They can hurt you, your family, and your friends. The best thing for a Tabia is to live in a sanctuary. There, they are not a danger to anyone. What's more, they are safe from themselves. Make the right choice. Turn yourself, or anyone you know who is a Tabia, in to the Authority. You are always welcome here."

The announcement is met with cheerful applause from the public. The screen goes black again, and The Plaza is once again filled with movement. Suddenly I'm being shoved, and a man grabs me before I fall backward. I'm about to thank the man when I noticed he's not letting go. I stiffen up. The man's cold hand permeates my skin and I feel chilled to the bone.

"Get ready," the man hisses. "Prepare yourself."

I'm speechless. The man's shoes are completely worn out, his hair is greasy, and his beard is scruffy. This man has no home. Constantly on the run from the Guardians.

"Get ready," the Wanderer says again. "Prepare yourself."

Just when I'm about to tear my arm out of his grasp, he lets go, enters the crowd, and disappears as suddenly as he came.

Embla, who didn't see what just happened, suggests that we hurry home before it gets dark, and no one argues. I can't let go of what Onni said on the roof, but now's not the time to continue that conversation. I'd rather just give him a hug, but my mind is full of questions.

What did the Wanderer want me to get ready for? Were those really Onni's memories I'd seen? Why? How? Onni had confirmed what I'd already known. But that's impossible. It's impossible.

It seems like I'll never know.

4

Whoever you are, I hope you're still interested in listening. They keep yelling at me to eat something, but I need to continue; there's too much at stake. I've already missed so many chances on this journey to stand up for myself and talk about what's important.

That same evening we had dinner together just like every evening, and I didn't have time to continue my conversation with Onni. During dinner, he wore his usual mask. The same charming, happy Onni as always. That was also the night we discovered something that would shape our lives forever.

"Today, we have reason to be extra grateful," says Apsel when he has everyone's attention, "because we got three barrels of fish from Portson's as a donation. He told me that these fish came from Mercaub, so they're not the same kind we usually eat. We'll eat some fresh fish tonight, and we can dry the rest."

The news gets a mixed response among the children, some of them love fish while others sigh at the thought of having dried fish for dinner several days in a row. After I serve myself some fish and carrots, I hand the bowl to Onni, who's sitting next to me. Before I let go of the bowl completely, I give him an encouraging smile, and he smiles back. He seems completely unbothered after our conversation on the roof.

I think everyone should be grateful that they get to eat fresh fish; usually, we only get the kind that comes in tin cans.

If I was going to complain about anything, it would be canned food, even though I understand the purpose of it.

I pour some of the garlic vinegar on the fish and carrots. I feel sore in my legs after today's walk, but more than that, I think it was the climb. I catch Onni's attention.

"It's nice that we have the day off tomorrow too," I point out.

Everyone in Ela, or at least in Efricia, gets two days off a week. But at Sethunya, we're usually lucky if we get one. Not because Apsel works us too hard, but because there's just so much to do all the time. How can the Authority think that one assistant is enough? The fact that they even approved one is a miracle. How did Apsel manage to do all this alone for so many years?

"Tomorrow, I'll do homework," says Onni decidedly.

I sigh. "Right. I should too."

"I can help you with yours," offers Onni. Even though he's three years younger than I am, he's probably always been smarter. At least smarter when it comes to the subjects we study at school, and it's probably because he's so much more interested in learning than anything else.

Since all of us orphans have to help with the work on the farm, we get two workdays a week as long as we do our homework. That's why we only go to school for three days every week, which suits me just fine. I usually do homework with the other kids and we help each other out.

"Please feel free to help me out with the equations," I sigh.

"Oh, we've just started with equations!" says Onni enthusiastically.

"There's probably no one as excited about learning things as you, Onni," I say.

Onni smiles at me.

"It's so much fun to learn new things," he says suddenly. "I want to learn everything!"

I laugh, but Onni looks down at his plate. "But in three years, I'll be in the same grade as you are now, and then it'll be the end."

"It doesn't have to be over," Marcell chimes in monotonously. He'd been listening in on our conversation. "You could apply for a scholarship to go to university and keep studying."

Even though Marcell is the only one of the kids who doesn't go to school, and never has, he obviously knows how the system works. I remember Marcell telling me that the only thing he remembers about what happened after the test was how they'd brought him into another room with a few other kids. They had to wait there, probably for some decision to be made, before being taken away to the train station. He hadn't even gotten to say goodbye to his parents or siblings. Straight to the train. Along the way, the group of small children became smaller and smaller until Marcell was the only one left. Once in Ithmah, they'd arranged work and housing for him. That's how he came to us.

I remember my own test. I was super nervous because I was so afraid to make mistakes. Apsel had done his best to give me a pep talk and Embla tried too, to some extent, but everything she'd said had only made me even more worried. She said that if I couldn't handle it, I might have to move and work in another place. Or be sent to Agnarr to start military prep training. But the test had gone well. They had tested my ability to understand and remember information, both written and verbal. I remember there being some math I had to do as well. The toughest part was probably the physical portion of the test. We were so small back then, but they still pushed us to run fast, jump far, and throw heavy things. I was sore for several days afterwards.

"Do you ever wish you could do that, Marcell?" I wonder.

"What? To go to some fancy university and act like I'm better than everyone else? No, thanks. I'd rather look forward to my first paycheck," Marcell says it quietly, so Onni won't hear him. I don't understand why he just suggested it to Onni if he hates academics so much.

Marcell has always been my polar opposite. He was really looking forward to turning sixteen – when you become an adult and make your own decisions. Children up to sixteen years of age work for free, but in return they get free housing and food. Of course, the Authority finds ways to avoid paying for it; for example, by sending children to orphanages instead. When you grow up, you have to do everything for yourself, and not everyone succeeds. Ithmah is filled with Wanderers who don't have a roof over their heads and have to beg for change.

Lately, Marcell and I have grown apart. From the moment we got there, he chose to go his own way. I don't blame him. We all have our own goals and driving forces that bring us closer to reaching them, and I know he needs to do things his way.

Just like I'm doing things my way.

Apsel says goodnight and disappears into his room while I cuddle up next to Disa and Kali, who share a bed in the dorm, to listen to a bedtime story. Every night Embla and I take turns reading. Embla blows out all the candles except the one she needs to see the book. Just like Embla, I don't like to read from a screen because I love the feeling of turning pages. It's dead silent in the room except the wind whispering through one of the open windows that isn't covered by wooden planks, causing the curtains to float in an almost ghostly manner. Like all the other rooms, the dorm has high ceilings and it gets really cold at night. Because of that, we've decorated the room with long swathes of fabric that hang from the beams, and across the room, the fireplace is lit. I ask a boy named Simon to close the window so that we won't forget later. If it's open at night, all the kids will have frozen half to death by tomorrow and I'll be busy curing colds. Ever since the epidemic a couple of years ago, I've been careful to make sure that all the windows are closed at night.

When the story is over, Embla closes the book. It's silent in the hall. None of the children are awake. I wiggle out from between Disa and Kali's sleeping bodies and accompany Embla out to the kitchen to make tea.

In the kitchen is the orphanage's only TV, which is screwed into one of the walls next to some bunches of garlic and dried fruits. It's small and over ten years old, but it works well. If it breaks, we don't have anything to worry about. A new TV is the only thing the Authority would help us with without protesting, because they want to ensure that the entire population of Ela can watch the news and speeches from the President.

Soon Marcell comes in and joins us. The door to Apsel's room is open and we can see him at his desk, where he sits bent over his screen. I think he's worried about how he's going to keep the orphanage on its feet in the years to come. If only there was something I could do.

Then the broadcast signal sounds for the second time on the same day. This time, it's much quieter and doesn't seem to be coming from the TV in the kitchen but from Apsel's screen. I immediately become curious. It's rare for the broadcasts to be limited to a selected audience. It's not like it matters in this case, because Apsel immediately comes into the kitchen with the screen and, with a motion of his hand, he sends the picture from his screen to the TV so that we don't have to crowd around the small screen to see.

Ela's eighth President, Didrik Daegal, is the focus of the broadcast. He stands on a podium in front of the Presidential Palace in Adali. He's wearing the same suit he always seems to wear when he speaks: a long, dark, thin coat in varying shades of purple. There's a light scarf around his neck. A light shirt and vest. Dark pants. His beard is short and well-trimmed, and his medium-length hair sways gently in the wind. Behind the President is his press officer, Erikk Aalarik. He's the one who had succeeded in passing the law, many years ago before he became head of the press, that made it mandatory to report people with powers.

"What's he babbling about this time?" asks Embla, with no particular interest in her voice.

"Shh," hisses Marcell, directing his attention back to the TV.

"Today, at three in the afternoon local time in Siverov, a group of terrorists boarded a train that departed from Bergh. The terrorists were carrying explosives, and their goal was to blow up the train upon arrival in Siverov," the President says in a calm, even tone. Video clips of the explosives are displayed on the screen.

"If they had succeeded, the train station would have been blown sky-high and hundreds, maybe thousands, of innocent people would have been killed," continues the President.

The train station in Siverov is now being shown in the video, but nothing seems to be out of the ordinary. The trains are coming and going, and the people look indifferent.

"The train station was never blown up. The bombs were not detonated. No innocent lives were wasted, and all members of the terrorist group are now in custody. A terrible catastrophe was prevented," Daegal takes a brief artistic pause. "Thanks to my esteemed EMES soldiers. They have been keeping a close watch on these people and suspected that they were planning something. When the terrorists boarded the train, the EMES soldiers were already there, disguised as civilians. They arrested the terrorists immediately. No passengers' lives were in danger, everything went quickly and smoothly and without incident."

Finally, video plays of the terrorists with black cloth bags over their heads, wearing handcuffs and being led away by the EMES soldiers. The soldiers are dressed in burgundy uniforms with gold-colored seams and details. Each of them wears a golden mask, which all have unique designs that set them apart from the others.

"Why do they always wear masks?" wonders Embla.

"It's because they're anonymous," answers Marcell. "So that they can pass as civilians if needed, like on the train."

I'm shaking. On the terrorists' jackets is the same symbol that had been scribbled on the wall in Ithmah, but this time the scorpion's poison tail is a bright, familiar burgundy color.

"Let this be a warning to others planning something similar. The EMES soldiers are always one step ahead. We will not rest until Ela is completely rid of terrorism and our people can live freely without fear," the President continues before ending with the words "Together for Ela!"

The broadcast fades to the sound of the audience's applause. A tone sounds, followed by a message in capital letters: "PLEASE HOLD FOR A MESSAGE FROM ADALI."

Apsel lays the screen on the kitchen counter. The letters now appear as a hologram, floating and rotating above the screen. The text changes from red to gold.

"Every time I see him, I marvel at the fact that looks almost exactly the same as he did around thirty years ago when he first became President," mutters Apsel.

"How old is he?" I wonder.

"Eighty-six."

"Ancient," notes Embla.

"Yes, there aren't many in our world who manage to get that old," Apsel sighs as he scratches his beard.

I had thought about this before, but I rarely dared to talk about it. The idea that the President looked too young. As you know, it's considered taboo to ask questions about the President even though it may seem innocent when it comes to something like his appearance. I thought back to the abuse we'd witnessed that afternoon. That night, I had convinced myself that it must just be good makeup and frequent dye jobs of the President's hair that made him look so young. Or maybe he's had surgery. That, or a good filter on the cameras, of course.

Now I know better.

"Twenty-nine years as President. I remember when a President was only allowed to sit for two terms, but that's changed since he came to power," Apsel tells us. "Not that it matters. Of course, there's rarely an opponent you can vote for anyway."

"I don't understand why you're so negative towards President Daegal," says Marcell. He's done a lot of good for this country."

Apsel's eyebrows shoot up.

"Oh, really?"

"All the restrictions and laws surrounding people with powers, for example. He's made our lives safer."

Apsel looks skeptical.

"That, and of course, he created the Tabian sanctuaries so that they can't steal our jobs—among other things. If it weren't for the sanctuaries, they'd be able to roam around getting anyone to do whatever they want or hurt people with their dangerous abilities."

"And I suppose you've never wondered why we don't even know where the sanctuaries are located?" Apsel continues to look skeptical.

"It's to protect the Tabians," says Marcell, sounding completely convinced. "Otherwise people who are afraid of their powers might attack them. Not to mention, the research they're doing there might be sensitive, so they could be keeping the location secret to protect us too."

Apsel shakes his head. Then he walks up to the two Presidents' portraits hanging on the wall and says: "I'm just saying that if we were to get a new President who's more like these two, then we would probably see changes in Ela. Positive changes. Both Adam and Elham had vision—they thought of the people and didn't give benefits to the rich. That's all I'm saying."

Marcell is unable to respond before the screen gives off another tone to indicate that the broadcast is about to resume. Adali's anthem plays, and after that a hologram is projected. It's the President's press officer, Erikk Aalarik.

"Discipline and Loyalty. These words are displayed on Bionbyr's coat of arms and symbolize the balance of qualities that an EMES soldier must possess. Every year, we examine between fifty and seventy soldiers who have undergone rigorous training under the leadership of Headmaster Andor Amaro." If I didn't know any better, I would think that it's really Erikk in miniature form on the desk above the screen. The hologram reflects him down to the smallest colorful detail. He has a bleak face, perhaps because he's always so serious, with his head bent slightly forward. His dark mocha-brown complexion is always smooth in the hologram. "To serve President Daegal and the country of Ela is a great privilege, and only the very best are bestowed with this honor. This year, as you know, it's Uropi's turn to show us what they can do when the admissions staff for Bionbyr comes to each of the cities in the province. But this year Bionbyr will be celebrating its sixty-year anniversary, and we are going to honor the occasion by training twice as many soldiers as usual. Since our recruitment pool has become larger, this year we will also be visiting Efricia."

The news is met with a mixed response. Marcell looks eager, while Embla and I each heave a deep sigh. Erikk continues:

"I urge all young people living in Efricia who are sixteen, seventeen, eighteen, and nineteen years old this year to seize this opportunity to become a part of this prestigious school. There, you will gain the skills needed to become an esteemed professional and serve Ela and its people more than anyone else. The Selections are tough, but with enough will, ambition, and potential, *you* can become an EMES soldier. Time will tell who among you are best suited for this monumental task. Ela's people, one people."

Adali's anthem is played again and the hologram ends. Apsel reaches his hand across the screen and it becomes a black mirror with four reflections. Apsel is the first to open his mouth:

"Well, what do you think of that?"

5

"Huh? Do you know what this means? They're coming here! This year!" Marcell does a little dance on the stool.

"Are they really coming here, to the orphanage? I ask, fidgeting in my chair.

"It's mandatory for everyone who's of age," says Apsel. "They said they're coming to Efricia, so that applies to us as well."

"I don't have to worry about it, though," Embla says, exhaling deeply. "Lucky for me, I turned twenty this year."

"When was the last time they came here?" I ask. "I can't remember."

"It was three years ago," Apsel answers.

"But I don't remember you taking part in the Selections."

Embla frowns, trying to think back to three years ago.

"I don't remember either," she says, turning to face Apsel. "What happened again?"

"You were sick," says Apsel, "so you couldn't attend the Selections."

"Hmm... that's right," Embla says thoughtfully.

"I've got to start training now!" exclaims Marcell. "Let's see... They test for fitness, swimming... Hey, you're good at that Freija! Muscle strength and hearing..."

Marcell is interrupted by Apsel grabbing his shoulders.

"Listen, Marcell, I know it sounds exciting to be a soldier, but keep in mind that this means you'll have to carry weapons, maybe even kill people... It's not like any other job.

If you get an invitation to Bionbyr — you can't say no. I don't have the money to buy a contract for you to work here.

Marcell wrenches free of Apsel's grip.

"Look Apsel, it's nice of you to look out for me, but I *want* to be chosen. It'd be so much better than my job in the harbor. As a soldier, I'll be able to travel around, see the whole world! And I'll be working for a good cause. Like that guy said, it's the greatest service you can do for Ela. It's a higher purpose. I would be helping to keep everyone safe, including you guys."

"Yes, but..." Apsel begins, but he's interrupted by Marcell as he holds up a hand and says:

"No. I'm grateful for everything you've done for me, Apsel, but I'm turning sixteen this year. It's not your decision."

"I don't want to decide for you, I'm just trying to warn you."

"Thanks, but I don't need any warnings."

Marcell gets up and disappears from the room. Apsel sighs deeply and looks down at the floor. I've been listening to the exchange of words between the two of them with a growing knot in my stomach.

Apsel sighs again and shakes his head. "No, I'm too tired after today's events. We'll talk more about this later. The only thing we can do now is prepare for the inevitable."

"Goodnight, Dad," Embla says, giving her father a kiss.

"Goodnight, darling," replies Apsel, "and goodnight, Freija."

Apsel goes into his bedroom, leaving Embla and I to sit alone in silence for a moment before we also decide to go to bed.

You got your wish, Marcell. Sometimes I still wonder if this life was really everything you wanted. Was it everything you thought it would be? If only you could look back on that night. Would you have said the same thing? I'm not so sure.

Everyone at school has already heard the news of Bionbyr's arrival and it's the only thing anyone is talking about. Every time I pass a group of city kids, they're chatting about Bionbyr and how great an honor it is to be selected. They gossip about how extravagant the military school is, how the dorms are really something else and the food is just "too good to be true." I have a hard time believing it. On the other hand, though, almost anything would be better than life in Ithmah and having to go to school here.

Instead of going home after school, I decide to find a quiet place to clear my mind. I start making my way towards my little "oasis" outside the city wall. On the way, I look in through the storefronts, keeping my distance from the stressed-out people crowding the streets as I observe Ithmah's dilapidated, rusty houses. The fact that so many people can even live in one place amazes me. And Ithmah isn't even the biggest city in Ela — far from it, in fact. As soon as I'm outside the city gate, a cool breeze blows in from the sea and the calmness washes over me.

On the other side of the bay, I can see the harbor. Two ships have just come in, so everyone is hustling and bustling to unload goods. Boxes and containers rattle and bang as they're lifted and lowered by small cranes and people the size of ants. Trucks are waiting to be loaded, and they each drive away when they're full. It might be my imagination, but I feel like there are a lot of scents traveling towards me. I can smell salt from the sea, but also fish, spices, oil, and other things I can't even put a name to. I wonder where all the goods come from and where they're going. Everyone in Ithmah will eat the fish, but most can't afford the spices. The boxes have stamps that show where they come from. Although I can't see them from here, I know they say Vallis, Eidyllion, Pari, and some might even be from the capital.

I put my bag down between the palm tree and fruit tree where I usually stash it and walk over to the pier. Here, the wind is fresher and the sun doesn't feel as hot. I sit down for a while, cooling my feet in the water as I take everything in, thinking to myself that this right here is enough. The world can come to me a little bit. I don't have to go to the world. Suddenly, thoughts begin to rush into my head. A job; moving; Bionbyr. I would give almost anything to know what's coming, to avoid wondering how everything's going to change soon.

Behind me, there are soft gnawing sounds. When I turn around to investigate, I see some animals climbing the fruit tree. It's a bunch of sugar gliders. Now I understand why the tree never has any papayas. The sugar gliders are running up and down the branches, looking behind every leaf to see if there's anything to eat. Any new shoots that have grown have long since been eaten up by the fuzzy little dodgers.

I squat down to watch the small creatures. They usually travel in small packs, even inside the city, searching for food wherever they can find it. I've seen them around trash cans and outdoor cafes, but they're always being chased away by people who don't think they belong in town.

I can't help but think that those of us from the orphanage were treated much the same way. We never fit in anywhere either, no matter how much we struggled to. We worked hard in school. We made sure Ithmah got food from our genetically modified crops. But somehow, that wasn't enough.

If I stop and reflect for a bit, I wonder if we could have done anything differently to become part of Ithmah? To fit in? I don't think so. The city kids couldn't see us orphans as anything other than unwanted, dirty, a waste. So, in the end, there weren't many choices for us other than to play the role they had assigned us.

As a matter of fact, I don't think the sugar gliders belong in town either, but that's because I know that they're supposed to live in forests. Here, however, there are no forests nearby. The closest thing to a forest we have around here is the actual oasis at the mount ranch. Just like here at the sea, there are palm trees, but there are significantly more of them there and the water always seems to sparkle. I've gone there a number of times to look at the animals. The sugar gliders were chased away from there too, and now they're doing their best to survive—just like everyone else.

One of them catches sight of me, glides down from a low branch, and scampers towards me. Its coat is brown except on its belly, which is cream-colored. The small back paws have four toes each, but the hands have five and almost look like tiny human hands. Above one eye, the sugar glider has a dark marking that gives the illusion that it's wearing a mask.

"Hey, you," I say.

The sugar glider cocks its head and looks as if it's trying to understand what I'm saying. It takes a little skip forward.

"Are you hungry?" I ask. "Can't find anything to eat?"

I remember that I have some biscuits in my school bag, so I make my way over to it to look for the package. There are only two biscuits left. I take one and hold it out for the sugar glider.

"Here ... Want it?"

The sugar glider comes towards my outstretched hand. It raises its head to sniff the biscuit. Then it stretches out its front paws, snatches the biscuit from my palm, and darts up into one of the trees. The other sugar gliders have seen what just happened, and they also want a piece, but the brave one with the dark marking above its eye doesn't want to share. I laugh and pull out the second biscuit.

"Here, come get it."

I divide the biscuit into small pieces and throw them on the ground so that the other sugar gliders can get a little bit too. *It must be nice to be a sugar glider*, I think when I see how they nibble at the biscuits, *no rules to follow, no obligations*. Sounds great, besides being poisoned and constantly fighting for survival.

Even these little sugar gliders remind me of what awaits me. In my frustration, I groan loudly and accidentally scare the sugar gliders, but it's quickly forgotten and they continue to munch on the biscuits. Suddenly, I get that feeling of emptiness again. The one that makes me feel like my soul is divided and that somewhere out there, the missing other half is waiting. I look at the sugar gliders again.

"Is it my mother?" I whisper to them without reply. *Is she alive?*

I remember every time Apsel and I talked about how I got to the orphanage. How my mom had come on a stormy night, and Apsel had thought that she only wanted to come in to warm up. She had shown me to him and asked Apsel to watch over me. *She had said that I was special.*

I try to remember more details about my mother, and I recall Apsel telling me that she must have come from far away. At first, she had looked like a Wanderer, but that illusion had shattered as soon as she had taken off her hood.

How had she talked? Apsel had said something about it. Was it Adalian? A Capital dialect? I sigh. Why would anyone travel from somewhere so far away to leave a child in an orphanage? There are orphanages closer.

Suddenly everything goes still in my mind. I try to remember what Apsel had said about my mother's appearance, but it's completely blank. Has he ever said anything about it? He must have. Why would he have left that out? How is it that I can't remember anything at all?

When I leave, I feel more lost than when I got here. I turn around to take in the view one more time and see one of the sugar gliders sitting on a branch looking at me. I suspect it's the brave one, but I'm not sure. I squint and see the mark on its eye, confirming my suspicion. It looks like it's winking at me.

My passion or motivation or whatever you want to call it was born that day. I didn't know it then, but I understood it a little later. Maybe it had always been there, waiting to for me to discover what form it would take.

On the way back to the orphanage, I can feel the weather changing rapidly. The wind is getting stronger, and that's usually a dangerous sign. I pick up the pace as I walk through the sunflower fields. At first, the wind is relatively gentle, but soon it begins to blow faster and faster. The danger is already beginning to appear on the horizon: sand.

I start to run.

As I approach the farm, I see Onni fighting with the goat, Freda. She doesn't want to go into the house, but we all know that she has to if she's going to survive the storm. The stable is too fragile. There are little compartments in the soil that the hens can hide in, but they're too small for Freda.

Onni's face is dirty, and I can see that he's been crying because of the stripes his tears have made in the dirt. The strong wind is now blowing so much sand towards me that I have to keep my hand over my eyes to shield them from the onslaught. I help him with Freda, and together we manage to get her inside.

Half the savannah blows into the hall with us. I shake myself off first and then brush off Onni and Freda. Freda seems to have hurt one of her front legs because she has a bit of a limp. I pull out an elastic bandage from the first-aid kit and begin to wrap it around the injured leg. Apsel has taught us a lot about how to take care of ourselves and the animals. Orphans and other people of low status can't really expect to be able to go to the hospital for emergencies.

"Come on," I say in the same fatherly tone that Apsel always uses, "we'll take it off later, but take it easy for now."

Outside, the sandstorm has increased to maximum force. It's critical to not have a small bladder because even the short distance between the house and the outbuilding can be dangerous during a storm like this. For the smaller children, we have to use chamber pots. Fortunately, the orphanage is already prepared for sandstorms. The windows are covered and Apsel has made sure to seal every possible nook and cranny. The sand grains are treacherous though, and they get everywhere inside no matter what we do to try to stop them.

Everyone sits in the dormitory, and Embla keeps them occupied by reading aloud. I close the door behind me and seal it tight. You can never be too careful. I sneak in quietly so as not to interrupt Embla's reading. She notices me and gives me her classic sly smile, but she doesn't stop reading. She's reading the legend of Anora and Dar. It's been a long time since I heard it, and I enjoy listening to Embla's performance.

What happened to you, Embla? Where did everything go wrong? When did I lose you? I'd give anything to be back in that room, listening to your stories, feeling your warmth. Don't you miss it too?

It's later in the evening now, and the storm has finally ceased. All of us "adults" are sitting in the kitchen with a midnight snack and some valerian tea. A gust of wind rushes past my neck from the open window, giving me goosebumps. I shiver a little and suddenly think of the Wanderer who grabbed me in The Plaza yesterday. I had totally forgotten about it.

"What do you think that Wanderer meant by, 'Get ready'?" I blurt the question out suddenly. Embla and Marcell stare at me.

"Who?" Embla asks after a few moments.

"What do you mean 'who'? The Wanderer who grabbed me in The Plaza."

"What Wanderer?"

I look at Embla and see that she's serious. She's not playing stupid. Had I really imagined it? He'd felt so real. The man had come out of nowhere. I hadn't seen him at all until he suddenly appeared in front of me, with a tight grip on my arm. He had been completely invisible before that. I remember being so scared when I saw the man's stare as he muttered the words "prepare yourself." Prepare myself for what?

Growing up, there have been several times when Wanderers have come to the orphanage. Sometimes they've been friendly, sometimes not. Wanderers have no homes and no jobs and are therefore illegal. The Guardians pick them up off the street, but Apsel always accepts them with open arms, albeit with some caution. "Remember that Wanderers are just like you and me," he used to say. "The difference is that they have even less."

But the Authority portrays Wanderers as lawless criminals, and I can't help feeling a little anxious when they come around. Most people just close their doors, pretend to not be home, chase them away, or worse.

"No one," I answer, avoiding the topic of conversation. I feel like what happened in The Plaza was real, but there's no point in worrying Embla if she didn't see anything. Marcell doesn't seem particularly interested in the subject either.

"Maybe you should get some sleep, huh sister little?"

"Yeah, I'm probably just a little tired," I lie. Come to think of it, it's probably not a lie anyway, and a big yawn confirms it.

I caress the bracelet that I fished up on my birthday and think about all the weird things that have happened to me lately. A Wanderer no one can see. A memory of something I couldn't possibly have experienced myself. A golden fairy tale bird. What's happening to me? Are these warnings that something's going to happen?

"Well, wherever you end up, you know we're here for you," says Apsel, who must have noticed that I disappeared into my own world for a while. "After Bionbyr has come and gone – and you're not recruited – you'll be called into the Labor Office, where you'll only have to take a few tests and complete an interview."

More tests? It feels like I've been taking tests all my life. Tests that will determine what path I take, what I can do; tests that show my knowledge and abilities. But can they really show who I am and what I want?

"I know it's scary, but that's what it's like to grow up. You don't get many choices," Apsel continues. "It's hard not knowing what kind of job you'll get, what kind of workplace or co-workers you'll have, but it might be something good. And if you don't enjoy it, you're not doomed either. Look at me, for example, I was assigned to work at the ranch – and I did for several years – but then I was told that the director of this orphanage had died. I applied to become the new director and, well, you know the rest!"

He throws up his arms and smiles.

"It's all right, sister little," Embla says.

"Yeah, you're right," I say. "I don't even know what kind of job I want."

"That's complete nonsense," Marcell chimes in, displaying his usual attitude. "They just want to fill empty seats."

Apsel gives him an angry look.

"We were just trying to cheer Freija up," he says, but Marcell rolls his eyes.

"But you're wrong," says Marcell. "The fact that you became the director of this place was probably just a coincidence. I know people in the harbor who've been trying to get relocated for years. Usually, they don't even get an answer, or they get excuses about the applications getting dropped or stock answers about there being no vacancies. It's all just bollocks. There's always free space somewhere."

"I understand your frustration, Marcell. You might be right that it was good timing or luck that made it possible for me. But there's still hope. Don't give up," says Apsel.

"Bollocks. It doesn't matter what you do. The Authority always does whatever benefits them. They don't care about what's good for each citizen, they only look out for their own. I'm looking forward to Bionbyr's arrival. I'll show them what I'm good for, and I'll make sure I get a ticket for that boat to the school."

"I thought you liked the President and the way he governs?" Embla says sarcastically when she sees Apsel looking offended.

"I never said I liked it. I accept it. I live by it. There's a point to the system. You can see it for yourself: lower crime, less starvation, and there hasn't been much sickness since The Late Epidemic. The system works. I want to do something more, absolutely, and that's why I want to be one of them. Bionbyr will help me with that."

"But how can..." Embla starts, but Apsel interrupts her.

"Let him be. He's already decided, and we all have the right to think and feel as we please. It's not until we can accept each other's differences that we can see each other as equals."

Nobody says anything else. I don't even try to get involved in the discussion. Apsel, Embla, and Marcell all have very definite opinions — and none of them are willing to concede to the others. I'm usually the one who mediates, but tonight I just can't.

6

The sun hasn't come out in several days, even though the sandstorm has long since passed. The swirling sand left behind a hazy darkness and a thick blanket of grains over the orphanage and fields. When we walked around the property to assess the damage, it quickly became clear that this had been one of the worst and most powerful storms we'd had in years. The tractor wouldn't start. Several of our chickens had lost their lives. Some of the hives had been toppled over and one had been completely destroyed. Large parts of the vegetable gardens and the crop fields were either blown away, torn up, or suffocated by sand and debris.

"I heard Dad talking to the Authority earlier," Embla says sadly. "He won't get much support from them. They said it was part of the deductible to grow in this environment and that the insurance won't cover it. It'll take several weeks, maybe even months, to get it all back on track again."

Embla and I are trying to clear sand from the vegetable beds. It's a lot harder than either of us thought it would be. I wish there was something more I could do. The knot in my stomach just grows when I think about the fact that soon I might not even be in Ithmah to help at all. Sure, Apsel has Embla and Marcell – and Onni and the other kids, of course – but like Embla said, it'll be months before they have anything ready to sell.

I rub my fingers against my black bead bracelet idly.

"I know it's not much, but maybe you can get a good price for this," I say as I give Embla the bracelet I found on the seabed. Embla takes the beads and squeezes my hand twice. I still wish there was something more I could do. We'll see what happens with the testing at the Labor Office at the end of the school year. Unless I'm admitted to Bionbyr.

I don't know if I'll be able to handle being away from my family. Or what it means to be a soldier. Carrying weapons, for example. Exposing myself to danger. Even if it means keeping Ela's people safe.

"Thank you, sister little," says Embla.

The representative from Bionbyr arrives in Ithmah by car early on Wednesday. Apsel has been notified to prepare those of us who will be undergoing the testing and make sure that we all have food in our stomachs before we get picked up in the car. I hear Apsel walking around, muttering that something seems strange. This has never happened before. Usually, he just has to send information about the kids who are the right age and make sure that they appear on time for registration at the testing location. Never, in all the time that Apsel has been the director, have they sent someone to personally pick up the kids. For security reasons, Apsel took down the Presidential portraits of Adam Simulis and Elham Donya and put up the hologram portrait of our current President. Just in case the representative were to enter the house. I understand his caution. We would be fined by the Authority if the portrait wasn't cared for and displayed properly.

"I know that neither Adam nor Elham are particularly high on our current President's list, and I don't want anyone to think that I have the wrong opinions or something," Apsel explains when Embla raises an eyebrow. He takes down the map of the Old World as well.

The representative is middle-aged, with light, almost pale skin, and his reddish-brown hair is combed back. Despite the heat, he's wearing a long, black coat. It's fairly thin, but underneath he has some kind of black robe with blood-red embroidery that makes it look expensive. Marcell and I sit on the stairs outside the front door of the orphanage and watch as Apsel talks to the representative. Some of the children are out playing, but they've already been told to keep away from the visitor. Embla is tending to the garden beds that are still partially covered by sand. We look at the representative as he talks to Apsel. He has this way of keeping his head high and looking down at Apsel when he talks that I instantly dislike. The two of them start walking towards me and Marcell. We quickly get to our feet.

"Like I said, there are only two. This is Freija and Marcell," says Apsel, gesturing to both of us.

The representative inspects us with a critical eye. He searches for something for a moment before turning back to Apsel.

"There should be three young people here. One is missing," he sneers. "Where is Embla Faas?"

Apsel looks at him, first in confusion and then in defeat. He takes a deep breath, and in a slightly shaky voice, he says:

"Embla is my daughter. She works here at the orphanage with me, and she's actually twenty years old."

The representative holds up his hand to silence Apsel.

"She should have attended testing three years ago. But she didn't."

"She was sick," insists Apsel. "Stomach flu. She wasn't called in because of it."

"Embla Faas will be tested with the other two," the man emphasizes each word individually to make his point really sink in. "That's an order."

The representative takes a step towards Apsel so that they're face to face. I look at him and notice that parts of his cheek, chin, and throat have clear burn marks. Sunburns are pretty common around here, but these burns are from flames. I wonder if there was an accident, or is this just what happens when the Authority punishes someone?

Reluctantly, Apsel calls a confused Embla over from the garden to join our little group.

"I'm sorry, I tried," Apsel whispers to Embla, who still doesn't understand what's going on. Before anyone can explain to her, the representative orders us all to line up in the yard. He makes himself extra clear when he says it to Embla. I don't know if it's fear or just nerves I feel right now. We haven't even begun the testing yet, and I already feel something within me telling me to get away, forget about Bionbyr, and move on with my life—whatever that would mean. As we stand there in the yard, I feel like a product that's being inspected to see if it measures up. Marcell is standing next to me with his back straight and his eyes staring straight ahead. I don't intend to put any effort into impressing the representative, and neither does Embla. Her eyebrows are arched, and I can see the gears in her mind already beginning to turn.

The representative doesn't seem like the kind of person to waste his breath on keeping a conversation going. It makes the situation even more uncomfortable. He walks around us and inspects every detail of our outward appearances. Is this one of the tests?

"What happened here?" the representative asks suddenly, as he grabs my arm and points to my forearm. His grip is so warm that I could have sworn he'd pressed a hot saucepan against my skin, but as soon as he releases his grip, the feeling is gone. I look at the spot he pointed out and see a small scar, barely visible, that I had completely forgotten I even have. I hardly know how to answer, but I give it a shot.

"The reeds can be really dangerous if you're not careful," I can hear how nervous I sound as I say it.

The representative stares at me but seems to approve of the explanation. After all, it's the truth.

"Okay, I've seen enough," the man finally says. "We need to get to the Selections."

He takes us in the same car he came to the orphanage in. Marcell and Embla are allowed to squeeze into the back seat. Squeeze is an exaggeration, actually. The seat could easily fit another person. It must be nice to be rich enough to afford this kind of luxury. The feeling gets stronger when the doors close and the car's air conditioning comes on. Just like Ithmah's trams, this car has no driver. When the representative gets into the car and presses a screen a few times, the car drives off automatically.

"He can't do this! Why do I have to go through the Selections? I'm already twenty years old! This is absolutely ridiculous!" Embla blurts out without thinking.

"Quiet, Embla!" I hiss, looking anxiously at the front of the car to see if the representative has heard her. Everything seems to be quiet. I look at Embla as her eyes fill with tears. I want to cry too, but I need to stay strong to get through this. I need to help Embla get through today too. Bionbyr is under the direct control of the President, you don't say no when they give you an order. It's just not possible. We have to go to the selections and compete in their tests. And we can't bomb them on purpose, or they'll know and we could get in trouble.

Marcell notices that Embla is taking this hard, and at first, he's offended that she's so upset to be taking the first step towards his dream career, but soon he seems more understanding.

"Come on, girls," he whispers encouragingly. "We'll go there, suffer through the tests, and then tonight we'll go home, and everything will be just like before. Remember, there's the interview as well. It's not enough to be strong and healthy, you have to have the right mindset too. If they notice that you're scared or unfit to be a soldier, they won't choose you."

I feel a little reassured by Marcell's words and nod to him. Embla wipes away her tears, but I can feel her pulse still soaring. I give Embla a kiss on the forehead and she gratefully accepts it.

The Selections must be in the field outside Ithmah, because we don't take the highway into town. Instead, we drive along the city wall, which extends high above us towards the sky. It would be nice if the orphanage had its own wall to protect it from sandstorms. Since we don't have one, our only option is to cover the windows with boards and wait until the storm subsides to see the damage. Ivy grows along the city wall and in the places the ivy hasn't already covered, the wall is filled with doodles and graffiti. The contrast between the rusty wall, the vibrant green plant life, and the graffiti with its bold black or brightly colored scribbles are beautiful in their own way.

Way out in the field, the sun shines on a long line of white tents that are arranged in a U-shape. There are a dozen Guardians patrolling the field for security. There's no sign that this is usually a place for children to play. Down by the water, where I always go to swim, there are more tents on the beach. I can see the Bionbyr coat of arms. The shield is

Bionbyr's signature navy blue, and it's enfolded in solid-gold wings. In the center of the shield is Bionbyr's emblem: a killer whale and a shark that chase each other's tail fins to form a circle around the letter B. Under the B, even though I can't see it from here, I know it says, "Discipline and Loyalty." It's the school's motto. Some of the young people are already in their places, and more seem to be walking over from the tram station. I take note of the fact that Embla, Marcell, and I seem to be the only ones to arrive by car. The selection area is full of pristine white officials. Their clean, bright uniforms make them look like a cross between soldiers and doctors.

The car parks in front of the largest tent, in the center. The representative gets out of the car and opens the door for us. We carefully step out and look uncertainly around us.

"You should go in there and get registered," says the man, pointing at the entrance to the tent.

Embla's eyes shift constantly, and she doesn't seem to be able to focus on anything. I've never seen her like this before. Most of the time, it's the opposite since I'm usually the one who gets insecure while Embla cheers up and supports *me*. Now I take Embla's hand in mine and say:

"Come on now. It's only one day. Tonight, we can go home. Just look at all these people. They'll never choose us."

I'm trying to convince myself as much as Embla. I squeeze her hand twice and Embla squeezes back.

Inside the tent, it's a completely different atmosphere than I'm used to at school. Here, everyone is treated exactly the same, whether they live with their family or in an orphanage. I recognize several people from my school and make eye contact with some of them. Nobody says anything. Here, no one can watch each other's back. It's every person for themselves. When I look around, it feels there are a lot more people that should be here. Some of the others from my class aren't visible. Actually, there are only a few hundred here, and there are way more people than that who are between sixteen and nineteen in Ithmah.

After standing in line for a while, we finally get registered, and we each receive a number: 113, 114, and 115. Embla and I are in group 6, while Marcell is divided into group 4. We're sent to one side of the tent where we can change into more suitable clothes before we sit next to the stage to wait for further instructions.

The clothes waiting for us look like they're made to fit ten-year-olds, and when Embla asks one of the officials about it, she just gets a cold look and an order to put them on. We soon discover that the clothes are stretchy and fit perfectly over our bodies like an extra layer of skin. The clothes are gray, but along both sides there are wide stripes that glow in Ela's bright burgundy. We attach our identification cards to our clothes. When Marcell tries to adjust his, he discovers that it's not possible. The I.D. can't be tampered with once it's attached to the uniform.

Embla, Marcell, and I sit together on an empty bench in front of a large stage at the back of the tent. The only thing on the stage besides the podium is a big screen and two large speakers that float above the podium. No one says anything. A frightening silence fills the tent, and the only thing that can be heard are the voices near the registration tables. White-clad officials patrol the entire tent, making sure that everyone is where they should be. The registration is efficient, and it won't be long before everyone has received their number and been assigned to a group. The benches in front of the stage are filled with young people, with exactly enough space for each person who's supposed to be here today.

"It's the representative!" Embla whispers to me, pointing discreetly towards the stage. We have to strain to see because the stage is a bit far, but if I squint, I can clearly make out the red details on his black robes. Standing next to him is a man who could be his twin, based on the way they're dressed. The only difference is that the embroidery on the other man's robes are blue and his hair is not styled as neatly. They're standing on the side of the podium, waiting for a third person. It's another man. I get the feeling that this man is much kinder than the representative who brought us here. He's also dressed in black, and he has medium-length black hair, with even paler skin than the representative's. *These people don't get out in the sun much,* I think.

When he starts talking, his voice echoes through the tent. It's not as cold and determined as the representative, and it makes me feel a bit more at ease about the upcoming tests.

"Welcome!" The man holds up his arms, as if to embrace all of the gathered youth. The screen behind displays him more clearly. There's a drone somewhere filming him, so we can't miss anything he says. "I am the headmaster of Bionbyr. My name is Andor Amaro." Spirited applause sounds throughout the tent. "Next to me, I have Domi Bern Cainea, the Social Studies professor, and Domi Esbern Cainea, professor of Criminology. Give them a hand!"

Embla and I reluctantly applaud the Criminology teacher, Esbern Cainea, who picked us up this morning. We both have the feeling that he already hates us. So he and the Social Studies professor *are* brothers.

"Life as a soldier in Ela's Military Elite Squad is a tough life. It's an important life. It's a job that's a privilege to have. But not everyone can become an EMES soldier. Today, you take the first step towards proving that you have what it takes to hold one of Ela's more important positions." Andor speaks every word with passion. I think he's probably given this speech countless times before, and I'm impressed that he still manages to say everything with emotion, without sounding like he's reading from a script. "An important job like this also requires many sacrifices. You'll be away from your friends and family for weeks – even months – at a time, but you'll be rewarded in other ways. Every month, an EMES soldier receives between 50,000 and 100,000 monetas. But of course, for us, it's not about the money. It's about standing up for what's right. Together for Ela!"

"Together for Ela!" thunders through the tent. The headmaster continues to explain the arrangements for the day and tells each group what they'll be starting with. There are eight tests we'll be taking today. Group 6, which is mine and Embla's group, will start with an endurance exam and Marcell's group will start with the swimming test.

A monthly salary of fifty thousand monetas? My thoughts are spinning. That's fifty times more than I could ever dream of earning in a month at a normal job. With that kind of salary, I could save the orphanage. If I can graduate and become an EMES soldier. Is that really what I want? I'll never be able to pay back everything Apsel has done for me, because I had a good childhood with plenty of food and love. But I can do this for him. First, I have to get through today. *Am I ready for all this?*

I look at Embla, nervously bouncing her leg and trying to think about anything else. As if someone has flipped a switch, everyone in the room rises in unison. Embla, Marcell, and I are caught up in the stream of young people trying to find their way to their first tests. Eight officials stand outside the tent with large screens that they use as signs, one for each group, held above their heads. Embla and I don't even get the chance to say "good luck" to Marcell before he's already gone towards the sign with the number "4" on it. We quickly spot our own sign and head towards it. The woman holding up mine and Embla's group number waits for everyone in the group to gather before she starts speaking to us. I'd guess that there are about thirty people in our group.

"Welcome, I am Yrsa, and I will be your guide today. My job is to make sure that you're in the right place at the right time during today's events. Keeping up with me will make it easier for both you and me. Questions so far?" Yrsa doesn't look much older than Embla, and her white hair feels unnatural compared to her dark eyebrows. I get caught in her ice-blue eyes. No one asks any questions. "All clear then. We're off to a good start. We've organized the tests today so that every other test will be a physical activity and the ones in between will be non-physical activities. You'll start with the endurance exam, which I personally think is the worst of them."

"It'll be good to get the worst out of the way first, at least," I whisper to Embla, but I get no answer. Embla is still really tense. I've never seen her break down like this before, and the day hasn't even started.

Yrsa leads us into one of the smaller tents that are adjacent to the big one. Inside, there are exactly as many machines as there are people in our group, and everyone stands next to one while a pale, round woman with thin, gray hair walks around fastening cords on the machines for each student. I look curiously at the others as they become... I try to think of the right word, but "connected" is the best I can come up with, to the machines. When it's my turn, I notice that each of the cords has a small transparent square attached to the end, made out of some material I've never seen before. It's soft, light, and thin. When it touches my skin, it feels really cold. I get ten of these attached to my body: one on each arm, one on each leg, and the rest in various spots on my chest. When the gray-haired woman is done hooking me up, another person comes forward and fastens a rectangular fabric bag with a weird gauge on it over my arm. It tightens so much that it almost hurts. I can feel my heart beating harder and wonder if the cords can detect it.

I'm only now starting to realize that I've never seen a machine like the one I'm standing next to before. It consists of a seat perched on top of a pipe. In front of the seat is a handle with enough room for both hands. When I see the other young people settling into their machines, I do the same and instinctively put my feet on each platform. When I relax, I notice that the platforms aren't stuck in place. The person who strapped the tight gauge on my arm now fastens my feet to the platforms and slips a blue mask over my face that covers my nose, mouth, and chin. Then he picks up a glass tablet that was stored in a compartment in the machine, stands next to me, and waits. All the other students have someone standing by their side as well.

"Try to breathe normally," the guy urges me. I turn myself around to see if I can find Embla and catch sight of her a little farther ahead. Like me, she's sitting on a machine with a mask over her face, with her hands clamped tightly around the handle in front of her.

"We're going to test your physical fitness, but before we get started, you'll have a chance to see how it feels. Partly to warm you up, but also to get the machines started. I know it might be your first time doing something like this, but you'll notice that it's not especially difficult. Tread with your feet just as you would if you were taking a walk. Go ahead and give it a try," Yrsa explains and sits down on a chair that's higher up than everyone else. From there, she has a perfect line of sight over the entire group.

I look down at my feet and feel uncomfortable. I try to tread, but nothing happens. I try again and succeed in taking a single step forward, even though I haven't moved an inch. I try to do it again, but it doesn't work as well this time. I groan.

"Bend your knees," suggests the guy who put on my mask. I follow his advice and bend my knees at the same time as I take a step. This time it works much better, and finally, I have control over the situation. It feels surprisingly easy now, and even fun.

"Now the test is really starting, so try to keep the same pace. You'll notice that it gets harder and harder. The test will only be finished once none of you are able to continue. Do your best! Get ready!" Yrsa says after we've practiced for a short while, and the test officially begins. By this time, I've already gotten the hang of the machine and I continue to pedal, despite feeling some resistance in my legs. But somewhere in the back of my mind, I hear: *Where have I heard that expression recently?*

It doesn't take long for the first person to stop, and after that more and more give up. I'm among the last to keep going, but I'm starting to notice that my legs can't hold out much longer and, finally, I have to call it quits too. The guy who's been standing next to me checks the gauge on my arm and takes notes on the glass tablet. It seems to be some kind of screen because it beeps when he presses the glass and continues to record his notes. Then he steps closer to the machine and scratches down something else that the machine has recorded while someone else starts gently removing the cords from my body, one by one. I try to step down, but I've forgotten that my feet are secured, so I stay seated. I get a little annoyed that the guy hasn't prioritized disconnecting me from the machine, but I understand why when he finally frees me and I step off. My legs feel unnatural, and every step I take is difficult. My leg muscles have turned to jelly, and I have to stay seated at the machine for a little while before I feel like myself again. I wave to Embla, who sees my wave but doesn't return it.

"Okay, follow me," Yrsa calls out, and everyone follows obediently. In the next tent, everyone is put into separate stalls. There are new people here to help us with everything we need for the next test. I was so out of it after the last test that I missed what this was for. The booth contains a small chair. A girl asks me to sit there and then put something over my ears. All sounds disappear. I can see that the girl is saying something, as her lips are moving, but no sound comes out.

"WHAT?" I yell, and the girl smiles and gives me a thumbs up. Apparently, I'm not supposed to hear anything.

This goes on for a little while, and then suddenly I hear a voice. I jerk, frightened at first. It sounds like the voice is coming from inside my head.

"You will hear some sounds, and when you hear a sound, we would like you to say loudly and clearly which ear you hear the sound in. Nod if you understand," the voice says, and I nod. "This is the sound you'll hear." I hear a discreet sound but can't tell which ear I heard it in. "Nod if you heard it." I nod again. "Good, do your best!"

For the next few minutes, I sit in the booth and say "right," "left," "left," after each beep. Before I can think about what the point of this test is, it's over, and we move on to the next activity, which will test our speed.

In another tent, they've set up a course for us to run on. I'm bad at estimating distances, but comparatively, it would be about the same as the distance between the orphanage and the stable, maybe a little more. Embla looks a bit better after the last test. I walk over to her and give her a supportive look.

"How are you feeling?" I ask, but Embla doesn't get a chance to answer. The group has already assembled and Yrsa gives us instructions.

"You'll start there," Yrsa says, pointing to a line on the ground, "and end there." She points to another line on the other side of the track. "You won't all run at the same time. I will come around and split you into groups of six. The number I assign you is your new group number, as well as the order you'll go in, understand? No one says anything, so Yrsa quickly approaches the group and points to each of us to assign our numbers. I get number 3.

The first group gets ready. It's a mix of girls and boys who advance to the starting line. One of the boys is limping a little and seems to have trouble walking. *Is he really going to run?* I wonder. The starting shot goes off, and everyone starts running. The limping boy is struggling to keep up, but he quickly falls far behind the others. But that's not the most startling thing about this race. I'm so busy watching the limping boy at first that I don't even notice that one of the others hasn't started running at all. A boy with dark hair stands perfectly still. He's as stiff as a board and it looks like his entire body is tensed.

"Come on!" shouts the official who fired the starting shot. The boy shakes his head. A Guardian comes forward and gives him a hard shove that sends him falling forward, but he regains his balance and stands completely still again. The boy seems to say something, because the Guardian leans towards him and shouts:

"What?"

"You don't own me!" The boy's voice cracks a few times, but he sounds determined. I'm holding my breath. The first group has already finished running, and I have no idea who came in first or how it went. All I see right now is another Guardian walk over to the track, quickly reaching the brown-haired boy. He has a whip in his hand.

"If they say run, you run!" He gives the boy a lash over his back. The boy screams but still doesn't move. Another lash, and another. Red lines begin to form on the boy's back. It glows through the gray fabric.

"You don't own me!" he screams again. The Guardian gives him a kick in the back and continues to whip him. "Run! Run! Run!" he roars with every lash.

7

The boy falls forward, regains his balance, and takes a few steps to escape the whip. He tries to stand still again, but he can no longer stand upright. He crawls on the ground until finally he just lays there, but the Guardian doesn't seem to want to stop whipping him. Then, one of Bionbyr's officials steps forward to call off the beating. I can't hear what they're saying, but they pick up the boy, each grabbing one of his arms, and pull him off the track. They disappear out of the tent.

The next group is getting ready to run, but everyone is still spooked by what they've just seen so they don't hear when the starting shot goes off. It's not until someone from the group after them urges them to run that they turn their focus back to the race and do their best to get to the other side of the tent. Everything happens so fast and my group is called too quickly. I can't understand what I just witnessed. I look at Embla as she leans towards me and wipes away tears that I didn't even realize were running down my cheeks. I think back to what had occurred to me earlier: that we can't perform *too* poorly. When I get to the starting line, I look around for the whipped boy, but the white-clad officials and the white tents merge into a dazzling mess and I can't tell the people from the surroundings.

The official with the starting gun walks in front of us to make sure that none of us are standing on or over the starting line, which is covered in some kind of red liquid. It smells like iron. When he's satisfied, he stands off to the side, raises the gun, and fires the starting shot.

I don't even have time to be nervous, my body feels numb. I need a break to recover from what I've just seen, but no one gives me a break. I run, taking in everything I can. It starts out pretty well, but soon I'm passed by most of the group. I try to concentrate on running, but all I can see in front of me is the boy on the ground with red covering his back. The thought of the whip makes me want to run faster, but at the same time, it makes my legs feel like spaghetti—and they're still shaky from the first test. I want to sink down to the ground, just like the boy. I want to look into his eyes and ask him how he feels, ask him how he can be so brave, so stupid, to just stand there and say what he did. Somehow, I manage to make it to the finish line, but I have no idea how I've performed. Embla's group is next. I've never seen her run as fast as she does during the test. A few seconds later, she too reaches the finish line.

I still have nightmares about the whipped boy. It was effective, I'll give them that. It made me not want to end up like him. The Guardians have always had that effect on us. They keep us in order by spreading terror. I keep thinking that it could have been Embla. If they had heard her in the car. If they had heard the criticism she expressed at the orphanage. If they could read her thoughts. That could have been my sister.

I know what awaits us if we continue, but at the same time, we have no other choice. They can't be allowed to get away with this. That's my promise to you.

Before lunch, we're each given a glass tablet with a number of questions that we have to answer to test our knowledge. My thoughts are still scattered, so I honestly don't know how I did. At this point, it's make or break. If I don't get sent to the school, I'll have to find other ways to help Apsel. Maybe there's still hope that Marcell will come around back around, feel grateful for his good upbringing, and donate some of his salary. It's probably too much to even wish for. Yrsa announces that it's time for lunch and that the tests will resume in an hour.

"Thank goodness," Embla says, and I feel the same way. Finally, a break. Sandwiches and juice are served in some of the tents. Even though the lines look long, we get our food pretty quickly. We each get a tray with the exact same amount of food and drink. Marcell waves both of us over to join him at one of the tables.

"How have you been doing?" he asks enthusiastically. He doesn't seem to be anywhere near as tired as we are, but I can see in his eyes that the day must have been heavy for him too. We shrug. Marcell nods and then looks around at all the young people surrounding us.

"I think I've done well," he says, "but there are so many people to compete against..."

Marcell doesn't notice our shock. How can he? He wasn't there. He didn't see the whip that was splashing red all over the track. He didn't see the boy who writhed in pain. He didn't see the abuse that was happening right in front of our eyes. Thankfully, Bionbyr's official had finally put a stop to it. What would have happened if he hadn't?

Even though Embla and I are hungry, we hardly touch our food.

"Aren't you going to eat?" asks Marcell, who eventually notices that something's not right. Embla and I nod and pick up our perfectly round sandwiches in unison. Embla takes a big bite of hers, opens her eyes wide, and looks between the two slices of bread.

"There's meat in these!" she exclaims. "A slice of real meat! Does yours have it too?"

I check mine and it's true: there's a thin slice of meat nestled in with lettuce, a slice of tomato, onion, and some kind of sauce. I take a big bite too. It's been a long time since we've eaten meat that wasn't one of the slaughter hens from the orphanage, or the old donkey an eternity ago.

"Do you think they get this kind of luxury food at Bionbyr?" wonders Embla.

The juice is also really good. It tastes like some kind of red berry that I don't recognize, but it's sweet and delicious, and soon I can feel my energy returning.

Over at the beach, we get split into small groups again. I'm looking forward to jumping in the water. We haven't gotten to be outside very much today, and the water is probably the only thing that can make me feel completely calm again. They've put flags in the water and set up lanes, just like the ones on the running track this morning. Here, too, there are white-clad officials in place. Some are sitting out on the water in small boats. Despite the heat, I feel goosebumps on my skin when I see the official with the starting gun. It's a woman this time.

"Group 6, listen up!" yells Yrsa. She's put her white hair up in a ponytail, revealing a strong jawline and long neck. "You'll go to the starting point on the beach and start by swimming in breaststrokes to the first flag you see out there. Then, you'll turn around and swim in backstrokes. Keep in mind that you can only use your legs for this part. You'll do this until you reach the second flag. When you get to that flag, you will dive down and pick up a doll from the bottom. You'll need to bring the doll back to the beach. Any questions?"

I go over what Yrsa said in my head. Swim normally to the first flag, swim on your back without using your arms to the next flag, dive and pick up the doll from the bottom, then bring it back to the beach. I understand.

This time, Embla is in the same starting group as I am, and she walks with determined steps over to the beach. She stands right at the edge of the water and shows no signs of nervousness when our turn comes, but I feel my heart beating hard in my chest. I'm good at swimming and I'm fast. Do I have to be good at everything, or will they choose people who stand out and do really well in a few specific events?

The sun's rays glitter on the surface of the water. When I turn to look back at the beach, I see something dark among the white officials. The headmaster is standing there in his dark clothes, and next to him stands the representative who picked us up this morning, I think his name was Cainea? Are they particularly interested in swimming?

He and Andor are just standing there talking to each other, but suddenly they both look in my direction. No, not in my direction, they're looking *straight at me*. I quickly look away. Was it just my imagination? I don't dare to look again. I think of the Guardian with the whip and decide to swim as fast as I can. The starting shot goes off. I get to the finish first, well ahead of the others.

The following two tests are in the same place. Just like the first test, I get a collection of cables attached to me. I have to stand in position near two posts that are connected to a bar. I'm instructed to take a wide stance in front of the bar and do whatever I can to lift it. I feel bad because I'm only able to lift it a few centimeters, but the official seems satisfied. I'd like to see the city kids try to lift it higher than that anyway. They've never had to lift anything heavy in their lives. Immediately afterwards, a doctor asks me to undress. The doctor pinches and prods, carefully inspecting every inch of my body. Still naked, I have to stand on a scale to check my weight. He measures my height as well and, before I leave, I have to complete a vision test.

Today's last test is the interview. I head into a tent where there's an elderly woman, also dressed in white, already waiting in front of a screen. In addition to the desk the screen is on, there are two chairs—one for the woman and one for me. She motions for me to come in and starts tapping things on the screen. The tent is no bigger than mine and Embla's room at the orphanage. The woman smiles at me and asks for my name. Of course, she's already seen my I.D. tag, but maybe she's trying to be nice.

"Freija Falinn." The official smiles again and looks at the screen. It occurs to me that we haven't been told what any of the officials are called, except Yrsa, and I get an overwhelming desire to ask the older woman her name. I'm guessing that she wouldn't tell me anyway, though, so I stay silent.

"You're from the Sethunya Home for Wayward Children, correct?"

I nod, but I'm promptly asked to answer out loud.

"Yes."

"Have you always lived there?"

"I was left there as a newborn and grew up there with Embla, my sister, and Apsel, who's the director. Marcell, who's also here today, didn't come to the orphanage until later."

"You only need to answer with a 'yes' or 'no' unless the question requires further explanation."

My heart rate suddenly increases. I feel like I'm being scrutinized from head to toe. Have I already blown it?

"How do you think your schooling has been?"

At first, I'm uncertain. It's not a "yes" or "no" question. Should I just say "good"? I do and am asked to explain what's been good about it.

"It's really been fine all around. The whole experience. Of course, I don't really have anything to compare it to. I've learned what I'm supposed to, I guess, but I do wish that I could have felt more welcome."

"In what way did you feel that you weren't welcome?"

"We orphans have always been treated differently."

"What makes you say that?"

"It's just a feeling. Every time they talk to me, or rather, don't talk to me. But it doesn't matter, I've had my family at the orphanage. They've always been able to help me with homework and problems if there was anything I didn't understand in school."

"Am I to understand that you haven't received education from authorized professionals?"

"Huh? No, what I mean is that those of us who went to school helped each other. We've always been corrected by the teachers when we get something wrong."

"Have you ever received education from the director? Apsel Faas?"

"If you count working on the farm, learning about the plant kingdom, animal and crops, and such, then yeah, but nothing about the subjects we learn in school."

"So Director Faas hasn't educated you on history or Tabians?"

"N-no," I reply. The whole time I'm wondering if I'm answering right or not, what is right or wrong here, and how the official is evaluating my answers. I try to read her reactions, but the woman's face is like a stone statue and gives nothing away. My insecurity must be shining through, because the official smiles and says:

"You can relax. This interview is just for those at Bionbyr to find out who you are as people. Not everything is about strength, speed, or how smart you are. It's also about who you are as a person. Just be yourself and answer honestly, everything will be fine." I relax a bit, but I'm not sure it's a good thing.

"What do you think of President Didrik Daegal?" the official asks then, causing me to jerk. This is a completely different kind of question.

"Well, I don't really know..." I begin. "I've never met him." I try to smile, but I can see that the official doesn't think I'm funny. I'm starting to fidget. It feels wrong to say that I think the President is good, but isn't that exactly what they want to hear from their future soldiers? To say that I think he's bad... I think of the people in Ithmah who I've seen being abused by Guardians because they scribbled something negative about the President. I think of Apsel, who took down the two Presidential portraits before the representative came to the orphanage. I think of the President's challengers during election years, who always seem to disappear under mysterious circumstances.

"I think he does a good job," I say in the end.

"At school, you've probably read about his work in providing security with regards to those who have powers. What do you think of it?"

"If they're dangerous, they need to be taken care of," I tell her, but my mouth feels really dry. "They have to be kept away from normal people."

"Do you know anyone who possesses a power?" I shake my head. "No, and it's a criminal offense to not report it if you suspect someone."

The official moves on to asking about Bionbyr. "How do you think you would feel if you were accepted?" This is it.

I've never seen myself as the kind of person who could hold a weapon, fight, go to war. Not for my country, and above all, not for the President. But if I don't get in, it'll be much harder for me to help Sethunya. I look at the woman and hope she can't read my thoughts. I answer as close to the truth as I can.

"I would be proud." The woman keys something in on the screen. There's a stone in my chest.

"I see that you did very well at swimming today. Impressive," the woman praises me.

Did she buy it? As a matter of fact, I would be really proud if I managed to go all the way. To not only complete the tests today and get in, but to get through all three years at the school, become a soldier with a great salary, and donate it to the orphanage.

"You know that Bionbyr is looking for all sorts of people, right? Everyone has something that they can offer. There are various duties that an EMES soldier can perform. Not all of them are out in the field."

I swallow hard and force a smile.

Embla's interview apparently went faster because she's already waiting for me after mine ends. We've been asked to find our assigned changing tent outside, where we'll be able to change back into our own clothes and wash up after today's tests.

"How did it go?" I ask.

Embla shrugs her shoulders.

"I might have gotten a little ticked off when I was talking to the interviewer. I mean, I didn't say anything stupid about the President or anything. But I told them that I'm already twenty, so it's not like I'll be selected anyway. I told them I'd never hold a weapon." She sighs loudly and looks around. "I honestly don't understand why they even bother running this whole recruitment thing. Why not just let people come to them? Surely they'd get their hundred and fifty students a year anyway, and then they'd be getting the ones who actually *want* to become soldiers."

"Three hundred students this year, don't forget," I remind her. Embla's eyes widen. It means there's a greater risk of being selected. Even though there aren't any officials nearby, I still get a little nervous about Embla's words. If she's going to criticize Bionbyr's methods, she should probably wait until we're far away from here. I think of the boy again.

We find the changing tent, which thankfully isn't too crowded. There are huge wooden barrels of water where we can wash ourselves. The water in the barrels has already been used by so many others that it's pretty cloudy, but that's nothing new for us. We strip off the gray uniforms and sit down in front of the tubs on teeny, tiny pallets. There's soap provided, and we use it all over our bodies. The water is still lukewarm when we each take a smaller wooden bucket, fill it from the barrel, and pour it over our heads. We continue like that, soaping up and rinsing off with the cloudy water a few times until we think that we probably won't get much cleaner than we are. We find our clothes, which are waiting neatly folded in a corner of the tent, and when we put them on, we begin to feel somewhat like ourselves again.

Marcell steps into the changing tent and begins to undress and work on getting as clean as he can. When we see him, we're both glad that he came in after us, because he looks ten times dirtier and sweatier than we were.

"I have a good feeling," he tells us when he sits down in front of the barrel to start scrubbing. "It feels really good."

Embla and I nod to him and leave him to his bath. We head back into the biggest tent, the one with the stage, to wait for our results. Both Embla and I have done our best today, though there are so many more who have generally performed better. Now, there's nothing more I can do. Either I'm selected and I can try to save the orphanage, or I'll just have to find another way. I just hope that there's a lot of people who performed better than Embla so that she can stay with Apsel.

When everyone has gathered again, we notice that the benches that were filled to the max this morning have now become sparse. I can see spaces between young people everywhere, and I wonder if they, like the boy, were dragged away. Earlier I heard Yrsa say that some of the recruits had to give up, that there were many who simply didn't measure up. Hopefully, they left the Selections unharmed.

Headmaster Andor steps up onto the stage. Just like before, he's being filmed, and his double appears on the large screen hanging behind him.

"Today, you have done your best. You came prepared. Good work!" Andor gives a round of applause to everyone in the room, and this causes all of the officials around the tent to applaud as well. I wonder if they really mean it or if it's just for show. "I know that you're all tired after today's tests, so I'm not going to put this off more than necessary. It has been an informative day for all of us. To be selected as a candidate for Bionbyr is a great honor, and these competitions serve to separate the chaff from the wheat."

"Can't he just cough up who's been selected?" murmurs Embla.

Andor holds up a glass tablet, presses it, and says:

"Twenty-two people have been admitted from today's Selections. When I call your name, I would like you to come up and stand on stage next to me."

Andor clears his throat.

"Abast, Albertina!"

Andor and the officials applaud. A girl with curly hair and freckles rises. I don't recognize her, so she must go to a different school. She walks carefully up onto the stage.

"Akula, Marcell!"

More applause thunders through the tent. I don't know if I should feel sorry or happy for Marcell's sake, but I decide to be happy. This is what he wanted. Andor continues to list off names: a proud Borghild, Vaino walks with determined steps up to the stage. He looks like he owns the ground he's walking on. Edur, Cyrus – a pale guy who barely looks sixteen – seems to want to disappear when he's called. I can understand that. I feel Embla grab my hand and hold it tight. They're starting to approach F.

"Falinn, Freija!"

Embla's grip loosens, and she stares at me in horror. But Embla wasn't selected. Faas comes before Falinn. I let out a sigh of relief. I know that I'll have to go to Bionbyr if I want to have any chance of saving the orphanage, but Embla belongs here. Here, she can help Apsel to restore everything that was destroyed in the storm, and I know that she'll be safe at home.

My joy disappears as quickly as it came. Just as I'm taking my place next to Cyrus, Andor clears his throat again.

"Excuse me, I seem to have skipped a name. Would Faas, Embla please come up to the stage?"

8

The selection was hard on Embla. The following days were tough for all of us. Embla tried to keep a brave face for the sake of the kids, but she could never hide her feelings from me. When the kids weren't around, she acted like her life was over. I don't know if she's ever managed to completely recover. Since then, she's changed, and it's tarnished our relationship. Embla is one of the driving forces behind me recording all of this. One of the reasons why it's so important for you to help us. Can you understand?

The mood didn't improve when Kali was adopted. She and Disa were the same age, and they've always been together. There haven't been many times when I've seen Apsel cry, mostly because he does that in his own room so he won't worry the children, but after the adoption went through, he wiped his tears away with his shirt sleeve and looked at us with red eyes. I was a little disturbed, seeing him that way. It always used to be the opposite: us kids would get upset about something and Apsel would comfort us. Sometimes I forget that even adults can be sad.

Even Marcell started acting differently. He had to keep working in the harbor up until our last day in Ithmah. Until the boat picked us up to take us to Bionbyr. Nevertheless, he still helped out with the small corn harvest that we had been able to salvage after the sandstorm. He and Apsel didn't argue anymore. No harsh words, no intense discussions, or derogatory comments about each other's political views. I'd almost dare to say that he was friendlier than ever. Maybe that was his way of saying thanks to Apsel, after all.

When Embla's name was called by Andor on the day of the Selections, the applause started ringing in my ears. All around me, everything seemed to dissolve away. The people. The sounds. It was a mess that I couldn't see or touch. I wanted to throw myself into her arms. I wanted to scream. I wanted to cry. Run far away from there. I wanted to tell Embla that everything would be fine, even though it would be an empty promise. I wanted to make her believe it. Still, I did nothing. I couldn't move, couldn't talk. Embla's eyes were vacant. They remained empty.

Andor, with his wry smile and glittering eyes, had praised me for my success in the swimming test. He had reached out a hand to me, and when I grasped it, my vision went black. At first, I had thought it was the same thing that had happened on the roof with Onni, but then I thought it must be the exhaustion from the day finally catching up with me. I wasn't dizzy but scared, and my heart was pounding—but as soon as he let go of my hand, my sight came back.

"I need to get out of here," Embla says. "The shed is messy. I'm gonna go clean up in there."

She and I have just finished cleaning up after dinner. Marcell and Apsel have their hands full putting the kids to bed. When Embla says that she's going out to clean, it usually means that she wants to be alone, so I don't go after her. After a while, though, I feel really alone in the kitchen, so I head out into the yard. The sun has almost completely set. I can hear rattling from the shed and there's a faint light coming through the small window. Embla is probably planning to completely re-organize the inside.

I stand there for a while, confused, trying to decide if I should go in and keep Embla company. Then I hear a sound from the bushes a little ways away. As I move closer, I can hear a child's voice. Behind the bushes, I find Disa sitting and playing by herself.

"Hey Disa, isn't it bedtime?" I ask as I sit down on the ground next to her. Disa nods but doesn't let go of the sticks she's playing with. There's a long stick and a shorter one. She's built a small house out of a few stones.

I get up and brush the dust off my knees. I reach out to Disa and say:

"Let's go get into bed."

Disa nods. Then she says, very quietly:

"I wish Kali was here."

"Me too," I whisper back. I wonder how Kali's doing now. I hope she's having a good time, but what do we really even know about the people who come to the orphanage to adopt? Is Kali's new family really kind to her? Do they love her for who she is? I have to believe that her adoptive parents are good people. For my own peace of mind.

Soon, it'll be my turn, I think. Only it won't be parents adopting me, but the Authority. The President. And they'll be able to do whatever they want with me. I have to believe that Kali is doing well. How else can I handle her absence?

When I've made sure that Disa is in bed, I go to Apsel. He's left Marcell to continue reading the story himself. There's a thought that's been haunting me ever since I fed the sugar gliders at the oasis.

"I wanted to ask you to tell me about my mom again. About when she brought me here to the orphanage. But I've heard you tell it so many times… I know the story by heart already."

"I'd be happy to tell you again, if you'd like."

I feel silly. I let my gaze sweep across the room and note that Apsel has moved the Presidential Portrait back in here. But the map of the Old World is still rolled up under his bed.

It strikes me how incredibly much I will miss this room. It's not the walls or the furniture or the things themselves I'll miss, but the calm I always feel when I come in here. This is where I've had all the wonderful conversations with Apsel, this is where he's listened to my worries and answered my questions. I think about the story of when my mom came here sixteen years ago. I know she came here, left me, and then went away. Apsel has no idea where she came from or where she went.

"Can you tell me again about what she looked like?" I ask finally.

"The woman looked determined. She had a straight nose and intelligent, but soft eyes. She was quite tall and slender. She had glasses," Apsel's tone is blasé, like he's reciting a list of chores that need to be done around the farm.

I bring my hand up to my nose and feel it with my forefinger. My nose is round and wide, not straight. Maybe I got it from my other parent?

"But what was her complexion like?" I ask. "Was it as dark as mine, or maybe a little lighter or darker? And her hair, was it black like mine?"

Apsel looks at me without meeting my gaze and swallows. He seems unsure, doubtful. Or is it just my imagination?

"You know deep down that it doesn't matter. But ... It was lighter," he says in the end. "Her hair too. Lighter."

I'm trying to think of one of the kids at the orphanage I can compare her to. Efram is a little lighter than I am, but his hair is the same.

"Was she more like Efram?"

Now Apsel is staring straight into my eyes. He looks almost scared.

"Apsel?"

"I don't really remember." He shakes his head. "Now, I actually have a few things I need to deal with..."

"But you must remember what her complexion was like?"

"It was dark in the kitchen. She had a hood on almost the entire time and I barely saw her face."

Apsel sounds annoyed, but I don't give up.

"Her hair then? What did it look like? Was it as thick as mine? Did you see her eyes? Were they dark brown like mine?"

"I don't remember. It was sixteen years ago, Freija. I'm sorry, I really don't remember anything."

"But you remember that she had glasses. That she had a straight nose. But you can't remember this?"

Apsel starts scratching at his arm, just like Embla does when she's nervous. He sees that I've noticed and stops immediately. He avoids my gaze.

"She was light," he finally says.

"Like Efram?"

"No. Like Disa."

I'm speechless. Disa's complexion is the same color as a fine sandy beach.

"And her hair was blonde," Apsel continues. "I never thought about her eye color, so I don't know that one, unfortunately."

I sit and stare straight ahead for a while.

"But..." I finally get out, "if she was so different from me... How can she have been my mother then?"

"I've already said too much, Freija—"

"Say it! Tell me everything!"

"Freija, you know children don't necessarily have the same skin color as their parents. Besides, we have no idea what your other parent looks like. Why is this suddenly so important?"

"'Cause it sounds like you're hiding something. Why else would you be acting like this? I want to know!" I'm screaming now. I don't care if it wakes up the kids.

"Everything I've done has been to protect you. All I know is that it wasn't your mother who came here and left you."

"What?!" I burst out. "Where's my mom then?"

Apsel sighs. "She's dead."

I can't stop them. The tears. My face is a river, and the current is strong. I want to get away from Apsel and his lies. I run out into the yard and feel the cold biting me, but I don't care. All of my energy has evaporated.

It might seem silly that I reacted so strongly over a person I'd never even met before. But for me, it was like my mother had died that day, even though she had actually been gone for sixteen years. I want to blame it on a mix of everything: Embarrassment; the pressure to save the orphanage; the responsibility of being an adult. I wanted to be a kid for a little longer. With the hope of someday meeting my mom. The feeling that my biological family was still out there, somewhere in the world, was still within me. Did I have two moms? Or was there a dad out there somewhere looking for me?

That thought had to wait. As I walked into our room, I discovered that Embla was there with a bag packed.

"I won't do it," Embla says.

I look straight into her eyes and see a lost world. The Embla I know, the one who's determined, strong, spontaneous, sly, loving – all the qualities that make up my sister, the things I love about her – they're all gone. In front of me is a scared, insecure, broken child. My body automatically moves towards Embla, and I might be embracing her a little harder than I meant to. She lets me hug her and gratefully receives my support. We sit down on the bed, with our arms still around each other, and Embla sobs so hard that she soaks my ragged clothes.

"Are you going to run away?"

I feel Embla nodding into my shoulder. I sigh. This is so unfair. After all, she's already passed the age of selection. She already has a job. An important one. Especially now, when so much of the Sethunya Home for Wayward Children has already been destroyed. Apsel needs all the help he can get to repair the damage from the storm.

"I'll be smarter this time," Embla whispers. "I'll think of something."

I wasn't really worried about Embla coming up with a plan. One way or another, Embla always succeeded when she put her mind to something. She had done it before. When Embla was eleven, she decided we would both go to Vallis because she wanted to see an even bigger city than Ithmah. Like an obedient puppy, I had jumped on the train, and that small taste of adventure was addictive. I'd felt invincible. I thirsted for more. But the adventure came to an end when Guardians searched the train and found us. If it hadn't been for Embla's ability to lie without getting caught, we would have been punished severely, even though we were still so young. Traveling without a travel permit or visa is totally prohibited. We had been put in the Guardians' vehicle, and it wasn't long before we were back at the orphanage. Apsel had grounded us both for two weeks.

What if Embla really did try again? Ran away? I wonder how far she would go. She probably wouldn't get very far before she got caught, and this time she wouldn't be able to talk her way out of the situation. When I imagine a life without Embla, my chest hurts. Embla should always be here; she's my sister, after all.

"No, we're going to do this together," I say firmly.

Embla lets go enough to look me in the eyes. For a second, I think I catch a glimpse of her old self. Our eye contact is interrupted when her gaze shifts towards the door.

"Dad?"

I turn around and see Apsel standing there. How long has he been there? My grief turns into anger when I see him. I haven't let go of our conversation from earlier, and I feel like I can no longer trust him.

"Come join me, Embla," he says melancholically. Embla dries her tears and gets up to follow him. I do the same, but he stops me.

"Just Embla. Wait here, Freija."

An unpleasant feeling wells up inside me. More secrets? Rage boils within me, and it takes an ugly form. I kick Embla's bag so hard that it goes flying into her bed.

By now, I've learned to control my emotions better. I have eyes on me at all times, which means I can't act anyway. So every time I feel unsure, scared, or unable to see where we're headed – where the future will carry us – I close my eyes. I force myself to think of happier days when we were little; when there was nothing for us to worry about except helping out in the fields, going to school, playing, painting, laughing.

When Embla comes back, I see traces of a smile on her face, but also something more. Has she been crying again?

"What did he say?"

The lone wax candle in the room lights up her pale face and closed eyes.

"Freija… We're going to Bionbyr."

"What?"

Embla takes my hand in hers and squeezes it twice, and my hand squeezes back automatically.

"We'll manage it together. You and me. It might not be as bad as we think. Plus, we'll get to see the world."

Embla tries to smile, but I can see that it's strained.

"Freija, it's not about whether you want to or not, it's about taking action."

I really have no idea what Embla is talking about, but somehow it feels better. Getting to Bionbyr is necessary if I'm going to become an EMES soldier and collect that salary. It'll be much easier if Embla comes along.

"What made you change your mind?"

"Dad reminded me to put the needs of others before my own. Going to Bionbyr could open many doors."

Whatever Apsel said to her, I'm glad he did. If Embla takes the lead, I can confidently follow her. And if Embla thinks we can do this, I think so too.

"It's worth a shot," Embla says.

Embla smiles and gets in bed. She seems to be at least as tired as I am. When I blow out the light and get into my own bed, Embla whispers:

"And if anything happens, I'll be there to protect you."

9

RAIJA.

The golden letters are gigantic. The white ship that's going to take us to Bionbyr isn't much bigger than the others in Ithmah's harbor, but its distinct appearance distinguishes it from the other ships: from above, the ship is almost an identical copy of a stingray. The narrow bow is partly submerged where the nose connects with two wings, one on each side of the body. The rounded wings extend all the way to the stern, where they form two pointed tails. The body that goes between the wings from the bow to the tails is five stories high, and I can see hundreds of windows along the sides. I don't know why a ship would be designed this way or what the function of the wings is, but it's not important. Under the name of the ship, it says "Baudier Transport" in slightly smaller letters that are just as neat. It's the name of the company that manages the Authority's transportation of goods. Is that how the Authority sees us? As goods to be transported?

Embla either isn't impressed with the ship or she hasn't noticed it yet. I watch as she looks at Ithmah instead. Her eyes are empty. She did the same thing at the orphanage before we left.

It took a long time for me to understand. It was her way of saying goodbye to places she would probably never see again.

It's early morning, and the gulls are laughing as they feverishly search for breakfast. People have stopped to watch the vessel. It's not every day that they see a ship like this one. A gangway is stretched out from the center of the bow, and harbor workers make sure that it's properly secured to the dock. My attention turns to a couple of barrels set a little farther away on the pier. Something had flashed past in my field of view. I giggle quietly when I see the same sugar glider with the dark marking over its eye sitting on one of the barrels. Spontaneously, I walk up to the sugar glider, who looks at me intently. Or rather, he's staring at my shoulder bag. I understand right away.

"Here you go."

I open my bag, where I packed some photos and food before the trip. I'm looking for a small biscuit from the package Apsel made me pack as a lunch, along with sandwiches, fruit, and water. The sugar glider takes the biscuit, completely fearless, and crunches it up immediately.

A signal sounds, and I say goodbye to the sugar glider. After that, my steps are lighter as I go back to join Embla, Apsel, and Marcell, who are all waiting at the pier. Apsel has put Onni in charge until he gets back. All of the "adult" children have now disappeared from the orphanage, and suddenly thirteen-year-old Onni has been forced to grow up.

"Remember to stay strong," Apsel tells us. "Don't forget that there's strength to be gained from each other."

Apsel's eyes are red when he hugs Embla goodbye. He's trying to be strong for us too. I kind of regret that our last conversation alone ended with me thinking horrible things about him. The man who's been a parent to me all my life. Who always made sure that I had food to eat, a bed to sleep in, and that I felt safe and loved.

I give him a hug and squeeze hard.

"Thanks for everything," I whisper to him, and I feel his grip tighten on my body.

"We'll see each other sooner than you think," says Apsel.

Will we? Does Bionbyr have holidays? Or will three years go by quickly? Right now, it feels like I'll be there for an eternity. I get sad when I think about the fact that the next time I come back, many of the kids might have new homes already. Onni has become an adult and who knows what'll happen to him. If he gets a scholarship, he won't stay in Ithmah. I wish I had hugged him more times before we left. Hopefully, there are ways to communicate with them from school.

Marcell gets a quick hug, and says, "thank you" and "goodbye then." With a quick nod, he takes his bag, turns around, and walks towards the gangway to stand in line. Embla, who has already hugged Apsel goodbye, gives him one last squeeze before she joins me in the boarding line.

Check-in goes fairly quickly, as there are several officials helping out. Just like at the Selections, everyone is dressed in white and they're all walking around with glass screens. I count six people standing in a row between us and the ship. Each of them has floating drones next to them that seem to scan everyone who boards. The flying machines seem to be a newer model of the ones the Guardians in Ithmah use for surveillance and crime prevention. These ones have long arms and look kind of like floating octopi. When it's almost my turn, I can see that the drones also do something to the forearms of the students who pass by, and it makes me a little nervous. It doesn't seem serious, though, because no one is reacting much to the procedure.

"Welcome. Put your thumb here on the screen," the official says to me when it's my turn, holding out the glass tablet.

"Where?" I ask when it's not clear. It's just a piece of glass. No text, box, or anything that suggests where to put my thumb.

"Anywhere."

Okay, I think and press my thumb against the glass. It's not long before the tablet lights up with my name, picture, and some information about me. The screen flashes green.

"Welcome, Freija Falinn," says the official, who then instructs me to stand on a cross on the ground. I hear the drone's buzzing sound as its white light shines straight down on me. I imagine that there's a little camera lens looking right through me and wonder what it's really registering. Can it read my feelings?

The drone that's scanning me gives off two quick beeps and the light changes to red. I'm starting to sweat. What's happening?

"May I look in your bag," the official says, ordering rather than asking. I hand over the bag and watch as it's searched. What could be in there that's dangerous?

"Food, drink, and animals are completely prohibited from being taken aboard the ship," notes the official after emptying my shoulder bag of food and water. I get the bag back and am grateful that I'm allowed to keep the photos. I'm asked to stand in front of the drone to be scanned again, and this time I'm approved. In the middle of it all, I had forgotten about the last part, and I'm shocked when the drone suddenly grabs my arm, presses a needle into my forearm, and injects something there before pulling the needle out again. I can't feel the needle at all.

"Give me your arm," the official commands, and I do as I'm asked. Other than a small drop of blood, you wouldn't think I just had a big needle inserted into my arm. The official moves the screen over my forearm and holds it there until it gives off a beep.

"There, you're done. Your cabin number is C0319. Thank you for your commitment," says the official.

My commitment? It wasn't like I really had a choice. I was just doing what I was told.

"What was that thing that got put in my arm?"

The official looks at me, trying to figure out if I'm joking or not. "It's your transmitter, your access card, your health card — your identification card, to put it simply."

"Oh, okay," I reply, but I still don't understand. Does this mean that we're always monitored? Now they know exactly where we are. I take a deep breath as I realize that there's no going back. I don't dare to ask any follow-up questions, though, and I decide that it's best for me to go ahead and board. The official has already called the next person over as I take my bag and move forward. I stop when I realize that it's Embla. She also presses her thumb against the screen, and the drone scans her and glows green, but when the drone tries to stab her with the needle, *it doesn't work.* The drone gives off some tones and releases its grip on Embla. Then it illuminates her in a flood of red light. I look at Embla, who seems worried, as the official approaches her. I can't hear what they're saying, but the procedure starts again, and this time it works. The drone sticks Embla, plants – *whatever it is* – and releases her. The official holds the screen up to her arm. Embla looks relieved.

"What happened?" I ask as we walk up the gangway and try to avoid getting dizzy.

"There was something up with the machine, nothing to worry about," Embla replies and starts to walk faster. She's not fond of heights.

Immediately upon boarding, we're asked to step aside to listen to the personnel who are going over the safety procedures with a small group. We listen, taking in all the information, and as soon as the instructions are clear they let us go.

The Ray – the ship – can't be compared to anything I've ever seen before. Of course, we have the mandatory technology at the orphanage, like the TV screen and Apsel's tablet, but they're nothing in comparison to this. Like in Ithmah, the ship's walls have displays with encouraging advertisements for Bionbyr, impressive slogans for the President, and video footage of EMES soldiers. Drones float around through the corridors. It's not just the technology that's overwhelming. The whole ship is white. Everything is clean and fresh, with running water and lamps that light up every nook and cranny, and everything is morbidly organized. What amazes me the most is all of the decorations that seem to have no purpose other than sitting there, looking beautiful. Chandeliers hang from the ceiling, dripping with glass or crystal. We could have renovated the orphanage several times over for the amount it must have cost to build all of this.

Before we try to find our cabin, we go to an observation deck near the bow. The deck is so big and airy that, at first, I'm worried about the ceiling caving in, but there are sturdy pillars of marble to prevent that. Here, many young people stand and lean against the windows. At first, I think they're students from Ithmah who want to say goodbye to their hometown, but when I recognize only a few, I realize that there are young people from all over Ela. From cities like Vallis, Wim, and Pari. Ithmah is the last stop before Bionbyr, and they've already seen more of the world on this trip than I have in my whole life.

"Hello!" bursts out a girl with dark, curly hair when we get up to our cabin. I notice that she has two different shoes on her feet: one black and one red. She walks energetically over to me and Embla. "Are you going to Bionbyr too? Yes, of course you are. That's where the boat's going. Silly me. My name is Tricia. I'm in the cabin next door."

Tricia points to her door, the cabin next to mine and Embla's. The door to our cabin is opened by holding my forearm – where the drone stuck me – over a panel. If you have the right to enter, the panel emits three short, rising tones and glows green. The door opens and closes with a "bzz."

Embla and I say hello and continue towards the cabin. Tricia comes along.

"It looks exactly the same as ours!"

Embla and I exchange a look as we put our bags away. We're both getting a little over-saturated with her seemingly endless energy, and I wonder if we'll have to spend the entire voyage with Tricia hanging around us. How long does it take to get to Bionbyr? A day? A week?

"You've come just in time for lunch. I'll go ahead and grab a good table, even though there's always room. You'll want to sit by the window, of course, or am I wrong?" Tricia laughs and leaves the room in a storm.

"Did you see where the bathroom was?" Embla asks and gets ready to go back out into the hall.

I point to the door next to Embla. "Is there a toilet in that room? You think all the cabins have them?"

She mutters something and goes into the bathroom. I sit down on one of the four beds and look around the room. It's about as big as Apsel's office, but the roof isn't as high. It feels claustrophobic, and had it not been for the big, round window, I'd probably be feeling pretty down. Upon closer inspection, I see that the window isn't real anyway, and I move over enough on the bed to reach it. It's fake. It's just a screen that reflects the environment outdoors. *Of course.* There must be hundreds of cabins, and not all of them can have windows facing outwards. What if we're even below the surface of the water?

I lie down in the bed that I've inadvertently chosen as my own and suddenly feel my bag moving. *Moving?* I sit up immediately and open the bag. I'm horrified when I realize it's the same sugar glider I fed before.

"How did you get past all the machines and officials?" I whisper.

The official who confiscated the food from my bag also said animals were forbidden, and even though I didn't intend to bring it with me, the sugar glider is still with me. "What am I going to do with you?"

I'm panicking. I can't really let it loose in the hallway, and I definitely can't keep a sugar glider in the cabin. Embla probably wouldn't have a problem with it, but can I trust our other roommates — who even are they?

"Back in you go!" I hiss and manage to get the sugar glider into the bag just before Embla is done on the toilet. "Ready for lunch?"

I can't really relax during the walk to the deck where the dining hall is because of what I have in my shoulder bag. Embla notices that I'm still wearing it. She comments that I could have left it in the room, but I shrug. She probably thinks I'm just nervous about the journey and what awaits us when we get there. I let her believe it, and when she squeezes my hand twice, I squeeze back.

We arrive at a place that must be a central part of the ship's elevators. There are probably ten of them here. I read on one of the screens that there are five decks we have permission to be on. Three of the decks all have cabins, then there's the dining hall and the observation deck, and on the top is a park with a pool.

"Should we go by the park real quick and check out what it looks like up there before we head to the dining hall?" Inside, I'm praying that Embla will follow along, and I'm relieved when she agrees to it.

"Don't leave me alone," she pleads, and we head to the top.

The park is much bigger than I thought. The trees look real, and some even have fruit. Now I just have to try to let the sugar glider go without anyone seeing.

"Well, that's it. Should we go eat then?" Embla asks the question too early. I haven't even found a good place. I look around fervently and ignore the question. Everyone is in groups around the park. I think I can see some similarities in their clothing styles and wonder if they're from the same cities. Some have strange hair colors that can't be natural. I get a little annoyed when I think about whether they paid for it or not. Why would anyone pay to dye their hair when you could spend that money on something else? It's inconceivable. But that's not why I'm here in the park.

"Look, a High Heel..." Embla sighs and nudges me with her elbow. "Why didn't his parents pay for him to stay at home? Clearly, they could afford it."

I get a look at the guy she means. His hair has black roots, but the rest is colored red and reaches a bit below his shoulders. His skin tone is somewhat lighter than mine, and he's wearing a white jacket in a glossy material that I don't think I've seen before. His black pants have metal details, and his shoes have such high heels that he must be at least six and a half feet tall when he's standing. I notice a dark mark on his cheek. No bigger than a pinky fingernail, but still visible from a distance.

I heard the phrase "High Heel" quite early from the few of Ithmah's city kids I spent time with. That was back when it didn't matter where you came from, when status didn't dictate who you could play with. They called people with high status "High Heels" because if you have high heels, you can't work in the fields like those of us who are poor. Heels are completely worthless in rural areas. Everyone with status has those shoes. Have you heard that phrase before or is it just something we say in Ithmah?

While Embla is completely occupied looking at the guy with the heels, I take the opportunity to open the bag. I sit discreetly on a low wall that curves around a tree and put down the bag with the sugar glider still inside. It jumps out, and I'm pretty sure no one sees me. I exhale. Hopefully, it's smart enough to stay away from the officials and other people.

Just when we start heading back to the elevator to take us down a floor to the dining hall, we hear a loud humming and the whole ship begins to shake. A signal loop sounds, and a voice comes on, telling us all that we're leaving Ithmah and that Bionbyr is our next stop.

10

Just like everything else on the ship, the dining hall is enormous and everything in it is white. We have to beep ourselves in before we can go up to a long counter to get food. Behind the counter, there are probably between twenty and thirty people working to make sure that every teen gets their own tray of food. They work systematically, and each of them has something to hand out: trays, cutlery, plates prepared with food, and water to drink. They're efficient, and I don't have to wait for my food at all.

The rest of the room is airy. Just like on the observation deck, the roof is held up by columns. The tables are placed in neat rows, each of which can seat six people.

"What's a *'good table'*?" I ask, referring to our cabin neighbor Tricia, who had said she'd save a table for us.

It's not long before I see a girl waving from a table on the windowed wall. Her complexion is quite pale and gives the impression that she's sick, but her smile spreads from ear to ear when she sees me and Embla. She bursts into a cheerful "Hey-o!" We settle in and start eating. Outside, Ithmah is getting smaller and smaller.

"What's this?" I'm referring to the food, or rather the artwork, on my plate. Nothing about it feels natural. On one side is a rectangular, clear orange slice with a sauce beautifully curled over it in a wavy pattern. On the other side, next to the orange slice, there are two globs of some kind of mash. One is a beautiful purple and it's a little bigger, while the smaller one is green, just like the peas at home.

"Fish!" laughs Tricia. "It's super good!"

I take a bite and agree with her. The green mash has not only the same color as peas but also the same taste. And the purple one tastes, weirdly enough, just like the carrots back home. It makes me feel a little calmer. Maybe it's not a completely different world we're in after all, and I'm grateful for the flavors from home. What are Onni and Apsel and everyone else doing now? And where is Marcell? I haven't seen him since he boarded the ship.

Embla stares out the window, just like she did earlier today. I'm taken in by the image. Not even I could swim back to shore from here. I'm filled with a mix of delight and despondency. I already miss the scents of the market spices, telling fairy tales to the children, and playing with Freda the goat. But I'm excited to see more of the world. Now, we have no choice other than to go there for ourselves. When Ithmah has gotten so small that we can no longer distinguish the city, Embla turns her attention to me and Tricia.

I feel like we should try to be nicer and talk to Tricia – try to make friends with our future classmate – but I feel like lead, and no words want to come out of my mouth. Fortunately, I just need to nod and smile when Tricia talks to us.

"Are these seats free?"

A boy and a girl have arrived at the table.

"Sure," I say.

The boy sits next to me and the girl sits next to Embla.

"My name is Ewind," the girl introduces herself.

"Ivalde," the boy says.

When I see the heels on his feet, I realize that he was the one we saw up on the deck earlier.

Ewind has ash blonde hair and spirited gray eyes. Her blue clothes aren't as exclusive as Ivalde's, but they're still good quality — not worn or dirty. I suspect that they're both dressed in some fashion I'm not familiar with. They're definitely not orphans.

"My name is Freija, and this is Embla." Embla has her mouth full of carrot mash, so she nods in greeting. "We came from the same orphanage outside Ithmah. Where are you from?"

I'd swear Ivalde flinches at the word "orphanage," but it might just be my imagination.

"I came from Tarara," Ewind says with a proud smile.

"Pari."

"I've never met people from so far away!" I burst out, my mouth agape. "How long have you been on the ship?"

"For almost three weeks," Ewind says. "Ivalde has been onboard for two."

Ewind has a way of smiling with her whole face that makes me feel a little more relaxed. Ivalde also seems nice, but a bit more reserved.

"The boat started in Tarara," Ewind says. "There were quite a few of us who boarded there. Ivalde was the only one from Pari. Not many would-be soldiers from there."

Pari is one of the richest cities in Ela. They live in exaggerated luxury with machines that do all of the work for them. Just like our farm, they sell from large farms and export all over the country. Pari's families always pay to keep their children from being recruited during the Selections.

I notice how Embla is looking at Ivalde, at his shoes, and I know that she's thinking the same thing as I am. That it's a little strange that he was the only one from Pari and that he wasn't "rescued" by his family. Did he want to come to Bionbyr that much? Like Marcell? Embla opens her mouth to say something, and I'm preparing to chime in if it's something inappropriate. But I don't have to worry. All she asks is:

"Do any of you know what Bionbyr looks like?"

"Well, the only thing I know is that the whole school is like a boat, it floats on the water."

"It's never in the same place for long," Tricia fills in. "For security reasons. And that's the same reason they don't want to show pictures of it."

I swallow. I didn't think that Bionbyr could be a target for terrorists. But of course. It's a school that trains soldiers to stop terrorists.

"But Bionbyr is one of the safest places in the world," Ewind says. "All of the students are trained to become soldiers, and the teachers there are the best of the best."

"As we assumed then…" mumbles Embla. I glimpse the old Embla, but I don't have time to stop her. "Is it common to have shoes like that in Pari?"

She's referring, of course, to Ivalde's heels. He seems a little offended at the question, but calmly answers: "Among some."

"Among those who can afford it," Embla says.

Ivalde gives her a look I can't interpret. Then he says: "Yes."

"We would never have been able to walk around in high-heeled shoes at the orphanage," Embla continues. "It's a little impractical when you're tending crops, fetching water from the well, and feeding the chickens."

Even though I'm glad that Embla seems to have gone back to her usual self, I think the taunting is unnecessary. After all, Ivalde can't help where he comes from any more than we can. Hopefully, we'll be spending the next three years with these people, and I'm worried about where her attitude will get her.

"Mm," says Ivalde.

It gets quiet around the table and the mood drops. I wish I could make her understand that we can't just make enemies wherever we go, we need to be smart. My goal is to get through school, and I need to make Embla understand that. Maybe Marcell can help?

"Has anyone seen a rather muscular guy with mousy hair? He boarded in Ithmah, just like us, and I'm pretty sure he was wearing a pale-yellow shirt," I wonder. They shrug their shoulders. I realize that it was a pretty unhelpful description. Well, he's on the boat somewhere, and I'll bump into him sooner or later.

"ATTENTION!" a voice echoes through the dining hall and causes every head to turn. "We are approaching a storm and must ask everyone to return to their cabins. Initiate safety protocols and wait for more information."

Like clockwork, everyone in the dining hall gets up and moves to the elevators that go to our cabins. Embla and I are hanging by Tricia, who's heading in the same direction.

When she sees Embla's worried look, she puts her arm around Embla and smiles wide.

"Don't worry. We went through a storm at the beginning of the trip too. They'll dive under, so you'll hardly notice it. You might want to cover your ears, though. Haha!

"*Dive under?* You mean the ship will dive underwater?"

"Exactly!"

Something strikes through my body when I think about it. The park at the top didn't have a roof, right? I really hope the little sugar glider managed to find safe cover, or that it somehow glided back to Ithmah.

When Embla and I get back to our cabin, we get another shock. Marcell is there. He looks equally as shocked to see us. I run straight into his arms, and he accepts me — if somewhat reluctantly. I've never done anything like this before, but he is, after all, part of "home."

"Marcell!"

"We thought you had dumped us…" Embla says it a little jokingly, but I notice a guilty look on him. He's already had time to unpack his bag, but he seems to have been a little unsure of which bag was his at first since Embla's bag is also open. It looks otherwise untouched. I look up at the fake window and notice how dark the sky has become. I'm fascinated by how the screens can depict reality so accurately. It doesn't feel like I'm looking at a screen at all but through a real window.

"ATTENTION!" the same voice as before echoes through the cabin. "Diving initiated. Get ready!"

I feel my pulse increase as I stare at the screen. We're on our way down below the surface. I can't help thinking it's tremendously exciting.

The ship tilts sharply, and I lose my balance. I fly straight into Marcell, who tumbles over. Embla crashes into the wardrobe. We had forgotten to start the safety procedures. It's hard to move, and every step I take to the bed is heavy. The floor has become a steep uphill slope. I can see on the screen that we're underwater now. Everything is dark and scary. Claustrophobic. I reach my bed and see that there's some kind of strap that I can fasten around my body.

An extremely unpleasant sensation suddenly presses into my ears. It feels like they're about to explode, and it renders me completely deaf. All sounds are muted, and there's an intense pressure. The same feeling always happens when I dive deep. I show Embla and Marcell how they should hold their noses and blow with their mouths closed so that their cheeks become like little balls. I do it too and hear a squeaky sound, followed by a "pop."

We finally manage to brace ourselves just in time for the ship to straighten up again, and the announcer tells us that we can move freely. Marcell is the first one out of the room. His bag is secured in the wardrobe. Mine and Embla's things are all over the floor. We both sigh, and start picking up our stuff.

"Oh, that's right!" Embla exclaims and waves me over to her. I sit next to her, and she asks me to hold out my hand. She holds her hand out above mine and drops a bracelet. I immediately recognize the beads: It's the same black beads I found in the ocean on my birthday. To think that it's already been two months since I turned sixteen ... I don't feel the least bit wiser or older. I think about the bracelet I gave Embla after the storm in the hope that she could sell it and get money for the orphanage. Back when I thought she'd be staying. The bracelet has been remade: Embla has strung the beads on a new, thicker, white string with knots made between each bead. She's also polished them so that they glitter even more.

"And look at this."

She holds up another bracelet, the same.

"There were enough beads for two new bracelets," Embla explains. "One for you and one for me."

"I love it."

"I have no idea what those words mean. Maybe it's the language of the sea people or something, hehe, but I thought my word was a little cooler, so I kept it for myself. I was going to give you this when you were chosen at the Selections and we were separated. I thought that it would somehow make you remember me and your home. Something like that. Then I forgot about it because I, well, you know."

"Obviously we stick together," I say. "Duh."

The word "*Matåv*" is engraved in one of my beads. I also wonder what it means. I don't believe it's the language of the sea people, though. I don't actually believe in the sea people at all. I know it was just something Apsel said so that I wouldn't swim out too far when I was younger. "*If you do, they'll pull you down under the surface and you'll never be seen again.*" Nonsense. I still smile when I think about how he said it. With the utmost seriousness in his voice. No, "*Matåv,*" that's probably some old language, or it's a made-up language. Maybe some kids invented it and we'll never know what it means. On Embla's bead, it says "*Fdokr,*" and it's impossible to pronounce.

"I know I probably shouldn't say this," says Embla after we've been silent for a while, "but I'm glad you're here with me."

"I know what you mean," I say.

The storm lasts for almost three whole days. Even though we were so far below the surface, I swear I could hear the thunderstorm above. It turns out that I didn't have to worry about the park. It was still accessible while we were underwater. Whether it was a real glass ceiling or just screens set up to look like one was hard to tell, but the entire park was covered with a dome of glass. It must have been under enormous pressure, but it held.

In the following days, we spend our time with Tricia, Ewind, and Ivalde. We never get a fourth roommate, which is nice. Ivalde doesn't seem to have anyone else to talk to, which isn't much of a surprise since he doesn't know anyone else. He was the only one to come from Pari, so he has a cabin to himself. It shows clearly on Embla that she can't handle being around Ivalde. Whether it's because he doesn't show much emotion or because he comes from a rich family, I don't know. He seems to understand it because he constantly keeps away from us, and sometimes it feels like he's watching us. Embla seems to find things to be bothered about with Tricia and

Ewind as well. When Tricia wants to hang out with us, Embla thinks she's way too happy and energetic. She jokes all the time, and even I can get tired of her over the top positivity. Tricia spends a lot of time in her cabin, though, because she often feels sick.

"We were in the same class, but we're completely different. Her family members are all Edenites," Ewind explains. We're sitting in the park and enjoying the fact that they've opened up the roof. The ship is not quite above the water's surface yet, and – if I was 10 feet taller – I could reach out and touch the waves. It's nice to feel the fresh sea air. Tricia is back in her cabin, feeling nauseated after breakfast.

"Edenites?"

"Believers. See, they believe that all the water that came from the ice melting was a punishment from some kind of higher power because we didn't take care of our earth. They're against all factories and avoid everything that has to do with technology. They live a simple life, to put it mildly. They only eat locally produced foods and avoid everything that's been genetically modified, whether it's food or any other products, in the hopes of restoring the earth to its original state. They call the earth 'Eden,'" Ewind explains. "That's why she's been so sick. Her body isn't used to this kind of food."

"Are you an Edenite too?" I wonder.

"No," she answers firmly, leaning closer to us. "And to be honest, I really don't like them. Back home, everyone is divided into two groups. The Edenites and the rest of us. They rebel against everything. Especially against the radio tower. If you ask me, it's just crazy talk. We all know what happened..."

I wonder if we really know or if we'll ever find out the truth. But I know what she's referring to: the Tabians—the Power People. Those with the inheritance of Kraften.

"I've heard that if we can cure them, make them normal again so that their powers disappear, then the world would be like it was before. I believe it, actually. It sounds about right," says Ewind.

Would the ice caps form again? Would the water levels fall? Would the weather become more stable? Would there be more landmass? The thought has never occurred to me. Embla is sitting with her arms crossed, and I can see how hard she's trying to stop herself from saying anything stupid. Ivalde looks exactly the same as Embla. He looks like a bomb that's about to go off.

"Well, that's just a thought. Are we going to dinner, Ivalde?"

"Cabin first," he forces out. His face is a redder shade now. Almost as red as his hair. It isn't red like Embla's, Ivalde's is more like a tomato while Embla's is more like a sunset.

"Okay, I'll meet you in the dining hall. Are you coming then?"

"You can go ahead, I just want to enjoy the fresh air first," I lie. I look at Embla, who's close to exploding. I'd rather her go off when it's just the two of us instead of making a scene in front of the others.

"Alright, I'll grab a table!"

As soon as Ewind and Ivalde are out of sight, she bursts.

"What did she even mean by that? Saying that they would become *normal people*? Tabians *are* normal people, just with powers. She talks about them like they're some kind of freaks."

"But if they're normal people," I say, "why do they have to live in a sanctuary?"

"You sound just like *them*," hisses Embla before she too leaves me. I freeze up for a moment after she snaps. Where did that come from? I sigh and follow her with my eyes and, as she walks past one of the trees, I get a glimpse of the little sugar glider I released here at the beginning of the journey.

"It looks like you're doing just fine, you little troublemaker."

I look around to make sure there's no one else here and let the sugar glider get closer to me. It purrs cozily as I scratch it gently on the head.

"I have nothing for you to eat," I whisper when I see the sugar glider's eyes start to take an interest in my pockets. Even though I don't have anything for it, the sugar glider stays with me. It creeps up into my lap and settles in. I'm a little flabbergasted, but I start scratching its back as discreetly as I can. I really hope no one sees me.

We sit for a while until I remember that it's already dinnertime. Dinner is only served for a certain amount of time, and if I miss it, I'll have to go without. Besides, I don't want to eat alone, so I say goodbye to the sugar glider and make my way downstairs.

Just before I enter the dining hall, I catch sight of a familiar pair of heels standing in front of one of the large windows. Ivalde stands alone, looking out over the sea. I clear my throat gently as I approach, and when Ivalde gives me a quick smile and doesn't say anything, I take it as a sign that it's okay for me to stand next to him.

The sky is becoming more colorful as the sun slowly begins to set. It would be nice to still be outside. I realize that I'm getting pretty restless and tired of being stuck indoors. I would easily trade this boat trip for a whole week's work in the fields at Sethunya.

"Do you miss Ithmah?"

I'm a little taken aback by the question. Apparently, he can say more than individual words and can actually put together a whole sentence. And it's a question! I think there's something special about Ivalde, but I can't really put my finger on what it is. Maybe it's just because he's so closed off and withdrawn that I want to know all about him. But I have no idea what to ask. He doesn't seem to want to talk that much.

"Maybe not the city itself," I reply, "but my family."

"But you lived in an orphanage, right? I thought you didn't have a family?"

I shrug.

"Everyone at the orphanage was my family, *is* my family," I say firmly. "They're my brothers and sisters, and I love them. Just because I don't have parents doesn't mean I don't have people I love and care about."

I find myself raising my voice just like Embla would have. I take a deep breath and try to calm myself down.

I was more upset by Ivalde's words than I first thought. Ivalde seems to have noticed my reaction, because he holds up his hands and says:

"I didn't mean to upset you. I've never met someone who was from an orphanage before. I don't know what it's like."

"Are there no orphanages in Pari?"

He shrugs his shoulders.

"Maybe there are. But not where I lived. I went to a school with only the top students."

"What do you mean? Can orphans not be top students?"

Ivalde furrows his brows, thinking. I feel the anger rising inside me again.

"I always thought that those who are poor don't perform as well," Ivalde finally replies. "That's why they're poor. They don't take control of their lives. But kids in orphanages don't choose to be poor… Huh, I hadn't actually thought about it before."

Ivalde talks as if he's thinking about the weather. It's hard for me not to just scream at him. Ivalde looks at me in complete shock, even though I haven't said anything.

"I'll go in and see if I can find the others, see you there!"

He leaves me just in time. If he'd said anything else, I probably would have dragged him by his goofy colored hair.

Well, now I know what's special about Ivalde, I think, *he's a total jerk.*

"All poor people are lazy? Onni does really well in school, and he's an orphan. Of course there are orphanages in Pari. There are people who are poor and weak everywhere!" I mutter to myself.

"There you are!" Embla comes over to me and grabs my hand to pull me over to the table where the others are already sitting. Just like so many weeks ago when I sat on the roof with Onni, a thousand pictures flash through my mind: an oasis, Ithmah's field, Apsel talking baby language, the toolbox that fell onto Embla when I thought she had broken her arm, a conversation between Onni and Embla where they discuss my surprise party. It all goes so quickly that Embla barely notices my focus disappear for an instant.

My anger eases and fear takes over. Fear of what, I'm not sure. What's happening to me? I don't have time to think it over. We're about to have dinner with three hundred other young people, and I don't want to worry Embla unnecessarily. More than that, something else catches my attention. Ewind points it out first.

There's a light gleaming on the horizon.

Bionbyr.

11

I'll probably never forget the first time I saw Bionbyr: a large glass dome makes the whole school look like a floating gem. I had never seen such a large building before, especially not a boat — which is what Bionbyr actually is. And how could the sea be so blue? All the colors seemed brighter and more vibrant there. Ithmah seemed brown, gray, and dirty in comparison. The evening sun was shining hot from the brightly colored sky, but it didn't feel as hot as it usually did when the sky was cloudless. The sea around us was cooling and the air was fresh.

The beauty of the school can't be described. Compared to the school I attended in Ithmah, a worn-out brick building covered in scribbles, broken climbing plants, and the various kinds of roofing that have been patched at different times, Bionbyr is something special. Something straight out of a dream.

The Ray has stopped a ways from Bionbyr. They've asked us to go down to the gangway to wait for a smaller boat to take us the rest of the way. I understand why. From here, I can make out a harbor in the school. Yes, *in.* There's actually a tunnel that looks like it goes right through Bionbyr, but despite it having high ceilings, the Ray is too big to fit in there.

Bionbyr's dome shines in the sunlight, and it brings my thoughts back to the black beaded bracelets Embla and I wear. I haven't had a chance to tell her that I want to avoid spending time with Ivalde from now on. It'll have to wait.

As we get closer, we see that the dome is made entirely of glass that doesn't have any noticeable seams, as if it were all a single piece of glass. Bionbyr is a perfect circle with wooden beams that reach from the lower floor to the top and support the weight of the dome. I can count seven pillars from here, and since Bionbyr is circular, I suppose there are a total of about fourteen strong pillars that hold everything up.

The boat ride that takes us all the way into the port of Bionbyr goes by really quickly. All of the incoming students can fit without the need to crowd. At first, I think we're about to collide with the glass dome, because the boat doesn't seem to be slowing down as we approach, but right where we flow into it, the glass is only an illusion. I imagine that I can *feel* the glass, and the first thing I notice is that the hot air suddenly becomes a little cooler. It's not cold, but comfortable. I can see the sun clearly through the glass, but it's not as intrusive.

And if Bionbyr was a nice sight before we entered this port-like area, that was nothing compared to what we're seeing now.

We've entered a port where there are already like fifty boats of all different sizes. Every one of them sits perfectly positioned to utilize every inch of the harbor. I was right when I thought the harbor seemed to go all the way through Bionbyr, because I can see another opening on the other side. On each side of the harbor, I can see all of the floors clearly. They stretch tall above us. Even taller than the highest houses in Ithmah. Including the floor we're on now, it looks like there are six floors. We stop at the dock, and I can see a huge gray screen instructing where to go in white letters. If I'm interpreting it correctly, there's a medical facility near here, as there's a blue cross on the screen with an arrow pointing to the right. There should also be a gym, a library, and a cafeteria on this floor. I try to memorize as many details as I can, so I won't get lost in the coming weeks.

We're led out of the boat and into the harbor, where we await the rest of the travelers. I catch a glimpse of the sugar glider but, thankfully, I'm the only one who sees it. Discreetly, I follow it with my eyes and marvel at how skillfully it climbs up each floor. There are plants hanging from the open floors above, which helps. The sugar glider gets smaller and smaller until, finally, I can no longer see it.

"Oh, so you thought you'd come here," I mutter to myself. Embla gives me a curious glance, but I brush it off. She doesn't need to worry about it.

Everything goes by pretty fast, and before I can get too caught up in all of the beautiful attractions Bionbyr has to offer, we go in unison to a woman who seems vaguely familiar.

Where have I seen her before? One look at the white hair reminds me of the official from the day of the Selections. But I can't remember her name.

The white-haired woman doesn't seem to waste time showing us around the place that will be our home for the next three years. She follows the harbor edge for a while until we reach a crossing tunnel. Describing it as a "tunnel" does feel quite right, as it makes it sound small and crowded. The ceilings are high and there's plenty of space. The tunnel is as wide as the orphanage, I'd guess. Maybe bigger. Here I can see a sign saying "Library," and two pairs of elevators. One is farther away and one is quite close to the edge of the harbor. The white-haired woman asks us to take the elevators to the second floor. Embla and I won't fit in the nearest pair of elevators, so we take the ones a little farther away, but it still only takes one turn to get everyone from the boat up to the second floor.

This floor also has high ceilings. I'm amazed at how clean and sterile the environment is. It's sparing with color, and the splashes of color that are around have been chosen with care. The majority comes from the neat floral decorations along the floor. Where we come out of the elevator, I read "01" and "03" on the doors on one side and "02" and "04" on the other doors. Farther away in the corridor, beyond the doors marked "03" and "04" where the first elevator pair is located, there's also a new group of people. I don't know what comes over me, but I suddenly feel nervous. When I get a closer look at them, I get the feeling that these are students who already go here. Everyone is dressed in the same uniform. It's reminiscent of the Guardians' burgundy uniforms, with only the golden helmets missing. On the shoulders is Bionbyr's emblem beautifully embroidered, though from here, the killer whale looks like a black slug. They're standing completely still, in perfect lines, and they don't move even when the white-haired woman leads us past them and into a large auditorium.

On the other side is the entrance to a part of the dome that extends along the entire outer wall and continues past the roof. Right in front of the dome wall is a large hole that makes the Auditorium feel like a giant balcony. I'm not entirely sure, but the port should be right below us. If I went over to the opening, I'd be able to confirm it, but since we've been instructed to find places to sit down, I don't dare to challenge fate. In many of the seats, there are already some people with a different kind of uniform. This one is more emerald green than burgundy.

Embla and I get seats next to a guy in a huge fur jacket, which takes up almost two seats. How had he not been sweating to death on the Ray in this tropical heat? Here, of course, it's the perfect temperature. Embla, who is closest, leans towards me to avoid getting fur on her.

"Check it out," she whispers to me, pointing to the scene right at the edge of the balcony. Up there, Andor – Bionbyr's headmaster – stands together with some of the professors. Among them is the representative who came to pick us up in his car: Esbern. I get an unpleasant feeling in my stomach. I still remember his red details from the day he picked us up. The professors on stage all have uniforms that are similar to each other, but each of them has something unique. Esbern's red details and Bern's blue ones, for example. Bern's blue hair almost blends in with the sky in the background. He looks younger than Esbern and feels somehow calmer.

The students standing outside the room enter the Auditorium and settle into their assigned places. The doors close.

"Welcome aboard Bionbyr!"

Andor's voice echoes through the Auditorium. There probably isn't a corner of Bionbyr that escapes his voice.

"Freshmen. This is what's going to happen. My colleagues here will call out your names. When you hear it, be prepared to join them. They will take you to your new sleeping quarters. There, you will have exactly two hours to freshen up, change into your school uniform, and read the rules in your IPKA. At 1900 hours, we invite you to a welcome party, in informal attire, on the terrace. Once again, I welcome you to Bionbyr."

"What's an '*ippka*'?" I whisper to Embla, who shrugs her shoulders. I guess we'll find out soon.

"Those of you who will belong to class Alpha are as follows," says Ebern, who wastes no time, but reads quickly, clearly, and firmly from the glass screen in his hand, announcing the names of those who will accompany him. I notice that many of those who are called start to get up, but when they realize others are still sitting, they sit down again. Are we supposed to go up now or later? When are we supposed to go? No one wants to make a mistake. My name isn't called, and Embla's isn't either, or any other names I recognize. I feel somewhat relieved.

Bern is in charge of the next group – "class Beta" – and he calls out his list of names, including Marcell's. I've been trying to locate him, but he vanished into thin air as soon as we left the Ray.

Bern takes a step back and one of the female professors steps forward. Unlike the others, she's wearing high, black boots, and her uniform jacket looks perfectly fitted to her body. Her dark brown hair is set in a ponytail that widens behind her soldiers. She, too, has a glass screen in her hand that she reads from.

"This means that those of you who remain will now belong to class Gamma, which I'm responsible for, but I'll read your names anyway, for the sake of doing things right," says the woman. Her voice seems to caress my soul. I get a warm feeling in my body from listening to it, even though it was so short and concise. This time mine and Embla's names are called out, along with Ivalde, Tricia, and Ewind, who we got to know on the ship.

"Thank you, Domi E. Cainea, Domi B. Cainea, and Domi Malimot," Andor says. "Students, please follow these three to your respective quarters. I hope you will feel welcome here. Get ready, prepare yourselves. Together for Ela!"

The students in the burgundy uniforms hold out their right hands with their fingers outstretched, clench their fists, and move their hands quickly to the left side of their chests.

I try to distinguish individual students, but they're too far away and look too similar for me to be able to tell them apart.

The sound of almost five hundred people banging their fists on their chests is so loud that I flinch.

This is the signal for everyone to get up. I hold Embla's hand tightly and walk towards the woman who called out our names. The woman is called Domi Malimot. When we're all gathered around her, about a hundred students, she briefly introduces herself as the one responsible for class Gamma.

"Follow me."

She takes us out into the same corridor as before and into the exact same elevator pairs that we took up to this floor. With us are some of the students in the emerald green uniforms. Did they come in another boat before us?

"Half of you, take that elevator, and the other half will take this one," she instructs, stepping into the last elevator she pointed to. "We're going to the third floor."

When Embla and I enter the elevator, I see that the other classes have taken different elevator pairs that are farther away. We are the only class that went back to the same place.

The third floor is very similar to the second floor, except that now "Hygiene Room" and "Gamma" are displayed above the nearest doors on each side of the corridor.

"Only first-year Gamma students have permission to enter here. To get in, just wave the chip in your left wrist over the panel. Your dorm is to the right when you enter. Be sure to read the list displayed on the screen on the wall near the dorms. Since there are twice as many first-year students this year, you'll need to share a room with a classmate in the beginning. You can't go wrong, thanks to the chip-locks. We'll see you in exactly two hours, up on the sixth floor, for the welcome party. Welcome!"

Malimot smiles as she walks past us and leaves to our own devices. Time for us to show responsibility for ourselves.

"Are they trying to save oxygen or something? They're so short with their words," Embla mutters to me. A student in our assigned class beeps us into Gamma's sleeping quarters, and we step inside. "And what did she mean by 'in the beginning?'"

The door gives off a little "bzz" when it closes again.

Just like the Auditorium we were in a second ago, this room is airy and fresh. We enter a common room with six lemon-yellow sofas with dark blue-green throw pillows. And just like the Auditorium, this room has the feeling of a balcony, as there's a hole going straight down in here as well. Embla and I go over to check out the railing, and we can see the water in the harbor at the bottom. Just below us, there seems to be a classroom because we can see the benches students probably occupy when class is in session. I get a little scared when I look down, but I quickly comfort myself with the fact that if I fall, at least I'll end up in the water. It'll still hurt, though. Embla doesn't dare to go near the edge, she takes my word on what's down there instead.

When I turn around, I see that there's a kitchen section of the room, with a splash wall in the exact same shade as the throw pillows on the couches. Near the couches, there's a large TV screen above a fireplace. It's an artificial fire, but somehow it still generates heat. There's a dining area with two long tables, filled with enough chairs to seat everyone.

Branching out from the common room, there are three corridors full of small rooms on either side. Those must be the dorms. Embla pulls me over to the screen by the dorms to find out if we ended up in the same room. She groans when she discovers that we've been assigned to different rooms. I'll be sharing a room with Tricia, who's somewhat familiar, but Embla will have a new person in her room.

"I hope this 'Vera' is a decent person," she mutters, "but at least our rooms are pretty close to each other."

The dorms here are very similar to the cabins on the Ray. Just like on the Ray, there's an artificial window here that seems to let in natural light. But wait. As I look closer, I see that this is a real window. I'm guessing that not everyone has one, but I'm glad it's a window I can actually open. I test it out and realize that it's actually pretty easy. I leave it open a crack. There are two beds, one in each corner of the room, and in the middle are two desks that face each other. At the foot of each bed is a set of wardrobes. The room is very simple and stylishly decorated. On each bed are three sets of school uniforms, workout clothes, and neatly folded underwear. There's also a set of party clothes, which are really just another kind of school uniform, except it's in a different color and there are more gold details. Next to the clothes, there's also a glass tablet.

As I sit down on the bed, I discover how soft the blanket is. I hardly want to take my hands off it. It feels just like downy chicks. So smooth. On the floor is a rug that must be made of the same material.

I pick up the glass and look it over carefully. At the bottom, barely visible, I make out the word "IPKA."

"Do you know how this works?" I ask Tricia, who's already started to change into her formal uniform. Since we only have two hours, I should really do the same.

"Do you think we really have to use those?" Tricia replies with a sad look. Her whole world seems to be falling down around her as she looks at the glass tablet.

"Yeah, I think so, but I don't know how to work it either, so we can learn together."

"I don't want to learn. It's blasphemy to use something like this."

Ewind had mentioned something about this on the boat ride here. It must have been the first time I had heard anything about technology being the reason why the world looks the way it does.

I'll have to learn by myself then. It's something we were told to look into during our free time before the party.

I hold the glass tablet in front of my face to see if I can find a button of some kind. To my surprise, the tablet reacts.

"Hello, Freija Falinn," the IPKA says, and I almost lose my grip on it in my surprise. I must have done something right. Maybe it detected my face or the chip in my wrist? "Starting installation."

"Heathen," Tricia mumbles and walks out of the room wearing her uniform.

"Welcome, Freija. I'm your Intelligent Personal Knowledge Assistant. What can I help you with?"

I hesitate at first. "We're supposed to read something before the welcome party."

"That's right. Clicking on this symbol will allow you to access your personal archive. What you are looking for is in the 'Administration' folder. The document is called 'Rules.'"

The IPKA illuminates the places I'm supposed to click on so that I can easily find the right one.

"Is there anything else I can help you with now, Freija?"

"No, I don't think so. Thanks."

"Together for Ela," the IPKA concludes, leaving me to read the rules in peace and quiet. I skim through them quickly and read that we have to be back in the common room by ten in the evening, before the doors are locked for the night, and that we can't commit acts of violence against other students without the permission of a professor in class. It also says that everyone should be treated equally and that all differences will be settled, which means that – among other things – there are to be no personal accessories or celebration of birthdays. I think of Ivalde's heels and mine and Embla's beaded bracelets. If we break any of the rules, we'll be punished with anything from a bad mark on our reviews to expulsion.

"Have you seen Ivalde?" asks Ewind, who soon enters mine and Tricia's room through the door that Tricia apparently left open.

"No, sorry. Not since the boat."

"Well, he was in the Auditorium, and then I lost him. We're assigned to the same room, but I haven't seen him at all. You think he could have gotten lost?"

"No clue. We still have some time to ourselves, so I'm sure he'll be up soon. Is Embla still in her room?"

"Last time I saw her, she was in the kitchen area of the common room. I'll keep looking."

I nod to Ewind, but she doesn't see it. My focus returns to the glass tablet. Maybe it's best to wait until later to explore what it can do? According to the IPKA's clock, there's about an hour left until we're supposed to gather for the welcome party, and I haven't even washed or changed yet.

Just like Ewind had said, I find Embla in front of the refrigerators in the kitchen. I can see Tricia standing on the balcony, looking out over the sea to the horizon. I wonder what she's thinking.

"So, check this out!"

Embla opens one of the coolers, which is full of packages I've never seen before. They're colorful, and some have pictures of fruits and berries on them, but it's impossible to tell what they contain.

"What is all this?"

Ewind produces a package and gives it to me.

"It's Ultrafood!" she exclaims. "It's the Authority's own food producer that specifically supplies food for the military."

"What's in it?"

"Depends," Embla replies. "Some are just drinks, and others are some kind of cookies with seeds, nuts, dried fruits, and stuff. There are also sandwiches with cheese, and ham, and—I don't even know what else."

"We need to get ready for the party. Should we go wash up and change?"

"Do you think our crops go towards this? Or is it something modified altogether? Shameless. What did you say?"

"Should we get ready for the welcome party?" I ask again.

"I guess so."

"How did it go with your roommate?"

"Okay, I guess. Vera was wearing a green uniform when she came in. What do you think that means?"

"You didn't ask her?"

Embla shrugs and grabs a set of her new clothes. Together, we walk across the corridor to where it says "Hygiene Room" above the door. The hygiene room, like the common room, is actually several rooms in one. There's an area for showers, one with toilet stalls lined up one after the other, and farther down, it looks like there's some kind of vanity area where chairs are lined up in front of large mirrors. There are reclining chairs placed here and there, and drones ensure that everything is kept clean. The shower here feels like a refreshing rain on a hot summer day.

The school uniform feels comfortable on my body. I take a few steps and can't think of anything negative to say about it. There's really nothing special about the clothes: pants, a long-sleeved t-shirt, a thin jacket in burgundy, and black boots, but they're soft and comfortable. Light. I smile to myself when it strikes me that I've never had the feeling of wearing brand new clothes before.

The top floor, floor six, turns out to be a single open space in the form of a park. Yeah, if you ignore the fact that we're completely surrounded by a dome. Here, it becomes extra clear, since you can see the top. At the top, it looks like there are air vents, but even though it's evening now and I know that it's frosty and terribly cold back home in Ithmah, I can't feel the cold here on the deck. It feels like a hot spring day.

There's a stage on one side and a pool on the other. Between the two are trees, flowers, some benches, and above all, over a hundred white tables with four or five chairs each. Above the tables, ropes are strung with lanterns hanging down from them. The tables are set with white tablecloths with Bionbyr's emblem embroidered on them. The porcelain and cutlery shine in the lantern light. Do I even dare to touch the glasses? I'd be so afraid to break one. I notice that even Embla is marveling at how elegant and stylish everything is. Wonder how much all this has cost the Authority. Not just the park, but our rooms, and the rest of Bionbyr. The idea is staggering.

I have to reach out my hand and touch the leaves of a bush just to make sure it's real. How is it possible for this to grow here on Bionbyr, which is actually a boat? I try to catch Embla's gaze, but it's stuck on the green grass. I've never seen anything so green before. Somewhere among the trees, I know the sugar glider is hiding. I'm not looking forward to the day when it's discovered.

In front of the stage, a buffet has appeared, so we head towards it. Even though we're several minutes early, there are already a lot of students here, and many have started to help themselves to the food. It smells incredibly delicious.

Embla spots Ewind at the buffet, so we decide to join her. She's standing there with a guy who has short, black hair similar to my own.

"Hey!" Ewind bursts out as we arrive. "I've added you to the Square, but you haven't accepted yet! Do it!"

Embla and I probably look equally as confused. "The Square?"

"The Square is a social app," Ewind explains. "Like, you can keep in touch with your friends there, write to them, things like that. Ivalde, have you added them?"

It's only then that I realize it's Ivalde standing next to Ewind with a plate in his hand.

"I'll do it soon," he chuckles. His gaze reveals a different feeling. Sorrow.

"Wait, did you get a haircut?" asks Embla.

"It's because he had to. Didn't you read the rules? Nothing that stands out too much is allowed. His lovely red locks got a reputation," Ewind says. In Ivalde's new hairstyle, the mark on his cheek is more obvious. Somehow, it's beautiful. "I can understand their point. It's important to show that we're united."

I discreetly touch the black beaded bracelet. I don't want them to take it away from me, so I slip it into my pocket, where I'll keep it from now on.

We find a table after helping ourselves to the buffet. It was hard to choose because everything looked so good, but it would have been impossible to take a little of everything. In the end, we had to settle without even getting a clear look at everything that was offered.

In front of me, I have a dark red soup that, like Ela's flag, is decorated with a miniature version of the country in gold at the center of the bowl. It tastes like beetroot with something strong mixed in, maybe chili pepper or something like that.

At one of the tables, a little closer to the stage, I catch sight of Marcell sitting and laughing with a group of other students. Among them, I see a guy who reminds me a little of Onni, in that they both have their hair hanging down in front of their eyes. Except this guy is blonde. When he sees me looking at him, our eyes meet for half a second before I look away. But I think I saw the hint of a grin on his face.

Andor is on the stage again. This time, he tells us again how excited they are about the new recruits and that it will be an intense year.

"We will place reasonable but high demands on you. In a sharp situation, you can't expect the enemy to wait for you to assess the situation and make a decision on how to act. You have to learn how to quickly gather information and prioritize what's most important," he says. "Tonight is the first of three parties we are organizing at Bionbyr. This spring, we will, of course, be hosting a graduation party for the third-years, and in between – to mark the halfway point in the school year and get some positive reinforcement – we'll be hosting a Winter Ball after the autumn classes have finished. This year will be extra special, as President Didrik Daegal will be attending, and since he is celebrating thirty years as regent next year, we will be the first to celebrate this right here at Bionbyr!"

All of the students applaud, and the older students make the same gesture they did in the Auditorium, which ends with the sound of a huge drum being struck.

Andor continues his speech, but my thoughts are stuck on one of the details. The President is coming to our school this winter. I get a knot in my stomach. It's one thing to see him speak as a hologram, but the thought of seeing or meeting him in real life causes my body to tense up for some strange reason. Everything suddenly feels so real. He's no longer a symbol, but an actual person. But when I look at Embla, she doesn't have the same anxiety in her eyes as I do. In her gaze is something I haven't seen in her in what feels like forever.

Purpose.

12

I find it hard to fall asleep after the many new sights and the massive amount of information we've received today. Tricia doesn't seem to have any trouble falling asleep, because it doesn't take long before I hear a sleepy yawn and a single snore. It doesn't bother me at all. I'm used to Embla's snoring. If you get used to it, you can fall asleep to anything. I've been staring up at the ceiling where my IPKA projects the clock in a glowing blue. 23:56. Four minutes to midnight.

Did Apsel manage to fall asleep okay tonight? Or is he lying awake just like me? Is he worried about whether he'll ever see his daughter again? Is it even nighttime at the Sethunya Home for Wayward Children? I don't know where Bionbyr is, but we're probably in a different time zone. I hate the feeling of being so far away from my family. It would have felt a little better if I was sharing a room with Embla like we always have.

The moonlight shines down, spilling into the room, just like mine and Embla's old room. At midnight, something soft lands on the blanket near my feet. I feel small paws approaching on my legs and then on my chest. I take a quick peek at the window that I left open before. How did the sugar glider know that this is where I sleep? Has it been looking for me, searching room by room?

My heart is pounding hard. My pulse is getting faster. I check on Tricia and see that she's still sleeping heavily. What if she sees it in our room?

"Do you want to sleep here?"

The sugar glider coos and crawls under the blanket, finding a perfect spot next to my chest.

"I feel like I should give you a name. I can't just call you 'sugar glider' all the time," I whisper, thinking. Apsel used to tell us about a spirit that saved children from drowning and then watched over that child for the rest of their life. I try to remember what the spirit was called.

"How about 'Aariel'?" I suggest. I think I see an expression of approval on my new furry friend. "Then it's settled. I like it."

Having someone to hold on to, even if it's a little furball, makes me feel more at ease.

Sleep welcomes me quickly.

When I wake up early in the morning, Aariel is gone. Tricia is already finished changing, and she's standing there, looking out the window. She's perfectly still until she sees me. Then she lights up.

"Good morning! Did you sleep well? I've probably never slept that well in my entire life. The mattresses are fantastic; they mold right to your body. Did you like it? I loved it. I wonder what kinds of lessons we'll have today."

Internally, I groan so loudly that part of me is worried she'll somehow hear it. Another advantage of sharing a room with Embla is that she's just as tired as I am in the morning. I manage a somewhat forced "good morning."

"Good morning, Recruit Terah. These are today's lessons. Your first lesson is 'Physical Education: Running' with Domi Amoz in the training center."

I sit up in bed and look around feverishly to see if there's anyone else in the room. When I'm sure that it's just me and Tricia, I stare at her. Was it her IPKA who answered her question, just like mine had helped me yesterday? Then I see that Tricia isn't looking out the window, or she did and accidentally started something up, because the window has activated as a screen. Her IPKA is still untouched on the desk. On the screen, we see today's schedule displayed and color-coded. After the Physical Education class, "*Hygiene*" and "*Breakfast*" are planned to immediately follow, and then "*Social Studies*" with Domi B. Cainea in "*Alpha 2*," followed by "*Lunch*" and a double-lecture in "*Medical Arts*" with Domi Malimot in the "*Medical Bay*."

I already knew about this because I had spent more time getting to know the IPKA when I came back to the room last night. At Bionbyr, there are eight days in a week. Three days of lessons followed by a day of self-study, then another three days of lessons followed by another self-study day. The first thing I noticed is that we have some kind of fitness class every morning before breakfast—every other day we have Physical Education and on the other days we have Strength Training. Even on the days when we have no other lessons.

Tricia is standing there, stunned at the "conversation" she just had with the window. I remember that yesterday she had expressed frustration with using technology and I have a strong feeling that this is only a small taste of all the modern technological features the school has to offer. Behind Tricia's smile, I can see how divided she is. I definitely can't relate to her feelings, even though we've lived a relatively techno-free life at the orphanage. There's always been some technology there and we've been dependent on the technology we've had access to.

"Should we go together then?" Tricia smiles and dons her mask of positivity again. She seems to have some pretty extreme mood swings.

"We should get Embla first," I reply, changing into my workout clothes.

Embla seems to have had the same idea, as she walks into our room. She yawns a "good morning" and gives me a hug.

"Sleep well?" I wonder.

"Oh, yeah. You?"

"I slept great, actually. The bed is wonderful."

"Mm."

"How's your roommate?"

"Vera? Yeah, she seems okay. She's from Agnarr. They were the students who were wearing the green uniforms."

"Yes, of course!" I burst out. I should have known that. It makes sense, after all. Agnarr is the military prep school. They're sixteen years old, but practically already soldiers. They have ten years of training before they even get here.

"But other than that, we haven't talked much. She spent most of her time with her IPKA yesterday," says Embla. "We'll see how it goes. I don't think we'll be best friends, but you never know."

Thanks to all the screens, we find our way to the training center surprisingly easily. Our Physical Education professor, Domi Amoz, is already waiting for us as we enter the room. It's a big room. There's only one wall that doesn't consist of floor-to-ceiling windows. On that wall, there are TV screens hung in front of about twenty machines that look exactly like the ones we used during the Selections. If we were to fall, we'd hardly hit the light purple floor because it's so soft that you almost sink into it.

Domi Amoz stands with his hands behind his back. His stern commands immediate respect, or maybe not so much respect as a bit of fear. The orange-red hair sits in a small, hard knot in the middle of his head. Gathered around him are the other students in our grade. There's plenty of room left over.

Amoz instructs us to line up in a row, and he goes back and forth along the line with his hands clasped behind his back. It feels weird to stand like this. Are we being inspected? Every now and then, he tells someone to raise their chin or hold their arms tighter against their body.

Embla and I do our best to fit in. I know I need to do this to get through the next three years and try to save the orphanage. I have to do my best. Will Embla do the same? We need to sit down and talk about it so that she understands how important it is for me to get through this.

I cast a glance at Ivalde. The workout clothes from Bionbyr look so out of place on him. I can see that he feels the same way, as he stands in perfect form but with a dogged expression. Without the heels and the brightly colored hair, he looks just like everyone else. Even though I'd rather not spend time with him, I still pity him for being forced to sever the things that made him himself.

Even then, when I really thought about it, I wondered if our physical attributes really contribute to our personalities. Was Ivalde really not Ivalde without the heels and colorful hair? Maybe not. Maybe that's what Bionbyr wanted to convey. That we're all the same despite our differences?

"This is Admin Halldora."

Amoz turns everyone's attention to the same white-haired woman we followed yesterday.

"Good morning, first years," she greets us and takes a step forward. Like Amoz, she has her hands behind her back. She stands near me and gives off a strange charisma. Jealousy begins to spark inside me when I look at her. How can she be allowed to keep her unnatural white hair when Ivalde had to cut his? Maybe she did something to deserve the privilege, or they want her to be recognizable in some way.

Domi Amoz presents two more people who greet us. I miss their names because I'm still busy thinking about Halldora, but I notice that one of them is the blonde guy who I had briefly made eye contact with last night. The one who was sitting with Marcell.

Marcell is also standing there, just like Ivalde, in perfect form with his chin up and chest out. His arms are tucked neatly at side sides. Unlike Ivalde, he has pride and ambition on his face.

The first years are divided into our respective classes. Since it's our first time, each class will follow one of the presented leaders for a run. On future runs, we'll have to fend for ourselves. Class Gamma will follow Admin Halldora.

We take a left out of the training center and run along the inside of the dome on a wide deck. It's at least sixty feet from the training center to the wall of glass. We run past the dining hall on the left, and – to my surprise – we don't take another left when we reach the bridge that goes across as the deck continues over the water so that we can cross over to the other side. The bridge is pushed out from the harbor's edge when there aren't any boats moving in or out.

I see the other two classes in front of us. It actually feels pretty ridiculous to run on a track. The black boots of our uniforms make the trip heavy and unbearable. Not as light as they felt the first time I tested them.

Jogging around the entire dome takes us about an hour.

"Ah, this is cotton for the soul," notes Ewind when we're all gathered in the hygiene room. I completely agree. My shower helps me cool down after the sweaty morning. I tap on the mirror wall and get shower cream from a spout. "Don't you think? I'm going to love this routine. Exercise every morning, followed by a shower and breakfast. Could this get any better?"

"I can actually think of a lot of things that are better," Embla snaps.

"Oh really?"

"Playing with the kids, taking care of the crops in the fields, reading fairy tales, hanging out with my family," Embla stares down at the floor.

"I didn't think you had a family, though? Aren't you an orphan?"

"My dad is the best person there is. You don't understand what he's done for me!" Embla sputters.

I see how much attention we're drawing and silently ask her to calm down. Marcell stands in a shower a little further away, pretending he doesn't know us. That blonde guy is there too. My gaze catches on him for a second, but I let it go and head to breakfast with Embla.

I knew she was missing Apsel and the orphanage, just like me, but I think being away hurt her more than it did me. She didn't talk during breakfast, only responding when she needed to. I never got a chance to talk to her about my financial plan. I needed to let her settle in a little first. Everything went by so fast that I couldn't stop and think about what was happening. The few moments we had to catch our breath in the beginning were the moments right before we fell asleep. It was plain to see that Embla didn't like being at Bionbyr. I know she tried, but sometimes her feelings got in the way, and the Embla who had been acting jaded before the trip resurfaced. She became bitter. Not even the yellow edible flowers we ate could put her in a better mood. But for me, it felt so nostalgic. Images of

how the morning sun made the succulent leaves sparkle like little
crystals. The sour figs from which Apsel had made good soup.
I was probably missing it more than I wanted to admit.

All of the students are already in their places when Domi Bern Cainea enters the classroom for our lesson in "Social Studies," and the temperature almost seems to drop as soon as he appears. The tables we're sitting at are neatly lined up, one by one, with exactly the same amount of space between each table. He goes straight to the big screen behind the large, shiny desk and writes three words in the air in front of the screen: "*Discipline and Loyalty.*" Bionbyr's motto.

"Good morning, class Gamma 1," says B. Cainea, sounding strained. His blue hair doesn't look as intense as it did at the Selections. Now it's more gray-blue. I like it somehow. But then I think of Ivalde and his hair. He couldn't keep his unnaturally colored hair anymore. There's no way Bern's blue hair is natural, right? Maybe there are different rules for professors.

"Good morning!" the class answers, a little half-heartedly.

"You've already made a mistake. Does anyone read the rules anymore?"

We look at each other curiously.

"When you speak to your professors, you must end with the word 'Domi,'" Bern continues. "Does anyone know why?"

I glance around me. Tricia looks scared, Embla sighs, Ivalde is absent, and Ewind looks like she should know the answer, but doesn't know why.

B. Cainea points to the first word on the screen: "*Discipline.*"

"Discipline creates order. Without order, there is chaos. Right?"

154

"Yes, Domi," I hear some answer. I'm not one of them, and immediately I feel like I've failed. I hear Bern sigh, but he continues.

"What do you think 'loyalty' means? You?" Bern points to a guy sitting right next to me. My heart leaps in my chest at first, until I realize he's not pointing at me.

"Uhh, maybe…" the guy starts, but he's quickly interrupted. Even though his head and face are shaved, you can see shadows of his dark hair that frame his face perfectly. In the middle of his angular face are two nervous eyes.

"Stand up and introduce yourself."

The guy stands up, much more steadily than I would have. I look at his still hands. Mine are trembling.

"Hakon Sanvi, Domi."

"Ah, you distinguished yourself at the Selections. It will be exciting to see your development here at Bionbyr." Bern says it as a compliment, but at the same time, he has a derogatory tone. "Well, Recruit Sanvi, what do you think we mean by 'loyalty'?"

"That we support each other, Domi."

"We can start from there. Loyalty means a community. That we're there for our comrades. Without each other, we are nothing. If we cannot trust each other, we can forget about the entire thing and do something else. It would create chaos. Here at Bionbyr, we show fellowship with our salute. Stand up and do as I do. Hold your right hand straight out and point it up halfway. Your fingers should be squeezed together with your hand outstretched. Clench your fist and then hit the left side of your chest. Like this!" Domi B. Cainea salutes us, and we mimic him. "Practice it until you have it down. And don't forget our motto."

Bern turns to the desk and motions over something with his hand so that the world map is projected into the air. At first, it's flat, but he quickly positions it upward so that everyone can see it, just like a painting.

"In order to gain an understanding of why our world is the way it is today, and how to continue moving forward to flourish, we must understand our history. We must learn from the mistakes of the Old World and do better. Does anyone know why there are so few cities in Ela?"

Ewind raises her hand, is granted the floor, and stands up.

"Ewind Dolon. It's because the majority of the earth is uninhabitable due to the toxins in the soil, the water, and in some places the air, Domi."

I wonder if she read that straight out of a book as she says it. Everyone knows this. Ela has a few large cities and a number of small ones. All of them are overpopulated, and many are forced to live outside of the cities — like at Sethunya. I wish I had gotten that question.

"Thank you, Recruit Dolon. Specify *why* the earth is uninhabitable."

"The ice caps melted, Domi," Ewind replies.

"Everyone knows that. Can anyone else tell me why the Disaster happened?" He sits down in a brown leather armchair and stares out over the class. I know what kind of answer he's looking for. And I know what Tricia is thinking. I raise my hand.

"Freija Falinn. The Power People, Domi."

A vague smile creeps across B. Cainea's lips. As I sit down, I catch Embla's gaze. Is it my imagination or does she look disappointed?

"The sea level was raised. Large swathes of land disappeared. Earthquakes, storms, fires, volcanic eruptions, diseases, death. Yes, this is something that didn't happen naturally. The power that many people possessed was devastating for our world," Bern adds.

Tricia is sitting a few tables away with her eyes fixed on her hands in her lap. I think she's trying to resist speaking out. According to her beliefs, technology is the culprit. I don't really know what to think.

"No one knows exactly how these individuals developed such powers. What we do know is that they were born with defects and couldn't control their powers. President Daegal is the first President to actually do something about the problem. Thanks to him, we can keep their powers under control, and he was also the one who started Project Medeor. Does anyone know enough about it to explain it to the rest of the class?"

Ewind is quick with her hand.

"Recruit Dolon?"

"Project Medeor is an initiative to keep the Power People together in select places to keep them under control, but also to use technology to clean the air and water, and make the soil fertile again."

"A perfect answer," B. Cainea smiles. I still think it sounds like Ewind is just regurgitating something she read in a text somewhere. I find myself getting annoyed with her. But why exactly? Because she had the right answer? Because I didn't? Ridiculous. "Project Medeor strives for all people in Ela to survive the illnesses that still exist, for our children to be able to reach their fifth birthdays, and for us to be able to live and grow everywhere. Once, this was possible. Then came the Power People. And now our world looks like this."

"I don't think Tricia will be able to stay on the list." Ewind waits until Tricia leaves us after lunch, probably to gather her thoughts before our double-lecture in "Medical Arts," before she says it. The rest of us have also finished eating, but we're still sitting and enjoying the day. We're perched at the edge of the dining hall, where there are open walls and the ceiling rests on pillars. The view of the sea is magical. I can see that we're moving because Bionbyr is leaving a trail of white foam, but it doesn't feel like we're moving at all. Between the white metal tables, there are birds flapping around to get their share of lunch.

"What kind of list?" I wonder. Embla is still angry about what she calls "Ewind's assault" during our showers.

"Wait, haven't you read anything? Haven't you checked your IPKA? Look, check this out," Ewind pulls up a list of the names of everyone in our grade on her IPKA. All of the names are white. Mine and Embla's names are somewhere in the middle. "There's a list for each year. After all, it's only been a day, so we haven't been evaluated yet. So the list isn't current, of course. But this is where you can see who gets expelled and who succeeds."

The Selections don't seem to be over. I read in the rules that you can be expelled if you violate the rules, but are there other ways to get expelled? I feel pressure; like there's a heavy stone on my chest. Ivalde seems to be feeling the same way. His grim facial expression is even clearer. I see worry in his eyes. It must be eating him up from the inside, because he doesn't talk much.

"Did you think it would be easy here?" Ewind smirks. "By the way, have you accepted my request on the Square?"

"No, I haven't even checked it out yet," I admit.

"Calm down. Give me your IPKA and I'll show you."

I hand over my IPKA so that Ewind can show me and Embla how the Square works. It's a platform where you can send messages to each other, to the professors, and to a forum for questions where we can help each other.

"How do you know all this?" I ask.

"Well, *everyone* in my family has one, actually. Of course, that was a much older model, but the idea is the same. Didn't you have one? Didn't you have something like that at the orphanage?"

"Well, we had a screen, which might have been sort of like an IPKA, but it was black and clumsy, and it didn't have any features like this at all," I tell her.

"Aha, so you probably only had a TeKA. Gotcha. Ivalde, you probably had an IPKA in Pari, right?"

Ivalde nods.

"Limited feature here," he says a little later.

"Yeah, but that's just because we haven't gotten permissions yet. We'll get more and more the longer we're here."

Ivalde rolls his eyes.

The pressure in my chest feels even heavier. Embla and I are so far behind everyone else at Bionbyr. Many of them come from wealthier families where they've gotten used to all the luxuries offered here, where they've had the chance to learn all the advanced technology and already have the answers to the professors' questions. This won't be easy to handle. But I have to. I'll just have to work even harder. Will Embla be prepared to try that hard? And if she doesn't, will I be able to do it without her?

Whatever she decides, I'm ready to take on the challenge.

13

"Embla, can we talk a little after dinner?" We're on our way to the lesson in "Medical Arts," which is across the harbor from the dining hall. The water in the harbor sparkles as far as the sunlight reaches.

"Okay. What's on your mind?"

"I'll tell you later. When it's just you and me."

Embla nods.

The Medical Bay is Bionbyr's infirmary. It's not so much a bay as a large room with several smaller rooms containing sick beds and equipment attached to it, similar to Gamma's common room. Along the walls are glass cabinets with medicines, jars, tubes, compresses, and other gear inside. Domi Malimot, who's our class leader, is waiting for us before the lesson begins.

"Good afternoon, class Gamma 1," she greets us.

"Good afternoon, Domi" we answer, much more enthusiastically than we were with the Social Studies professor. I say it too, loud and clear.

"We won't always be in the medical bay, so pay attention to the schedule to see which room is assigned for each class period. Since you're new, it's important to show you what's here," Domi says. She speaks much more calmly and with more warmth in her voice than B. Cainea.

She shows us around the medical bay and carefully explains what kinds of medical care are offered and how fast the rehabilitation can be thanks to the officials and technology in place here. The dome not only protects against the sun and controls the temperature, but also acts as a safety net against, among other things, air pollution and UV rays, which means that Bionbyr can go to places that would normally be completely unlivable.

Part of life as a soldier is that we can expect to be injured in some way. I'm not looking forward to it. But I'm relieved to hear Domi Malimot tell us about the skilled medical drones that can perform advanced surgical procedures, and the medicines offered here that can cure just about anything. She tells us about how they can grow organs like skins, livers, and hearts here.

When we got sick at the orphanage, we would mostly rest. If it was serious, Apsel would boil a broth or a special herb drink. The drink helped, but it tasted really bland. I remember one time when Onni got pneumonia. Despite resting and drinking the herbal brew, he didn't get better. Finally, Apsel took him to the hospital in Ithmah. We had stood in the yard listening to Onni's coughs until they were out of earshot. At first, the hospital hadn't wanted to help because neither Apsel nor Onni had insurance, money, or high social standing. Apsel had been forced to negotiate with the Authority, and finally, they had agreed to give Onni the care he needed in exchange for cutting Apsel's food rations in half for two months. Just when he thought the money problem was solved, the next problem came up. Apsel wasn't approved as Onni's guardian, even though he was employed by the Authority to run the orphanage. It took a few more days to get the paperwork certifying that he had the right to take care of Onni, and by that point, it had gone so far that Onni was on the border between life and death.

"Once upon a time," Apsel told us, "the state existed to keep people healthy. Adam Simulus, Ela's first President, made it a law that everyone should have the right to healthcare and that the

Authority would help those who needed it. For children, it would be completely free up until they were six years old. It didn't take Didrik Daegal more than a year before he abolished that law and turned healthcare into a profit-driven business."

It was times like that when Marcell would protest, saying that, "It's better for the money to be used to heal the world instead," or some other reason, and so the debate between them started.

Domi Malimot shows us into one of the rooms that connect to the medical bay's main entrance room. Plants are growing from floor to ceiling along the walls, and in the middle of the room is a large cultivation of herbs. I see how happy Embla is at the sight. It reminds us of home.

"I've already talked about all the advanced medical techniques and medicines that we have to offer at Bionbyr. From my experience, however, I know that the home remedies used around Ela work at least as well, which is why I've turned this room into an herb garden," Malimot says.

Several of my classmates look skeptically at the green leaves that sparkle under the big lights. They probably belong to families that have never had to grow their own food or rely on home remedies because they had access to healthcare and packaged foods. They don't even know that food comes from the earth.

"The advantage of growing here at Bionbyr is that it's always the right season. The temperature is favorable for plants, and water is always available, even if it doesn't rain for a while."

When I first read that we would have a double-lecture in "Medical Arts," I wondered how we would fill three whole hours, but the time actually goes really quickly. Domi Malimot goes through easy ways to treat wounds with an herbal cream that we can mix ourselves using herbs from the greenhouse room.

"I understand that this is a school," Embla says in a somewhat quiet voice, "and that it's run by the Authority and all... But everything feels so excessive. If we could get just half of what's here at the orphanage, or even just a quarter... Dad complains all the time about how little help he gets from the Authority, how it's never really enough, how he always has to turn over every single monetas to make sure we get what we need. Why are orphanages so much less important than the rest of the world?"

I have no answer, and I can't help but wonder the same thing. It's not just the medicine, but also all the food from the buffet we indulge in every day. Meat, fish, poultry, rodents and fried insects, about twenty salads and mixes, soups, bread with so many toppings that you can't taste them all at once. At Bionbyr, not one goes hungry. No one is sick.

"What did you want to talk about?" Embla says sourly. I get a little annoyed at her tedious attitude, but I shake the feeling off as best I can. I explain my so-called "plan" to her.

"What?" snorts Embla. "So you actually *want* to be here?"

Whether I *want* to or not, it's not like we have much of a choice.

"I just think that while we're here, we should do our best so that we can graduate. Then we'll be able to make a difference."

"Do you actually believe that? You're so naive sometimes. You can do whatever you want, but I just want to get out of here. I want to go home."

"I don't want you to go. I need you here," I say.

Embla says nothing. She stands with her arms crossed, barely looking at me.

"Before we left, you said you'd give it a try, and —"

"I have given it a try," Embla snorts. "This whole place is corrupted. Don't you see it? Double standards everywhere. And we're just supposed to stand in line and take this crap? Are you really fine with this?"

"I don't think it's that bad. I —"

"You're being brainwashed, Freija. Wake up."

"What do you want to do then? Run away? Do you think that'll help Apsel and the orphanage? Will it help you? If you want to get out of here, make sure you do poorly so you get expelled. But in the meantime, it would be nice if you and I could get along. You're my family and I want to be with you."

Embla sighs. "I'll never be a soldier with no free will. I'll never be someone else's pawn."

"I don't think so either. So, does this mean you'll stop being a sourpuss and pushing me away?"

"We'll see."

"Okay, that'll do," I reply, a little disappointed.

Gamma's common room is homey, despite the sterile environment. The darkness of the night has settled over the glass dome-like a blanket, and I imagine that if anyone saw Bionbyr in the distance it would look like a ball of light on the horizon. In the common room, there's cozy lighting and the students in our class are using every conceivable seat. It's pretty crowded, probably because there aren't supposed to be this many people here at the same time. Out on the balcony, just below mine and Tricia's window, which is still open so that Aariel can come and go as he pleases, five of us sit together and read about the professors in our IPKAs.

Ever since our lesson in "Medical Arts," I've been very curious to know more about our class leader. Her name is Malva, and it turns out that she was born in Calli, which isn't far from Adali, the capital. She used to be a doctor in Vallis, one of the bigger cities in Efricia. That's where Embla and I tried to go when we were little. That must be why I felt like I recognized her at the first lesson. At one point, we'd made eye contact, and when I looked into her eyes, something awoke within me. Her eyes were dark blue, like the sea. They didn't tell me everything, but I got the feeling that she recognized me too. Just like the ocean, her eyes hide secrets, and I'd love to know what they are. Have we met before? If she was a doctor in Vallis, it might not be entirely unreasonable for her to have been in Ithmah as well. Would I have this feeling if we had only seen each other occasionally in passing?

Bern and Esbern come from the capital. Esbern was trained as a Guardian and has worked as the President's bodyguard, while Bern became a professor at a university in Calli. There, he got married and had a daughter. When she died at the age of five from an infectious disease that had been caused by a Tabia, he did everything possible to ensure that Project Medeor was a success. He and Esbern both got positions at Bionbyr after several years of working on the initiative.

"Now I understand why he was so intense when he talked about the Power People and the initiative today," Ewind says. "If I'd lost my child... Well, I don't know if I would have the strength to do anything about it. I'd probably just be so heartbroken and devoid of energy. I know it sounds harsh, but sometimes I *hate* the Power People. For the Disaster. For all the suffering we've endured."

"You're wrong. It wasn't the Power People who caused the Disaster," says Tricia. "It was us humans. Because of all our technology and lack of respect for nature."

"I actually agree. We don't know what caused the Disaster. It could be like Tricia says," Embla chimes in, unusually calm.

"But do you, like, have any proof of that? If so, show us. Like, it sounds pretty unreasonable that technology could cause all this devastation. You've seen what the Power People can do. Or have you not seen the news?"

"Do you believe everything you see on the news? Can't you think for yourself? They only show you things that support their own story in order to convey their own message," Embla retorts.

"Yeah, but tell me then, how could technology cause an infection in Bern's daughter?"

"I'm not sure exactly how, but..."

"No, that's just it. You talk badly about the Authority and the President, and that's all you manage to cough up? It's so not okay."

"But... That doesn't mean that we should just buy into everything they say without thinking for ourselves, right? I don't think anything much has changed in recent years. The majority of Ela is still uninhabitable, poverty hasn't gone down, people are still dying of the same diseases. If we don't do anything about it, nothing will ever change. You don't know what it's like to grow up with starvation as a big part of everyday life."

"Since the Power People were rounded up, things have actually gotten a lot better. But everything can't happen overnight. It'll take time. We're here at Bionbyr now, we'll be able to make a difference. You want change? Make sure you get through the next three years here and go out into the world as an EMES soldier. That's how you make a difference."

The conversation reminded me of the many debates Apsel and Marcell had after the kids went to bed. I have such a nice image in my head when I think of all the times before the debates started. I didn't think about it then, but we actually did have a story about a Tabia that was good. And a man who was evil. You've probably heard it before, but if you haven't, you should give it a listen. Otherwise, you can fast forward four minutes and six seconds.

"There were once three friends who walked the earth together long before Ela got her name. They were called The Three Salvines, an old word for protection and healing, because they spread light and love wherever they went. The Three Salvines – Anora, Dar, and Carita – helped the elderly and healed the sick.

Dar was strong and would defend and protect the weak.

Carita was wise and could find solutions to problems that no one else had thought of.

Anora was different from the other two. She was special. With her bare hands, she could heal the dying and helped the lame to walk. Of The Three Salvines, Anora was the most honored with gifts and gratitude. She always shared the gifts and food with her two friends.

Time passed, and jealousy began to grow within Dar, but he kept it hidden from Anora and Carita. Deep down, he felt that the strength he had was not enough, and he became jealous of the gifts Anora had received and the Power - the Kraften - she possessed.

Jealousy continued to grow within Dar over the years. He was the first to leave The Three Salvines. While Carita and Anora continued to spread light and love, he chose to find his own path. He wanted food to fill his empty belly, beautiful fabrics to adorn his body, glittering jewelry around his arms and neck. He wanted everything he saw, and he would never get it if he continued to stay with Anora and Carita.

Another few years went by. Carita missed her friend and wanted to look for him. Anora wanted to continue helping those in need. Carita felt that after all the years they had spent spreading light and love, it was time for someone else to take over. They had done their part, but Anora was determined to keep going. Carita left Anora in search of Dar.

After a while, Anora began to notice that the number of people and animals in need of help was increasing. Forests began to burn, the sea boiled over, and all across Ela, fear and death spread among the people and animals. A rumor began to spread about a great evil that had descended upon the earth, devouring everything in its path.

Anora started to feel lonely, and it was then that Carita returned to her. Carita told her of how Dar had stolen something from the earth and was looking for the last thing that could pose a threat to his power: Anora's Power of healing. Carita begged Anora to hide. Anora looked around, at the scorched ground, at the grieving people, and the extinct animals.

Anora didn't want to hide. She wanted to meet her old friend and put an end to all the evil.

Dar had thought that he would destroy Anora so that no one would look up to her or admire her anymore. With her out of the way, people would worship him because they would fear him. But when she stood in front of him as they met at Solhöjden, he no longer felt as sure. Up there, her warm gaze made him feel sheepish and he didn't know what to do anymore. Anora asked him to stop what he was doing.

He threw himself forward to attack Anora, but she grabbed his arm and he became petrified. Anora looked into his eyes, but she couldn't find any goodness left in them. The desire for power had taken over everything that Dar once was. With all her strength, Anora pulled Dar down into the earth, but she couldn't do it without disappearing into the earth with him.

Dar and Anora were gone forever. The Three Salvines would never be the same again.

Grieving over the loss of her two best friends, Carita was determined not to let their sacrifice be meaningless. With all her wisdom, she traveled to Måndalen to commune with the earth, and she felt how its power was transferred to her soul. Carita felt that

Dar and Anora had been united with her own soul and that The Three Salvines were together once again.

Carita has since disappeared, but it's said that from time to time she returns to perform miracles. Those who have been laid at death's door may live for a hundred years, and the lame may walk again."

I never told the story to Ewind or Tricia. I was afraid that their relationship might become even more toxic, and I didn't want that on my conscience. If you use your power for good, then aren't you good?

My thoughts culminated in a dream that night. I remember it as clearly as if I'd just dreamed it.

As soon as Tricia falls asleep, Aariel sneaks into the room and climbs into my bed. I hope this will be a recurring routine, but at the same time, I feel scared. What if someone catches us? He crunches on a piece of bread with sour figs in it. I brought it with me from dinner when no one was looking because I don't know how many edible plants there are in the park on the sixth floor.

Aariel falls asleep, and I feel his heavy breathing against my chest under the blanket. It must be warm and comfortable under there. It makes me feel calm. My eyelids are getting heavier and heavier, and soon I'm back at Sethunya with Apsel, Onni, Embla, and even Marcell. We work in the fields in the afternoon sun and finish the day's work before darkness falls.

"So, you've lived here at the orphanage all your life?"

The voice comes from a raven. I can barely make out its black eyes among the cloak of black feathers. Two pins glittering in the sunlight and staring straight at me.

"Yes…" I answer doubtfully and ask why the raven wants to know.

"Who were your parents, then?"

"I don't know."

"You must have found out who left you here? Or were you left outside the door without so much as a little note?"

The raven lets out a cackling sound. It scares me.

"I should probably go in now before it gets too late," I apologize.

"Wait. I'm just curious, just curious. Don't you have any siblings?"

"All of the children here are my siblings."

"But nobody like... *you*?"

"What do you mean?"

The raven's black eyes are searching my own for an answer. I don't know what kind of answer he's looking for. His gaze is mesmerizing. In the end, the eyes are the only thing I see. The rest of the body seems to fade away.

"Get ready. Prepare yourself."

14

The dream of the raven became a forgotten memory, and the rest of the week flew by, but lately things have been happening that have brought the dream back to mind. I can't really tell you what it means yet, but I'll continue with my story of what happened at Bionbyr.

I must say that it's much easier to live at Bionbyr than I had feared at first. We have eight different kinds of lessons: Social Studies, Combat Training, Criminology, Medical Arts, Law and Order, Weapons and Equipment, three different Physical Education classes (Running, Cycling, and Swimming) and Strength Training.

Getting to swim in the sea brings a feeling of incredible freedom. So far, we've only had one class period like that, but I'm looking forward to doing it every week. We can't reach the seafloor, of course, and it makes the open water feel infinite. Getting out into the cold water is a privilege. Even though Bionbyr is probably twice as big as the main plaza in Ithmah, if not even bigger, nothing can match the open feeling of the sea.

Although Social Studies is interesting, and I've actually gained more respect and understanding for Bern after what we learned about him at the beginning of the week, my favorite subject is Criminology. The cases we look at and learn about in Criminology are so interesting that it's hard to think about anything else. Embla's favorite class is obviously Medical Arts.

On Tuesday, when we had our double-lecture, Esbern talked about how the Authority has been able to prevent terrorist attacks more and more effectively with each passing year. It started with the Guardians using glasses that could recognize people's faces. The tiny computers in the glasses could perform real-time comparisons of faces to a database that stores tens of thousands of pictures of criminals. Because of this, they've been able to prevent crimes before they've even begun. I think it's fascinating, but Embla really doesn't like Esbern. According to her, she wouldn't even be here if it weren't for him.

Domi Niilo Telum's lessons in Weapons and Equipment are also interesting, even though I expected it to be my least favorite subject. Niilo is the shortest of the teachers and probably the brightest. Like Embla, he has freckles on his face, but he has way fewer—only a light dusting over his nose. These are the lessons I was afraid of before we got here, and I know that Embla doesn't like them for the same reason: learning to hold a weapon. Knowing that I'll probably have to use it. Maybe even against another person. Will I be able to handle it? I don't know. This is probably my biggest fear about graduating from Bionbyr. The salary is fantastic, and I know I have to get through school to reach that goal, but what is this school going to make me into? Will I be the kind of person who won't hesitate to use a weapon?

Fortunately, this class isn't just about weapons. In the first lesson, Niilo shows us the garage that's hidden under the water's surface. I still marvel at Bionbyr's size. Just below the library and the medical bay, there's a large area held up by huge marble columns. Between the pillars, parked with precision, stands all the school's vehicles. There are cars, tankers, trucks, and plenty of other military vehicles.

"I miss our horses," Tricia tells me after the lesson.

"You have your own horses?" I wonder.

"Our tribe shares them. It's a great feeling to ride, and they're really strong."

"Is it a big tribe?"

Tricia shrugs her shoulders casually. "There's less of us than the number of students here, but it somehow makes it feel more like family. Do you miss your family?"

"Oh," I sigh deeply. "I think about them almost every day. But I'm glad to have Embla here. I'm even happy to see Marcell around," I giggle.

"I don't think Embla is very popular."

"Really?"

"That's the feeling I get. I know I'm not very popular either. We actually have a lot in common, Embla and I."

"I like you both," I assure Tricia. She smiles.

"I still miss the horses."

Three days a week, we have Combat Training with Domi Myra Manar. Myra is small but muscular, she comes from a poor family, and according to her professor profile, she used to work at the hospital in Vallis, just like Malva. She's won several martial arts championships, and I can see why. It's been really challenging to get through her lessons: we spar with each other and practice our kicks and close combat skills. It's way outside of my comfort zone.

The professor I find most fascinating has to be Domi Eilif Faris, who teaches our Law and Order class. I'm probably not alone in my interest, as several of us first years turn their eyes to her as she passes by. According to her profile, she apparently lost both her arms and legs in a natural disaster outside Siverov, where she comes from, I have a hard time believing it after looking at her. She seems to be the youngest of all the teachers. She looks a lot like Marcell, with her angular face and long nose, except Marcell has mousy brown hair, while Eilif has gray, almost silvery hair.

She walks, moves, and looks just like any other person, but a lot of people say that she's a mix between a human and a robot. The topic that's most often discussed is actually her dentures, which she must have if she'd been in an accident that serious. They're so skillfully made that you can't tell at all from looking at her. Or is healthcare so advanced in Siverov that they managed to heal her arms and legs without prosthetics?

"Good afternoon, first years," Andor welcomes us to the Auditorium. I feel pretty tender after Combat Training, which we just had before this, but in general, I feel good. It's our seventh day here, and I thought I'd feel more worn out than I do. Embla and I are just behind Marcell and his gang. The blonde guy is there, and two others. I recognize one of them from the Selections in Ithmah.

"I have heard that there's been talk in the corridors about the list in your IPKAs, and it is true that we will now start the evaluations," says Andor. "To kick things off with style, we'll start the evaluations with a field test in the simulation chamber. Alpha will start at 1400 hours, Beta will start at 1500 hours, and Gamma 1600 hours. When you're not engaged in testing, I suggest you continue with self-study here in the Auditorium, or in your common room. I hope you're all in top form! Make sure that your names on the list stay white. Good luck!"

I stretch out my right arm with an open hand, clench my fist, and pound it against the left side of my chest, just like we learned earlier this week. At first, it was difficult to decide how hard I should make the salute, but now I've gotten more used to it. It's a great feeling to be part of something bigger. I hear how it echoes through the room and feel admiration for our community.

"Come on, go already!" orders one of the guys in Marcell's gang. He's bigger than Marcell, with small eyes that sit close together on either side of his big nose. He's the one I recognize from the Selections. He picks the guy he's trying to boss around, who's considerably smaller and very timid looking, up by the collar. He almost looks like he's Onni's age, even though I know that's impossible.

"Take it easy, Väinö," the blonde guy says.

"Stay out of it, Nói, I want to hurry up and start the test so I can show everyone who they should watch out for. I'll win easily," Väinö says, putting the smaller boy back down. Embla and I follow the stream of people leaving the hall. The simulation chamber is just across the corridor, but only a third of us are going there, the rest will probably go back to their quarters.

"Still, we're not the first group, we won't even start for another hour," Marcell concludes. It's been a long time since I heard his voice. I've barely even seen him this week, and on the few occasions I have seen him, he's been with these guys. They crowd past the others and leave the Auditorium. Secretly, I think I now know what the blonde guy's name is. Nói.

Just before 4 o'clock, Embla and I meet up with Ivalde, Ewind, and Tricia outside the simulation chamber. Everyone has the attitude of never wanting to be too late or too early for meeting times. The day before yesterday, one student in our class was told that she was too early for our morning lesson with Anze. He said that she was out of sync with the rest of the group and that it could result in her being left out. It was especially a problem in the morning because she could have made sure she got the sleep she needed instead. I felt sorry for her.

At four o'clock, the doors to the simulation chamber open, and out comes the white-haired girl who escorted us around on the first day.

"Welcome to your first simulation test. My name is Yrsa, as some of you may already know. You can call me Admin Halldora. Some of you already met me at the Selections," she speaks in a monotonous voice, "while others may have greeted me at the reception office on the fifth floor, where I work as an administrator. Now then, this test will be based on a real scenario. Once you're in the simulation, you'll forget that it's a simulation — which is, of course, the idea. You'll be divided into groups A through J with ten students in each group. Discipline and loyalty are the keywords here. Don't forget to work together. This test is about life and death. Each group leader will have access to an IPKA with additional instructions. Are we clear?"

"Yes, Admin!"

Yrsa reads the group assignments from her IPKA. I end up in group B with Ivalde, and our group leader is Hakon. I'm grateful that there's at least one person I know in my group, but I'm a little disappointed that it's Ivalde. I still haven't let go of what he said about the orphanage, even though he hasn't said anything like that since then. Yrsa locks us into the simulation chamber in groups.

It's a large room with hundreds of chairs lined up. At the far end of the room is a giant screen with about twenty other screens floating around it. We're instructed to sit in the chair, and we're strapped in. The chairs support our whole bodies, and I notice how flexible it is. When I move an arm or a leg, the chair moves with it. The last sensation before everything goes black is a mask being pulled over my eyes and plugs inserted into my ears.

It's dark for maybe half a minute before I can see again. I'm no longer at Bionbyr but in a dilapidated neighborhood. *We're on land.* Around me, I see the other nine members of my group. Hakon is holding an IPKA. This place was probably once filled with streams of people passing through day and night. Now that lively scene has been replaced with concrete, steel, and the smell of the burnt skeletons of cars. Weeds grow among the rubble, and it's unnaturally silent.

"Huddle up," Hakon says, clicking on the instructions on his IPKA. "Our goal is to locate this apartment. Does anyone know where to start?"

Hakon clicks on a hologram of a house. We look around us and see some high-rise buildings a little ways away from us. Only now do I notice that we're fully equipped with weapons and protective suits. I touch my sleeve and marvel at how real everything is. The material feels rough.

A tall guy with a sad expression looks down a pair of glasses sitting on his face and fiddles with a round piece near his temple. I feel my head and realize that I have a pair too. I pull them down onto my face and see a whole new world in front of my eyes. Everything is green now, and clearly defined lines turn the real environment into smooth, clear contours. I look around at my group members and see their silhouettes. They're brighter than the environment. Everything makes me feel a little dizzy.

"There Hakon, four kilometers south," the guy says, pointing to one of the high-rises. "I see three people. Two adults and one child."

"Good work Ask. Okay, group, let's go!" Hakon exclaims.

I wonder where the other groups are, but I think they might have ended up somewhere else entirely.

Making our way through the ruins doesn't take too long. The hardest part is having to climb the dilapidated buildings and watching our steps carefully. It's the only way forward, and one mistake could cause us to fall to our deaths.

We make it to the high-rise we're looking for, and Hakon asks us to stay put. He holds a finger to his mouth and urges us to be quiet. We take out our weapons and walk carefully into the high-rise's large entrance. The room is bare. There's a corrosive smell. It's pitch black, and we have to turn on lights on our glasses to see anything. The only things that reveal that people have been here are some moldy fruit and rat-eaten bread. I feel my heart pounding harder and harder, and I hope no one else can hear it. Then they'd know how scared I am. I make eye-contact with Ivalde, who seems to be thinking the exact same thing. He's sweating, and his eyes are giving away more than he'd probably like.

Suddenly we hear a scream. It comes from one of the guys in our group, who has now taken a few steps back and is pointing in front of him. We all jerk when we see what he found. There's a body facedown on the floor. There's no visible damage.

"A Wanderer?" suggests Ivalde.

Hakon asks the person closest to examine the body.

"Is he alive?" someone wonders. I feel like I already know the answer. The lifeless body gets turned over on its back and we gasp as we see how grossly deformed the face is, along with the stomach and chest. I quickly look away but force myself to slowly look back at it.

It looks like the man exploded from the inside out. His intestines have been pushed out of his stomach. His clothes are torn. A big boil-like thing sits on his cheek like a big slug. We get a closer look and realize that it's his tongue, which has enlarged and penetrated his skin. No signs of external violence are visible, this is something that happened supernaturally.

"Stay on your guard!" Hakon orders us. I grab my weapon like it's the only thing that can save me and keep up with the group. I make sure Ivalde is near me as we move up the building. There are no working elevators, so we have to take the stairs. Somewhere above us, two people are still alive, and they might be in danger.

It's not long before we start to approach our target and we have to stop again. We hear voices. A child crying. It sounds like it's suffering. I immediately feel worried. What's going on? Hakon counts to three, and then we open the door and see a woman with tangled red hair standing there, pointing a gun at a child.

"Don't come any closer!" the woman screams. She has ten guns aimed at her, but she still holds her own gun aimed at the small boy. His face is filled with tears. He's sitting on the floor in tattered clothes. He's really skinny.

"Papa…" the boy sobs over and over. "You killed papa…"

"Don't listen to him. He's dangerous!" screams the woman.

"Put your weapon away," Hakon orders. "Put down the gun so we can sort this out."

"No, I'm not letting him out of my sight!"

Hakon moves slowly towards them but freezes when the woman screams at him to stop.

"Don't come any closer! I'm warning you! He's dangerous!"

"You killed papa!" the boy sobs louder.

"Is that the man down there?" Hakon wonders.

"I should have done this a long time ago. Back when I found out what he was," the woman releases the safety lock on the gun and gets ready to shoot the boy. Everything goes so fast. She doesn't get the chance to shoot before she has several bullets in her, and she falls to the ground. She's dead. The boy lets out a heartbreaking scream and rushes to the woman.

"Mama!"

The boy is shaking the woman. It doesn't help. She can't come back. The gun is still gripped tightly in her hand.

"Come with us," says Hakon. He's lowered his newly fired weapon and is approaching the boy. He's greeted with an angry look. The boy takes a step away from his mother's body and one moment, he's standing right there, but the next moment he's gone.

Like the rest of the group, I'm looking around feverishly, but there are no traces of the boy. It's not until one of our group members falls to the ground shaking that I realize how dangerous the situation still is. It's Ask, the guy who found the high-rise. He's lying on the ground, emitting inhuman screams and splashing like a freshly caught fish. Hakon and two others grab him and try to calm him down.

"What happened?"

"It burns!" screams Ask. Suddenly, he tugs on his uniform to try to get to his body. He tears violently at his face and leaves deep, bloody wounds on his cheeks. As if he's getting an electric shock, his chest flies up, and then he becomes completely still.

"OUT!" orders Hakon, and we all run from the room. We still don't know where the boy is. I'm among the last to leave the room when I realize that there's still someone there. I turn around and see that Ivalde is standing still, clasping his chest.

"Ivalde! Come on!" I scream at him, but he doesn't move so I run up to him and try to drag him out.

"The pain," he hisses. He's crying. He's in pain. Was he attacked too?

"Come on, now!" I scream again, but he's petrified. I have to make every effort to pull him out of the stairwell. The others are far ahead of us. I hear more people screaming. Weapons are fired. People are crying.

Before I can do anything, everything goes black again, and someone takes off my mask. I'm back in the simulation chamber.

My breathing is out of control. I can feel my lungs struggling to get enough air. I turn around and twist my head. I see Ivalde a few chairs away, and he appears to be unharmed. Ask also appears to be okay, albeit a little shaken.

When I've managed to gather myself, I see that there are still some groups left in the simulations. Everything is being displayed on the screens. They're in the same high-rise building as we were, but I don't want to see it again. I refuse to experience it so close up. Instead, I look at another screen that lists all the groups. I give a disappointed sigh as I read next to "Group B," the words "Operation Failed."

15

After our workout in Strength Training, I shower and head straight back to my room. There aren't any lessons today, so I have some time to reflect. Yesterday's incident has given me a thousand things to think about. What was the purpose of that exercise? Where did we fail? I'm glad I wasn't one of the ones who fired. Then I would have felt even worse. I look at Tricia's side of the room. She's been under her blanket ever since she got back from breakfast.

Embla comes in after a while to pick me up. Ivalde and Ewind are sitting in the park on the sixth floor, and I think it would be good to have some company and talk about what happened. We ask Tricia if she wants to tag along, but when we get no answer, we leave her in peace. I take an energy bar from the pantry and a cup of tea that's supposed to taste like valerian root, but it must be different from the kind we have back home because it tastes mostly like water. We quickly find Ivalde and Ewind in the park and settle in next to them.

"I heard that Ask was discharged from the med bay this morning. What happened?" Ewind sees that the guy who was "killed" in our group is heading towards us.

Ivalde looks away with a shameful expression. Although I have my own thoughts about Ivalde, I can't help but feel sorry for him. Ask's death in the simulation had hit him hard in the moment. So much so that he himself had felt pain. If I hadn't pulled him out, he probably would have stayed there. It turns out that all the groups got the same assignment in their separate simulations. Ewind's group had arrested both the mother and the boy for questioning, which had turned out to be what was required to pass. Ask wasn't the only one who needed medical attention afterwards. Just as he passes Embla, he says something to her that I have difficulty making out. But Embla heard him clearly. She rushes to get up.

"Is there something you want to say to me?" Embla screams at Ask.

"People like you and that weird Edenite don't belong here at Bionbyr. You're a danger to us all."

"Oh really? Well, at least we survived!"

Ask takes a few steps towards Embla, but she doesn't move.

"Watch yourself."

"Or what?" Embla hisses as she takes a step towards Ask. He pushes her so hard that she has to take a step back to avoid falling. Just as she pulls back, Domi Malimot comes over and separates them.

"Alright, that's enough. Recruit Faas, you can stay here. Recruit Wakiza, you can follow me. We have some tests we need to take care of in the medical bay," Domi Malimot orders, leaving with Ask.

Embla groans loudly.

"Wonder how serious his injuries were to have to go through so much testing," Ewind remarks.

"Are you okay?" I ask Embla, but she doesn't hear me. "What was that even about?"

"How can they think that was okay for first-year students? And during the first week?" Embla says, ignoring me.

"It was pretty traumatizing," agrees Ewind, "but we learned something from it."

Embla snorts and rolls her eyes. I shoot her a meaningful look and she makes a face that says, "sorry, I'm trying." She's not giving these new people a chance, especially not Ewind, with whom Embla seems determined to be at odds. Usually, I love her clear opinions, but now I'm just annoyed.

"I never thought that powers could be dangerous like that. I mean, sure, the President talks about it all the time and all... but I've never seen it," I say instead.

Although that's not really true. All this has made me think back to a time in Ithmah when I was eight years old and had sold some of the harvest at the Plaza with Marcell and Embla. It was an incredibly hot summer day, and just as we were on our way home we walked across The Plaza, and I saw a crowd standing farther away on one of the side streets. It made me curious, so we all went over and saw a dozen Guardians standing outside one of the high-rises. We heard screaming from the building, but I couldn't tell what they were saying. Some people in the crowd whispered that there was a Tabia in there. I had never seen a real Tabia before, so I was fascinated.

Suddenly, it had become terribly cold. Had the sun already set? How long had we been watching? But then someone shouted "look!" and I saw the Guardians dragging away a boy my age. He screamed. His parents stayed in the background and watched. They didn't do anything. I got scared. Some in the crowd couldn't bear to look, Embla among them, but I was hypnotized. There had been smoke coming from the boy's hands, which the Guardians had made sure to hold high in the air with the help of steel poles. His feet had dragged on the gravel. One of the Guardians lost his footing, and this resulted in a relaxed grip on the boy's hand, which had been freed. The boy had managed to grab hold of the Guardian, who turned to ice in front of us. I had seen ice cubes before, but nothing like the ice statue that had been created in only a few seconds. The other Guardian had shot the boy in cold blood. I don't know if it was out of justice or revenge. I'd forgotten about it until now. A repressed memory.

"Well, that's exactly why the Tabian sanctuary is necessary," says Ewind. "And hey, we're only first-years, we've only spent a week here at Bionbyr. After we've been here for three years, we'll have learned everything we need to know to deal with terrorists."

"You really don't hesitate for anything," Embla says. I hear criticism in her voice.

"Nope," says Ewind. "I trust the President and Bionbyr."

It looks like Embla is about to say something else, but then Marcell and his gang pass us. Nói is with him.

"Hey Marcell!" I call out in greeting. The words are flying out of my mouth before I have time to think about it.

Marcell shrugs and stops. The others keep going.

"Oh, hey!" he says after a few seconds. "I didn't see you. Gotta get to class. Later!"

He hurries after his classmates.

"Does class Beta have lessons today?" I wonder.

The others shrug. Marcell's behaviour makes me sad. We've lived together under the same roof for ten years, and now he's treating us like strangers. I want to know how he feels, if he's doing alright.

"Who was that?" asks Ivalde.

"We come from the same orphanage. I wonder if he even misses a single thing from home," Embla replies, shaking her head.

"He might feel like this is his home now," Ewind suggests.

"Maybe you're right," I say. My gaze lingers in the direction Marcell disappeared. "At least it was his dream to come here."

"I think some people are so ungrateful," says Ewind. "Like, I get that not everyone wants to be a soldier, but if you're selected to come to Bionbyr, it's because they know that you'll make a good soldier. So if you don't trust your own judgement, you should trust Bionbyr's."

"What do you mean by that? How is that about being grateful?" says Embla. She's about to say something else, but Ewind, who hasn't noticed Embla's irritation at all, speaks first.

"Yeah, but take Tricia, for example. She didn't even want to take her IPKA, and I heard that during the test she totally refused to use the scanner glasses or her weapon. I know it's because she's an Edenite, but I actually thought that when it came to life and death she'd see reason. Because of Tricia, one of her group members was attacked. You can't trust her. That's what I think they were trying to show with the test. Our loyalty and dedication. I love that they drive that hard from the beginning. It makes me feel like a whole new person. Now, I'm soldier-Ewind!"

"Good for you. It's really nice that you've found your calling. But there are a lot of people who haven't been able to settle into all this yet. For some people, it's actually really difficult," Embla explains.

"Yeah, I heard what happened during your test," Ewind says with a superior look on her face.

"What happened?" I ask.

"Your sister froze in the middle of everything and allowed that boy to kill one of her group members. She should be grateful that it was just a simulation. If it had been real, I don't know how I would have lived with myself," Ewind says.

It's the last straw for Embla. She gets up quickly and starts walking towards the elevators. I hurry after her.

"Embla, wait!"

If Embla can hear me, she ignores it. I speed up and catch up to her just as the elevator doors open.

"Em-em, you can't run away every time a discussion doesn't go your way!" I'm breathless from the chase. We get in the elevator and hit the button for the third floor.

"I can't sit and listen to that. She just sat there and criticized me too. Don't you understand? And don't get me started on the view of the Power People Bionbyr shows us. It's driving me crazy!"

"Aren't you being a little paranoid when you say things like that? I'm glad we got to see it. It makes me really think and analyze things. We have no idea what these powers can do, and it scares me. You should have seen what happened in our simulation. If you had, I don't know if you'd be so quick to take sides."

"I don't need to know exactly what happened in your imaginary scenario since they programmed what they wanted to show and not what's real! You're starting to sound like Marcell, you know that? You and I used to be fascinated by powers, fantasizing about what it would be like to fly or breathe underwater."

"Back then, we had no respect for the force behind those powers. Don't you remember the boy who was arrested at his home in Ithmah? The one who froze a Guardian to death with his bare hands? I'm terrified that something like that could happen to you, sister big," I say, taking Embla's hand in mine. I squeeze it twice, but Embla pulls her hand back instead.

"Just say it. 'Round up Tabians, send them to the sanctuaries, eradicate them.' It's because of people like you that this witch hunt even started. But I don't intend to sit and watch while the Authority commits mass murder. What you do is your business."

The elevator doors open again and Embla storms out.

"But Embla!" I say, reaching for her. I'm just barely making contact with her arm when I'm transported to a small room lit by wax candles. It's diffused and blurry except for a clear shape: Apsel. He's staring straight at me.

"You must protect her. You're the only one who can."

Suddenly, I'm back on Bionbyr's third floor. I stand there, leaning against the elevator and feeling nauseated. A figure comes towards me and asks how I'm feeling.

When I manage to get my focus back, I see that it's Marcell's blonde friend standing next to me. Embla isn't visible.

"How's it going?" Nói asks again.

"I haven't eaten very much today," I lie. "I probably need to sit down."

Nói helps me over to a group of sofas that's neatly positioned between the elevators near our quarters. He sits down next to me.

"I recognize you!" he says, smiling. "We've seen each other a few times, but never introduced ourselves. I'm Nói Tosh."

"Freija Falinn."

"Actually, I already knew that. Marcell told me that you come from the same orphanage. You and that girl with the fiery red hair."

"Embla."

I haven't even been able to make sense of mine and Embla's conversation, and now I'm having a new one with a complete stranger. My head feels foggy and Nói seems to notice.

"Are you sure you're okay?"

"Absolutely. I feel fine. Just a little low blood sugar. How have you been liking the first week?"

"I enjoy it here at Bionbyr! But this isn't my first week," laughs Nói. "I'm a second-year."

"Then why...?"

"Hehe, why am I hanging out with Marcell and the guys? Me and Maté, the little guy, have known each other since Agnarr. We stayed friends, but since I'm a year older, I ended up here before him. You could say he's like my little brother."

Nói's broad smile disappears in just a second. Instead, grief washes over his face. When he sees how worried I probably look, the smile quickly returns again.

"And you? How are you feeling about the first week?"

"Surprisingly good actually. Although I'm a little scarred from yesterday's test, I think. I haven't been able to let it go," I reply honestly.

"Mm, I can understand that."

"But this has to be a regular routine for you, right? Considering you already grew up in a military school?"

"I guess you could look at it that way. We've been trained, to be sure, but we never got to do simulations like that at Agnarr."

"Did you have a good childhood? I mean, it must have been tough and full of exercise, but what was it really like? Your life as a soldier was already determined when you were six years old." My question is genuine. Although we haven't had a fantastic upbringing with barely enough food on the table, long work days, and a lot of studying, we could still move around pretty freely. Growing up in a place like Bionbyr, where everything is predetermined when you're just a child. Without having the chance to even dream. It sounds unbearable.

"For me, it's never been a difficult choice. I wanted to go to Agnarr. I wanted to come to Bionbyr," Nói replies.

"What for?"

Nói smiles. "It's a personal story. But I can tell you more about it over a cup of tea later. Tomorrow night?"

I accept his invitation.

"Alright, well, I should probably get some food in me now," I apologize and thank him for helping me to the sofa.

Dreams are just an illusion, just like everything else in life. But if I could, I'd like to study to become a teacher. Getting to work with kids and spreading knowledge would have been fun. Speaking of dreams, I can't think of any more excuses for the visions I keep getting. But I'm afraid of what they mean. I don't want to say it out loud because it makes it feel too real. There's no other logical explanation. It wasn't me that Apsel was talking to, but Embla. All these visions do is pose more questions. Who is Embla supposed to protect? Me? Why do I have these visions? Is that why she has to protect me? But that would mean that she knows I have them. Why didn't she say anything about it? No, she can't know. If that were the case, she wouldn't have stormed off like she did. We've always been able to talk about everything, so even if it was difficult to deal with me, she would have done it. I wish she had.

I look down at my hands. They look perfectly normal. Five fingers on each hand. But I'm not normal. I just have a lively imagination. That's it. It can't be true because I've seen what powers can do, and it scares me. What would that mean for me? Will I hurt people? Maybe I can push it away until it finally disappears?

16

I'm about to put my toothbrush in my mouth when I see that the list has been published today. The first evaluation is complete. I ask the mirror in the hygiene room to display the list. My name is in yellow. Embla's, Ivalde's, and Tricia's names are too. Seeing the names color-coded this way makes it feel so much more real. Simple, tiny mistakes, and we could be expelled. How many chances do we get?

"Have you seen the list?" I ask Tricia.

"Yeah," she says indifferently.

"Aren't you worried?"

"No, I'll finally be able to go home." Tricia shrugs her shoulders and leaves the room.

I wonder what happens when you get expelled. It sounded like Embla was also aiming to get expelled so she could go home again. I didn't even know that you could be expelled because I've never met or heard of anyone who was. I think the chances are pretty low that you actually get to go home. I wish I could talk to Embla about this, but she avoided me last night and I haven't seen her today. I hope she understands that I'm not using the kind of reason she accused me of. If only she would listen. I'm glad she's not completely alone, though, in any case. Last night she sat with her roommate and several others from Agnarr. She seems to enjoy the company of Vera and her friends.

I'll give her time.

"This is Uri Mikkson," says Esbern during our double-lecture in Criminology. "He worked in a mine outside Calli. Lived a normal life with his wife and children. Do you recognize him?"

No one answers. A hologram of a steady man with dark hair and a tired expression appears on our IPKAs. He could be anyone. If I'd seen him in The Plaza, he would have passed me completely unnoticed.

"Maybe you recognize him better like this?"

The hologram changes shape and instead we see the deformed body from our field test. I'd forgotten how bad he'd looked. With his swollen tongue and intestines hanging out of his body.

"An investigation revealed that Mikkson had been on the run with his family for a couple of months before his death, never in the same place for more than a few days. His son Flora – thirteen years old – had been revealed as a Tabia, and instead of handing him over to the Authority, the family chose to flee. Due to the starvation and stress they were exposed to, Flora's power became unstable, as you saw. In addition to his camouflage power, he had also developed an incurable poison."

I look for Ask, who experienced the poison firsthand. His jaws are tense, and he can barely look at the hologram of the corpse. I try to remember if his name was yellow on the list too, but since I wasn't really looking for his name, I can't recall.

"If you see someone who's deformed like Uri Mikkson, or seems to have been injured by something other than a weapon, you can always count on it having one of two causes: illness or a power. In fact, they're one and the same. Personally, I think the Power People are a disease that infects the human race, although they're obviously useful in their own way... This case teaches us something important. The truth always catches up in the end. Uri Mikkson wanted to save his family, and that was his downfall. That's why it's so important for Tabians to be brought to the Tabian sanctuary where they can be investigated, observed, monitored, and kept safe for their own good and the good of others."

Ewind raises her hand and Esbern gives her the floor. She stands up neatly next to her seat.

"Excuse me, Domi, but it sounded like you said 'sanctuary,' as in singular. Is there only one, Domi?"

"Good observation, Recruit Dolon. The general knowledge is that there are several sanctuaries around Ela. Once there were over twenty. Today there is only one."

Ewind takes her seat again, and the lesson continues. We get to experience the field test again, this time in the smallest detail. Where were the warnings? How should we have acted and when, are some of the questions answered.

What's your opinion of Tabians? Are they scary? Are you fascinated? Curious? I realize that you might've come to realize a thing or two as you've listened to my story, but I want you to know the whole truth and not a censored version where I present myself and what I want you to think in some perfect production. We're far from perfect. And everything we're revealing in this recording is something we can be punished for. But it's worth it. Sorry for the interruption, I just had to ask the question.

After lunch, Domi Myra Manar walks us through different techniques we can use to avoid being captured by an enemy and how to escape different grips. I'm always nervous about her lessons, despite her disarming smile. Myra is really strong and agile, so it's no wonder she won several championships.

"The most important thing," she says after calling on Hakon to demonstrate, "is to try to read your opponent. What will he do next? Will he go left or right? Will he strike or hold fast?"

She shows us some techniques for evading maneuvers on Hakon, and even though he's struggling so much that he starts to sweat, he can't manage to catch Myra as she avoids his grip with lightning speed. Next, Myra lies down on her stomach and instructs Hakon to place himself over her. Hakon looks a little embarrassed, but he does as he's told.

"If you get taken down, you need to know how to free yourself," Myra says from her place on the floor. "Here's where your training and strength will come in handy. The important thing is not to panic. Relax and everything will be fine."

I have a hard time seeing how Myra's supposed to get up from the mat, where she's lying on her stomach with her arms along her sides and Hakon on top of her. Despite Myra's physique, Hakon is bigger and taller than she is.

"Don't hold back, Recruit Sanvi," Myra says, "or I'll subtract points. Let's go!"

The whole class gasps as, in only a few seconds, Myra is able to escape Hakon's grasp and get to her feet. Hakon obviously wasn't holding back, because his face is completely red from the effort.

Myra fixes her ponytail – which is slightly out of place – and tells us to split into pairs and start practicing. I turn to Embla but find that she and Vera have already started.

"Spar with me," says Ewind, and we move away a bit so as not to collide with the rest of the class.

We're the same height, and we also weigh about the same. It turns out that we're also equally skilled, or not so skilled, at holding each other down and getting out of each other's grip.

"How did she say we're supposed to do this, again?!" I gasp when Ewind manages to get me down on my stomach on the mat and pins my hands behind my back.

"First, you have to relax."

Even though my hair is pulled back into a ponytail, it's hanging right in front of my face, but I can still sense Myra's legs a few feet away from us. I'm even more anxious to escape Ewind's grasp now. I'm gripped by a desperate need to be able to prove myself. I try to wrench my hands free, but Ewind has them locked in a rock-hard grip.

"I said, relax." Myra sounds so determined that I follow her direction. I fall completely still, but Ewind doesn't let go.

"If the enemy had something to tie your hands with, you would have been captured already," Myra says. "Then you would have to rely on your colleagues to come and rescue you."

"Yes, Domi," I say, exhaling.

"I didn't tell you to give up, Recruit Falinn," Myra says, crossing her arms. "I'll stay here until you get back on your feet."

I have no idea how to get out of this. Ewind is putting all of her weight on me, and it feels like I'm completely locked in. I blow my hair out of my face and see that some of the other students have stopped practicing to watch. I want to shout that I give up, I've been captured, it's over. But Myra stubbornly remains.

Relax, relax...

I think back to our previous workouts and the videos we got to watch of Myra's competitions. *I need to get back on my feet...* With great effort, I manage to get my legs under me without Ewind being able to stop me. Now I can push myself up. Ewind tries to push me back down, but my legs are stronger. In the end, we're locked in a standing position and

I'm able to get a leg behind Ewind, catching her by complete surprise and dropping her to the ground. This causes Ewind to lose her grip on my arms, and I regain my balance. I turn to Myra.

"Nice," she says, "but now your enemy is on her feet too."

Ewind has risen, but we're both too tired to go for another round. Myra laughs, says that we've fought well, and moves on to the next pair. As soon as she's gone, we sit down on the hard mat to catch our breath. Ewind looks just as strained as I feel. Her blonde hair has come loose from her ponytail, her face is swollen and covered in sweat. Several of the others are also taking a short break, but most are still sparring. I feel like I should also keep going, to avoid having my name in yellow. Ivalde seems to be thinking the same thing, because he's still going. His opponent repeatedly tries to catch him, but he's too fast and always manages to slip away. Ivalde turns his head towards me and meets my gaze, but I quickly look away. When I look back, I see that he's still looking at me, which gives his opponent an opening, and they start an intense struggle. I giggle. Did I judge him too early, back on the Ray? I haven't really given him a chance, and we haven't had much time to really talk since then, even though he's always with us. Although he doesn't say much, so it's a bit difficult to hold a conversation. Regardless, it's not like me to freeze anyone out, and now that Embla is doing it to me, it feels even worse. No one deserves to be sentenced without being given a chance to explain.

In the hygiene room, I walk over to Ivalde. He's standing there, pressing both of his hands against the wall and hanging his head. Then he puts a hand on his stomach and grimaces.

"How are you?"

"I don't know," he replies. "It feels like something is trying to dig its way out of my stomach with a spoon. The pain came out of nowhere."

"Have you eaten anything strange? Should we go to the med bay?"

"I don't think so. No, I'll probably just sit down for a while, I'm sure it'll feel better."

I'm just putting a hand on his back when he asks me not to touch him. It'll make the pain worse, he claims.

"I'm here if you need help," I assure him, and leave him to his shower. A little farther away, Marcell is showering too, and I'm reminded of my meeting with Nói tonight. But we never said where or when. He might have messaged me on the Square, so I shower quickly and head to my room.

Tricia isn't in our room, and when I think about it, I never saw her in the hygiene room either. Her stuff is still here. Ewind passes by the room, so I get her attention.

"Do you know where Tricia is?"

"Yeah, she's in the medical bay. She got menstrual pain in Combat Training and was excused. Terrible cramps, the poor thing," Ewind says, continuing to her own room.

Even though menstrual pain is nothing to joke about, I exhale. At least that means she'll still be at Bionbyr for a little while. Above all, I'll have time to say goodbye.

I ask my IPKA if Nói has written anything on the Square. Indeed, there's a message asking me to meet him in the park at 1900 hours. The IPKA tells me it's in twenty minutes. Before I leave, I take one last look in the mirror and meet my own gaze. I feel beautiful today.

"Good evening," Nói greets me and does a little half-bow. Usually, I would have thought it was a bit goofy, but he does it in a charming way. I smile and greet him back.

"Have you had dinner?" he asks.

"No, not yet," I almost reveal that I had forgotten about our meeting and had planned to eat with my friends like we usually do around this time.

"Perfect."

Nói takes me to one of the tables, where he's laid out tea and sandwiches. I get nostalgic as it makes me think of all the evenings Embla and I sat up after we put the kids to bed, munching on sandwiches and drinking tea.

"I promised you a story," Nói says, "and I can't tell it without a good cup of tea or on an empty stomach. In this case, we'll have to settle for food in our stomachs and a mediocre cup of tea."

I giggle because I completely agree. The tea at Bionbyr is probably one of the few downsides. Nói pours the tea into two cups on the table. His movements are soft and precise. His hands look strong and, even with his clothes on, you can see his muscular arms. I notice that the tip of his tongue is sticking out between his lips as he pours the tea. Yet another similarity to Onni. He does the exact same thing when he's concentrating. Oh, how I miss everyone back home.

"Please, Recruit Falinn," Nói says, handing me a cup. I thank him. "So, you wanted to know why I want to be an EMES soldier. I come from Tarara originally."

"Like Ewind and Tricia!" I interrupt without thinking, adding that they're my friends when his face turns into a question mark.

"I'm the youngest of three brothers, but I also had a little sister," he says sadly. I notice his use of the word "had," but I'm already ashamed for interrupting the first time, so I let him continue. "Every spring, the Edenites have a great feast to honor the earth. By the way, do you know what an Edenite is?"

"Tricia, my roommate, is one."

"Oh, that's right. I've heard of her. Very strange that she was even chosen to come here, considering her beliefs. But anyway, when I was four and my sister was three, the whole family was watching the bonfire they lit on Höjden. Mom asked me to hold Pascha's – my sister – hand and to stay close. The Edenites danced around the fire in colorful costumes and horns on their heads. They sang and shouted to burn the old to give way to the new. I was completely engrossed in the show, and I lost track of Pascha. She had let go of my hand and walked towards the fire. Dad lifted me up and we went to look for her. My brothers and mom were looking somewhere else. But when we found her, it was too late."

Nói stares into his teacup. He didn't drink at all while he was telling the story, except a sip at the very beginning. I want to know more, but I don't want to push him. It's probably been a while since he's told anyone this. It must be like tearing the wounds open again.

"The festival was interrupted by an attack. The rebels came to Höjden, filled with hatred and aggression. They wanted the radio tower there. Back then, I didn't understand who they were or what they wanted, but their symbol has haunted me ever since that day. You know what I'm talking about, right? A mongoose eating a scorpion? As soon as I got access to a search database, I looked it up," Nói says. "In the chaos, everyone ran around with no kind of plan, trying to avoid being hurt in the explosions of anti-Tabian bombs and all the supernatural power the Tabians could muster. That field test you took last week is *nothing* compared to what they can do. They can summon fire, some can break bones with one hand, others can destroy objects just by touching them. Even though Pascha didn't die from any of their powers, it's still their fault that she's dead. She didn't have a chance."

I take Nói's hand in mine and give him a comforting look.

"Of course, my mother blames me because I should have been watching her. I understand that. Sometimes I blame myself too. But I swore that if there was any chance for me to prevent terrorist attacks, I would take it. So when it was my turn to take the Six-Year-Test, I was set to end up at Agnarr so I could come here. My brothers had told me about it."

"Do you have any contact with your family?"

Nói is surprised at my question.

"We can't have contact with outsiders until we graduate. They had the same rule at Agnarr. Didn't you know?"

"Oh, of course, I just meant—would you like to have contact with your family, you know, if you could?" I try to smooth over my mistake with a white lie, but I don't know how well I succeed. Nói seems to buy it anyway.

Is it really true that you can't have contact with anyone outside the school as long as you're here at Bionbyr? How did I miss that? The only thing I want to do right now is talk to Apsel and the others back home. I want to know how they're doing and tell them about how things are going here. But it's forbidden.

"Of course I miss them. But my mission is more important."

"I just wish there was an alternative. One where we don't have to fight," I say. It's a gamble. This is absolutely not something an EMES soldier should be saying.

"I understand what you mean. I wish the same; that we didn't have to resort to violence, that everything could be solved through talking, discussions, negotiations. But no one has time for it. People want everything to be solved in a millisecond. Patience is seen as overrated. And if the other party doesn't *want* to listen, it doesn't matter what you say. If they close their ears, there's nothing you can do to get them to listen without using force."

I understand what he means.

"Is there really no other way to get them to listen?" I wonder.

"Look, I've been out in the field for a long time now. I've done things that I probably never would have unless it was absolutely necessary. I remember my first kill shot," says Nói. He doesn't seem too affected by the memory. "It's important to remember that it's for the best. We're fighting criminals. We're the good guys. We're doing what's right. For the good of Ela."

Is this what I can expect after only a year at this school? Do I want to be the kind of person who sees the world in black and white? Is it worth saving the orphanage if I have to lose myself in the process?

"Maybe we need both? Pacifists like Tricia and soldiers like you."

"Maybe."

I thought I'd never hold a weapon, but when I was in the simulation, it was inevitable. It made me feel safer in that situation, knowing I had the upper hand, but is that really the upper hand I want? It's not a question that can be answered with a "yes" or "no."

Unless you're Tricia or Nói.

17

Are you still there? Unfortunately, I can't move faster through this story, because it's important for you to know everything. I know I haven't been able to reveal where we are now, and I still can't. Not until you understand. But if you want to affect things, if you want to make a difference in the world, listen to my story. That may be our only chance.

Even though it's the fourth lesson with Domi Eilif Faris in Law and Order, I can't stop looking for signs of her prosthetic arms and legs. There are rumors that students saw her by the pool one time, where she proudly showed them off. Oh, and apparently everyone could clearly see the metal that replaced her limbs.

"Last week, we talked a lot about how important it is for all soldiers to keep track of the laws and regulations in effect. Since Ela was founded 75 years ago, these have been developed. We must also keep track of what we're allowed to do. In war situations, little else matters aside from ordinary people's lives. As an EMES soldier, you have enormous power. But with that power comes responsibility."

"And those in power are using that power," Embla mutters. She sits next to me, still completely ignoring my presence. Thankfully, Eilif didn't hear what she said.

"Before I became a professor at Bionbyr, I was a student here, just like you, and I became a group leader for the Espionage Division. I loved it because you work from the shadows. A well-executed espionage mission is neither visible nor noticeable. It can have tremendously positive results as it can be used to avert terrorist attacks and even the capture or execution of terrorists. It can save the lives of many innocent people. But ordinary people don't even notice it. It's good for people to understand that the world is full of dangers, but they don't really need to know about every single one of those dangers. If they did, they'd panic. So you can't be looking for glory and fame if you engage in espionage. A job well done is one that's not visible, remember that."

Spying sounds a little like something I might be able to do. It doesn't seem like there'd be as much killing in that. It also feels good to see someone who's actually attended Bionbyr. Could this be the path for me? Being an EMES soldier for a while and then becoming a teacher? I allow myself a small smile. Not everything has to end in war and misery. It can end in something good.

Embla and Vera rush to the dining hall after Eilif's lesson. If she hadn't been ignoring me for the last few days, I'd think they were in a hurry to get good seats for all of us. I have to talk to her, force her to give me a chance to explain myself. I also want to know how she feels. How is she? Does she know that we can't contact Apsel and the others? How does she feel about our education, the training, and the fact that we're stuck here for the next three years? Is she longing for home?

Once I get to the dining hall, I'm drawn to the usual group and allowed to sit with them. Tricia is with us today. Embla and Vera are a ways away. She doesn't look in my direction once. I know this because I keep staring at her the whole time.

"We don't really know that much about the hierarchy of EMES soldiers," I say. "Eilif's profile says that she's a rank B. What are the ranks here?"

"There are seven ranks," Ewind says. "They don't have special names, they're just called rank F, rank E, and so on. Rank S is the highest rank. We'll be rank F when we graduate."

"If you graduate," Tricia smiles. She seems pleased that her name is yellow. "I'm looking forward to going home."

No one answers. Do we really know that you get to go home after getting expelled? A lot of the information we've received here at the school might not be good for us to have access to when we go home. Maybe they have some way of making you forget? A way to turn back someone's mind to how it was before they came here? Or do you end up somewhere else? Can you work in a secluded place with others who've been expelled?

"You advance through the ranks by distinguishing yourself during assignments. The more skilled you are, the higher your rank will be. Higher ranks also bring more responsibility. I think I read that if you're promoted to rank D, you can lead a group all by yourself. It's all in here."

Ewind picks up her IPKA and asks it to produce a list of the various ranks and what their responsibilities are. Only rank S can act as bodyguards for the President. Compared to the others, rank F seems pretty simple. At that rank, you can go on patrol trips, help keep track of large crowds as the President gives speeches, make sure that the equipment for the entire elite squad stays in good condition. Being an EMES soldier at rank F doesn't sound dangerous at all.

"The higher rank you are, the higher your salary is," Ewind says. "Check this out." Numbers pop up after each rank on the list.

My eyes catch on rank F first. Even that salary is more than what Embla earned at the orphanage or what Marcell earned in the harbor. The salary for an S-rank EMES soldier is so high that I have to rub my eyes and double-check that I'm not reading it wrong. Ranks A and B also have really high salaries. Only at rank D would I be able to afford to support myself and still send a decent amount home to Sethunya. It would save the entire orphanage, save Apsel and all the kids.

The numbers are motivating. I'll get my name out of the yellow and fight my way up the list. There's no other option. And if Embla doesn't want to help, I'll do it myself.

During our lesson in Weapons and Equipment, we each get a picotechnological pistol that we're supposed to take apart and put back together again. Embla and Vera aren't really listening to Domi Niilo Telum.

"It's no wonder that you're at risk on the list since you don't even listen to the lessons," I hear Ask whisper to Embla.

"Oh, be quiet. Don't you have anything better to do than terrorize me all the time?"

"Are you calling me a terrorist?" Ask stands up so quickly that his chair falls to the floor with a loud bang.

"What's going on here?" Niilo reaches Ask in less than a second. It's difficult to take the situation seriously since Ask is twice as tall as Niilo, but Ask calms down immediately, picks his chair up off the floor, and sits back down.

"And you two. If you don't stop, I'll have to send you to the headmaster. He'll have to determine the appropriate punishment."

Embla and Vera remain silent for the rest of the lesson.

After what feels like an eternity, all the students in our class, even Tricia, have managed to take their guns apart and reassemble them. However, Niilo isn't content with this. He activates a drone that's been sitting in the corner of the classroom and lets it scan all the guns. In the process, he discovers that several of the students failed to assemble the gun properly. One of them is me. I feel my cheeks get hot. I thought I'd been so careful and done everything right. Maybe I was too distracted by Embla and Vera. Vera looks disappointed when she learns that her gun wasn't approved, but Embla just shrugs. I had thought that a person like Vera, who comes from Agnarr, should know this task like the back of their hand. But maybe they haven't had the chance to practice on such advanced weapons — or Embla distracted her too much. It might be a good thing that Embla isn't talking to me right now. I don't want to be distracted.

"The next test will be a little more difficult," Niilo says as the door opens and several drones enter the classroom. At first, it looked like a group of insects was flying in. They look just like dragonflies, but instead of the buzzing of wings, there's silence. "Now, you won't have to take anything apart, just put it together. But you'll have to do it without any instructions or a physical model."

The drones hold a number of cloth bags that they drop in front of each student before leaving the classroom. When we open the bags, we see that they're full of weapon parts.

"You'll still get some help anyway," Niilo says. "The model is called E-75, and it looks like this."

He pulls up a model of a machine gun on the hologram, which slowly rotates so that we can see it from every angle.

"Get started!"

"So, how the heck are we supposed to put this together?" I hear Embla mumble, but I'm not going to let myself get distracted this time.

Some things are obvious, but it's the fine, internal mechanics that are the hard ones, and you can't see these parts in the hologram. The whole class sits in silent concentration while Niilo walks around inspecting. After half an hour, I pull everything apart to start over for the second time.

"Domi, I think I'm done."

The whole class looks up as Niilo goes over to Ivalde. Ivalde has already stood up, and he hands the weapon over to the professor.

"No bits left over anyway, this bodes well, Recruit Pelerin," Niilo says as he squints down at Ivalde's empty space. Niilo twists and turns the gun, opens the magazine, closes it, examines the sight, tests the trigger. Then, he lets the drone scan the weapon.

"Incredible." Niilo can't stop looking at the gun in his hands. "In all my years as a professor here at Bionbyr, I've never heard of someone succeeding. Not even the most intense weapons buffs..." He looks up at Ivalde. "Have you undergone any special weapons training, Recruit Pelerin?"

"No, Domi," Ivalde says, shaking his head. "I'm just interested in technology."

After the lesson, several of our classmates go over to Ivalde to look at the gun he put together and ask him for tips. I think I really should ask Ivalde for help too, and I'm just going over there when I see Malva entering the classroom.

"Excuse me, Domi Telum. I need Recruit Terah."

Everyone's eyes shift to Tricia. She gives us a smile and goes with Malva without any awkwardness. Malva lets Tricia walk in front of her on their way out of the classroom and follows closely behind. As soon as the door is closed, Ewind and some of the others check their IPKAs.

"Her name is in red," Ewind reveals to us.

We didn't even get a chance to say goodbye.

Our room feels empty. Now it's just my room. Tricia's bed is gone, along with her personal belongings. I've never had my own room before, and I feel insecure. Alone. Thank goodness Aariel still comes to join me at night. He gets something to eat and I get warmth. Of course, it'd be better if he could answer when I talk to him, but it's enough. At least I get to vent.

Tricia had left me a message on the Square. But it was sent from Malva's IPKA. I guess she held on to her principles of not touching her IPKA 'til the very end. She thanked me for being her friend. It's kind of strange, actually. I barely knew her. Was I really her friend? Maybe. There's still so much I wish I could ask her. Questions that I probably won't get answers to now. I stare at her last message for a long time. Maybe we were friends after all. We were roommates, if nothing else. We were at least closer than Embla and I are right now. I think she's acting childish, if I'm being honest. It's such a stupid misunderstanding that she's blown completely out of proportion. Suddenly my thoughts are interrupted when the screen turns black and the wine-red words MANDATORY TRANSMISSION are lit up. Everyone is supposed to be able to keep up to date on what's going on in the capital, what's going on with the Authority and the President, so any space on Bionbyr that can be a screen is a screen. The words appear on the window too.

I set my IPKA down on the bed and watch as the President appears in hologram form. He clears his throat.

"Last night, Central Samriga was hit by a powerful earthquake. It was the most forceful we've had in many years."

The President's hologram is replaced by a map of Samriga. An animation shows how the earthquake spread across the western half of the country and reached all the way to Piedra in the east and Orado in the north. It also spread far south, where there used to be a city called Dimmasti. Several years ago, another natural disaster happened there, and it's been uninhabitable ever since.

"Samriga, I want you to know that we haven't given up on your province. We will continue to do everything possible to get you back to your daily lives soon. I also want to take the opportunity to reject the wave of recent rumors. It can't be denied that this disaster is reminiscent of what happened in Petram."

The story of Petram is one that everyone is familiar with. I put my chin on my hand and listen as the President reminds us of his hometown and how it had once been the safest place in Ela. Petram was on an island in northwestern Uropi until the day an earthquake sunk the city into the sea. The President's friends and family had perished, but he had been at Adali's University when it happened.

Daegal pauses and looks down at his clasped hands. Then he looks up with a serious expression.

"But it was no ordinary earthquake that took those innocent lives and devastated an entire city. It was a Tabia. When I became President, I had several goals set right from the start. One was that every citizen of Ela should have access to daily news broadcasts so that everyone can find out what's happened in the world. The second was to keep the Power People in check, for everyone's safety. And the Tabia responsible for the disaster in Petram has already been punished. What happened last night was just a natural disaster. Together for Ela. Thank you."

The screen turns black and the room becomes quiet again. I look up from the screen out of habit, expecting Embla to be quick to comment. But of course, she's not in the room. Neither are Apsel or Marcell. Or Tricia.

It's terrible with all these natural disasters that Ela suffers. None of them are better or worse than the others. A sandstorm causes just as much damage as an earthquake.

I hate that Embla is mad at me, especially over a misunderstanding. I'd never be able to lose her. Why does she have to be so stubborn?

I pick up the black beaded bracelet from my pocket and put it around my wrist. The beads are so clear that I can see my reflection in them. I caress one of the beads, and my room transforms into Ithmah's harbor. I'm back on the docks, right before we boarded the Ray, before we got scanned and those chips were inserted. This view is different from before. It feels like I'm in someone else's head. Who am I? Far away, I can see myself standing on the gangway. Is that really how my hair looks? Maybe I should try to brush it more often.

A white glow surrounds me. The color quickly turns to red, and a loud beep indicates that something is wrong. The drone that scanned me alerts me that I need another check.

"Embla Faas, please stand still," I hear the official say to me. *To me? I'm seeing through Embla's eyes.*

The official comes up to me and asks what happened. I answer that I don't know, but the voice isn't mine. It's Embla's. *But I do know,* I hear Embla think. *The drone couldn't stab me.* They need to try again. *Let it stab me, let it stab me, let it stab me,* I think, as Embla, over and over. It works.

The scene changes and I'm at Bionbyr. Am I still Embla? I'm in Gamma's common room, sneaking away from the kitchen area towards the dorms. My left hand stays locked on my stomach, and I proceed carefully, so as not to lose what I have under my uniform. Vera is sitting on the couch with some friends. I think I have the room to myself and hurry to get to it. So I really am still Embla.

Once inside, I dare to bring out what I smuggled in. The knife gleams in the dim glow of the lowered lighting and the stars that shine through the fake window. Carefully, I run my thumb along the blade. *It's sharp enough.*

I feel the tears coming. I feel betrayed by my own sister. *This could be it for us. Would she accept me if she found out?* I shake my head. *I have to concentrate on what I'm doing. It's better to get it over with.* I bring the knife to my wrist, stop, close my eyes, and take a deep breath. With great concentration, I press the knife's edge against my skin and feel the pain burning as blood seeps from the wound.

With a jerk, I'm back in my own room. I feel around my body and jump up to look at myself in the mirror. It's me, Freija. Aariel is sitting on the bed, looking worried. I tear open the door and rush out. I run to Embla's door and knock frantically. No one answers. I scream her name.

"What do you want?" I hear her voice coming from farther down the corridor. I walk towards her with determined steps and look at her arm. It's completely untouched. No blood. No scars.

Where do I start? I can't find the words, and when Vera comes to keep Embla company, I don't dare to continue.

"Nothing, I just needed to know that you were there. You know, with Tricia leaving and everything."

"I'm still here," Embla says, going into her room and closing the door behind her. I stand there for a while. Did the things I saw really happen? In reality, I don't know if these visions are just my imagination or something more. It couldn't really have happened anyway, because there was no evidence that Embla had cut herself. But if it hasn't happened already, is it going to happen? Did I somehow look into the future?

I go back to my room, where Aariel is still sitting, looking worried. He leaps up to me and nudges my hand. My other visions have been about things that have already happened. And they've always proven to be true. Like with Onni's parents. They've also always been more spectative, more diffuse. *This was something completely different.* I was actually Embla. I could feel her, hear her thoughts. I'm going crazy. I thought it would be easier to push this away, but instead it's getting worse.

And I'm worried about Embla. The last thing Tricia said in her message was that her expulsion was perfect because she didn't like long goodbyes.

I'm not going to let that happen to Embla. Whether she wants my help or not.

18

Between the lessons, and especially when I'm outdoors, I find myself looking for two people: Aariel and Nói. The latter of the two mostly hangs out with Marcell, Maté, and Väinö, and at those times, I dare no more than a discreet wave. I always make sure I have dried fruit or biscuits so that I can sneak it to Aariel, but the little sugar glider is more interested in sweeter things like candies or cakes. I can't understand how he's managed to stay hidden for so long. After dinner, I find Aariel in a bush in the park. Since no one is around, I venture over to him and give him something to nibble on. I sit down on the low wall in front of the bush. The coast is clear, so Aariel comes to me and sits down in my lap.

"I'm glad I have you after all," I whisper.

"Have who?"

I get up so fast that Aariel falls off my knee and rushes back into the bush. Ivalde looks like a dark shadow in the twilight.

"What's that?"

He furrows his brows and squats down. I took the victory in advance. Sooner or later, Aariel would inevitably be discovered.

"I don't know…" I begin, but give up at once.

We sit down in the same place I rushed up from. Aariel is left under the bush with a piece of cake in his arms.

"He came from Ithmah. I have no idea why, really. I found him on the Ray, and then he came aboard the school. It's quite incredible that he's managed for this long. No one seems to have discovered him. Until now. It's like a bit of home has come with me here."

I expect Ivalde to get up and leave at any time to go report Aariel's existence. Instead, he sits down too.

"I wish I had it too. A bit of home here."

Ivalde carefully stretches his hand out towards the bush. Aariel, who thinks there's more food, comes out of his hiding place and sniffs at it. Ivalde scratches behind his ear. At first, Aariel looks a bit skeptical, but he soon accepts the scratches.

"When I was a kid, I wanted a rabbit," says Ivalde. "You know what those look like?"

I nod. "I've seen them in pictures."

"I thought they were so nice. But around Pari there are a lot of wild rabbits, and they're a pest for agriculture. I think I wanted a rabbit just after I had heard about a new type of pesticide. I had some idea that I would rescue all the wild rabbits and they would live in our house."

I laugh at that. "You must have had a big house."

"Yeah, pretty big. But I didn't realize that there were thousands of rabbits. Nowadays, most of them are probably dead."

"So you never got a rabbit?"

Ivalde shakes his head.

"What fascinated me most was probably how angry my dad got. I didn't understand it then, but later I realized that it wasn't just the fact that I wanted a pet that made him angry. To him, I think the rabbits symbolized everything that was bad about society. The lazy mass that destroys those who work hard and just want the fruits of that labor." It's as if Ivalde comes back to himself suddenly, and he lowers his eyes and says, "Sorry, I'm just rambling. You probably don't want to hear about my tragic childhood."

Yes, I do, I think. It's as if Ivalde has transformed in front of me and become a whole new person. He's never spoken this much to me at once.

"You said you'd also like a bit of home here," I say. "What would you like to have? What do you miss the most?"

Undisturbed, Ivalde picks up a few blades of grass from the ground and twists them between his fingers.

"It's hard to say. I've tried not to miss anything. Everything gets so much more difficult when you do. But what I miss most is Levente."

"Levente?"

"My boyfriend."

I believe I understand. Just the thought of being in love with someone, being hundreds of miles away from them and not having a single way to communicate with them, gives me a stabbing sensation in my gut.

"The worst thing is that we didn't even get a chance to say goodbye," Ivalde continues, then shakes his head. "We have the Square, but it's only for internal communications in the school, *but* I think it might be possible to hack it so that you could message someone outside the school."

"Can you do that?"

"I don't know. But I'd probably never dare to try. After all, they keep track of everything here."

A few voices nearby cause us to fall silent. A little ways away from us stands Domi Malimot. It looks like she's staring in our direction.

"It might be time to go in," says Ivalde.

We pat Aariel goodbye, and he quickly disappears into the bushes. On the way to the elevator, Ivalde asks about what Aariel has been eating.

"Mostly sweets and cookies."

"That doesn't sound very healthy," laughs Ivalde.

"No. I wonder what he does out there all day."

"He probably knows all the secrets of Bionbyr."

We stop at one of the elevators.

"Hey..." I say, "Do you know what happens to students who get expelled?"

"Are you thinking about Tricia? I think it's probably best not to think about it. She's gone, we're here. We have to think about ourselves."

"What do you mean?" I wonder.

"I didn't mean to sound cold, but... My dad's business has a lot to do with the Authority and the President. I don't know much about it, but... I don't think the President has any problems with getting rid of people. And if the President doesn't, Bionbyr doesn't either."

I swallow. "But what do you think could have happened?"

"Maybe she was sent to a labor camp. They often send people there when they don't know what else to do with them."

"Then she'll stay there for the rest of her life..."

Ivalde has been thinking along the same lines as I have without us having previously talked about it. Could this mean that we're not far from the truth? About what happens to students who get expelled? I wonder if there's any way to get away from the labor camp that Ivalde is referring to. *What does that even mean? What kind of work do they do there? But belonging to the Authority's camp can't be much worse than Bionbyr*, I think. As long as they aren't only working with technology there, maybe Tricia will be much better off there than here. All she wanted was to go back to her family, just like Embla. I wonder if there was anything she could have done to escape her fate? I wonder if I could have done more.

"Come on, Freija." Ivalde holds his left wrist up to the chip reader to open the door. "Try not to think about it anymore.

You couldn't have saved Tricia. You have to think about yourself."

We step into the elevator to head back to the common room.

"But there's another thing I'm thinking of too. Embla."

Ivalde is quiet for a while.

"You want to save your friends," Ivalde says thoughtfully. "I hope you don't think I sound too harsh, but it doesn't seem like Embla has accepted it."

"Accepted what?"

"That you can't win. They do what they want with us. The day you cease to serve a purpose is the day you're gone."

When the elevator doors open again, we're greeted with a big smile. Nói stands before us.

"Recruit Falinn! What a surprise. Shall we take a stroll?" he asks. I exchange a look with Ivalde to see if he wants to join us, but he raises one hand to his forehead and gestures goodbye.

Nói and I head down to the first floor. I appreciate walking by the water. The sun is sinking low and colors the sky with different shades of yellow, orange, and red.

"Have you had a good day?"

"Yeah, I liked today's Social Studies lesson. I never knew that there was so much history we never learned in Ithmah," I reply.

"A lot of the information is classified. You've probably heard parts of the story."

"Yes, of course. How was your day?"

"Exciting. We just found out that some of us second years will be sent out to Samriga for a real field test. Us and our teacher will be allowed to accompany some graduated EMES soldiers to investigate what really happened."

"But the President said that it was a natural disaster."

"That's what he told the public, yeah, but it's not true. They've never captured the Tabia that caused the earthquake in Petram. You don't actually have the clearance to know this, though, so I'd appreciate it if, well, you know…"

"I won't tell anyone. I promise."

"Thanks. I know I can trust you. We'll travel to Dimmasti first because the odds are greatest that the Tabia is there."

"Dimmasti? But there's nothing there, right?" I ask, surprised.

"But haven't you learned yet? Of course there's something there," Nói says, continuing in a whisper. "The President doesn't want anyone to know about it because the city is completely lawless. It's rife with crime there."

It makes me think back to Kali's adoption and the conversation we had that day.

The car rolled gently into the vicinity of the orphanage. Dust swirled around in the air, and it took a good while before it settled back down nicely on the ground again. Everyone, including Apsel, stood looking at the car from inside the orphanage. It was a holiday, so all the kids, including Marcell, were home. The car parking in a dust cloud and two women stepped out of it.

The women – who looked to be in their late thirties – were tall, and around their necks they each had colorful shawls that fluttered freely in the wind. Embla pointed out that they must be from the very richest layers of Ithmah, as few can afford to buy such fabrics. Of course, Ithmah has no great elite class to speak of, but it's definitely noticeable who belongs to the upper crust. The "high heels." The last similarity the women shared was that both had makeup around their eyes, something I reacted to because I had only seen it on people on TV, mostly people from the capital. I would never think of it.

It doesn't seem very practical, especially when you work out in the sun and you're sweating a lot.

Another status symbol, I thought. One woman had light hair and a smoother smile than the other, who was a little rounder around her stomach.

As the two women approached the front door, Apsel gained momentum. He'd been nervous and stressed out all morning, which was most evident when he panicked and woke me and Embla up because he'd lost Disa's folder. It turned out to be where it had always been: in one of Apsel's filing cabinets. After that, it was stressful to arrange breakfast for everyone, as we also needed to make sure that Disa and Kali were properly bathed and looked presentable. They were then banned from going outside, to minimize the risk of them getting dirty again.

Disa and Kali were standing in front of Apsel, each with a ribbon in their hair, as the women came over into the shade. The round woman burst into a smile and walked over to Apsel with determined steps to shake his hand, while the other woman gently looked around at the orphanage with a small smile.

"Hello, I'm Elice Strauss," the round woman introduced herself, "and this is my partner Urma Strauss. So, are these the children we're here to look at?"

Apsel nodded.

"Yes, that's right, ehm, we can go in here," stammered Apsel, and he began to move towards the large study. It's not often that adoptive parents come to the orphanage. "This way."

The two women and the two girls followed Apsel. Disa and Kali each had a bag on their backs that we had packed that morning. Neither of them had clothes or toys in any quantity, but Apsel thought that it was important for them to bring something from the orphanage, something that could give them some sense of security. They looked the most confused then, but they did their best to try to be extra kind and behave.

"So, now we need to leave them alone," I had told everyone in the hall. I'd forced myself to say it, as I was also very curious as to what was going on behind the closed doors. I shooed them all into the playroom, where I asked everyone to produce papers and pencils so that we could stay busy in silence.

"Strauss. Hm. It doesn't sound like a name that's from around here," Embla had pointed out after a while.

"What does it matter?" Marcell groaned, the only one not sitting with a piece of paper in front of him. Instead, he sat in the windowsill, staring out over the yard.

"Yeah, but I wonder where they'll live. If they end up in Wim or Siverov, which it sounds like they're from, then it'll be really far away," Embla defended her thought, but Marcell ignored her.

"Another thing I've been thinking about it..." Embla had begun to tell me, but she was interrupted by Marcell:

"What? What have you been thinking about now? Can't we just accept that, I don't know, life goes on?"

"What's with you today?" Embla had almost shouted. No one else dared to say a word.

"Nothing, forget it," murmured Marcell, jumping down from the windowsill and leaving the room.

"Was it something I said?" Embla was astonished. She'd always known Marcell's temper, but this was something more than the usual outbursts. I shrugged my shoulders. I didn't think Embla had said anything disturbing, but that it really had nothing to do with Embla. Something was gnawing at Marcell, I just didn' know what.

"What was it you were thinking about?" I tried to turn my focus back to my thought about Embla.

"Yeah, what was it again? Oh, yes, that's it. If adoptive parents really want a child, they must want it no matter what it looks like. Right? Why should we keep bothering with bows and flowers and all that stuff?"

My shoulders shrugged again. I thought for a second before answering that it was because Apsel says the children have the greatest chance of being adopted then. Maybe people would rather have children who are whole and clean. Even Embla agrees that there's a point to it, even though it makes her angry.

"I hope they're good moms. That it's a good family."

"Have you gotten a dose of Marcell today?" I teased. "Why are you so bitter?"

Embla was the closest thing to a mother any of the children at the orphanage had. And she was a bit like a big sister. Apsel was definitely like everyone's dad. We were a family, even though it was an orphanage. I had seen how Disa had lit up when she saw that two women were getting out of the car, and I understood her delight. If I was her age, I'd probably also be overjoyed at the idea of getting not just one but two moms.

But even though the orphanage was a kind of family, it was something I had always missed. I always thought about what it would be like to be adopted, but above all, how it would feel to be part of my biological family. The family that Apsel eventually told me didn't exist. I hoped that the mothers weren't looking to adopt children just for the workforce, that they'll actually love them. Maybe Disa and Kali would end up with a good family that could pay for them to get out of future tests and involuntary work.

"Wonder what they're talking about?" I said after a while.

"If I know Dad right, he sitting there apologizing again and again for things being broken here at the orphanage, for the lack of irrigation on the farm, for the facade of the main building that needs to be replaced, for not repainting for so long, and so on." Embla became more annoyed as she thought about it because she didn't think you should have to apologize for your home, but she regained control of herself, took a deep breath, and walked to one end of the room where there were a couple of armchairs. She picked up a book and read it instead. When I followed Embla with my eyes, my attention caught on Onni, who hadn't said much during the day and had mostly kept to himself.

Everyone reacts so differently when a family comes to adopt. Especially when they've already told us what they're looking for in advance. Some find it exciting, others get jealous and angry, and some of them wilt with sadness.

I went over to Onni and took my drawing with me because I wanted to keep working on it.

"Can I sit here?"

Onni didn't notice that I had approached him, but he nodded his approval. I put the drawing in front of me and grabbed one of the pens to finish it.

"Ooh, that's cool! What kind of bird is that?"

"I don't know... I probably just made it up," I replied.

"It's so beautiful."

"It really should be more gold-colored, I think. But we don't have any gold crayons."

Onni tried his best to give a smile in response.

"How are you holding up?"

"I'm good," Onni lied. I saw it on him. I knew what it was about, but I didn't think that day was the best day to continue the conversation I'd had with Onni on the roof. Our conversation had had an abrupt ending, and when we'd gone home on the tram, he'd been his usual happy self, as if the conversation had never taken place. But that day I understood: it had just been a mask he'd put on. Protection against the outside world so that his sadness wouldn't be visible.

Just like Tricia.

"Should we go for a walk?" I suggested, no longer thinking about finishing the drawing. Onni nodded.

Fortunately, Embla was too busy with her book to notice us sneaking out of the room. Had she seen it, she probably would have wanted to come along even though someone needed to stay and watch the kids.

"Is everything really okay?" I asked again. We had sat down next to the barn, near the hens, where there were two logs to sit on. "You can talk to me."

Onni was still silent.

"Is it about your mother?"

Onni nodded.

"Is it because Kali and Disa are being adopted by two moms? Are you wondering where yours is?"

Onni began to sob. First a few tears and then a whole river. I grabbed Onni and lifted him into my lap. Even though he was younger than me, he was already almost as tall. At first, it felt strange, but that feeling quickly disappeared when I noticed that he was calmed by my presence. In the end, he became too heavy anyway, and Onni sat next to me, but I kept one hand resting on his back.

"Where do murderers end up?"

"I don't really know," I replied. I'd never thought about it. There's no reported murder or violence, or even theft. When anything is said about it, it's mostly in passing that something out of the ordinary has happened, but no one needs to worry about it because it's already been taken care of. Those who

223

commit the crimes usually can't even flee the crime scene before they're taken care of by the Guardians. But I've never thought about where they'd end up. I'd probably assumed there was a place where they were kept locked up, but I've never thought any more about it than that.

"Do you think she's alive?"

I was uncertain. I didn't know how to answer. I felt like I wasn't really prepared to handle these issues. I didn't know. Yes or no? Which was a lie and which was the truth? Onni needed an answer.

"She's safe in Terraus." We hadn't noticed that Marcell had been standing around the corner feeding the hens.

"Terraus? Isn't that a myth?" I asked.

"You can believe whatever you want, of course. When you work in the harbor, though, you can't help but hear people talking. A lot of stories circulate down there, if you can believe it," Marcell replied nonchalantly.

"What do they say? Have you heard anything about murderers?" Onni was keen on his question.

"Yeah. It's said that those who commit crimes are never seen again."

"Ah," Onni sighed.

"Some say they disappear without a trace or receive a death penalty, and some say they're sent off to a place where they can live lawlessly. There's a lot of talk about that place, and everyone thinks something different about it. But many people say that this place isn't lawless at all, that it's actually really strict. That it's a prison of some kind, where they stay until they die."

"And that place is Terraus? But it's just gossip and myths." I was skeptical.

"Yeah, more precisely in Dimmasti. The other week, an elderly woman was walking around the harbor, asking if any of the ships were going to Dimmasti. As you know, there are no ships that go to Dimmasti, since officially there's nothing there. People thought she was kooky, but when no one wanted to help her, she got angry and pulled a letter out of her pocket. She claimed it was from her husband, who had been gone for five years."

I was still skeptical of what Marcell was telling us, but Onni was convinced. Every word Marcell uttered stuck in Onni's mind, and he tended them carefully. At school, we learned that Terraus was a continent without vegetation, or animals, or anything. How could anyone survive there?

"Five years ago, this particular man had vandalized one of the market stalls, after taking part in a bad deal where he thought he'd been cheated."

"I remember!" exclaimed Onni. "It was talked about at school for several weeks."

"Yeah, and do remember what happened to that man?"

Onni thought about it.

"No…No, I don't," he replied gloomily.

"Disappeared without a trace. He was gone. And everything continued as usual," Marcell said dramatically.

"And now you're claiming that this woman had received a letter from her husband saying that he was in Terraus? In Dimmasti?"

"Exactly. A letter! From the man! After five years! When no one in the harbor took her seriously, she picked up the letter to read it out loud."

"What did it say?"

"She barely had time to start before the Guardians came and carried her away. There was a small note about it in the newspaper the next day. If I hadn't been so bored and skimmed through the paper, I would have missed it because it was so small. It said that a woman had disturbed the work in the harbor with her startling behaviour and was carried away by the Guardians. Nothing more."

I agreed that it sounded strange. But why would the Authority withhold information about where criminals were held captive? To reduce the risk of them getting outside help to escape? And how had he managed to send the letter?

I was interrupted in my thoughts when the women came out into the yard again. They had Kali with them, and they put her into the car and waved goodbye to Apsel before they got into the car too, and drove away. Disa didn't appear. It was something Marcell also noticed because he mumbled her name and decided to go back into the orphanage. Onni, who looked a little better, followed Marcell and, in the end, I did too.

Inside, everyone had gathered around Apsel. Disa was still nowhere to be seen. Embla came over to me.

"What happened?" I whispered.

"Dad just told me that they only wanted one of them in the end. Disa has locked herself in Dad's room. He told me as quickly as he could that she's inconsolable and asked me to go check on her later."

"Oh, honey," I groaned, hugging Embla.

I couldn't imagine how Disa felt. During the sixteen years I had lived at the orphanage, not a single family had ever come to see me. Not even the ones who didn't have a clear idea of what they wanted before coming to the orphanage had ever given me a second look. I'd never felt as abandoned as I did during those times. I used to pull my thin blanket over me and disappear.

Nói and I are right below the balconies, here in the harbor. I can see Gamma's terrace three floors up, and there she is. My sister. Nói follows my gaze.

"You came from the same orphanage, huh?"

"Yeah."

"I've heard a lot about her. She hasn't adapted very well to the school, has she?"

"She's probably just having a hard time..." I begin but interrupt myself. *Let people in? Listen? Think first and then act?*

"It's hard when you first get here," Nói says instead. "Some people don't handle it that well. I've also had friends who disappeared. The best thing you can do is just focus on the goal."

Focus on the goal? That's exactly what I've decided to do, but it still doesn't feel good. Nevertheless, I'm grateful that Nói is trying to cheer me up.

The sun has just sunken down over the horizon. The school is really sparsely lit at night, but the light is bright enough that the stars aren't as clearly visible here as they are back home in Ithmah.

"Do you ever miss Tarara?"

Nói shrugs his shoulders.

"Not so much. It's best to not think about it. If you look backwards too much, you can't move forward."

"That sounds very philosophical," I laugh.

We sit in silence for a while and let our feet dangle down to the sea. Suddenly, I feel Nói take my hand in his. The sensation of his skin against mine sparks a tingling that spreads throughout my body. I glance at him, and he glances back and smiles. I don't know what to say, so I look away, but I don't let go of his hand. But he doesn't know what that means, of course.

It's lucky that it's starting to get dark, I think, *because there's less risk of Nói seeing this silly smile I can't get rid of.* My stomach is filled with a blissful joy, and I allow myself to think that this is a wonderful evening.

19

Nói and the other representatives from the second-year class left yesterday. He'll be gone for four weeks, and it might sound strange, but I already miss him. Eilif is with the second-years on their assignment, so her lessons are canceled in the meantime. It's pretty nice actually because now we'll get some more time for self-study. Before Nói left, I took the opportunity to be with him as often as I could. He's been helping me train, so after last week's simulation test I managed to get my name white on the list again. I'm still pretty far down, though, so I don't dare to allow myself a sigh of relief just yet. Ivalde has also proven to be pretty good, but Embla's name is still yellow. I'm just waiting for the day when Malva comes in after a lesson to pick her up for expulsion.

I'm actually looking forward to today's double lesson in "Weapons and Equipment." Niilo told us last time that we're gonna get to go jet skiing. Therefore, we're not in our regular classroom "04," but instead we've gathered around him in the harbor. He points to the various boats and briefly tells us about their names, how many people they can hold, and what they're equipped with as far as weapons.

"Today, you'll get to have some fun," Niilo laughs with a snort. "Split up into pairs and choose a jet."

"Come with me," Ivalde tells me, and he climbs into the driver's seat.

"Have you ever driven one of these things before?" I ask as I fight with a lifejacket. Ivalde already has his on, seated comfortably in front. I climb on behind him with unsteady legs.

"A few times. There's a facility near where my family lives that has them. Isn't there anything like that in Ithmah?"

Now that Ivalde is only wearing his uniform all the time, and his hair is dark and lacking the styling products he used before, I sometimes forget that he's from Pari – one of the richest cities in the world – and that his dad works with the Authority.

"Are you ready?"

I don't get the chance to answer before Ivalde starts the engine and slowly pulls us out of the harbor. He turns his head to the left and right, and when we've gone out a ways and no one else is close by, he hits the gas as hard as he can.

The watercraft bounces up and down over the small waves. Very quickly, we end up outside Bionbyr's climate protection system. The heat feels sharper, but our speed generates a cooling wind. Water is also splashing up and tickling our faces.

I hold on tight to Ivalde's waist, but I start to relax after a while. My stomach is tingling so much that I soon begin to laugh out loud. Ivalde then starts to speed up to make me laugh more. At some point, he turns around so that Bionbyr is right in front of us. It's been a long time since I've seen the school from this perspective. I realize that part of the thrill I feel depends on the feeling of freedom. We've already moved over a larger area by now than we do in a whole day at school.

Ivalde lets the jet idle, swaying in the waves for a little while before making a reverse turn and driving at full speed away from the school. I adjust my grip around his waist. What is Ivalde doing? The sound of the engine mixed with the wind makes it too loud to hear anything else. What if he doesn't turn back? What if we keep going and continue across the blue sea until we reach land? I'm filled with a strange mixture of panic and delight. Soon, something in the watercraft screams at us. It's a warning that we're too far away. It goes on for a few infinitely long seconds, then Ivalde turns sharply, and I have to hold onto him extra tight so I don't fall off the jet. I gasp.

Once again, I'm in someone else's consciousness, but I don't know whose. I'm in the corridor outside the common room. I check one more time to make sure the coast is clear before making my way to the hygiene room. Inside the room, I turn a quick eye towards the mirror and see that I look tired. I take in my face and sigh at the dark mark on my cheek. The person in the mirror is Ivalde. *I'm inside his consciousness.*

Ivalde is nervous. Carefully, as Ivalde, I sneak into one of the toilet stalls where I know there are no cameras, as it would be pretty shameful if there were. Thoughts of Levente flutter by. What's he doing? Is he thinking of me? How is Mom? And Dad? Do they miss me?

I double-check that the door is locked and listen to see if there's anyone else in the hygiene room. I have about twenty minutes to spare before I have to be back in the common room, so I need to use the time wisely. I pull out my IPKA and a small black memory card. I place the card on the glass screen and watch as the IPKA registers that an external device is trying to access information. It glows red at first, but then the screen is filled with coding language, and finally the IPKA approves the memory card.

Remember when we did this back home, Levente? Dad got so angry when the Guardians came knocking. He was so ashamed.

I click into the Square, where there's a draft in the outbox addressed to Levente. I haven't managed to get my codes to work so I can send it yet, but there are still some things I haven't tried yet.

Suddenly I hear someone dragging their feet outside the booth. My blood turns to ice. Carefully, I look through the gap into the room and see Hakon standing there. He has no clothes, no towel. His gaze is empty. His irises are almost gray. They're so cold.

I stash the memory card and get ready to head back. Hakon walks over to the sink with a swaying gait and looks at himself in the mirror. But does he really see himself? How long is he going to stand there? The common room will be locked soon, and if they find us outside it won't look good in the registry. Should I do something?

Finally, I gather my courage and leave the stall.

"Hakon?"

I get no answer. I walk up to him and immediately start feeling dizzy. Did I get up too quickly? No, this is something else. My thoughts go blank, and I barely recognize myself in the mirror.

"Hakon!"

He still doesn't seem to hear me. I give him my uniform jacket, which reaches down to his thighs because he has a shorter torso than I do. I grab his shoulders and lead him back to the common room.

A bright light dazzles me as I open my eyes.

"Good morning, Freija," I hear a familiar voice say. I feel someone near my face and the light shines even more in my eyes. "It looks like you're starting to focus. Can you tell me your name?"

"Freija Falinn," I answer.

"You'll be fine," says Malva. Her face seems huge. As always, she has her hair pulled back into a tight ponytail, and today she's wearing red glasses that frame her beautiful face. As my eyes adjust to the light, I start to see more of the room. I'm in one of the exam rooms in the medical bay. Malva lets an IPKA scan me by holding it over my body. I've seen her do it before, so I know that she's looking for internal injuries. She seems pleased, because she smiles and walks out of the room. Then, I see Embla sitting in a chair near the door.

"Sister little. You scared me," Embla says, picking up the chair and moving it next to my bed. She grabs my hand and squeezes it twice. It makes me shed a tear of joy.

"What happened?" I ask.

"You had some kind of episode and fell off the jet. Ivalde was driving so fast that it was difficult to determine where you'd fallen in. We found you floating on your stomach and thought you'd drowned."

Embla starts to cry.

"I thought you had died. I was so angry at Ivalde. I shouted at him and said a lot of ugly things. I beat him. Repeatedly. Hard, I think. A professor had to get *between* us. I wouldn't blame Ivalde if he's afraid of me now. I got a warning. They chalked what happened to you up as an accident because they can't link his carelessness to your seizure, but he's banned from any kind of excursions for a while."

Ivalde. Ivalde's perspective. Images come flooding back to me.

"Have you seen Hakon?"

"Hakon? He was here earlier, checking on you. It's noon now, so everyone is eating. But I wasn't really hungry."

"How is he?"

"How is who? Hakon? Fine, I guess. A little shaken, like the rest of us. But don't worry about that now, just focus on yourself instead," Embla says. "I'm so sorry about how I've been behaving towards you. I never gave you a chance to explain. It's self-study tomorrow, but I think maybe we should take it a little easy instead."

I'm grateful for Embla's apology. But even though we have a lot to talk about, I can't let go of the image of Hakon. Could he have been drunk? No, that's not possible. There shouldn't be a single drop of alcohol in the entire school.

They let me stay in the medical bay all day for self-study. Embla, Ewind, Ivalde, and even Vera come by to study in my room. It feels really nice to have Embla back, and it'll be interesting to get to know Vera as well. Ivalde has such a guilty conscience about what happened that I have to keep reassuring him over and over that it wasn't his fault. He couldn't help it.

When I finally get discharged in the evening, I'm really looking forward to sleeping in my own bed. Aariel must have been worried about me not sleeping with him like I usually do, because now he's staring at me with his glittering black eyes and vibrant nose.

"How am I going to sort out everything that's happened lately, Aariel? Where do I start? How do I begin?"

I decide not to say anything. I want to know for sure what I'm experiencing before I reveal anything.

It's a restless night. I wake up several times, and finally, I can't fall back asleep. I sit up in bed and stare into the dark room. Aariel also wakes up. He creeps up to me from his place by my feet and hands me a fig. I smile at his attempt to comfort me.

"You should keep it for yourself, but thanks anyway," I whisper to him and pat him on the head. He doesn't understand and puts the fig in my hand anyway. I'm wide awake now. I look at Aariel and wonder if we can make the morning come a little faster. I look around the room for something we can distract ourselves with.

"Should we play?" I ask Aariel, as if he can answer. He looks at me incomprehensibly. I put the fig he gave me on the floor.

"Can you get the fig?" I ask, pointing to the fruit. He looks first at me and then at the fig. He jumps down from the bed and scampers toward the fig, picking it up, returning to the bed, and handing it back to me. I laugh.

"Good! Very good! On the first try too!"

I put the fig back in the same place.

"Can you get the fig again?" I point at the fig once again.

This time, Aariel is very uncertain. He doesn't move at all. He's confused about what I really want. I imagine he thinks I'm crazy and can't make up my mind.

"Can you get the fig?" I repeat, pointing again.

Carefully, he goes over to the fig and picks it up. But this time he stays put.

"Come on," I urge him. "Bring it back to me."

After a second, he starts to move again and finally hands the fig to me.

"Good Aariel! Very good boy!" I gave him several pats and then scratch behind his ears. He purrs happily.

"Shall we see if it works with other things too?"

I look around again. Then I realize that I have a packet of biscuits in the closet in case there's a day when I can't steal food for Aariel. I pick up a biscuit and put it on the floor with the fig.

"Can you get the biscuit?" I ask Aariel.

He goes to the fig and picks it up. I sigh a little impatiently.

"No, the biscuit. Can you get the biscuit?" I point to the biscuit and realize that it might be cheating. But he moves towards the biscuit and picks it up.

"Good job Aariel!" I burst out. "Come here!"

He comes to me with the biscuit, and I break off a piece for him. We keep going like this until I need to get ready to go to my first lesson. After some training, Aariel has become very adept at fetching things.

The day is going well despite my lack of sleep. We have both Cainea brothers in their respective classes today and end the day with Combat Training. Myra thinks I should take it easy considering my stay in the medical bay.

"You can learn a lot from observing others too, don't underestimate it," she says after asking me to take a seat on the floor near the wall, where no one will trip over me.

I look particularly closely at the students who grew up in Agnarr. Their attitude when they're hit is somewhat more stable than the others. Despite sitting on the sidelines, I try to imitate as best I can. Hands high.

"You have to use your whole body. Work with your torso as much as with your arms," I hear Myra instructing Embla. She's boxing with Ask. He's great in comparison to the others. His light hair is well-combed.

When Myra moves on to instruct another pair, I see Ask mumbling something to Embla. Something that gets on her nerves. Her eyes say more than a thousand words. She seems to be in control, though, which I'm glad about since her name is still in yellow on the list. I've offered to help her so that she stay and I told her it's important for us to stick together. She's really reigning it in.

Ask seems to continue to provoke her because she makes some mistakes, which allows him to get some really good hits in. She shakes herself and keeps going. I want to tell Myra that Ask isn't fighting fair, but then I realize that the past few lessons she actually told us that nothing is off-limits. Out in the real world, no one is playing by nice rules. It hits me that I can't do anything about it.

Come on, Embla, I think, and I try to send her encouraging vibes. It seems to be working. Embla skillfully avoids Ask's attacks and get in some good hits that make him lose his footing.

But then he says something definitive that causes Embla to burst. She rushes forward and throws herself at him. They roll around on the ground and wrestle. She ending up straddling him and gets in hit after hit until he manages to turn the tables and repay the blows. I'm on my feet, approaching them. People all around have stopped what they're doing to observe the situation. Myra has noticed it too, but she's letting it go on. Until Embla gets in a kick that causes Ask to spit up blood. Then both Myra and I get involved in the fight. I get a punch in the face from Ask that was meant for Embla, but I don't let it stop me.

We finally manage to get them to calm down. Ask looks completely beat up, but the only damage visible on Embla is some blood running from her nose.

"You come with me," Myra orders Embla and Ask. "You come too!"

Myra points at me, and we all go silently after her. We walk out into the corridor and over to the elevators, and we head up to the fifth floor. I can guess where we're headed: to the headmaster.

It's all over now, I think. *Embla is going to be expelled.*

20

Embla, Myra, and I are sitting outside Andor's office waiting. Ask had to go in first. Neither Embla nor I say anything. I don't dare to break the silence, and Embla is quietly fuming and trying to control herself. Myra looks indifferently at Embla. She had moved Embla away from Ask so easily that it might as well have been a palm leaf she lifted from the ground. I wouldn't want to face her in a martial arts competition.

"You did pretty well," Myra tells Embla.

"Sorry?"

"Ask is pretty muscular. You must have been pretty agile to manage to escape his blows."

"I guess so."

Andor's office door opens. A raw Ask comes out and walks straight past us. We're not worthy of a glance. I can see that he has dried blood around his mouth and that one of his eyes has begun to swell. He must have been sent off to the medical bay.

I'm instructed to go into the office. Embla is allowed to remain in her seat.

The temperature rises slightly as I step into the office. Although the large windows on the opposite wall let in plenty of sunlight, the room is much darker than any of the other rooms in Bionbyr. The walls are a sandy color, broken up with pitch-black pillars. On one side of the room is a glass table that's almost twice the size of our dinner table back home.

There are nine leather chairs around the table. They look comfy.

Andor is sitting behind another glass table. There are few decorations in here, but I notice a large painting on the wall. At first glance, it looks like a picture of an eye, but when I look more closely, I see that the iris is really a person standing with their hands cupped, looking down. At each end of the eye, there are two more shapes: one wrapped in light and the other in darkness. They're reflections of each other. Scattered around the scene are nine symbols I don't recognize.

"Do you like art, Recruit Falinn?" Andor asks me.

"Yes. It's a beautiful painting, Domi," I reply.

"I think so too. Go ahead and take a seat," Andor beckons me, pointing to a chair in front of the desk. "I'm pleased to see that you're spending time with Recruit Tosh. He's one of our top students. There's a lot of potential in him, and I think you can learn a lot from him. You also have great potential."

How does he know about Nói and I? The only times I've seen Andor have been when he gives us instructions for the simulation tests in the hall.

"Let's be efficient so that we can continue with our day. Let's return to why you're here."

Andor taps his IPKA, and it begins a playback. It's a little scary to see such a perfect image of Embla. I didn't understand how effective the holograms are until now. I've always known that the images are high-quality, but they're unimaginably detailed. It's really Embla in miniature. She's in a defensive position, just as she was a few minutes ago.

"The orphan who can't control her emotions. This is gonna be easy," Ask says, mocking Embla.

Even in the recording, you can see how annoyed Embla gets, but she restrains herself. It's not until he says, "A little strange that an orphan is doing so well in close combat," that she becomes distracted, and Ask gets a hit in. She regains focus and dodges his attacks. Here, it's clearer how agile Embla is and how strong she must be when Ask has to lean a hand on the ground to regain his balance.

"Everyone knows that you only win fights because you're a Tabia," Ask says, and Embla rushes forward, throwing herself at him.

Andor turns off playback and puts the IPKA away. He leans back and rests his gaze on me.

"Is it true?"

"No, I don't think so! It's absolutely not true."

"He has a broken nose. She barely has a bruise."

"Embla has always been better than Ask in training. She avoided his blows really well, as you saw."

"So, you deny the charges?"

"What charges?"

"The accusation made against Recruit Faas before she went in for the attack."

There's a pain in my thumb, and I realize I'm sitting there, tearing away at the skin around my nail. It's become a small wound. I take a deep breath.

"When I observe the situation, I see a person who's at a disadvantage in several ways: he's been performing poorly, is at risk of expulsion after the last simulation test, and then he ends up in a situation where he has to compete with someone he knows performs better than him. Then, he uses a tactic that backfires on himself."

Andor's eyes are still on me. He tries to read my facial expressions, and I do my best to look as innocent as I can. Andor seems to buy my answer and gives me permission to go.

I hardly dare to look at Embla when I leave the office, but I can see how insecure she looks as she enters. Myra asks me to go to dinner, but I have to rush to a toilet because I feel so nauseated. Thankfully, nothing comes up, but my stomach is still doing somersaults.

I sit down on the toilet and lean my head against the wall. Do they really think she's a Tabia? It's over after all! Or? Or maybe not. In truth, I've never seen Embla injured or even sick. But's that not a power, is it? Isn't she just healthy? However, that wouldn't explain all the times I clearly saw her have an accident, and I can barely count them on one hand. Like the toolbox this spring. Her arm had looked broken. Maybe she has healing powers? Why wouldn't she say anything to me if that was the case? On the other, I haven't told her about my visions, if that's even what they are. Episodes. Dreams. I'm not sure if that's even a power, and even if it is, it's not something you can just tell people. "I have powers." You'd get reported and sent to a sanctuary.

In the end, I force myself to head to the dining hall to get some dinner. I can't let myself worry on an empty stomach and I'm *very* worried about Embla.

I sit down at a table far from anyone I recognize. I don't want a lot of questions. Questions that I still have no answers to. What was it I'd seen? If Bionbyr thinks that she's a Tabia, that might have been the last I'll see of Embla. Her worried face as she was left to face sentencing.

When Embla doesn't show up to dinner, I go up to our common room to see if she's there. She isn't there either, so I knock on her door.

Vera opens it.

"Come on in, Freija," she says, and I step into the room.

Embla is sitting curled up in her bed with bleary red eyes.

"Are you being expelled?" I get a little annoyed at my own tactlessness, but I'm so nervous I can't help it.

Embla shakes her head.

"No, and Ask will be punished."

"But isn't that good?" I allow myself to exhale.

"I've never been so humiliated in my entire life," Embla sniffles.

"What happened?"

"He asked such abusive questions. About me, about Apsel, about you, about the orphanage, about whether anything strange had happened, and I just sat there and took it."

"But you're not getting expelled?" I ask to reassure myself.

"No, but I don't know how long that will last. It's pretty clear that I won't be able to make it through the year."

"Oh, don't say that, sweetie," says Vera. I'd forgotten she was in the room.

"Vera is right. We'll get through this, sister big," I say, squeezing her hand twice.

A few days later, we have Medical Arts class. Embla and I are working together. It feels really nice that she's found her way back to me. It feels like how things were before.

Everyone is working in pairs, and today's test is to follow a recipe to produce a material that resembles skin. Embla is still shaken after what happened, so I do most of the work. It doesn't bother me. I want to do something for Embla, and even if it's as simple as classwork, it's still something. In addition, it's quite fun to mix the various liquids and chemical substances. With a cell extractor, I collect some cells from my arm. It looks like a thick pen, and when I press a button on one end, a needle retrieves the cells from my own skin. I can't feel it at all. The extracted cells are transferred to a large glass box to grow in. There, they germinate for an hour.

This is an advanced assignment, and we need to focus carefully on the equipment to make sure that nothing goes wrong. I wonder how this can be applied when we're out in the field and need the new skin urgently. This process seems better suited for hospital care.

As the lesson draws to a close, we check out the results of our cultivations. A jelly-like membrane has formed where we planted the cells, and depending on how well each pair mixed their concoctions, some are more or less successful. Some created a square of the material that both looks and feels like real skin. Some have gotten too thick, and a few failed in forming a cohesive surface, but Embla and I receive praise for ours.

"Next time, we'll go over how synthetic skin is used to heal wounds," Malva says, ending the lesson.

Embla goes away with the other students to save the piece of skin in a cupboard while I pick up after our experiment.

"Can you stay for a while?" Malva asks me.

"Absolutely," I reply, continuing to clean. When Embla has finish putting the skin away and signals for me to follow her, I tell her to go on without me.

"Good work today with the synthetic skin, Recruit Falinn," Malva says as she walks around the desk, crosses her arms, and leans against it. We're alone in the classroom. "But I noticed that you did most of the work."

"Embla isn't in top shape today, Domi," I say. "She's still a bit flustered."

Malva lets out a long sigh and her arms fall down to her sides. I'm very surprised. Then, she points discreetly up towards one of the cameras.

"Come with me," she says, and I accompany her out of the room. She takes me a ways along the harbor and we stop at its outer edge.

"Listen up. I know that Embla is your friend and that you grew up together. But she's not good for you. You have to surround yourself with those who can move you forward and upward."

I'm totally stunned.

"I have to help her," I say. "She's my sister."

Malva sighs again. Is it out of understanding or annoyance?

"Unfortunately, here at Bionbyr you have to focus on yourself and no one else. Believe me, it would be best if you let go of Embla. It could be a matter of life and death."

I stare at Malva. Frantically, I search for some sign that she's joking. I can't find anything.

"Thanks for your advice, Domi," is the only thing I manage to say.

"That's all. Thanks for listening. And Recruit Falinn? That's a nice bracelet, but the rules clearly state that you can't wear accessories."

She smiles, almost apologetically.

"Thanks for the reminder," I reply, touching the beaded bracelet. I've had it on me since I got that vision of Embla. Especially now, lately, it's reminded me of what Embla means to me. I put it back in my pocket.

Rumors of Embla's fight lasted for several weeks. Ask's name turned to yellow on the list, and after that, he avoided us as much as he could. It wasn't until the semester was coming to an end, when more and more people were expelled and students started talking about the Winter Ball, that the fight was forgotten. Then, only the President's arrival was of interest.

Embla and I haven't really talked about the incident. Back then, I was more focused on sorting out my scattered thoughts. Was Embla a Tabia? It wasn't impossible. But how could we have a conversation like that at school? We were monitored there. Later, we learned that not even the toilets were safe.

The last week will be over soon. Next week, winter break begins, which means that we'll get two weeks without classes or studying – provided that you're not lagging behind. I wish we could have had contact with our families, even if it was only for a day, but that's not how it works. If you've been selected, you have to give three years of your life to Bionbyr. Soon, half a year will have passed.

But before the break, there are two big events coming up: the Winter Ball, when the President will come to visit, and an upcoming simulation test. We've had a few simulations since the case of Uri Mikkson, and I feel like I've started to get the hang of them. It's actually quite nice to disappear into another world.

"Here you are, Recruit Falinn," says Nói, handing me a cup of tea. It takes me back to our first meeting in the park. This time, the environment has changed to the library and we have to whisper.

The library is a complete contrast to Apsel's bookshelves. There are no real books here; everything is digitized and packaged. There are long rows of compartments with screens and databases. Some of the shelves are lined with old artifacts or robots. It's like a museum.

Since Nói came back a few weeks ago, he's been a little different. Not towards me per se, but he seems more determined now. Whatever happened out there is confidential, so he hasn't been able to tell me anything, but I can feel the impact it's had on him.

"Are you looking forward to the party?" Nói wonders. A little ways away from us is his gang. Marcell looks indifferent, as usual. He's really in his element here. Sometimes I find it sad that he can barely be bothered to say hello to me, even though we grew up together. I understand him though. If I was in his shoes, I would have felt like Embla and I were too much of a reminder of "home."

"I'm looking forward to the break," I reply. It'll be nice to actually get a vacation. I'm imagining sleepy mornings and cuddling in the park.

"Recruit Falinn?"

"Yes, Recruit Tosh?"

"I know it's not really *that kind* of party, but it would still be nice if you wanted to go with me. Like a date. What do you say?"

It warms my heart and I laugh a little too loudly, causing some students to cast annoyed glances in my direction.

"Certainly," I reply. His hand finds its way to mine, and we sit there for a while. Until my hand starts to get too hot and sweaty and I have to pull it back to wipe my palm on my uniform.

My jump into the simulation goes painlessly and the test begins.

This time I'm completely alone; there's no group. Now I know enough to know that I shouldn't rush. Inspect the environment. What's around me?

I'm in a desert. In the sky above, the moon is shining brightly, and it's the only light source I have. I turn on the lights in my glasses and try to determine if there's a clear target. Even with the X-ray function of the glasses, I can't see anything. The sky is full of stars, and I can point out several constellations that we learned from Bern in Social Studies. There's one constellation that stands out from the others, even though it's only four stars that form a cross together. Very quickly, I find two other bright stars directly below the cross. With one hand, I make a straight line from the lower part of the cross and let it cross the line I'm making with my other hand using the other pair of stars. South. A direction. So I start heading that way.

It's not long before I arrive at an oasis. In the middle of the oasis is a deep pool of water. I immediately understand that I need to dive down. I'm beginning to feel like it's a test designed for me to pass, but then I realize that I'm going to have to dive so deep that I'm not sure if I'll be able to hold my breath for long enough. I look around to see if there's anything that can help, but then I remember from another test that our protective suits are usually equipped with exactly what we need.

I feel around for something that can help me breathe underwater and find a nozzle near my collar. I put it in my mouth. I can't breathe at all. I try again, this time with my head underwater, and immediately it works much better. I'm looking forward to diving.

Had it not been for the lights on my glasses, I wouldn't have been able to see my hand in front of my face. As I swim, I pop my ears to relieve the pressure. I go deeper and deeper. I don't really understand where I'm going, so I keep swimming. There are no stars here to tell me if I'm on the right track. It must be some kind of cave I'm swimming through. I try to memorize some benchmarks, like changing colors in the rocks or how the algae is growing in particular areas.

But after a while, it seems like I'm not getting to where I'm supposed to go. I feel my breathing getting heavier and heavier. My mouth feels drier and drier. There's a burning in my chest, and I panic for a second.

It's part of the test, I remind myself. *Just part of the test. It's going to be fine.*

I swim upwards, but I can't go very far. The roof of the cave is blocking the way. And now I've swum so far that I can't turn around, because there's not enough air left. The only way to go is forward. A second wave of panic hits me and it's hard not to give in to it. I force myself to push forward along the cave roof, and finally, I can see the roof curving upwards further ahead. It's only a few more yards. I kick as hard as I can with my legs and pull myself forward.

Finally, I rise above the water's surface and can breathe in. I take several hearty breaths of fresh air. Where am I now?

Still a cave. A shadow sweeps past me. My hand goes immediately to my weapon, but I stay in control. I lift myself up onto land, paying extra attention to my surroundings. There's a long corridor, and it's the only way out of the cave besides the pool of water I just emerged from. With a firm grip on my weapon, I walk into the corridor. I'm not alone.

Something is moving towards me. Something big and red. It looks like a snake with two large antennae, but the way it moves is reminiscent of an ant. An ant of human size and with over a hundred toxic yellow legs. I stop and stare at it. It crawls along the wall, and I can clearly see its fangs. I aim the weapon at it but stay perfectly still. The insect stops and acts like it just discovered me too. I don't know if it can see because I can discern any eyes on it. Can it smell me? I continue to stand still, even though my heart's pounding must be loud and clear.

Nothing happens. The insect crawls on, straight past me, and I exhale. I continue further into the corridor and reach a door. I open it and walk through.

I end up in an old room, probably in an old house. It smells of damp wood. A dim light from a window illuminates a table and chair in the middle of the room. I approach cautiously and find that the chair is occupied by someone with a hood covering their head. The body is completely still. On the hood is a note with the word "enemy" written on it.

I walk around the table and the person to see if there's anything else I should be aware of. There's nothing. I don't understand. What am I supposed to do? Shoot the person just because they're marked as an "enemy?" Is this a loyalty test? Well, I'm not going to shoot anyone without more information than this.

I take a deep breath and tear the hood off.

The cry that escapes my body surprises me as much as it surprises the girl in front of me.

The girl is me.

21

It's me, but at the same time not. The Freija Falinn sitting in front of me has a cold look and a stiff smile. My hair – or her hair – is in a ponytail, and it makes her look more aggressive than I usually look.

I don't like the way this version of me is looking at me. It's like a shadow of me, but at the same time, it's off. She's sitting with her shoulders drawn tight, she's dirty, and her smile is crooked. Do I even dare approach her? She doesn't seem to be bound. What exactly am I supposed to do? I look around the room again. The door I came through is gone now. The window is the only way out. I walk over to it and sigh. I should have realized it's just a fake window. I turn to face Shadow-Freija again. She's still just sitting there. She leans her head in my direction and inspects me from head to toe. An acrid smell is coming from her. The scent of ashes.

She gets up. She's approaching me now. Growling. She falters as she walks. What kind of test is this? Am I supposed to shoot myself? Should I fight myself? How?

Shadow-Freija becomes more and more threatening as she approaches me. I back up more and more until I'm pressed against the wall. I have no choice. I shoot her in the leg. It causes her to stop, but no more than if it had been a fly that hit her leg. She takes a shot at me and rips the weapon from my hand. She grabs me, and I try to wrestle myself out of her grasp. As if I was nothing more than a sack of potatoes, she throws me straight into the wall. I slam into it with such force that my vision turns black for a couple of seconds. Her hands find their way to my neck and she starts to press. Hard.

I feel my chest starting to burn, the same feeling that I usually have to get used to when I'm underwater for a long time, but this time it happens too fast and I can't think. Her grip tightens and I can't get a grasp on her or the wall. My hands are scrambling to tear her off my neck, but it's worthless. It feels like my eyes are going to explode at any moment.

I use the wall as leverage to push her away. Shadow-Freija loses her balance and her grip on my neck loosens. She no longer has the upper hand, but I'm shaken. We're both down on the ground. I have to catch myself with one hand to regain my balance. It still feels like there's not enough air. I try to breathe frantically, trying to get as much air into my lungs as possible. But I still feel like I'm suffocating. As if someone was holding a pillow over my face. My throat is burning.

Focus, I order myself. I won't let her out of my sight. I slip a knife out from one of my boots. She does the same. We get up and circle the room with the knives held high. She makes the first slash but misses. Immediately after, she lashes out again, and we enter into a battle of life and death. I find myself repeatedly noticing that my knife is slicing her, and there should be cut marks. But nothing happens. No blood is spilled.

She lunges at me, but I manage to parry and get a perfect thrust into her abdomen. It should have been enough to make anyone falter. Not her. In shock, she takes the opportunity to stab me in the shoulder, and I scream. I stumble away and have to lean one hand against the wall. The pain is unimaginable.

I see my weapon lying on the floor some distance away and take off towards it. It slides perfectly into my hand, and I turn around, firing three shots at Shadow-Freija that send her flying across the room. I'm surprised by how good my aim was, considering my shoulder feels completely messed up.

With the weapon pointed at her, I cautiously approach. She's on the other side of the room. The wall she flew into has a large hole, revealing concrete on the other side. The room is fake. The wood is just a facade.

My heart leaps as Shadow-Freija rises again. Completely unharmed. I'm back up. I can't win. Just like an endless dance, she charges at me again and takes me down to the ground. There's still a fighting spirit in me, and I continue to wrestle with her. She gets in some well-placed blows and so do I. We get to our feet, and with a well-aimed kick, I send her crashing into the chair. Wood scraps fly in all directions.

Every inch of my body must be covered with bruises. I can feel that my lip is cracked, and blood is flowing from my nose. Shadow-Freija is back on her feet.

Do they want me to fight until I can't continue? Is this a test of my willpower? What if I'm not good enough? I could be expelled.

Sorry, Apsel. Sorry, Onni. Forgive me, everyone.

Who is Shadow-Freija? Who is the girl standing before me? Is it me? Is that who I've been? Or who I will be? Apsel, will you recognize me when I return? I know I'll never be able to go back to the same Freija I was back then. And if I'm going to move forward, I *must* accept who I'll become. There'll be times when I have to do things I don't think are right. But I'll get stronger because of it. There must be a balance between darkness and light within me. Is that the test? Overcoming our fears? Can it be that simple?

I lower my guard. Shadow-Freija threatens me again, but this time I welcome her. I stretch out my arms as if to embrace her and she goes right through me.

When I open my eyes, I'm back in the simulation room. I look directly at the screen that's been following my progress and see that I passed. I exhale and lean my head back on the chair.

What happened? My head is spinning. My body is shaking. If I get up now, I'll fall over — that much I'm sure of. But that's probably the only sure thing. I want to swear loudly. What actually happened?

I close my eyes. My neck feels okay. I can breathe normally again. What was the point of this test? Who was she? And what will Bionbyr think about me letting her become a part of me? So many questions. I doubt I'll ever get an answer. I wonder if it was really me that I saw. Surely they wanted to see my "A"-game. Still, I can't stop thinking about what this will mean for me. If this test reflects a kind of future Bionbyr has envisioned for me. Have I started down a road that will turn me into a killing machine in three years? Will I lose my humanity?

There must be a balance within me. It's up to me to make sure that neither takes the upper hand.

I see that Embla is still in the room and her test is over. My heart breaks when I see that she failed the test. What'll happen to her now?

All of Bionbyr's students and teachers gather well ahead of time in the harbor. A murmur spreads among the ranks when the President's black boat comes into view on the horizon. As it approaches, you can clearly make out the silvery details. The boat is elegant with its soft lines. The nose is slightly pointed, and there are many similarities to a large car. It looks like it's about twenty-five to thirty-five feet long and twenty feet wide.

Ivalde, who's standing next to me, lets out a sound of admiration.

"So that's the Victoria then."

"Victoria?"

"I read about it in one of the Weapons and Equipment lessons. It's the President's personal means of transportation. Really, it's just a prototype. Top-secret.

"I don't really understand what's so special about this boat," I say, and Ivalde scoffs at me. "What's the difference between that one and the rest of the boats in Bionbyr's harbor?"

"It's an amphibious vehicle. A vehicle that works both on water and on land," Explains Ivalde. It's kind of cool, I guess, but not worth fawning over.

The Victoria pulls in to dock. On the long side, a door opens and a gangway is pushed out of the vehicle. Ela's burgundy adorns a mat on the dock. From the dark insides, Press Officer Erikk Aalarik steps out first and comes ashore. He looks more worn in reality than in the hologram. It may be due to his beard, but I'm not sure. His dark complexion and black hair are contrasted by the bright suit he's wearing. Under one arm, he holds a briefcase. Close behind Erikk, President Didrik Daegal steps out into the sunlight. As always, he has his hair lightly combed back and he's wearing a dark suit that almost reaches down to the ground. He has the same gentle smile he always wears when he's not talking about anything serious. He looks even younger in reality, if that's possible. There are no signs of old age in his face.

When the President sees Bionbyr's inhabitants, he raises his hand and makes a few gestures with his palm. We greet him with our drumbeat on our chests. The President smiles.

Andor joins the President, and they shake hands and exchange a few words. I'm too far away to hear, but something the President says makes the headmaster laugh.

The President is shorter than I expected. I was expecting to see a big man who would make me feel small in comparison. He certainly doesn't need to be any bigger, because he still has a strong presence and it's difficult not to give him my full respect.

In the following days, every first-year student analyzes the test. The bottom line is that it was a difficult test and only half of us passed. Some were poisoned by the red nightcrawler, some had drowned, and several hadn't even managed to get past the desert. It feels good to belong to the half that passed. I'm probably doing pretty well on the list. If I continue like this, it seems likely that I'll be able to pass my first year. Then I'll only have two years left.

Tonight, I'm lying in bed, staring at the ceiling. Aariel is at my feet, munching on a fig. I'm nervous about the list and hope I've got a good ranking on it. My IPKA is on the desk, but I can't get up.

"Can you get my IPKA?" I joke. Aariel looks at me and leaps cheerfully over to the desk and fetches my IPKA. I'm surprised. "Thanks!" I burst out afterwards. "It was mostly a joke, but you did so well!"

Aariel returns to his crunching, and I click onto the list. I'm completely filled with joy when I see that I've managed to keep my name in white since Nói went off on his assignment with the other second-years. It feels like it's been an eternity since he left. If I'm interpreting the list correctly, I actually did surprisingly well. My name is among the top ten, along with Ewind's. Ivalde also did well, but his name is in italic. It means that he's still on probation for the incident with the jet.

It feels like that was so long ago that it should have blown over, but apparently not. Ask's name is also italicized because of his fight with Embla. Out of pure habit, I check the bottom of the list for Embla's name in yellow. She's not there!

I get up quickly. I scroll up and down. She's not among the yellow names. I check among the names of the people who've been expelled, but her name's not there in red either. I go through the list carefully from the bottom up. In the end, I find her at number eighteen. Top twenty? I allow myself a light sigh. Embla is safe for the moment. She must have done something *really* well, otherwise they wouldn't have rewarded her with so many points. It feels so nice to see. I send her a message on the Square to congratulate her.

I have some free time before the winter ball starts, so I decide to wait for Nói up at the park. The preparations are almost finished. The park has been decorated for the party, just like the first night we arrived at Bionbyr. The music is lovely, and they haven't been stingy with the food and decorations. The decor is at least as beautiful as that first night on Bionbyr. This time, all the tables are draped in cloths of Bionbyr's signature deep blue that reach down to the ground. Diamond-shaped crystals light up the center of each table, surrounded by green plants. Everything feels even more extravagant this time. Probably to impress the President, but it makes me feel a little annoyed. Will we even be able to eat all this food?

Then, I see it again.

The bird from my birthday. The same swan-like golden bird that had perched a few inches from Embla. She hadn't seen it, and I thought it was an optical illusion or something. I look around to see if anyone else has noticed it and stop to ponder when I see that everyone is ignoring it. As if it's not even there.

Just like on the pier, it spreads its wings, lets out a scream, and disappears. It soars up to the top where there's room for it to fly out. Then it's gone as quickly as it came. *How could no one have noticed the scream?*

Nói comes over to me and gives me a gentle kiss on the cheek. He takes my hand and whispers that I look fantastic. I'm embarrassed but thrilled at the compliment. Nói and I have the same formal uniforms, just like all the other students, but he still makes me feel unique. I can't really let go of seeing the bird again, but I feel like I have to. There must be something in my head. But what?

"Won't your friends be mad if you hang out with me tonight instead of them?" I ask.

"Oh, they can fend for themselves. Even they understand that it's not every day you get to dance with a beautiful girl."

I allow myself a little giggle and have to look away. The whole situation is so unusual. It makes me happy. When I told Embla that I would be going with Nói, she just gave me a cocky look and said, "good luck." I think she's disappointed that I didn't come with her. But she has Vera, so she won't be completely alone in any case. The thought hits me that we haven't really talked about Nói. I wonder what she actually thinks about him.

There are so many people here that Nói and I are blending in with the crowd. It makes me feel calm. Embla and Vera are at the buffet, and I can see Ivalde and Ewind by the pool. Nói greets Marcell and Väinö as we pass by. I was told that Maté got expelled. According to Väinö, he was "too weak" to become a soldier.

Nói and I each take a drink made with matcha tea and mint. It's refreshingly cold, which I welcome because I feel like I'm getting sweaty from nervousness. Nói arouses something in me that I can't quite identify.

Away from the stage, the President sits with his staff and all the professors. Their plates are filled with food, and I doubt they'll even be able to finish half of it. Drones move between the students, refilling the buffet to make sure that it always looks full.

"Shall we dance?" Nói asks, stretching out his hand. A number of students have claimed some floor space and are dancing suggestively. I agree, and he leads me out onto the temporary dance floor. I feel his body against mine. He must also be a little nervous, because his back is kind of sweaty, but it doesn't matter. It feels nice to be this close.

After a couple of dances, the hunger begins to take over. We help ourselves to some food and find seats at a table quite near the stage just in time for the President to take his place at the podium.

"Good evening!" the President begins, raising his arms. "What an honor it is for me to come here to celebrate Bionbyr's sixtieth anniversary!"

He receives a storm of applause.

"What's achieved here at this school is one of the things I'm most proud of in our country. We train soldiers, but not just any soldiers. You are so much more than the Guardians in the cities. Thanks to you, everyone in Ela can sleep peacefully in their beds without being afraid. It's worth everything. You should be proud of what you're fighting for, just as I am."

Nói stands up and applauds. Half a second later, I also stand and applaud with a proud heart. I feel like he's talking directly to me, and his words excite me. They make me feel like I can do wonders. The President bows to the applause, thanks everyone, and goes back to his seat.

The food goes down quickly. The music begins to play a little louder. Nói asks if we should go for a walk, and we end up by the pool. He takes off his boots, rolls up his pant legs, and lets his feet cool off in the pool. He grabs my hand and pulls me into his lap. It's a bit uncomfortable.

"Is this okay?" he asks when he sees my reaction.

"Oh, yeah, absolutely. I'm just not used to it," I reply. It's true.

"That's right, you were never held by your parents… Sorry, that was really clumsy of me. I mean, wasn't there anyone who held you and made you feel safe when you were little?"

"Yes, of course," I reply, thinking of all times Apsel kissed me on the forehead and all the embraces we gave each other, and of Embla, who was always there with open arms and endless love. I hurriedly explain this to Nói.

"It sounds like you got more of that than I did," he says a little gloomily.

Sitting in his lap feels less uncomfortable after a while, but still unfamiliar. I take the liberty of resting my head against his shoulder.

"Didn't anyone care for you?" I ask.

"When I was little. But then I lost my sister and hugs became rarer. They weren't wasted on me, I'll say that."

I give Nói a hug. Even though he's been so forward towards me, holding my hand, giving me a kiss on the cheek, I feel his whole body stiffen. He's just as uncomfortable as I am, but I also feel a willingness in him. His body relaxes, and he gratefully receives the hug.

"Are you sure we should sit and cuddle like this instead of acting professional, like soldiers?" Nói teases.

"We're teenagers, let's act like it for once," I laugh.

It's so true. Some of us grow up so early that we forget that we're children who need to be young, make mistakes, and all that. It was nice to be teenagers instead of soldiers for once. We all had to grow up way too fast, we've missed so much. I try not to think about it, try not to be bitter about it, but sometimes I think back on that night with Nói. I wish that evening could have lasted forever. Back then, we had no obligations, no coercion, no worries about the future.

I wish I had more memories like that to go back to.

Suddenly the music turns off, and all the attention is turned to Andor on stage. He asks everyone to gather around and listen up. Everyone does as he asks without hesitation. There's a serious tone in his voice.

"I regret to inform you all that I must cancel the celebrations," he says. "I must tell you that an hour ago, an act of terrorism occurred. We must send students out to investigate what happened. First and second-years, if your name is in the top twenty on the list, you should gather in the hall and prepare for departure to Ithmah."

22

I feel myself go ice cold. *That can't be true,* my mind insists. *He must have misspoken. Not Ithmah, that's not possible.*

Nói brings me back to reality by grabbing my arm. He looks at me and says clearly:

"Don't let the location distract you from doing your job. Come on, we need to gather in the hall."

"Wait, where's Embla?"

I have to make sure she's okay. I'm grateful that she's in the top twenty because it means she's one of the students who'll be going. If I were her, I would have broken down with worry if I had to stay behind at the school.

"Okay, but then we have to go."

Nói helps me search for her. The news of the attack has received mixed reactions. Some look angry or upset. Others seem determined. But no one is upset as Embla and I. Finally, I catch sight of Vera comforting Embla near the buffet. I run towards her.

"Embla!"

I don't have to say anything else before Embla's arms surround me. She's crying. She doesn't need to say the words because we're thinking the same thing: did Apsel and the others survive?

"They're probably not in danger, Embla. The orphanage is an hour away from the town," I try to comfort her.

"Freija, we have to go now. Otherwise, we'll be late," Nói urges.

I get annoyed with him. How can he be so cold? Had it been his family, he probably wouldn't have been so eager. Or maybe he would have. I get ahold of myself and, together with Embla and Vera, we hurry off towards the hall.

"I'm in 17th place," Vera says when I shoot her a surprised look.

Good, I think, *Embla needs all the support she can get right now.*

Our briefing in the hall goes by quickly. We receive instructions on which boat to take and how to get there. They give us equipment that we'll be responsible for and remind us that this isn't a simulation. If we get hurt out in the field, we'll get hurt for real.

Everything is going so quickly. The second-years – who've been through this before – know exactly what to do, and the rest of us do the best we can to catch up. When we're all changed and ready, we head down to the harbor where Yrsa is waiting. She directs us to the two boats we'll be taking. A smaller one and a large one.

All of the students, along with Eilif, Bern, and Esbern, board the smaller boat. The big one is for transporting the vehicles. Eilif and Bern are already aboard, and they give us orders to take our places. Embla and I sit down in the boat and hold each other. She's shaking. The boat we're on is a miniature version of the Ray. There's room for about fifty people on the boat, and nearly every space is filled. We're sitting along the wall, and in the center of the boat there's a display table. The only thing the screen is showing at the moment is Ela's flag. Esbern comes aboard too and closes the door behind him.

In the hall, they told us that we're in the east, off the coast of Eisa, and that our fastest route is to go to the mainland and take the express train from the city of Bergh to Efricia. Although our boats are fast, going by water would require a detour, not to mention the fact that the sea is more unreliable than the train. The express train can only be used by the Authority, for whatever purposes they want. Everyone else has to apply for a permit if they want to use the track.

"Freija…" Embla whispers.

"Yeah?"

"What do you think happened?"

"I don't know," I reply. "We shouldn't worry about it yet. The attack was surely on the harbor or the Plaza. No one at the orphanage will have been injured."

I don't know if I believe everything I'm saying, but I have to keep Embla with me. I need to cheer her up to show her what she's fighting for.

That's what I told myself. In fact, I was at least as worried as Embla, but if I broke down then she would have done the same. It had been a one-way ticket from Bionbyr and we couldn't afford to falter. The power of your thoughts is much stronger than you think, and that thought made me more focused.

In retrospect, I can reflect on why they chose to send students on such an assignment, especially first-years who had so little experience. Was the threat in Ithmah really so small that Bionbyr thought they could keep students safe while offering field experience? Or was this just another way to separate the wheat from the chaff?

Just like the Ray, our boat dives under the water. The difference is that this time we don't have screens to show us the outside world. A claustrophobic feeling slowly creeps up within me. Being under the surface of a cave in total darkness isn't as difficult as being in a confined space with over forty others competing for oxygen. Of course, I don't have to worry about the boat's technology, but the feeling is hard to shake off.

We must have been very close to the mainland because, within an hour, we've already arrived. The strange thing is that I barely felt the boat's movement. I was probably so focused that I shut everything out.

Eilif opens the doors, letting in a draft of fresh air. I gratefully accept it into my lungs. I didn't even notice that we had come back up to the surface. Embla and I follow everyone else as they follow Eilif ashore. The boat has pulled up on a beach and we're able to jump down directly onto the sand. Although the time must be closer to eleven, it's still reasonably bright outside. This twilight is different from those I've seen before. The air is warm and humid. I feel myself starting to sweat, and it's getting a little harder to breathe. It's stressful.

Neither I nor Embla have ever seen such a beautiful setting before. An explosion of green amazes us. Not even the park on Bionbyr can be compared to the fantastic forest that now lies before us. Strong floral scents tickle our noses. The leaves on the trees are large, but look much softer than the palm leaves back home. The trees are so dense that we can't see past them, just more trees. Between the trees, there are even more plants that resemble the laundry lines strung between the apartments in Ithmah. Deep inside the forest, I can hear chattering, and I assume it's from some kind of animal. It sounds shrill.

We follow Eilif, who leads us into the city that I hadn't seen until now because of the dense forest. It's a total contrast to the beautiful scenery of our landing site. Steel, concrete, barbed wire. Nothing natural. Beyond the beach, a wall rises around the city. At least, I assume so because I can barely see the houses. Near a large opening in the wall, three Guardians stand on either side with weapons at the ready. I actually feel uncomfortable as we pass them. It feels like we're criminals being taken to a prison camp. Just inside the wall, there are several large vehicles parked which look fit for battle. They're compact with two large wheels at the front and two larger ones at the rear. The shape is similar to a wasp's head. The armor looks like it's strong enough to pass through concrete without taking any significant damage.

I turn one last time to glance back at the greenery, to cement the image of it in my memory. Then, I watch as the larger boat unloads vehicles that are nearly identical to the ones parked inside the wall. They're similar to the vehicles we learned about in Weapons and Equipment.

On a sloppily suspended, broken sign on the wall, I read: "歡迎來到" which I suppose is the name of the city, although I can't remember ever hearing of a city with a name that looks like that before. And weren't we supposed to take the train from Bergh? The sign is dirty and clearly hasn't been maintained for several years. It may have been the name of some ancient city that stood here before, which has now fallen into oblivion.

The town is filled with low wooden houses. Most of them have porches, and it looks like they can accommodate two smaller families in each house. I'd probably enjoy living here if I could get used to the humidity.

It's hard to believe that anyone lives here, though. Everything is so quiet. The only trace of humanity is the Guardians who patrol the city. Sometimes I catch a glimpse of someone inside a house, but as soon as they notice that we can see them, they always back into the darkness.

We're still following in Eilif's wake. The Cainea brothers also have their own group following them in the direction of the train station. I can see it now. A long mechanical staircase rises up to a platform above the treeline. There, under a sign marked "Bergh Train Station," the train awaits. It's beautiful. Very shiny.

We step up onto the stairs and stand completely still. The staircase moves by itself, and the higher up we go, the more we see of the city. It's much bigger than I thought. What we walked through was only a fraction of the whole city. The rest seems to fit in much more with the natural surroundings than the part we entered. I see a large square where people are moving, although there are also a number of Guardians there, and a large wooden building painted in red. The ceilings have an interesting design, and I appreciate the artistic design of their wavy patterns. Another building that catches my attention is a totally charred house in a glade in the forest. There's no vegetation for several meters around the house.

"What do you think happened there?" I ask Embla. She probably hasn't noticed anything around us; she's been focusing on putting one foot in front of the other.

"Oh! I know about that, actually. We read about it in my school in Tarara. It was once one of the Guardians' headquarters in Eisa, but a rebel burned it down. Well, as you can see, it's not completely burned down. Like, she only managed to affect a small part of it before she got caught. She still managed to sabotage them, though, because no one can live there now due to toxic fumes," Ewind responds. I have no memory of learning about anything like that in Ithmah. Maybe it was mentioned on one of the days we had the day off to work at the orphanage.

The vehicles from the boat load into an elevator that raises them all the way up to the train. Even though the train looks pretty narrow, the vehicles have room to load without any issues. Everything has been perfectly calculated. When we get up to the platform, we have to hold our wrist chips against a screen Eilif is holding in order to access our compartments. The screen indicates room 122 for me. Embla ends up in room 134, in the very last carriage. We're asked to go to our respective rooms to drop off our backpacks and then report to conference room 2 in trolley 4.

"I'll wait for you outside my room so we can go together," I say, and Embla agrees. My trolley is closer to the conference room.

I step onto trolley 12 and enter a large, airy room. There's not much here except a few screens on the walls and a pair of doors similar to the ones I just stepped through on the other side, as well as two more doors on the remaining walls leading to each corridor. On the right, it says 121-124, and on the left, it says 111-114.

The compartment I'll be sleeping in is a bit larger than the entrance room. Just like the cabin on the Ray, the walls have beds that fold down. I count eight. Under the window on the other side of the room is a white sofa. The walls are clad in purple and blue shades, and it feels great to see the Authority furnishing a space in something other than white for once. They've been decorated with plants and elegant lamps. I pull down one of the beds and put my backpack on it. Two other students come into the room and greet me briefly. They're in the middle of a discussion. I recognize the girl from the Selections in Ithmah, and from school, but we've never spoken before.

"So, do you think you're prepared for this, Albertina?" the guy asks, taking down one of the beds.

"Are you talking about the fact that I did poorly in the simulations or the fact that we're headed to Ithmah?" Her voice is harsh, but I think I can detect an underlying uncertainty.

"Both. But shouldn't it be easier now that you have a connection to the attack? You know there's pure evil behind it."

"I'm still on edge," Albertina replies. "I just hope my family is safe."

As I exit the room, I run into a fourth person as they enter the room. We nod to each other and he lets me pass. I don't have to wait long before Embla comes to meet me.

Good and evil. Black and white. It's easy to choose one or the other, and back then, I would have been quicker to agree. Especially at that moment, when all I could think about was whether Apsel and the others were okay. And about who could have been behind the attack. I've learned since then that right and wrong aren't what separates us from them. Our enemies. It's just like Apsel and Marcell's endless discussions, all political debates: different perspectives. Two sides that have different opinions.

The problem only arises when one begins to accuse the other and starts acting based only on his or her own perspective. Without considering the collateral damage that occurs as a result. It's only recently that I've begun to wonder if there's really a good side or bad side. And what's the difference between wanting to do the right thing and pure evil?

We were about to experience it for ourselves.

"How are you?" I ask.

"I just want to get there. I need to know."

Me too, sister big. Me too.

During the walk to trolley 4, we hear a shout announcing that the train is preparing to depart. Shortly after that, we can see the train's movement as we look out the many large windows that line the carriage walls. The train is moving fast, but softly. The students' dorms are in five carriages in the back of the train. The last trolley is a common room that's a more luxurious version of Gamma's common room at Bionbyr, according to Embla. There's also a carriage with a laundry room. Trolleys 6 and 7 are cafeteria carriages. The kitchen is in trolley 5, and both trolley 3 and 4 contain conference rooms. I don't know what's in trolley 1 or 2, but I would guess the teachers' dorms and the garage are there.

The conference room is reminiscent of Andor's office, except that it's furnished in warm, red hues. A large screen table occupies the majority of the room. Around the table are just over fifty chairs. On one of the short sides, Eilif and Esbern are busy conversing. Not everyone has arrived yet, so Embla and I manage to find seats easily. Soon Vera and Ewind join us. The room is quickly filled by students, but I don't see Nói anywhere. None of the second-years are in the room.

Eilif gets up and the room because silent. She brings up a map of Ela on the screen. The train route is marked out on the map.

"Listen carefully. In twelve hours, we'll arrive in Ithmah. We suggest you take this time to eat and sleep until we get there. At 1115 hours, you need to go to the garage in trolley 1 to be assigned a vehicle. We don't know if the train station outside Ithmah is completely intact, and we might have to travel by car for the last stretch. We don't know what kind of powers we'll have to face in Ithmah, so it's especially important that you don't go off on your own and instead just follow your orders. You're not fully trained as soldiers yet, remember that. You've been selected because you performed the best during the last semester. Don't let it go to your head. Also, remember that everything you discover during this assignment is strictly confidential unless otherwise stated," Eilif says, making hard eye contact with some of us one by one.

She taps the screen, and the map changes to a hologram of a jellyfish with long, flowing tendrils.

"This is a Medusa. It's a battle droid whose primary function is monitoring. When they find a perpetrator, they can give off a gas that solidifies the perpetrator's muscles. It's harmless, and the effect goes away after a while or with an antidote. We'll search the area with these to get a better understanding of the situation."

How do the robots know who the perpetrators are? I think, but I don't merit the idea with much importance. Bionbyr wouldn't risk civilians being targeted.

"Stick together. It's more difficult to snap sticks when they're bundled. Together for Ela!"

Eilif ends the briefing and asks us to go to the cafeteria in carriage 6 to get some food before we go to bed.

The second-years seem to still be in a briefing as they're still nowhere to be seen. Theirs is probably more in-depth. I hope to see Nói before I crawl into bed. Everything has happened so quickly that I haven't been able to reflect on the embrace and our intimate moments at the party.

"Come sit with us," Ewind says, leading us to a table where Vera is already seated. The food has already been served. It looks like long, narrow larvae covered with broth, along with a green salad. Even though we ate at the party, I can feel my stomach rumbling.

The salad is amazing. It's a whole new flavor to me. It's strong and has a citrusy tang to it. Embla, on the other hand, doesn't seem to like it. She spits some of it out and removes the rest from her plate.

"It tastes like I rinsed my mouth out with soap," she muttered, noticing that I was watching her with amusement. "Oh, there's Nói."

I turn around and spot him. He seems to be looking for someone, and I'm pleased to find out that it's me. In my mind, he walks up to me and gives me a hug, but in reality, he sits down in a vacant seat and greets the others quickly.

"How are you feeling?" he asks. He takes my hand.

"Okay, I think. It'll be nice to get out there and see what's actually happened. I hate that we don't know anything," I reply.

Nói digs into the food, which is still on the plate.

"This is no different from Samriga. We didn't know what we were walking into, but we managed it anyway. Just a group of rebels with powers."

"So, I don't really understand," Ewind says. "Why are they so bent on destroying the rest of us normal people? It feels the world is riddled with Power People who only want to sabotage and terrorize us."

"But Nói, how do we know who's behind it? Shouldn't we know exactly who's behind the attacks?"

"A target is a target."

I hear Embla snort, but thankfully she holds her tongue. She should see it as a privilege that she's even on this train.

I hope she thinks carefully and doesn't risk her position.

The train goes into a tunnel. It feels like I've gone blind, but the tunnel doesn't seem to be very long because we're soon out in the open again. Now it looks like we're soaring through the air, and I *have* to go to the window to see that we're not floating, but on an elevated section of track. The track here is built on a metal structure above a long stone wall. The wall appears to be several hundred – maybe a thousand – kilometers long. It looks ancient. We're surrounded by green trees, just like we saw in Bergh. I never would have believed that something so enchanting could exist in the same world I grew up in. There's so much life and vegetation here. Dusk makes it even more magical. The red sky contrasts the green nature in perfect harmony. I make a mental picture of the beautiful scenery and go back to the table.

"So, you're saying that as long as you're following orders, you'll fight anyone?" Embla exclaims. I shouldn't have left the table.

"That's how you survive," Nói answers indifferently.

"Is Marcell on the train?" I interrupt before the discussion has a chance to get any more heated.

"Yeah, he and Väinö are at the other end."

"How did he take the news?"

"Well, he doesn't usually show that much emotion, but I think he's just as determined. He's looking forward to showing what he stands for," Nói says, smiling.

I manage to get some sleep, and the hours before we need to gather in the garage pass quickly. At 1110 hours, Embla and I have already been notified that's time to meet up and directed to the vehicle we'll be riding in. I have to remind myself that we're not in a building but on a train. The garage contains five cars. The space is compact but precisely calculated.

At a quarter past eleven, all of the students have taken their seats. Each car has ten seats. The three from my room are in the same car as me, but other than them, there's no one I know.

The train stops at the train station outside Ithmah. It seems to be undamaged. Shortly after we come to a stop, the wall opens and forms a ramp for the cars to drive down. Screens in the car show us what's going on outside. Reality has caught up with me. Only now do I understand what's actually happened. A terrorist attack in Ithmah. I'm getting nervous. My body is shaking.

On the screens, we can see Ithmah's walls rising up in the distance as we approach. We drive into the city. It's Ithmah. It's home, but also not. Just like in Bergh, the streets are empty of people other than the Guardians patrolling.

The cars park in the Plaza and we stand outside. The jellyfish robots are activated, and within a few seconds they've disappeared from the site.

Eilif orders us to spread out. We march through the ghostly deserted city. I had always thought that the noise and rattle of the city was exhausting, but now I'd give anything to see people out and about. I even miss the rusty rattle of the tram scraping by.

Everything is so strange. Ithmah seems to be completely intact. What kind of terrorist attack was this? The buildings look pristine. I'm starting to have more and more trouble controlling my breathing. I'm already sweating. My heart is pounding.

"There!" one of the students bursts out, drawing the focus towards them. We've arrived at the field where the Selections took place. My gaze shifts in the direction the student is pointing, and suddenly I see what he's seen. On the horizon, beyond the sunflower fields, there's a pillar of smoke.

23

I hear Embla scream. Her cry cuts straight through my heart.

Eilif orders us back into the vehicles. When Embla doesn't move, I rush to her and force her into one of the cars. I don't care if it was the right car or not. We're heading towards the one place I had hoped would be safe.

"Embla, we can't give up hope yet."

Embla doesn't make a sound.

"Embla, can you do this?"

Her eyes go blank. But I know that her anger isn't directed at me. She grabs my hand and squeezes it hard.

"We can get through this together," she says. "Let me do this."

"Can you do this?" I repeat.

"It's not about whether you want to or not, it's about taking action, do you remember?"

I nod and squeeze her hand twice. In truth, I feel like vomiting. I'm so nauseated. I'm so scared. I want to cry, scream, tear out my hair, but I can't. This is a moment where I have to show the side of me that I'm afraid of. The one that Nói invokes so easily.

The ride to Sethunya Home for Wayward Orphans seems to take an eternity. My body feels more and more like lead. The whole time I feel like it's a dream; like it's not real. It's a wonder that Embla and I have managed to stay in the car instead of throwing ourselves out the doors. When we finally do step out, I immediately wish that I had never gotten out of the car.

I can barely process what I'm seeing. It's not possible. This place *can't* be Sethunya. But there are the cornfields, still intact, and they look exactly the same as I remember. I try to figure out where the dormitory was, the kitchen, Apsel's room, mine and Embla's room, but all I see is rubble. Charred, razed to the ground. It's almost impossible to say where the stable used to stand, or the outhouse. Everything is a single black pile.

It smells of soot and ruin. A fiery smoke boils around us. An intrusive odor lies in the air, a mixture of burning and something else. We're ordered to enter the area and gather around Bern and Eilif. It's hard to stay on my feet.

"The Medusas have found three adult bodies. One in the house and two outside. According to the report, there should only be one adult stationed at this orphanage," Bern told Eilif. He releases the Medusa he received the intel from.

"The terrorists didn't escape the explosion," Eilif says.

Have they found Apsel's body?

"Attention!" Eilif calls out to the students. She divides us into groups and asks us to search the area. The first-years must find out whether there are any survivors and take care of the victims. The second-years are assigned to look for clues about the attack. I don't even dare to look at Embla. I don't remember who's in my group. Everything becomes hazy. I follow someone who's walking towards the house without a thought about whether it's the right group or not. I need to know.

"Help me out over here," someone orders me. I stop and turn my attention to the voice. It's Nói. What is he thinking? Doesn't he understand that I'm... What am I? Shocked? Angry? Sad? He's found one of the children. The body is more like a cloth doll than a child, and I'm forced to help. I don't dare to look at the face. Who is it? I don't want to know. I have to get through this. "You can't break down right now!" Nói commands me. His cold face stares at me. He's right. I can't break down right now. Not yet. I feel the grief wash over me like a waterfall, but I have to drain it. It's not the time for this.

The only thing that seems to be intact is that rusty tractor parked out by the field. An image of Marcell and Onni driving it before the summer harvest appears in front of me. I wonder if Marcell also remembers it? Does he remember all of the nights he and Apsel argued about politics and all the times I had to mediate between them? Where is he? I can't see him anywhere. Is he sad about what's happened here? If so, is he letting his feelings show?

Another explosion is triggered, and we all throw ourselves down to the ground and cover our heads. We end up in the center of a deadly rain of glass and debris. Planted bombs, someone guesses. Or a rocket launcher. It's over in a few minutes, and no one seems to have been injured. It was probably just an aftershock. Many areas are still on fire, and I can feel the scents of ash, burnt wood, gasoline, and something else burning my nostrils.

The ground feels strange. This isn't the same place I grew up in. It's dry and lifeless. Hard. The explosion gives me a few extra minutes to collect myself. I feel the tears burning my eyes, but I hold them back. I can't show how much this is really affecting me. We don't get a free pass just because we're from the orphanage. We're soldiers. We have to act like it. But I don't want to. Where is Nói? I need him to cheer me on right now. I look wildly around me, but I don't see him. *Where are you now when I need you?*

Then I catch sight of Embla. She's not walking towards the house, but away from it. *What is she doing?* I leave my group and follow her quickly.

"I don't want to see," she whispers as I catch up to her. "I don't want it to be confirmed."

"I know," I reply in the absence of comforting words. "I know."

But I want to know. I look over at the ruins of the orphanage and see that a group has begun to pull bodies from the wreckage and line them up on the sand outside. Another group covers the bodies with green cloths. I feel nauseated.

"Come on. You don't have to look, but if the teachers see us standing here and not doing anything, it could be a problem for us later. Can you do it for me?" I plead. Embla sighs.

I want to get away from here too. I understand her. I don't want to be here! What's the point of doing a good job now, anyway? What am I trying to tell myself? The orphanage is gone. I can't save it anymore. What's the point of being an EMES soldier now?

I don't know where my power to keep going comes from. We're struggling to pull the bodies from the charred remains of the orphanage. Each body feels heavier and heavier. In the end, I have to accept that no one seems to have survived. They may not have even had a chance. There was no time to escape. In any case, they died quickly and – hopefully – painlessly. *They're dead.*

I avoid looking at their faces as best I can. As long as I do that, I can pretend that this is just another simulation test. That I don't know them. That they're not children. *Who kills children?* It's easier to avoid seeing the faces when the green sheets are placed over each of the bodies. They hide them, making them look like small green hills. When they start wrapping the sheets with cords, they look kind of like packages, but it becomes immediately clear that they're children's bodies again. My eyes catch on one of the bigger ones. It feels like I'm moving through syrup as we move towards the green cloth. I can't explain why I'm doing what I'm doing, but I step forward, grab one corner of the sheet, and pull it away.

The question is: what's worse? The sight of Apsel's stiff, burnt, deformed face, or Embla's icy scream. I throw myself back to my feet and catch Embla in my arms before she collapses to the ground.

"It... It's my fault!" gasps Embla.

"What do you mean?" I say.

"It's my fault," she says again, tears streaming down her cheeks. "I killed them all."

My ears are ringing. In my peripheral, I see Eilif come towards us and pull us up again. I can't hear what she's saying, but she looks angry. She points to the bodies and then to one of the vehicles. Do we have to carry them there now too? Is it their goal to break us even more? Can't they see that it was a mistake to bring us from the beginning? Why do we have to do this? Do they not understand that we've lost our father, our childhood, our family? Can't we have a second to pause and cry out? Is that too much to ask?!

Eilif's look scares me. I force Embla to help even though I find it difficult. Our mantra echoes in our minds. This is definitely something we have to force ourselves to do. I calm down. Embla takes up one of the smaller "packages." She sways on her way to the car, as her eyesight is probably blurry with tears.

The sun is high in the sky overhead. We must have been here for several hours. I try to do everything as quickly as I can so that it'll be over. I just want it all to be over.

I want to be with my family.

On the way back to the train station, we're ordered to ride in the cars we were first assigned to. I have to force myself to stay calm because I just want to sit with Embla. Vera is in the same car as Embla. At least she'll have someone who can comfort her. Good. Nói didn't say anything. He's sitting in another car too. Some of the students comfort Albertina, who seems to have been greatly affected by the attack. She's crying and saying that it's unfair. It's her hometown that's been affected. I get so annoyed that I sit there and tear the skin off my fingertips so that I won't tear something off her. What does she know? We didn't even go to the same school. What's her connection to the orphanage? Has she looked up to Apsel like a father, like Embla and I? Has she been nursing the children and reading them bedtime stories *every* night? Has she worked day and night just to make sure we have food on the table? No, she hasn't. She has nothing to do with this! Rage boils within me.

I was going to save the orphanage. The words cut through me. It hurts. *I was going to make it through the years at Bionbyr and straighten everything out. Everything was going to be fine.* I can't hold my tears back.

The car starts to lurch and shake.

"What's happening?" someone asks.

"We're taking a different route," Eilif says, reprogramming the car's route. On one of the screens, I can see that the train station is a good distance from us. Instead of the usual road, we're heading towards the cliffs and driving uphill. I have to hold on as we get to the steepest part. I see two of the other cars, one of which is the one Embla is sitting in. They're dangerously close to the edge. The remaining two cars must be pretty far behind us.

There's a loud bang. Then there's a bright light that spills over everything, followed by an explosion. It's impossible to know where it's coming from. As the dazzling light dies down, another explosion comes from the direction of the other two cars. One is so close to Embla's car that it's forced off its route and rolls uncontrollably down a hill. Two fireballs fly through the air. One almost hits the car in front, but the other seems to have found its target: Embla's car.

I scream internally. *Have I lost my sister today too?*

Eilif takes over the car's controls and drives it manually. She drives the car at full speed towards some rocks and places it in a safe position behind them.

"Get out of the car and ready your weapons!" orders Eilif, and we do as she says. The adrenaline kicks in and I prepare myself for battle. Eilif releases some Medusas that disappear into the savannah.

I run after them.

"Recruit Falinn!" Eilif shouts, but I don't listen. I don't know what's going on with me. It's like I'm chasing a thief through a market. I'm angry. I'm sad. I want to save Embla. Even if it's the last thing I do.

There, below the hill, I see the wreckage of the car. There are no signs of terrorists or anyone else. The wreckage is still burning, and I feel my body continuing to run on its own.

"EMBLA?!"

When I finally get down there, there's nothing but a fragile black shell left. *How could anyone have survived this?* From the corner of my eye, I see something else: a person who's slowly crawling away from the car. I run forward.

"Embla!"

I can't believe it's her. I get down on my knees and hold Embla's upper body in my arms.

"Are you hurt?"

Tears start streaming down my face and blur my vision as I examine Embla's body in the ever-darker evening light. Embla is shaking, but she says:

"No. I'm not hurt."

Her uniform is largely burnt, and she has traces of blood and black soot on her hands and face. Maybe she's in such shock that she can't feel the pain.

"The others," Embla gasps. "The others..."

"I can't see anyone else."

"Vera..."

Embla tries to get up, but I hold her down.

"Don't move."

"I feel fine."

I'm amazed at Embla's strength as she rises to a sitting position. She can only look around as voices approach. Eilif, the Cainea brothers, and the other students come running. Some have their glasses lit, and the light from them flickers jerkily as they run.

"Running off like that..." Eilif gasps as she comes up to us. She casts a glance at Embla, who's laying in my arms again, then at the car. "Look for other survivors! But stay away from the car. We don't know if it could explode again."

There's an uproar as the students run around to look for survivors. I sit there with my arms around Embla. Embla holds my arm tightly as she watches the scene before us. Finally, it's determined that the car has burned out. They've identified seven bodies in the car: Vera and the other six who were riding in the same car. Eilif and Esbern come over to me and Embla.

"How did you manage to survive?" Eilif asks.

"She must have been thrown out a window during the crash," murmurs Esbern.

Eilif bends towards Embla and angles her flashlight so that it shines over Embla's body. I think I see wonder and doubt in Eilif's facial expression. She pulls out an IPKA and lets it inspect Embla. She looks skeptical.

"She doesn't have any life-threatening injuries, it's safe to move her," she tells Esbern. "A medical droid can examine her further on the train in case there's anything the IPKA missed."

"Then, we should hurry. We have to move while the area is secured."

Eilif orders us back to the remaining cars to drive the final stretch to the train station. I do as I'm told and watch from my seat as Embla's limp body is lifted by drone and put into another car. Esbern deliberately sits next to me and puts a hand on my back. It's uncomfortably warm, so I move over, and he quickly removes his hand. He unbuttons his uniform—because of the heat, I guess. The mark on his face reaches down to his chest, where I can see a charm. It briefly occurs to me that the rule against accessories doesn't seem to apply to professors, before he interrupts the idea with a question.

"What did the scene look like when you arrived?"

I shake my head.

"There was the car ... It looked the same as when you arrived. But it was burning a little more then. And then I saw Embla..."

"She was lying on the ground?"

"She was crawling away from the car."

I look up at Esbern and see that he's nodding.

"Did she complain about having pain anywhere?"

I frown, furrowing my brow.

"No ... But I could see that she was injured. She was lying in my arms."

Esbern nodded again. To my surprise, he asks nothing more. We approach the train and soon leave Ithmah.

Was it all just a dream? If so, I want to wake up as soon as possible.

24

It's been two days since Ithmah. I'm grateful that Nói forced me to get myself under control during the assignment, but now I'm annoyed that he hasn't come to me and asked how I'm doing. We haven't talked since we were standing in the ruins of the orphanage together when he told me that I couldn't break down. When can I? Now? Embla's been in the medical bay since then. I've tried to visit her, but every time I've been denied. Each time I sit on a bench outside the medical bay and wait. Our classes will resume in a week and a half, so I don't have to worry about missing anything yet. Fortunately. I can't think about anything else right now. Not what I saw in Ithmah, not what might have happened to Embla or why I can't visit her.

If she had had healing powers, she should have woken up by this point. Has Bionbyr been wrong about their assumptions? Have I? Or was the accident so devastating that her power wasn't enough to save her this time?

Yesterday afternoon I shut myself in my room and didn't answer for anyone. I fell asleep at three o'clock at night, exhausted from crying. Aariel tried to comfort me as best he could, but it was useless. I feel completely drained of emotion. What am I supposed to do now?

Dad's dead. Onni too. The kids. Will I be able to continue without them? Without Embla? She has to survive this. It'll be hard to find the will to live without her. Still here. I don't care about anyone else, unless she is next to my side, nothing matters anymore. She is my big sister and must show me the way now that Apsel can no longer. She needs to be my compass.

My thoughts are scattered. Everything around me is gray. I'm totally exhausted. I close my eyes. It feels good to rest my eyelids for a minute. But every time I do, images of Sethunya flash before me again. They're a constant reminder that this is all real. If I hadn't seen it with my own eyes, I don't know if I would have believed it. But it's hard not to trust what you see.

"May I sit down?"

I didn't notice Ivalde approaching. When I finally look up, I nod and try to smile. Ivalde settles in beside me.

"Thank you," I say.

"For what?"

"For not trying to comfort me with empty words."

"No news yet?"

I shake my head.

"I don't understand why I can't see her." I try to hold back my anger, but it's difficult. "She seemed okay when I found her. I don't understand why she's being locked up."

"Is the rumor that the whole car exploded true?" Ivalde asks, and I nod. "Then maybe she got hurt anyway. She may have had internal injuries that weren't apparent. I don't mean to worry you," Ivalde adds quickly. "I just think that's probably why she's still in the med bay. But we do have access to top care here. She'll be fine soon."

I nod again. I need to see Embla to be convinced that she's doing well, but it still feels nice that Ivalde is here. I feel a little calmer somehow. We stay sitting on the bench, but we both fall silent.

Until I see something that makes me feel like I'm hallucinating. I have to rub my eyes to be sure, and when she's still there, I run to her. To my sister.

"Embla!"

"Take it easy," Embla tells me when I cling to her. She's got a clean new uniform. Were it not for those tired eyes that reveal the effects of recent events, I'd think she was all right again.

Ivalde cautiously approaches. Then he gives her a hug too. "Welcome back," he says.

"Thanks. Hey, Ivalde, would it be okay if Freija and I spend some time alone for a while?"

"Absolutely," Ivalde says, leaving us. "It's good to have you back."

Embla suggests that we go to my room where we can talk undisturbed. She wants to be some peace and quiet away from the other students. I understand that. If I was her, I probably would've snuck up to my room as soon as I had the chance and stayed there for a while.

"What a piglet you've become," Embla says when she sees all the nutshells on the floor.

"Yeah, it's not usually like this." I haven't told Embla about Aariel, and with everything that's happened, it hasn't been a priority. "You could say that I have a small pet, but it's top-secret, so you can't tell anyone. Okay?"

"Okay," Embla says unenthusiastically. I don't think she believes me. I close the window so I won't have to worry about anyone listening in. I hope Aariel doesn't decide to try to come in while it's shut.

"So," Embla begins. "I need to talk to you about something."

I sit down on my bed. Embla gets up. She looks nervous. The old Embla was never nervous about anything. Bionbyr has changed her.

"I don't even know where to start." Her green eyes avoid mine at all costs. I don't want to sabotage her courage, so I try to sit still and listen. Let her take the time she needs. But I'd be lying if I said I wasn't worried.

"There's a reason for my behaviour this semester. But it's not easy to talk about, not even to you. I was hurt that time when we argued about our views on the Power People. You were afraid of them. I took it personally. And then there's the way everyone here at the school talks about the Power People, saying they're evil, that they're not normal, not human. Even though there must be Power People who are human, right?"

I don't know how to answer. It feels like there's a war going on in my head. Everything feels like mash. I know where she's going with this, but I don't know if I'm ready. And how can I have a genuine opinion when all I've got is information from a third party?

"Right?" she repeats.

"Yeah, maybe... I don't know, Embla."

"Because otherwise..." Embla's face becomes a flood of tears. They don't seem to be able to stop. "Otherwise, I don't know if I'm human or good."

I'm losing my breath. Embla sits down on the floor where Tricia's bed once stood. She looks so small and lonely. But she's far from alone. I know what she's trying to say. So I try to confirm it in the best way I can.

"You're good." I walk up to her and sit next to her. Her hand is cold. "You're good." I'm starting to cry too. "You're good."

"But don't you understand?" exclaims Embla. "I'm one of *them*. I'm one of Ela's greatest enemies. I'm a monster. I'm a Tabia!"

"I know," I say. "Embla, I've probably always known."

Those beautiful green eyes find their way up to my own brown eyes.

"But why didn't you say anything?"

"Would it have been right for me to force it out of you? You've got to come to me when you're ready. I only wish you had come to me earlier. We could have gone through this together, instead of having to feel bad about it alone."

Embla cries even more. I think she's relieved and that this is her body's way of telling her. I hug her, and we sit for a while until she manages to calm down a bit.

"Before we went here, Dad told me something. I swore not to tell you about it until the time was right," she says.

I let go of her and listen. My uniform acts as a tissue in the meantime.

"It was about my powers, but also about you," she continues. Embla takes a deep breath and blows out all the air. "Do you remember the oasis on the Ranch? The one that Dad worked on before becoming the director? One evening, Dad heard a child's scream coming from the oasis. He thought it was strange because there were no other people living on the farm in the area. He got curious and crept closer to the oasis, where he saw a man trying to drown an infant. The man kept the baby under the water for a long time, but every time he raised the baby, it cried. Dad screamed at the man to stop, and then the man panicked, threw the baby into the lake, and fled the scene. Dad rushed out and began to search the water. It took a long time before he found the child, and, against all odds, it started screaming again. *I* was unharmed."

I stare at Embla. The world around us has currently ceased to exist.

"I think the man who tried to drown me was my *real* dad, and Dad – Apsel – thinks that my mother must have revealed herself as a Tabia, consciously or unconsciously, and that the man killed her. And we know that he had the same plans for me." Embla manages to say it indifferently. She's had many opportunities to reflect on the information. I, on the other hand, can only manage to sit there with my mouth hanging open.

"Your power ...?" I finally manage to say. My voice is dry, and I have to clear my throat.

"Exactly. I can't get hurt. Not unless I want to be."

"What do you mean?"

"Do you remember the drone who failed to stab me before we boarded the Ray?" I nod. "It couldn't stab me until I told my body to allow it. I didn't even know if it would work back then. When we arrived at Bionbyr, I had to test my theory, so I borrowed a knife from the kitchen and cut myself. I allowed the knife to do it, and it became a wound. But the wound healed really quickly."

I remember the vision I had that showed me exactly what she's describing. My vision must have been interrupted before the wounds healed, and it must also be why I couldn't see any scars.

"I got so angry when Dad told me this. I mean, how could he hide the truth for so long? But then he told me about his own mother – who was also a Tabia – and all the abuses she had to live with, the abuse she had to endure, until the day she was sent to a Tabian camp."

"Does that mean Apsel's a...?" I ask.

"No, he doesn't have powers. He just wanted me to grow up without having to endure all that crap. For me to have a normal upbringing." I can see that Embla's tears are making a comeback. "Thanks, Dad."

"What made you change your mind about coming to Bionbyr? Was it because of what he told you?"

"Yes and no. It was because of you."

"Me?" I burst out in surprise.

"Yes, you. Dad..." Embla lets out a deep sigh. "He told me you'd had a conversation just before and that you had asked about your mother."

"I remember it well. I was so angry that he'd made me believe that my mom was still alive."

"But have you ever thought about your dad? About who he was?"

"Yes, of course. But I wasn't even sure if I had a dad. Nobody knows anything about him, right?"

"I don't know *who* your dad is, but I know what he used to be."

I'm completely shocked. "What?!"

"The woman who left you at the orphanage told Apsel that your dad was in high standing with the President. She asked Dad to make sure you were kept safe and told him that it was critical that no one would find out who you were or that you were there. Haven't you ever wondered why no one wanted to adopt you?"

I'm at a loss for words. I don't know what to say. How to formulate a response. Where to direct my anger. At Apsel? At Mom? At Dad?

"It's because Dad made sure you stayed at the orphanage. Because it was the only way to protect you. When you were selected for Bionbyr, he didn't know how to do that anymore. And since I was also selected, an opportunity was created. That's why I changed my mind. He asked me to protect you."

"Protect me from what?" I almost scream. I've never felt as stupid as I do right now.

"The Authority. Bionbyr. The President."

I shake my head. Over and over again. Pretty soon, I have no skin left on my fingertips.

"Think for yourself, Freija. Rebels don't attack orphanages. They go after the Authority's buildings or transports."

"What are you implying?"

"Listen. This is what I believe, and I think you'll understand that it's not so far-fetched. I haven't been performing well at school, I've been yellow on the list, I didn't pass the end of semester test, and *yet* my name turned white. In addition, I was promoted to the top 20 so that I could go to Ithmah. The same goes for Vera, she was also on the verge of being expelled. Even though she's from Agnarr, she's always known that this life isn't for her, so we found each other through that connection. Now she's gone. And I'm still here. In addition, first-years never go on assignments. That doesn't start until you're in your second year."

When Embla sees that I'm still not with her, she says:

"Have you not thought about what happens to students who get expelled? I know that we've talked about it before and concluded that they can't go home. They know way too much."

"Yeah, but you're not saying that Bionbyr *kills* them, right?" I'm thinking of Tricia. She didn't even want to be here. She wanted to be home with her family, away from all technology. Does Embla mean that she's not alive anymore?

"That's *exactly* what I mean. The Authority has no problem getting rid of loose strings. Take the Tabian camps. Why do all news clips say that there are more camps than there are? There's only one, which we've confirmed right here at the school. They gather together all the Tabians, voluntarily or involuntarily, and cover the whole thing up by saying that it's what's best for them. That it's safe. But I'll tell you what it really is: extinction."

"But you don't know that."

"It's a massacre dressed up as a sanctuary. And if they have no problem getting rid of Power People, then think how easy it is to get rid of expelled students. Call it an accident and the rest of the students will buy it. I think the attack on the orphanage was an indirect attack on me. They haven't been able to reach me so far and needed something to get me out of the game. It worked for a little while. But then I realized something when I was in the medical bay, and everything made sense."

"I still don't really follow," I say.

"Why was my car the only one hit? And why weren't there any other attacks after it got hit?"

I try to remember. Another car was attacked but never hit. And the area was secured very quickly. It's true. But why would they go so far just to get to Embla? It's not at all reasonable. Which I point out.

"I think this goes back further than the events here at Bionbyr. It's about you, but I don't think they know it's about you," Embla says. "That's my theory anyway. They took in twice as many students this year. Nevertheless, they chose me, even though I didn't do *that* well on the tests and also explicitly said that I don't want to be a soldier. That I'll never bear arms and that I'm the worst at following orders. So why was I brought along?"

"Tell me." My mind is completely devoid of thought.

"I think they were able to find out which orphanage you ended up in, but they're not sure if it's you or me. That's why they took us both."

"But you're older than me, they should have excluded you based on that."

"Dad may have lied about my age in the official records."

"But what you're saying doesn't make sense, Embla. I don't know what to believe. Why would they want me?"

"That's ... Well, I don't know yet. But I think Andor..." Embla says. "I don't know. Maybe it's just my imagination, but when I was in his office being questioned after the fight with Ask, it felt like he was waiting for me to say that I am one ... And what happened in Ithmah doesn't feel like a coincidence either. It's more like they wanted my powers to stand out when we were there or something. And in a way, it did, just not clearly enough for them. I'm grateful that I was knocked out for so long that it could indicate internal injuries. There's not a mark on me."

I say nothing; instead, I just listen.

"I know this is a lot to take in. But I really feel like I'm right, or at least really close to the truth."

I can't take it. I want everything to end. I hate this situation and these thoughts. I want to stop thinking. Would the school really murder our family? Why? To find out if I have a power? All they would need to do is run some tests and see the report to find out what I am, in that case. Or maybe it's not that simple? But everything seems so unreasonable and very drastic. Kill a whole orphanage for what? To get a reaction from me? From Embla?

Embla's a Tabia. My sister. She's one of *them*. Those who terrorize the world with their powers. The ones we have to blame for the fact that we no longer have a home or a family. I've always known she's a Tabia. And I have never doubted her goodness. She's *not* one of them. She's my sister, and I love her. She may have received more information from Apsel regarding this conspiracy, but is it just a conspiracy or is it something more? I don't know. But I do know that I no longer have a reason to stay in school. What do I have to lose now? Except Embla.

"If what you're saying is true, or as close to the truth as possible, you're in real trouble."

"I know."

"We have to make sure their suspicions are diverted. We have to make sure we become star students. Every time you fight in Combat Training, you have to allow yourself to get hit sometimes. In the meantime, we need to find facts that substantiate what you're saying. If we're going to do anything about it, we need to do it right. We can't rush."

"I'm glad you're my sister," Embla says, squeezing my hand twice. I squeeze back. Our home is gone forever. Our family, our dad. But we have each other. I no longer have an orphanage to save, but I can save Embla.

25

I know what you're thinking. Why didn't I tell her about my visions? Wouldn't that have made it easier for Embla? But try to put yourself in my shoes. I was scared. Not of what Embla would think, but even though the window was closed, I couldn't be 100% sure that no one else was listening. Embla was already under Bionbyr's magnifying glass. I could help her through school hours, but I couldn't do that if I was being watched. At least, that's what I told myself back then. I still don't know if it was the right decision, or if it was a decision based on cowardice.

Bionbyr's classes will start again tomorrow. I've been thankful that we've had the last week off. On the one hand, we've been able to move freely without having to worry about being late for classes, and on the other hand, the library has been much quieter. Almost all of the students have been spending their time in the park on the sixth floor, enjoying the pool.

Embla and I have spent all our time in the library, searching for information that can prove Embla's suspicions. I don't know if we'll ever find anything, but we have all the time in the world to look. As long as we do well as soldiers, we may be able to influence the system from within. Assuming that we don't get caught, of course.

The change Embla has undergone in recent days is wonderful to see. Our "mission" has engaged her and given her a new glow. We can't turn back time and save the orphanage, but like Embla says, we can try to prevent similar events from affecting others.

"Do you remember Project Medeor? We learned about it in Bern's class," Embla asks, catching my attention. "I think I've found something about it. Project Medeor," she reads aloud. "An initiative undertaken by President Didrik Daegal in year 52 during his first term in office. President Didrik financed about twenty machines that were tasked with cleaning the polluted air and soil that arose after the Disaster. Since the Disaster, pollution has caused fatal infections, diseases, and other symptoms in people that primarily affect children at an early age. The project has proven successful in several places around Ela. Where previously it was not possible to grow or breathe, this is now possible. Today, there are over a thousand machines that continue Project Medeor's work for a fruitful future."

"We already knew that," I say.

"Yes, but then I read this in another place," Embla continues. "PTI — Picotechnological Immunodeficiency Virus. Little is being researched about the children's disease PTI. A debate is underway about how much the technology affects organisms and the ecosystem after a number of cases have been recorded that have shown that interaction with picotechnological materials has caused complications in cells and DNA in humans, animals, and plants. It can take up to four years for the deadly symptoms to appear, and usually, it's too late by then. Common symptoms such as fever, swollen lymph glands, skin rashes, muscle aches, and mucous ulcers are treatable and can be transient. If no action is taken against PTI, the immune system breaks down and the patient suffers from one or more additional diseases. The majority of the diseases are infections, tumors, and fungal inflammation.

Most are incurable, and the patient's life span is an average of one year after the outbreak of the disease."

"Could that be what Bern's daughter died of?"

"Probably."

"But in his presentation, he said that it was a Tabia that had caused the infection. This can contradict that claim."

"Exactly!" Embla looks satisfied. "Can we prove it in any way?"

"Where was he living back when his daughter died?"

Embla quickly looks it up on her IPKA.

"Calli. Why? What are you thinking?"

I check the database for reports of outbreaks in Calli. I find what I'm looking for in an instant.

"There have been a number of PTI outbreaks in Calli. What year was it, though, when the daughter died?"

"Year 50. What have you found?" Embla asks curiously.

"Wait," I ask as I look through the entries by year. "I've got it! His daughter died the same year that one of the biggest epidemics in Calli happened. Could that really be a coincidence? But why blame the Power People?"

"Because technology is so important to society, especially to the Authority with their surveillance, weapons, robots and all that, they can't acknowledge that there's a disease being caused by that technology. Which also kills children!"

I'm starting to feel like Embla is on the right track. So was Tricia. Her faith. She said it all the time. It wasn't the Power People, but the technology. What we've found doesn't contradict the theory that Power People caused the Disaster, but suddenly I feel much better. If the Authority's claims are even true, then at least we know we're not alone.

"I don't think we'll find more than this no matter how much we sift through the databases. All the texts are just short summaries. If we're going to dig deeper, we need to access the restricted section, and we don't have permission yet. And if we're going to lay low, we can't directly ask a professor or even Yrsa for permission. Even if they don't catch on right away, it'll only be a matter of time before they understand that we're spying," says Embla.

I agree. It also wouldn't make sense for Bionbyr to have their weaknesses available to everyone. We need help. Someone who's good at hacking and knows how to avoid getting caught.

"We could ask Ivalde for help," I suggest.

"Ivalde? Are you sure we can trust some rich guy's kid?"

"Yes, he's not like you think. Besides, he's really good with technology," I say, without revealing that I saw him in one of my visions when he hacked his IPKA.

"I'm still not completely sold," Embla says.

"Sister big, I wouldn't suggest Ivalde if I didn't trust him completely."

"Alright, if you trust him, then so do I."

It turns out to be difficult to catch Ivalde alone for the rest of the day. Eventually, we come to the conclusion that we need to wait for an opportunity to arise naturally instead of rushing to find a time to talk to him.

I haven't seen any of the teachers since we came back from Ithmah. They need a break just as much as everyone else, of course. But because we haven't seen them, the shock becomes even greater when Esbern steps into the classroom for our first lesson in Criminology after the leave. His scar has become redder, and the left eye that the marking frames has an eye patch over it.

"Good morning, class Gamma 1!" Domi E. Cainea greets us, and the class greets him back. "Everyone should know about the Power Registration Act, which means that by law you have to register your power as a Tabia or report to the Authority if you know someone who has a power. Does anyone know when that law came into being?"

Ewind raises her hand in less than a second.

"Recruit Dolon, go ahead."

"Seventeen years ago, Domi. It was because Erikk Aalarik filed a motion on this. The proposal went through a lot because of the rebellion in the capital the same year, in which many people lost their lives. The President said that the incident was a strong argument as to why powers must be controlled; because they're harmful to the environment and to people."

"As always, well said, Recruit. The majority of crimes committed are by Tabians. Therefore, it's important that we, as much as we can, keep track of who has powers. Can you give some examples of crimes? Recruit Dolon?"

Ewind stands up. "Burglary and vandalism, Domi."

"Very good. What else?"

"Abuse, trafficking, and cybercrime, such as identity theft, Domi," Hakon says, after being called on.

"Good, Recruit Sanvi. These are just a few examples of the crimes committed daily. During the last semester, we talked a lot about what we can do *after* a crime has been committed." Esbern pauses and gently raises his hand to his left eye. He quickly turns around and starts tapping on his IPKA, but I guess it's just to hide the fact that he's in pain from us. A number of holograms appear in the classroom. There are about twenty people circulating so that we have the opportunity to see them properly.

"This term we'll be talking a lot about how we can *prevent* crime. I won't go into the details of all of these cases because today you will get to work in groups with each of them. Those you see in front of you have each committed a crime. To give you some examples of what you will be working on, I can tell you that this person has the ability to destroy objects with a single touch. His crime was ruining a government building, which cost fifty lives. She took someone else's identity by simply changing her appearance, and his power gives him control over technology. He got caught after reprogramming the droids that distribute food rations so his village could get more than their share, which resulted in another village starving. What if he had thought bigger and, for example, affected Presidential elections or the security around the Tabian sanctuary? Your assignment is to read about the various powers and crimes so that you can then make a plan for how you would stop the crimes before they've even begun."

Esbern divides us into groups. I end up with Ivalde and Ewind. Embla ends up in another group. None of the criminals have names, only a number assigned to each. We've been assigned a woman who looks like she's our age and comes from Sainlie in the province of Jues.

"Telepathy. Direct mental contact between two consciousnesses. Telepathy is the ability to read another individual's thoughts or transmit their own thoughts to others without the aid of speech, signs, codes, or other physical signals," Ewind reads from her IPKA.

"The crime?" Ivalde asks.

"She was the leader of a rebel group in Sainlie and organized the group to sabotage a weapons transport to the Guardians' headquarters in Jues."

The report doesn't say where she came from, what her family situation looked like, what she did before, or her goals and dreams. The only thing that is clearly described in detail is the degree of the crime, how the organization had taken place, and where and when the crime took place. I get curious about something and raise my hand.

"Recruit Falinn, please," says Esbern. The class is silent, and everyone's attention is on me.

"What happens to the criminals after they are arrested, Domi?"

"Thanks, Recruit. First, a trial is held, and – depending on the degree of the crime – the penalty varies. Many end up in a secluded part of the Tabian sanctuary where they can't be harmed by anyone else. But Tabians whose powers are uncontrollable, such as your criminal or the one who can control technology, are brought to a special prison where their powers no longer work. The prison inhibits the powers so much that the Tabians could be mistaken for ordinary people, but we all know that they can never be normal."

"Thank you, Domi."

Ewind and Ivalde spend the rest of the lesson discussing how we could have countered the rebel leader's coup. But I have trouble concentrating. I try to remember everything that has been said about the Tabian sanctuary here at school, and it sounds more and more like a prison than a sanctuary. And a prison that has the ability to inhibit powers? Where is it?

"What do you think happened to Esbern?"

Embla wastes no time before asking me the question right outside the classroom. I want to talk about that too, but we have to be careful when we talk about it. We take the elevator up to our family room and sit on the balcony, far away from anyone else.

"What do you think?" I ask, continuing the conversation from earlier.

"I don't know, but it wouldn't surprise me if he was punished for the mission in Ithmah not going as planned."

"Mm, maybe. In the car on the way back to the train, I saw that the scars cover his chest as well. Wonder if the rest of his body also has scarring?" I say, shaking my head. Thinking of Esbern's body is not something I really want to do. "What about Eilif and Bern?"

"What about them?"

"Well, shouldn't they have been punished too if that was the case?"

"Maybe they were ... Or maybe Esbern was the only one responsible. I'm not sure."

In the distance, we see Ivalde walking alone. He seems to be deep in thought and jumps when we call him over. I realize that Embla and I haven't gone through how much to say or what we should reveal to him. So I quickly tell her that I'll take care of everything. She looks offended but agrees.

"Hey!" says Ivalde as he sits down on one of the loungers.

"Hey!" I say. There's an awkward silence as I try to come up with a smooth way to bring it up. "So, we've been talking about the crimes we read about in Criminology. I was really curious to know more about the history of the criminals, but as you know, the information isn't readily available to everyone, and we thought that because you're so good with technology, maybe you'd be willing to help us access the information."

Ivalde says nothing at first, but sits quietly, looking back and forth between me and Embla.

"You're lying," he says after a moment. "What do you really want to find out?"

I'm flabbergasted and completely speechless.

"Alright, it's like this," Embla sits next to Ivalde, whispering in his ear. The more she says, the wider his eyes get, but he never looks surprised. Then he sits quietly again.

"You may be right. I've seen a lot too. One of the scariest things was one evening when Hakon walked into the bathroom, completely naked and behaved oddly. He wasn't himself, and when I tried to talk to him the next day, he didn't remember any of it. Or he didn't want to remember."

"When was this?" asks Embla.

"Right after our first simulation test."

"He was our team leader," I say. "Do you think it was a punishment? But why would anyone punish him by stripping him naked and getting him drunk?"

My heart jumps. Ivalde didn't say anything about Hakon being drunk. I only know this because I saw it in a vision. Did I just expose myself?

Luckily, no one seems to notice. Ivalde shrugs his shoulders.

"So, you'll help us?" Embla asks discreetly.

I look at Ivalde's dark eyes and try to guess what he's thinking. It'd be really nice to have the power of telepathy right about now. We took a chance. Ivalde's face is blank, but I can see his thoughts rushing inside his head. Then he suddenly stands up and smooths down his pants legs.

"I'm sorry. I can't help you. I can't risk it. Sorry." He turns around and hurries away. Embla stands up, but I stop her from going after him.

"He won't reveal us," I whisper. "There's something else that's stopping him."

"I don't like that he knows about our plan now," she sighs. "Well, at least he still doesn't know the most important thing."

"Besides, we haven't done anything stupid. Yet."

Ela's signature anthem suddenly begins to play and gets everyone's attention. Then we hear Yrsa's voice informing everyone to come to the Auditorium.

Something has happened.

"You don't think...?" I ask.

"They're fast, but there's no way they could be that fast ... right? Surely they can't punish us for something we haven't done?" Embla doesn't sound quite sure when she says it.

"Welcome!" the headmaster greets us when everyone at Bionbyr has gathered in the Auditorium. I'm beginning to believe less and less that we're here because of Embla and I. "I apologize for having brought you here on such short notice. You will soon understand why. A unique opportunity has arisen. Listen carefully and have a look at this!"

He gestures behind him. A large square in the glass dome, which is of course also a screen, zooms in on something far away on the horizon. A ship is clearly visible. It's heading straight for us.

"This ship belongs to the rebels," Andor says, and he receives engaged murmurs from the students. I look around. Everyone is fascinated, excited, and looking forward to finding out what comes next. I get a bad feeling in my stomach.

"The ship can't see us thanks to our camouflaging glass screens. It gives us a huge advantage. I'd like to show you today what Bionbyr is capable of and what happens to those who oppose the system."

Andor nods to someone further back. Soon a rumble can be heard from some large machinery. We can't see anything except the rebel ship that's quickly approaching. Soon, we don't need the zoom to see it clearly. They have no idea that they're plotting a course right for us. If we stay still, it'll pass without any idea that it has passed the Authority's military school.

It's a ship like any other. A silvery, smooth gray woodlouse that almost hovers over the water. It moves quickly without causing big waves. The sun bounces off the metallic surface.

Andor nods again, probably to the same person, and turns quickly to look at the ship. Do I detect a smile?

The machinery roars again, the seats vibrate, and a red light fills the room we're sitting in. We can see the red light shooting out of Bionbyr. It takes half a minute before the laser – or whatever it is – hits the ship, and there's a huge explosion. The laser pulverizes the ship almost completely, and the residual remains have disappeared deep into the sea within seconds. The vibrations stop. Everything happened so quickly. I'm shocked by how powerful the attack was.

The room is filled with cheers and applause. The attack was a victory for the Authority. I elbow Embla to remind her to applaud too.

"Thank you, you can now return to your day," Andor says, and he's met by a respectful roar from the students beating their chests in salute.

Embla and I go to my room, shocked and nauseated. What had the ship done besides passing through? Could they even be sure it was a rebel ship? And was this their punishment? What happened to all the talk about trials? How many lives did we witness come to an end today?

"What should we do?" exclaims Embla. She frantically paces back and forth in the room. I sit down on the bed and stare out the window. Far away on the sea, where the ship was. There are no traces of it now. "What if they heard us on the balcony before? They wanted to show us what happens if we defy them. What should we do?"

"Even if they heard us on the balcony before, there's no way they could have arranged this in such a short time. I think the ship passed us by chance. But I think you're right in that we were supposed to see what happens if we don't follow orders. They wanted to scare us. It's effective," I say. "But it didn't work on me."

"Freija?"

"I'm with you. I don't want to follow this kind of abuse of power. Whether your theory is right or not, I'll do everything I can to try to influence the system. Try to make a difference. But it won't be easy."

"You have me, sister little."

"We have each other. But we need to do more. And we need help to be able to find the information we need to be able to do anything," I declare. I really wish Ivalde had wanted to join us in this.

"Aren't you pretty close with that blonde second-year?"

"You think Nói would help us? I have a hard time believing that. Nói is the definition of a loyal soldier, and with his history, it's very unlikely that he would even consider joining us."

"You don't have to include him in our meetings; instead, you can take advantage of your position with him to get the information we need without him really knowing why we need it."

I let out a deep sigh. Play double agent? It'll be a major challenge. Do I even have the ability to play sly and get information from people without giving myself away?

Yes, I do.

If anyone can do it, it's me. All I have to do is touch them, or at least I think that's how it works. Can I conjure visions if I want to? And if I choose this path, if I choose to do this, what will happen then? Can I do this without losing who I am?

26

One of the best things about Bionbyr has to be the early morning swims. To watch as the sun rises high in the sky and the sea glitters is like being in a dream world, and sometimes it's difficult to focus on swimming around Bionbyr. If you're not careful, there's a risk that you'll float off course as the school is constantly moving.

I'll probably never get tired of the sea. Regardless of everything going on at school and our plan, it's a privilege to be able to roam around Ela. And despite the fact that I have conflicting opinions about the food here at Bionbyr, I don't miss the days we had to eat gull in the absence of other ingredients at home in Ithmah.

Today I have an annoying feeling in my body. During the evening, I thought a lot about what Embla said about using Nói as a source of information without his knowledge. How should I start that conversation? And how do I go about it in a way that won't make him suspect anything? I've unknowingly avoided him since Ithmah for other reasons as well. I was probably a lot angrier at him than I thought when he didn't come to comfort me while Embla was in the medical bay or when he didn't seem to show any sympathy during the attack in Ithmah.

However, my reasonable side reminds me that he was just doing his job. He's a soldier and a good one at that. The fact that he didn't come to comfort me could be due to a lot of things, and above all, I think it has more to do with his friends not liking Embla. But he should have been there for me anyway.

I'm a little shocked that no one seems to think the attack on the rebel ship was anything but impressive. I've been listening to students talk to each other about it, and I haven't yet heard anyone who thinks it was unprovoked, wrong, or unethical. It makes me feel uncomfortable. Worried.

During lunch, I find Nói with his gang. Marcell ignores me as usual, barely saying hello. Väinö, on the other hand, I wish had ignored me. His gaze makes me extremely uncomfortable.

"Can we take a walk later?" I get straight to the point so I can get back to Embla.

"Yes, absolutely." Nói smiles. Charming, in a way that makes me feel a little weak in the knees if I'm being completely honest. I smile back shyly.

"Great," I half giggle and leave before I do anything stupid. Why am I doing this? It's hard to be angry with him. My heart and my brain are telling me different things. My heart causes me to giggle and my body to tingle, while my brain wants me to be more careful. But obviously you can't control who you have feelings for.

Embla is in a good mood during our lesson in Medical Arts. We're down in Malva's herb garden. I, on the other hand, feel melancholy. I don't know, maybe that's not the right word. What I feel is a mixture of incredible sadness but also some joy. I remember every time we worked on the farm, how we planted, harvested, nurtured. It's something we'll never do again.

"Curadnox is probably the most important plant you'll ever learn about. Does anyone know what it is?" Malva has gathered the class in front of a long bed of green plants with star-shaped leaves.

Ewind's hand flies up faster than anyone else's.

"Recruit Dolon?"

"I've never seen Curadnox myself, but I've heard about the subject. It's used in medicine to reduce anxiety, Domi."

"That's correct, Recruit. But Curadnox in its natural form, which we have before us here, can be used for a different purpose," says Malva, and she goes to fetch a bowl. She shows it to us, and there doesn't seem to be anything special about it. It could be a cup of tea. "This is an infusion of the herb. On your field equipment, there are small bottles attached to the belt which contain this mixture. If you take it, it'll counteract hallucinations and prevent others from tapping into your consciousness — via telepathy, for example."

Embla and I are fascinated by the plant, but those in the class who haven't had to grow anything before look skeptical. Sometimes I forget that not everyone is used to natural cures.

"The effect lasts for ten to fifteen minutes, but it may be enough to get you out of a life-threatening situation." Malva sets down the dish with the Curadnox tea. "Over the next two weeks, you will be responsible for ensuring that these plants thrive." Malva points to some young plants further back in the room. "If you bring up your IKPAs, you can find recommendations under the Medical Arts section. Choose a station and get started!"

Embla and I each take a cloth pot and make sure to set up next to each other. We need to oil the fabric bags with a special plant oil before we put in the small plants. Embla gets to oil them while I read the instructions from an IPKA. The plants are so cute in their pots. Small, green leaves on a thick stalk. We read in the IPKA that we have to make sure they get a lot of light, and if we were growing them outdoors, we would have made sure they grow in a place that gets at least eight hours of sunlight every day. Since the herb garden is not in sunlight, we'll need to set the lights so that they glow for eighteen hours each day. Over the next two weeks, the plant will thrive and grow as large as the other plants Malva showed us. But we can't harvest them until after they've bloomed. The IPKA has a picture of a flourishing Curadnox, which looks almost exactly the same, except that the top has white tendrils that extend towards the sunlight. When the tendrils have become purple and curly, you know it's time to harvest.

"Are you doing all right, Recruit Falinn and Recruit Faas?" Malva stands beside us.

"Yes, Domi," I reply. Embla nods. I hope Malva doesn't take offense or think that we're being short with her because she's unpleasant. Malva's warning that Embla isn't good for me hangs in the air. She hasn't said anything since then, but it feels like she's checking to make sure I'm not doing all the work again this time.

"Did you manage to get a pump for watering? It looks like they're all gone."

Embla and I look at her incomprehensibly.

"No, we don't have anything like that, Domi," I reply.

"Not to worry, I probably have some extra here somewhere. I'll get one so you can share. Can you keep the pot ready until then, Recruit?"

Malva enters a separate room. I quickly check the IPKA to find out about the irrigation system. We need to attach the fabric pot with the plant above the water so that the roots are constantly absorbing liquid. The pump should ensure that air enters the water.

Malva comes back and gives us a pump. I take it because Embla's hands are still pretty greasy.

"This one actually came from Adali. It's a specially ordered pump from there, so it's a little better. Andor brought it to me after his recent visit to our President. Be careful with it!"

"Thanks, Domi." Embla and I say at the same time. Malva goes on to other students and makes sure that they get set up properly.

Embla reads the instructions carefully and tells me what to do. It goes pretty smoothly, and, in the end, everything is in place. What we can do now is monitor it and make sure it gets enough light. Embla looks satisfied. It makes me happy.

I meet Nói after dinner, and we take the same walk as we did a few months ago. He's wearing his black, short-sleeved uniform top. It looks tailor-made to his body. Despite the pressure from the *assignment*, I feel relaxed in his company. We hold each other's hands, and it feels natural. It feels wonderful.

"Why didn't you come and keep me company while Embla was in the med bay?" I ask.

"I wanted to give you some time. I was tough on you out in the field."

"I needed it."

"But I was ashamed. You had just lost your family. The place where you grew up. I had no right to tell you what to do. Or how to feel."

I lean my head on his shoulder.

"I'm glad you did," I whisper, hugging his arm. "Do you think about your family often?"

"More or less every day. I think about my family and how I can protect them," he answers. He doesn't ask the same question back, probably to avoid making me sad. It wouldn't have done anything if he had asked. I think of my family at the orphanage often, and every time I get equally confused. I'm regretful and sad, I'm angry and I want justice. Then I think back to what Embla said about my dad, that he was high up with the President. Was that a long time ago? Is he still there? Is he one of the provincial leaders?

"What would you do if you lost your family?" I know I'm out on some slippery ice. Is it a leading issue? Was I too transparent?

"I would want justice. And I wouldn't hesitate to get it myself." Nói sounds determined. I hear in his tone that it's a sore subject.

"How?"

"I would find out who or what was behind it, and then I would find them," says Nói confidently.

"But what if it turned out to be a power greater than you, who had much more resources and was difficult to access? What would you do then?"

Nói doesn't respond as quickly. His grip on my hand releases a little, but not completely. He's probably wondering what I'm looking for. Have I ruined everything for myself and Embla now?

"The terrorists themselves died in the attack. Justice has already been served." Nói stops walking and takes a harder grip on my hand. "Don't blame yourself. It's not your fault that the orphanage is gone."

Did he misunderstand me or does he just not want to understand? Do I dare to continue?

"I know, but I'm not asking because of what happened in Ithmah."

"Why are you asking?"

My heart starts beating faster. I can feel sweat starting to run down my forehead, and I discreetly wipe it away.

I decide to switch tactics. "'I don't know if I'm going to be a good soldier."

"Why not? After all, you're high on the list and you've done well on your tests!" Nói lets go of my hand and asks me to sit down on a bench. He sits close to me and holds me with one arm. He puts his free hand over my cupped hand, which I have resting in my lap.

"I don't want people I care about to get hurt because of me," I sigh and try to look sad. What I'm saying is true, but I want him to get the impression that the issue is with me instead of Bionbyr and the Authority. And if *they're* listening in, that's just fine.

"Listen. We're your family now, and we all know how our lives will be shaped. Loss is part of the job description. Hard to get away from it. But you can't take on everyone else's feelings alone."

"I know, but…"

"No buts, Recruit Falinn. I'm here for you."

It's not going at all like I thought. I wonder if I should try to elicit a vision? I touch his hand. It's soft and warm. I run my fingers over the smooth skin and try to concentrate. Nói gets goosebumps as I move my fingers along his forearm. He moves closer to me. I put my head against his shoulder again and can almost hear his heart beating. It feels good. He caresses my cheek, and a vibration goes through the body. Suddenly I get the urge to kiss him. A second later, I taste the kiwi from the fruit salad we had at dinner on his lips. They're moist and soft. Our hands interlock with each other. Our eyes meet. There's a sudden silence. It's hot. Our hearts jump to each other. He kisses me back. I can't get enough. I don't care if there are students passing by and watching us. It feels right. Everything feels wonderful. Until…

Until I'm back in Gamma's common room. Actually, it can't be Gamma's because the couches are dark blue with orange pillows, but also because Marcell is sitting on one of the couches. Väinö is with me and that short guy who was expelled — I forget his name.

"I dunno. As long as I can remember, I think," says Marcell. "Things have happened that can't really be explained, but there's always been an explanation anyway."

"Have you reported her?" asks Väinö, smacking. He has several energy cakes in front of him and his mouth is filled with one of them.

"Yes, I already did that during the Selections. When we were interviewed."

"Then Embla must be normal," I say firmly with Nói's voice. "After all, if she was selected, then she can't be a Tabia."

"Yes, you're right," Marcell says, and he lays down on the sofa.

The vision ends, and I'm back with Nói. He doesn't seem to have noticed anything, and I don't feel as dizzy as I usually do. I stop kissing him. He looks happy.

"Will I see you again tomorrow? I'm going to go back to my room now to prepare some things for tomorrow," I lie.

"That sounds good," laughs Nói.

I give him one last kiss and head to the common room. I hope Embla is there. She needs to know. I scream internally. Marcell *betrayed* us.

Before I go into the common room, I have to stop. There's one big, important thing that I've forgotten that I have to take into account: Embla doesn't know that I can see visions.

In my retelling, I say that Nói had mentioned everything in passing and that I didn't catch much more than that Marcell had reported Embla as a Tabia. Embla sits quietly when she hears what Marcell has done. Embla doesn't even look angry. There are many emotions on her face, but anger isn't one of them. Injured, disappointed, sad. A dose of abandonment.

"That must be why he's been acting so strangely towards us," she says finally. "He's ashamed. What else did Nói say?"

I wish I could tell Embla that it was a vision I had seen and that that's why I couldn't ask follow-up questions. It would be great if we had access to real, normal paper so I could write it down. I think that would be the safest way. I'll try to find something similar. I don't dare to do what Embla did and talk openly about it in the room. You never know who's listening. Carrying this secret inside hurts me.

"He didn't say much more than that," I sigh. "But Bionbyr can't have ignored the notification, I'm sure of that much. You may be right. All the tests and trials we've undergone are to prove that you have powers. The problem is that it's not visible if you don't know what you're looking for. It's said that Bionbyr is the safest place in Ela. For you, it's the most dangerous."

27

I get to train with Ivalde during our lesson in Combat Training. He's distracted and fails to fend off my attacks. I start to feel guilty as I manage to get in several hits. Even though the blows come from me, it's still gotta hurt. When the lesson is over, we're finally out of the room. I consciously waited with him and signaled for Embla to go ahead. I have an uneasy feeling, but I don't know what it is.

"You don't have to worry about me," Ivalde says, as if he can read my thoughts. "I've just had a lot on my mind lately."

"Did something happen?"

Ivalde leads me out onto the bridge. We hurry away towards the outer edge of the harbor, right where the opening for the boats is.

"We can talk undisturbed here," he says as we come to a stop. I recognize the place immediately. It was here that Malva took me that day when she warned me not to hang out with Embla.

We lean towards one of the pillars right at the opening. I look at him curiously. "This is a dead zone. The opening cancels out the frequencies of sound recording. As long as we whisper, they can't hear what we're saying."

"Are you sure about that?"

"I'm good with technology." Ivalde smiles confidently.

"What was it you wanted to tell me?"

"I'm sorry that I just bailed after what you told me. I was afraid of getting involved in something."

"I understand," I say, though I wish there was something I could say to change his mind.

"But after we saw the ship explode, I was reminded of something I'd been suppressing."

Ivalde looks ashamed.

"What do you know about Pari?"

"It's an agricultural town. Much of the country's food comes from there. I don't know much more than what's shown in the pictures, like the Opera House. So I'd guess you have a good music scene." I feel like I'm being questioned.

"What would you say if I told you it's not just an Opera House, and that agriculture is just a cover?" Ivalde looks serious.

"Okay?"

"Pari is a wealthy city thanks to arms exports. We're the ones who make all of the Authority's weapons. We're the ones who built Bionbyr. And my dad is at the top of the hierarchy there. Or was. Actually, I don't know anymore. The Opera House is a casino. Do you know what that is?"

"I've heard that word before, but it's not something I recognize immediately."

"It's a place where you play for money. However, in this case, we're not just talking about money but also people and weapons. Much of Ela's human trafficking happens there. People go around to Ela's orphanages and buy children to use them to bet."

"Human trafficking?" I can't even form a whole question.

"Labor ... prostitution..."

I'm feeling nauseated. Did Apsel know this? Was that why he was always so nervous every time someone came to adopt?

"I was also involved," says Ivalde. A lone tear runs down his cheek. "My job was to make sure the right person got the right payout. I was in charge of the betting lists. And in the beginning, things went well. I didn't think about what I was doing, I didn't think about the lives I was helping to destroy. I just did as I was told. Until the day Levente's name appeared among the entries. His family is one of the real farming families, and they weren't doing very well. It's common for those families to become pressed for money, especially when they lose laborers in the games. They have to borrow money and end up in a vicious circle."

"You love him."

Ivalde nods. I get the feeling that Ivalde isn't telling me the whole truth, so I let him talk and just try to take in everything he's saying. I grab his hand.

"When I saw his name on the list, I went crazy. Thanks to Dad and all the weapons we've built over the years, I've become very knowledgeable when it comes to technology. So, I hacked the system and made sure that Levente was freed."

"Isn't that a good thing?"

"Certainly. But it also backfired. Because I was cheating, someone else had to lose. And apparently, I chose the wrong person."

"Who was it?"

"Someone from the Authority. Dad got the blame, and his punishment was to send me here."

"How is that a punishment? Isn't it a great honor to be selected for Bionbyr?"

"Not for people like me. They've never said it out loud, but they don't expect me to survive when I end up in the field for real. I'm not cut out for hard work. You know that. And Dad says it's a good opportunity to learn 'discipline.'"

I pat him on the shoulder. Bionbyr has transformed right in front of my eyes. Day has become night, and in front of me, I see a guy who's Ivalde's age. He's shorter and lighter than Ivalde, but still, they're the same. Levente has purple hair on one side that covers half of his face. He has makeup around his eyes in some dark color, high heels on his feet, and his clothes are sparkly and colorful. It makes my chest tingle. A warm feeling arises, and I can almost *feel* my heart beating. The feeling is stronger now than when I'm with Nói.

The vision is short, and I quickly come back to reality. I'm close to saying something about my vision before I stop myself. I'm grateful for it. It was filled with warmth and love. I think of Nói and how I feel when I'm with him. Maybe Ivalde and Levente's love is stronger because they've known each other longer. Will Nói and I feel that way someday?

"What happened to Levente?"

"He was fine," says Ivalde. "Thanks to my intervention, his family didn't have to use him as collateral anymore. I don't know what things are like now, but I hope they don't try anything like that again. I miss him so damn much. He's the only one I wouldn't be able to live without. If I get caught opposing the Authority here too ... If something happens to him..."

"Stop. Nothing will happen to him." I try to sound as confident as I can. Internally, I'm boiling with anger. Everything is becoming clearer and clearer. We must put an end to the power the Authority exercises against us. They use us as something they can easily get rid of if we don't play by their rules.

"I'm also angry," says Ivalde. "But I want to focus my anger on something productive. That's why I'm telling you all of this. I want to help. I want to help you."

"I don't know what to say," I reply. "Thank you!"

"But don't tell Embla that I was involved in human trafficking, okay?" asks Ivalde.

I don't even have to ask why he doesn't want me to say anything because I already know the answer. She would distance herself from Ivalde, and it would be difficult to work together. If we can avoid it, we will. But I don't like having to keep another secret from her.

"And don't tell anyone else either, just so I'm clear about it," Ivalde continues.

"Of course. Although no one would believe me even if I said something."

"Embla would."

Ivalde is right. Not that I would tell anyone, but if it came out, it wouldn't be long before Embla found out.

"Shall we go to her? There are some things I'd like to tell you both at the same time," Ivalde says, and I nod.

"But wait. Why did you tell me all that? It was enough for you to say that you wanted to help us. If it's so important to keep all that secret, why tell me?"

"I don't really know. I feel a special attraction to you that I can't really explain. It felt important for you to know as much as possible," Ivalde tries to explain. "Not to mention that it's better that you find out now instead of in a crisis situation."

I agree with that. I like to be prepared.

Embla looks surprised when Ivalde and I knock on her door. Even though she has the room herself, she doesn't want to be in there when she can avoid it. The memory of Vera is too fresh, and she misses her too much. That's why she accompanies us to my room. As soon as we close the door, she gives me a questioning look.

"It's all good. He says that he wants to help us," I say, to ease the tension in the room. We sit on the floor with my IPKA in the middle as the only light source apart from the dusky sky outside.

"What makes you want to help us now?" wonders Embla.

Ivalde repeats enough of what he told me to help Embla understand, but omits what he revealed about children being used as collateral. Instead, he makes it sound like his dad made a mistake and that's why the Authority chose to punish him.

"I was the only one from Pari, everyone else paid their way out, as you know," says Ivalde when he's done.

"You're here as a hostage?"

Ivalde shrugs his shoulders.

"If I do well here at Bionbyr, and if Dad does everything right ... Then *maybe* I can go home when these three years are over."

"Then why would you want to help us?" Embla gets an angry look on her face.

"It's true that I want to go back to Pari and live a normal life. But I can no longer turn a blind eye to what's going on there. I've seen through Dad what the Authority and the President are capable of. One day, a delivery of gas bombs will be sent to Kaju on behalf of the Authority. Shortly thereafter, Kaju is affected by a terrorist attack in which gas bombs played a significant role."

Embla jaw drops. My eyes widen.

"They stage the terrorist attacks themselves..." Embla says, barely audibly.

"I can't swear that all attacks are like this," Ivalde says. "But the attack in Ithmah, against your home, was certainly not carried out by any rebels." Ivalde sighs deeply again and looks thoughtful. "When I've seen my dad, I've thought there is nothing we could do about it. We're all in the President's grasp in one way or another. But with what you've told me..." He looks up and meets our eyes. "Maybe it's time to try to do something about all the injustices."

Suddenly, Aariel jumps down from the window. This causes Embla to get to her feet in less than a second. I'm grateful that she didn't scream in her surprise, but she's not far from it.

"Calm down, Embla, calm down," I say before it's too late. "I already told you a little bit about him, didn't I?"

"But, but..."

"Hello, Aariel," laughs Ivalde. "It's been a while. How are you?"

Aariel scampers up to Ivalde and nudges his hand. Ivalde pets his soft fur and Aariel purrs, pleased with the attention.

"But how?" asks Embla, and I tell her about how Aariel came to Bionbyr.

"It's a wonder he hasn't been caught yet. It's not safe here for him, but I don't know what I can do. So, for the time being, he comes here to sleep at night," I say.

"This makes me nervous," Embla says seriously.

"I know. Me too."

"But who knows? Maybe we can use his help one day?" says Ivalde, trying to lighten the mood somewhat.

Neither I nor Embla say anything.

"So, what's the plan?" says Ivalde.

"We need to find evidence, but all the information we have access to is just too general. What we need is restricted, and that's why we need your help."

"Okay, what have you found out so far?"

Embla briefly recaps our discoveries in the database in the library. There's not much to celebrate.

"Then, we went through all the teacher profiles to see if there was anything we missed." Embla pulls up everything we found on my IPKA and reads:

"Esbern. He studied at the Guardian College in Adali, later he became a Guardian, specializing in criminals. Worked at

321

the National Security Department before becoming a teacher here."

"Bern. Graduated from Adali University, Ph.D.... Worked as a professor of social sciences in Calli before coming here."

"Andor. Also studied at AU. Worked in the Security Department. Do you think he and Esbern knew each other back then?"

Ivalde compares the years.

"They worked there at the same time, so it's very possible."

Embla continues: "Eilif. Went to Bionbyr, but we already knew that. Was an EMES soldier until six years ago when she started working as a teacher instead."

"Myra. Worked as a nurse in Vallis. Has come second, first, and then fifth in the Elan Championship in martial arts. Then we have Anze, who worked as a teacher, but then became a physical trainer for the Guardians for a while. Then came here."

Embla takes a short breath and continues. "Niilo. He graduated from the Technical University of Takai. He was a technology teacher in Takai before coming to Bionbyr."

"Finally, our class leader. Malva. Served as a doctor in Vallis and worked at the hospital until she started here. It was last summer, just before we got here."

"Yes, she is the newest professor," says Ivalde.

"Yeah, but what can we learn from this?" Embla asks with a sigh.

"The only thing I can think about," says Ivalde, taking the IPKA, "is that Niilo and Anze are the only two who actually worked as teachers before they started here."

We sit in silence for a while and ponder all of it. One headmaster and five professors who've never taught before or even worked at a school. It sounds weird, but I can't draw any conclusions from it.

Embla pats Aariel and feeds him some sweets. Ivalde sits with his eyebrows furrowed in deep concentration.

"We need more information," he says in the end.

"But how?" I ask. Then I think about my vision where Ivalde tried to hack his IPKA. And he also told me that he'd managed to hack the system in Pari. "Can you hack the IPKA?"

"It's going to be difficult. Once the IPKA is registered to a student, firewalls and system barriers are set up that make it almost impossible. They'll notice immediately if someone tries to influence their IPKA. But if I could get a blank, which isn't activated, then it should work."

"But how do we get ahold of an unregistered IPKA?" wonders Embla.

Ivalde looks at me and then at Embla.

"We'll have to steal one."

28

We start the plan to steal an unregistered IPKA at once. Last night, Ivalde told me that while we were on assignment in Ithmah, he and some other students had to go to a storage room on the fifth floor and organize a new delivery of technological goods. When he was there, he noticed a secluded room full of IPKAs. But without a proper code, it'll be difficult to enter. In addition, we must have a legitimate reason for visiting the storage room or even being on the fifth floor. Yrsa is up there with the administration, and she receives students daily, and although we discussed some pretty good excuses, we didn't come up with any that were good enough. We said we would sleep on the matter.

Our first opportunity comes during a double lesson in Weapons and Equipment with Niilo a few days later. We've been assigned the task of connecting different eavesdropping devices. We work well during the first half of the lesson, but then Ivalde tells me that I should deliberately sabotage the device by disconnecting the cords. I do, and the device shorts out and dies. Niilo gets noticeably annoyed, but he asks me to get a new one from the storage room. This was Ivalde's plan from the beginning.

"Yes, Domi. But, Domi?" I say.

"Yes, Recruit Falinn?"

"I don't know where the storage room is."

"I can show Recruit Falinn, we were there organizing things during the winter break, Domi," Ivalde says quickly.

"Okay, but come back quickly," Niilo sighs irritably and asks Ivalde to put his wrist against his IPKA. "I'm giving you temporary access to the storage room. Bring some extras, Recruit."

Ivalde and I leave the classroom and head to the elevator. In the elevator, Ivalde discreetly takes out that black memory card I saw in my vision. He lays it against the wrist, which he then lays against the elevator's dashboard.

"It's probably best if you do it too," he tells me and slips me the memory card. I place it against my wrist the same way he did, press it against the scanner, and return it to Ivalde. I feel the adrenaline pumping in my body as the elevator arrives on the fifth floor. I like the excitement. Ivalde leads the way, and we don't stop until we're standing in front of the white door to the storage room. He unlocks the door, and we go in.

The room has to be about as big as our common room, I would think. Besides that, instead of the open floor plan of the common room, there are shelves in smaller corridors on each side of a long corridor. At first glance, I see helmets, sleeping bags, uniforms, training gear — and, of course, weapons.

"I saw the door in one of these hallways," Ivalde says, looking around. "You'll know it when you see it."

It's not long before Ivalde calls out that he's found the right one. I run towards him. He stares at the glass door. On the other side, there are hundreds of untouched IPKAs neatly stacked.

"How do we get in?" I ask.

"Hang on."

Ivalde inspects the door, muttering to himself.

"I need a few minutes. You should go find the eaves-droppers in the meantime and come back here when you're finished," says Ivalde, and I do as I'm told.

When I come back with a bunch of the devices, Ivalde is still standing in the same place.

"There's a panel there next to the door, but I would assume that if someone who doesn't have access to the room tries to use it, an alarm will go off. I could try to disable it, but the risk is the same with that. Do you see those?"

Ivalde points to something inside the room. I have to squint to see what he's talking about. Inside, small, narrow beams shine across the room at various heights.

"Even if we can get in, it'll be difficult to get past them. I don't think any of us are that stealthy."

"So, what should we do?"

"We have to go back to class," says Ivalde. "Come on!"

"But...?"

"We can't do anything right now. We need to hurry before Niilo becomes too suspicious. Come on!"

We return to the lesson. Niilo thankfully doesn't point out that we were gone for too long, so we get back to working on our assignment. Embla looks at us eagerly and has to hold herself back from asking questions. We'll tell her everything later.

"So, how do we get in there?" Embla utters the exact question that's been on my mind. We're sitting on the floor in my room again. Embla scratches Aariel behind the ear. He gives off a cheerful purring sound.

"Getting into the storage room will be easier now," says Ivalde. "I copied the authorization code Niilo gave me. But the question remains as to how we're going to get into the IPKA room. I think it'll be difficult to open the door without being noticed even if I manage to short circuit or hack the panel."

"Then the next problem is the lasers," I agree.

"Can't you disable them too?" Embla asks, in a voice that indicates that it'd be as easy as chopping wild onions for lunch.

"No," replies Ivalde. "I know that the technology they use here at Bionbyr is advanced, and I certainly could, but if I *do*, it'll activate some *other* security measure. I'm sure of that much. They're paranoid when it comes to security."

"So it's over?" sighs Embla.

"Not necessarily. The first door is a challenge I'd be willing to face. We just need to find a way to get past the lasers. Something small and stealthy."

"Like?"

"I don't know. We'll have to think of something."

Embla giggles. I know she wants to get everything over with. Waiting and planning aren't her strong suits.

"Recruit Falinn, you have received a message from Recruit Tosh," my IPKA announces. I ask it to read it to me, and Nói's voice begins to emit from the screen. "Good evening, Recruit Falinn. I wonder if you would like to have tea or take a walk with me tomorrow night? All the best, Nói."

Suddenly I feel guilty. Last time we met up, I said we would see each other again the next day, and then I forgot about it. I was so focused on what Marcell had said that I didn't think about it. But he didn't sound angry or hurt anyway. Embla rolls her eyes, and both she and Ivalde look jealous. Are they annoyed that I'm making plans to do something with Nói?

"Yes, please," I reply to the IPKA.

"Well, shall we get back to addressing our problem?" says Embla. "Gah. I don't know what it is with me, but I'm craving biscuits. Can you get some biscuits?"

The question is addressed to Ivalde, and just as he's about to leave the room, Aariel scampers over with a biscuit and gives it to Embla. Her eyes find mine.

"Did you know he could do that?"

"Do what?" Ivalde asks.

"Didn't you see that? I asked you to get the biscuits and then he got one for me."

Ivalde gives Embla a skeptical look.

"But it's true! Freija, can you tell him?"

"It's true."

"But...But...But can't we use Aariel then?"

"Stop joking, Embla," says Ivalde.

"No, I'm serious. After all, he's managed to stay out of sight the whole time we've been here. He's small. Stealthy. And look."

Embla gives Aariel my IPKA. He grabs the glass screen without any problems.

"He can grab things," Embla says excitedly.

"But can we really trust him to do this?" Ivalde sounds extremely skeptical.

"In Ithmah, they're actually known for seizing anything they can get their paws on," I say. "And one time he actually did fetch my IPKA."

"See!" exclaims Embla.

"Can we really rely on a sugar glider to do this for us?" asks Ivalde. I notice that he's sounding more and more convinced that it sounds like an idiotic plan. I don't know if I think it's our best bet either, but it doesn't sound like we have many other options.

"We can't afford to fail," Ivalde continues. "But if you believe in Aariel, it's two to one." He sighs. "Tomorrow, we'll have another simulation. We need to be careful, but I think we should try to do it during our free time while the other groups are running through their simulations."

Embla and I agree. But I have a bad feeling.

After our morning cycling workout, we're back to Medical Arts class to take care of our Curadnox plants. After only a week, they've already gotten pretty big and produced many leaves. Embla's plant also has a bud that will soon flower. Mine is a bit behind.

"Will you clean the pump, or should I?" Embla asks with a tone that suggests she absolutely doesn't want to do it. I chuckle and offer to do it.

I roll up my sleeves and fish up the pump from the tub. A shock passes through me, and the herb garden transforms into Andor's dark office. Everything looks exactly the same as when I was there being interviewed after Embla and Ash's fight, except for one thing. The President is there. He's wearing the same clothes as he wore on his visit during the Winter Ball. I welcome the sight even though it's an unpleasant feeling to see the world through what must be Andor's eyes. I'm curious.

"And the girl?" The President's lips barely move, but the question definitely comes from him.

"We haven't been able to prove anything yet. I suspect that Malva didn't do all the tests properly. She's far too soft, I've always said that," I reply as Andor.

"It was Myra who recommended her?"

I feel Andor snort. "I know you should never go on friends' recommendations. But we needed someone urgently. She does a good job in general. Next term, she'll continue with the remedy."

"And the other girl?"

I'm quiet for a moment before answering. I pace a few steps back and forth across the room.

"Very competent student. But no signs of what you're looking for."

Daegal looks thoughtful for a while.

"Yet," he says.

"It sounds a bit far-fetched if you ask me," I say.

There's a knock at the door, and the press officer – Erikk – enters the room. He gives me a look before he walks over to the President and whispers something in his ear. The President laughs.

"Thank you, Erikk," he says, and the press officer leaves the office. The President sits in the headmaster's seat behind the large glass table. He crosses his legs and leans back. "The solution to the problem has presented itself, Amaro. If it's the right girl, we must force her power. You know as well as I do that the most effective way to do this is by playing on emotions. They came from the orphanage outside Ithmah, right? Good. After the sandstorm this spring, work there has been much worse, so it won't be a big loss."

I can tell that Andor doesn't really follow the President's monologue. But I think I understand what he's saying between the lines. In the present, I feel my own body shaking, and I struggle to stay in the vision.

"We've initiated two missiles with the orphanage as the target. During the Winter Ball, you will announce that Ithmah has suffered a terrorist attack and that students in the top twenty from years one and two will be allowed to go there."

"Recruit Faas is far down the list, so she wouldn't be able to go."

"Did you not have a simulation test recently?"

"Sure, but she didn't do well."

"Well, now she has," insists the President. I nod. "Do you know why we have the Tabian Sanctuary, Headmaster?"

"Yes," I reply. I hear Andor's thoughts, and the words sanctuary, research, and weapons stand out the most.

"People are afraid of things they know nothing about. They live in constant fear of the terrorist attacks eventually hitting them. They're tired of it. Through the sanctuaries, they get a sense of security and power. If we remove the monsters from the streets, they sleep like babies."

"Sorry, I'm not really following," I say.

"Recruit Faas and Recruit Falinn expect us to have answers about the terrorist attack. They will not be able to move forward unless we can prove that we've captured the terrorists," the President says calmly. "They have to find bodies in the explosion. Someone has to be sacrificed."

"I understand, Master."

The President dissolves in front of me. My thoughts are torn from Andor, and I find myself back in the medical bay. I remain in the same place and the lesson seems to have continued as usual. No one seems to have noticed anything. Except Embla. In her green eyes, I see fear and confusion.

"What happened?" she asks. I still have a hard grip on the pump I was about to clean. I look at it and then at her. I feel spiteful and whiny. So many emotions within me that I just can't get out right now. I must continue to be strong. And how should I bring all this up to Embla? And why does it have to be so hard for me to talk to the only person I know would understand?

"I think it's low blood sugar," I lie. I can hear for myself how worn out the lie is starting to become. How long can I keep using the same lie? "Nothing to worry about. Let's continue."

I see that Embla doesn't believe me, but I ignore her and start cleaning the pump's filter instead. I'm ashamed on the inside, but it's not the right place to explain myself to her yet.

I avoid talking about what happened in Medical Arts during lunch too. We sit down with Ewind and Ivalde, and the time goes by quickly. I notice that Embla tries to hint at me on several occasions, but I ignore it.

During our lesson in Combat Training we practice sparring with two opponents. Embla ends up with Hakon and another girl, so she has no opportunity to continue chatting about what happened in Medical Arts.

"In class, we work by the book, but we must be prepared for situations outside this room as well. That's why we're going to work two-on-one today," Myra instructs. "Go ahead and get started!"

I'm the last in my group to defend myself two-on-one. My opponents are circling me and making some awkward attacks, but I avoid them smoothly.

"You can't win a fight just by defending yourself," I hear Myra shouting from somewhere in the hall. I'm probably not the only one who hasn't dared to do more than dodge. But she's right. You have to be willing to take risks if you want to have a chance at winning. I'm not even thinking how my feet should move while the footwork is fully underway and I circle my two opponents. Assessing. My fists are raised up near my face, and although I wish I had protection or some of the gloves that we usually use, I know that I won't feel anything until after class. The adrenaline has taken over my emotions. I see their blows coming before they even realize they're attacking. I get in some good hits. I feel like a fish in the water. Invincible. We continue that way until I'm the only one still on my feet.

In triumph, I look around the hall to see how the other students are holding up, and my breath catches in my throat. Embla is lying on the ground and taking hit after hit as the others strike, but she refuses to give up. She sits up a little and tries to fight back, but every time she gets knocked back down to the floor again. In a pool of blood. *You have to allow yourself to get hit,* echoes in my head. *But not to any limit,* I want to add, but it's too late. I said what I said. I can't take it back now. I want to scream her name and tell her to give up. But she allows herself to receive blow after blow.

Until Myra steps in and says that it's enough. She orders us all to go to the hygiene room and wishes us luck on the simulation test this afternoon. It doesn't even take a second before I rush out of the hall and run to the railing. But I don't throw up like I thought I was going to. My stomach is reeling up and down. Embla, limping and injured, comes over to me and puts a hand on my back. I shrug and refuse to meet her gaze.

"What's wrong with you? First, you were acting strangely in Medical Arts, and now this," she mumbles. She doesn't understand. How can she understand? I want to tell her everything, but how can I? They say the truth will set you free, but how can that be when it causes pain and sorrow for others?

I'm crying. My tears are flowing down my face. It's a torrential downpour. All the feelings I've been holding back all year are finally coming out. It's like someone has pressed a button and sent missiles straight into the dam that's been holding it all back.

"Come on," I say, sobbing. I take Embla to the same place Ivalde took me. The dead zone. But the tears don't want to stop coming. My body is shaking. In any case, it's still liberating. Cleansing.

"Sister little, tell me what's happening."

Embla grabs my hand. She squeezes it twice and I squeeze it back even harder. Twice.

"I forced you into this. I shouldn't have done that." I'm impressed that I even manage to say two sentences that Embla can understand.

"But I'm okay, look, I'm fine," Embla says. "It sounds strange, but I'm actually looking forward to getting a little bruised up. Although they certainly won't last long."

"It's unfair for me to put you in that situation."

"It's okay. I promised Apsel that I would protect you."

"I know why."

"You do? How?"

I wipe my snot on the sleeve of my uniform and sniffle. I feel like a slime bomb, but I try to calm down as much as I can.

"I'm like you. I've known it for a while," I say, before falling silent. Embla holds my hand in hers and nods empathetically.

"What's your power?" she whispers, glancing around discreetly.

Yeah, what is my power, really? How should I explain it without making it sound silly? Have I ever proven if any of my visions have really occurred? Yes. Yes, I have. I saw Embla cut herself, which she later revealed. I saw Ivalde in the toilet with the same memory card he later used to clone the codes with. And besides, he told me that Hakon had been acting weird and naked, just as I had seen. But what does all this mean?

"I get visions," I finally say. "But I don't know why I get them. Sometimes it's enough for me to touch someone or something that someone else has touched. Like the bead bracelet or the pump in Medical Arts."

"Oh! Was that a vision you got in class?"

"Yes," I answer, but before I can explain what I saw, Embla quickly says:

"It was really scary to see you that way. You were you, but at the same time not. Your eyes were looking straight at me but also straight through me. But what were you seeing?"

I tell her about my vision. When I'm reminded of the orphanage and the ruins, the tears come back. Just when I thought I'd already drained my body of fluids.

At this moment, Embla and I have switched roles. I'm full of emotion and she's calm. It's needed. I need it. But the silence worries me. I'm not used to her not announcing what she thinks right away.

"People really hate Tabians, huh?" I sniffle since Embla doesn't say anything.

"I don't know if 'hate' is the right word. Rather, I think they're scared. Here at school too. If they only knew that two Tabians were among them, they'd be wetting their beds."

I let out a laugh. "Thank you, sister big."

I've always blamed the fact that I didn't tell Embla sooner on security concerns. I told myself it would be too dangerous if we were both interrogated, that I could do more for her if I hid. But it's not until now that I realize that it was because I didn't accept who I was. I knew Embla would have no problem with that, and that may be one of the reasons I didn't want to tell her. I was ashamed, and I wanted to be allowed to be ashamed. Embla would never allow it.

Every day of our lives, we're told that Tabians are evil. That they're the ones we have to blame for the life we live. I didn't want to affect you the way they do. I wanted you to get your own idea of who we are. But I understand your doubts. I've had them myself. Sometimes I still have them. I'll also tell you – without revealing too much – that nor all Tabians are good, just as not all people are good.

Darkness exists within all of us. Our lives are not defined by how we accept darkness, but by how we fight against it.

I'm grateful for my tears the day I came out to Embla, and for my doubts. In them, I found strength, and with that strength, I found myself in a whole new way.

The journey had only just begun.

29

"There you are!" Ivalde erupts. His steps are fast as he makes his way towards us. I quickly wipe away all my tears but understand that my face must be pretty red still. He says nothing about it. "The simulation test is about to start. We have to get ready to assemble."

I shake myself off as best I can, take a deep breath, and together we go to the Auditorium for instructions. It feels hard to have to face everyone, as they can all clearly see that I've been crying. Embla is with me, so I manage to muster up the strength to do it.

I'm surprised that Embla took the news about the vision as well as she did. If she's angry or frustrated, she doesn't show it at all. It feels very strange. I was expecting her to scream. But it's like she's traded roles with me and is keeping all of her emotions under control. But sooner or later it'll all come out. And what will happen then?

Andor welcomes everyone as usual. By this time, it's become routine, and these gatherings really aren't necessary. We can get the same information through our IPKAs. I creep down into the chair so that as few people as possible can see me. It might be silly, but all I really want right now is to be invisible.

Marcell is sitting with Nói and Väinö. When I see Marcell, I just want to go up to him and slap him. He looks completely unmoved. Does he even care that the orphanage isn't there anymore? That the person who supported him for ten years is no longer there to support him? Does he regret reporting Embla? Embla, who has been like a big sister to him?

Embla grabs my hand and I calm down. She's also looking at Marcell, and I feel the frustration emanating from her. Her free hand is a hard knot.

As always, Gamma is the last to take the test. It buys us a lot of time. Ivalde, who is the most sensible of us right now, takes the lead up to the park where Aariel probably is. We go to the place he usually hangs out, and we can barely see him in the bush. If you didn't know he was there, you wouldn't even notice him. What else are we missing out on just because we're not paying enough attention to the things around us?

I ask Aariel to come to me and he leaps happily up to my arm. I open my uniform jacket and he crawls in against my chest. Just as we're leaving the bush, I see Malva looking at us. I feel petrified but try to pretend like nothing's happening. She's still looking at us but does nothing. She's sitting at a table by the pool with several plants in front of her. I look away and keep going. We're already at the elevator when I dare to look again. Malva is focused on the plants, and I allow myself a sigh of relief.

She can't have seen Aariel, right?

The door to the room full of IPKAs looks exactly the same as the last time. It's cool in the storage room, but not cold. It's quiet. I'm nervous. Embla is looking around awkwardly, standing with her arms crossed. Ivalde gets down on his knees in front of the panel and pulls out something similar to a screwdriver. He opens a small door on the panel and pulls out some narrow cords.

"This shouldn't take too long…"

My fingers fall victim to my nervous habit again. Embla elbows me to get me to quit. This is much more nerve-wracking than I had imagined. I just hope it goes according to plan.

We hear a click, and the door slides open. I listen anxiously for an alarm, but we seem to have managed not to trip it. No one dares to move. Even Aariel is completely still. His big eyes look from one person to the other.

"Alright, little buddy, we'd like you to jump into the room and grab an IPKA for us. You have to be careful and avoid the lasers. Can you handle it?" I don't know why my voice got a childish tone all of a sudden. I'm not talking to a baby.

"Are you sure we have to rely on Aariel? After all, he is an animal," Ivalde points out.

"Can you turn off the lasers without the alarm going off?" asks Embla.

Ivalde shakes his head.

"We don't have many other options, and it's a little late to come up with something else now anyway."

"I don't like it anyway," says Ivalde.

"Too late," I say, pointing. Aariel has shot into the room and is gliding smoothly past the lasers. He's so small that they don't have a chance to reach him on the floor. I hold my breath. Ivalde doesn't even dare to look. Will he succeed? My heart is pounding in my throat.

Aariel makes it to the shelf and takes the first IPKA he can reach. It hits the floor with a bang. I let out a loud yelp in shock. It seems to have survived. Aariel jumps down on the white floor and picks up the IPKA again.

"Good! Now bring it over here," I call out as loud as I dare.

It turns out to be more difficult to carry the screen across the floor than to just grab it. When he's halfway, it looks like he's about to give up and stand up. The lasers are frighteningly close to his tail.

"Come on, Aariel, come on now!" I encourage him. I'm sweating.

Aariel looks at me and then at the screen. He takes a step away from it as if he's about to run to me and leave it behind. But then he turns around and grabs it and brings it with him the rest of the way.

We all give small cries of joy and pepper Aariel with kisses, making him pretty uncomfortable. Ivalde takes the IPKA, inspects it, and slides it under his uniform.

Behind us, the doors are closed again, and it's as if nothing has happened. We leave the crime scene faster than anyone can say "sugar glider."

After the simulation test, I meet up with Nói in the park. In reality, I'd rather be with Ivalde and Embla as they go through the unregistered IPKA, but when I see that Nói has prepared tea and sandwiches, I'm a little happy. My heart feels really warm. He pulls out a chair for me to sit on before he goes to his own chair and starts pouring tea into our cups.

"How was the test?" he asks.

"It was good. I passed it. At this point, I've started to understand what they're looking for, so it's just a matter of thinking logically," I reply. "Oh sorry. That wasn't meant to sound so cocky."

Nói chuckles. "That's what I like about you. You keep a cool head under pressure."

"Well, I wouldn't say that. When we left the orphanage and Embla's car was attacked, I ignored orders and ran straight to the danger."

"And? You have flaws. It makes you human." Nói takes my hand and strokes it softly with his thumb.

Human? Am I human despite being a Tabia? What is it to be human, really? If someone cut us up here and now, would we bleed in the same way? Am I human because I feel, love, think, and breathe just like you, Nói? Yes, in that case, I am a human being. Just a human with some extra qualities.

"Where have you disappeared to now, Recruit Falinn?" asks Nói. "You look sad. What is it?"

"Oh, uhm, nothing," I reply quickly. He won't go for it, so I have to come up with something to say. "Well, I wish I could talk to Marcell. There's so much I want to ask him."

"Like what?"

"Among other things, I want to ask how he feels after the incident. I know how I feel, and even if he only feels a fraction of what I do, he needs someone to talk to," I say.

"He doesn't say much. I can see it's taken a toll on him, of course, it would be strange otherwise. But he's brave and seems to have put it behind him."

Nói makes it sound like Marcell is an emotional person, and I know he's not. Has Bionbyr shaped him that way? If so, I want to find him, shake him, and tell him he's a real piece of crap. We can all mourn on our own terms, I suppose. But no. He must know something.

"Can you tell him hello for me anyway and tell him that I'm here for him? And that we forgive him."

"For what?"

"He'll know."

"Okay, I'll say hello. Are you looking forward to the end of the year party then?" says Nói, changing the topic. Talking about Marcell on our date is probably not what he had hoped for.

"I haven't thought about it very much. As I said, my thoughts have been occupied with other things. Right now, I'm just trying to cope with every day, one day at a time."

"I understand. I remember the end of our first year. It felt really nice to have made it all the way through the first year.

But it's probably not until you graduate in the third year that you can really relax. Students are expelled in their second and third years as well. The first year is a pure honeymoon in comparison to others."

"Sounds encouraging," I say sarcastically. "But I guess as long as you're here by my side, I can handle it."

Nói leans forward and gives me a kiss. I welcome it. How can it be possible that despite everything horrible that's happened lately, despite the grief Embla and I have been through, the constant fear of them finding out what I am — I can still appreciate this? Should I have a guilty conscience for feeling good at this moment?

Right then and there, I was feeling so many things all at once. Primarily, I wanted to go to Embla's room and see how things were going with the IPKA, but part of me wanted to stay with Nói and forget all our problems, but then I also wanted to be completely alone. Alone with my thoughts of Apsel, Onni, the kids. I wanted to know more about my parents. But if there was one thing I had learned from my breakdown that day, it was that I needed to let myself process my emotions.

I was with Nói for a while after he kissed me. The evening offered many pleasurable moments until I had to force myself away from him.

"We started to worry about you," Embla teases when I finally knock on her door. "Ivalde has managed to get it started. Ivalde! Freija is here, come on, we can go to her room and you can tell us what you've done."

We walk out into the corridor and over to my room. Aariel is sitting on the bed waiting for us calmly when we come in. I rush over to him and give him a hug that may be a little too rough, but he doesn't complain.

"You're the best!" I burst out and produce several energy bars that I brought from the kitchen. Aariel gives a joyful smile and starts to munch on the cookies immediately.

"So, tell me!" I say, sitting down in bed next to Aariel. It feels great to be able to sit there. A little while ago, Nói and I took a walk and my legs felt like jelly. His lips have left imprints on mine. I giggle when I think of it. It's so bizarre that I've kissed anyone at all.

"Are you listening then?" Embla says, squinting at me.

"Yes, absolutely," I say, focusing. "But wait. If we really find something here, I mean something really valuable ... What do we do then?"

"We have to share it," Embla says, "with the world. Everyone has to know."

"But how?"

We sit quietly and ponder it for a while.

"Maybe..." Ivalde finally says. "Maybe we could collect everything, texts, pictures, videos—whatever it is ... We collect it in this IPKA ... And then we transmit it."

"Transmit?"

"We broadcast it to every screen and source of information in the world." Ivalde looks determined, but at the same time, uncertain. I know he's thinking of Levente and how it will affect him if we get caught. He has a lot more to lose than Embla and I.

"But how can we pull that off?"

"I don't know yet," says Ivalde. "I'll come up with something."

"It's not like we've found anything big yet," Embla says.

"About that, what have you found?"

"Not much so far. Ivalde found a folder labeled 'CONFIDENTIAL,' and we figured it would make sense to start there. Most of the folders are still locked, and we think we need some kind of code. But! We found information about something called the Nine Elements. Let's see, what was it now ... Fire, air, earth, water, metal ... What else was there, Ivalde?"

"Wood, electricity, light and darkness," Ivalde adds.

"That's right, thanks!"

"Wait, things are going too fast. What does all that mean?" I wonder.

"There is a report called 'Forbidden Teachings,' but we can't access it. All we can see is a note that the idea of the elements comes from the 'Lynxes.' But we don't know what the Lynxes are."

"Why is it confidential?" I wonder. "It just sounds like they're powers, several of which we've already seen. Did you say something about 'Forbidden Teachings'? What does it mean?"

"Yeah, at this point, we can only guess," says Embla.

"Can you learn powers?" I wonder.

"No," Embla answers at once, but then becomes uncertain. "You can't, right? Ivalde?"

"That would explain why it's 'forbidden' teaching anyway," replies Ivalde thoughtfully. "It may have to do with the technology that uses artificial powers. I don't know if people – that is, non-Tabians – can have artificial powers, but it's possible to transfer them to machines. When I think about it, I'm not surprised. I've seen it before. We all have."

"We have?" asks Embla.

"Yes, we have," I say. As soon as Ivalde mentioned it, I realized what he meant. "The Medusas, for example! Those jellyfish-like robots we had with us in Ithmah!"

"And don't forget Bionbyr," Ivalde points out. I think about it, and I can see that Embla is also trying to figure out what he means. Her eyebrows are furrowed dramatically.

"The dome! It's made of screens that have camouflaging properties. That's why the rebel ship couldn't see us!" erupts Ivalde. I remember the boy from our first simulation test. One of his powers was camouflage. Have they taken the power from him?

"Isn't that just technology, though? Is it impossible to think that they can create these effects without powers?" Embla is skeptical.

Ivalde shakes his head. "Sure, there are technologies that can reflect a surface to make it look like the surface is invisible, but Bionbyr is too advanced for that. You know the school is big, really big. The boat we shot down should have seen waves in the water, heard us, or seen some kind of disturbance in the forcefield. Technology can't make things disappear altogether. So that there's no trace of its existence."

"But where do they get the powers from? Can they absorb them from Tabians or ... How does it work?"

"I don't know," replies Ivalde.

"Are you sure that, as a human being, you can't have artificial powers?" I wonder, thinking of a certain professor.

"I think it'd be difficult for a person to receive a power like that. Much of the body is required. A machine is much more durable. It's not as fragile."

"But it's not impossible?"

"No, I don't think so."

"What are you thinking, Freija?" asks Embla.

"Esbern. Haven't you noticed how he radiates heat? The few times he's touched me, it felt like someone put a boiling pot right on my skin," I shudder.

"And his scars..." Embla hisses.

"It could be an effect of his body rejecting the power. But, are we saying what I think we're saying? That one of Bionbyr's professors has a power?" says Ivalde.

"Or more? Esbern probably isn't the only one in that case," says Embla.

We say nothing but let the thought sink in.

"But that doesn't make sense. Why would Bionbyr argue that Tabians are a danger to the public and then use powers themselves?" Ivalde looks upset.

"And if they're hiding this—what else are they hiding?" says Embla. "Ivalde, do you think it's possible to get into those locked folders? Do you have any way to hack it?"

"We need a fingerprint," says Ivalde.

"What do you mean by that? Whose fingerprint?"

"Someone high up in the school. I think it's enough to get one from one of the professors, the only question is how to get it."

"Yeah, it feels pretty impossible. So this whole plan is out the window. What should we do? Ignore everything? I don't want that. I want to see them burn for what they've done to the orphanage and other innocent lives," says Embla.

"We made synthetic skin in one of our Medical Arts lessons, do you think that would work?" I'm thinking. If we could only get an imprint on the skin in some way, then it should work.

Aariel jumps into my lap and finds a spot to rest in. His soft fur is so nice to pet. It makes me calm. In another world where I grew up with my mother, maybe I would have laid in her lap the same way?

Everything goes black. I can't see anything. But the scent is strong.

Sulfur. No. Burnt plastic. The smell stings my nose and the sweat is worse than ten wasp stings on the arm. Where is the smell coming from? It's difficult to turn my head. The stress almost causes me to lose consciousness. The only thing I can focus on at this moment is the life that wants out of my body.

How come I've been able to put hundreds of people to sleep without problems, with only a slight movement, but being able to calm my own body even with the greatest effort isn't possible. It's beyond all logic.

I scream. The pain I'm suffering is greater than anything I've ever felt before. Worse than the long days I had to spend fleeing through a forest with broken shoes, feeling the sharp stones and roots tearing my feet; the hunger that twisted and turned in my stomach like hard punches and kicks because I haven't eaten since I fled; the pain of realizing that I'll never be able to return. Neither I nor the child I carry.

The child. The child who wants to come out right now.

In the corner of my right eye, I can see the flames from the fire next to me. The smell must be coming from there. Why was it so important to burn things right now? Why was I in a hurry? I know why. There must be no traces left.

I scream again. The hunger I felt before is nothing compared to what my body is suffering through at this moment. Others have told their stories of giving life, but I never really believed in them. They must be exaggerated. Now I know. Nothing was exaggerated. It's quite the opposite.

My eyes darken and blur. I feel that when what I'm carrying leaves my body, it's not the only thing that will depart. My soul is ready to move on. I just have to deal with this last task. Soon it'll be over.

"I see the head!" someone wheezes. The person probably screamed it actually, but all I can hear now are dulled sounds. And a buzzing in my left ear. The smell starts to diminish. The material possessions that accompanied me during the flight begin to disappear completely. Soon there's nothing left to prove my identity. I will fade away, as will the objects in the fire.

"It's a girl!" says the same voice as before.

A girl, I think. *Just like I always wished for.* Not that it's any consolation now. She will grow up without her mother. Without a family. Without an identity. She will never know who or where she belongs to. Not until *they* manifest, at least. She'll never know that her mother loved her. More than anyone or anything else she loved.

"...Freija..." I whisper before it's too late. My last wish is for my daughter to be called Freija. My last mark. Maybe the name could be a compass in my daughter's life. Make her wonder who gave her this divine name.

Hope is a consolation in my last moment of life. I'm ready to let go of the world. I've done what I can. Now I can't smell anything at all. My vision is no longer blurred but completely black. The last thing I hear before my consciousness fades completely is surprising:

"There's another one!"

30

The shock is too great. The pain is too real. I scream. Embla has to throw herself at me and hold her hands over my mouth so that no one outside hears. My body feels broken. My vision is blurred. I'm sobbing. Snot and tears are everywhere.

It takes a long time before I manage to come back to myself, and I can feel Embla sitting close and caressing my back, hugging me soothingly. I see Ivalde on the floor. He's lying in a fetal position and crying. His eyes are jumpy.

"What. *Happened*?" Embla asks as calmly as she can. The words are heavy. She moves her face close to mine and whispers, "You got a vision, didn't you? As soon as you started, he fell over and started screaming. I had to keep his mouth shut too. Then he got quiet and started shaking."

I look at Ivalde, who doesn't seem to notice anything happening around him at the moment.

"Words can't even begin to describe what I just saw. I honestly don't know *what* to feel. What I saw... what I felt... it was... I saw..." I stumble over the words. How can I get it out? No matter how I try to describe it, they'll never understand what it was I experienced. "I saw, no, not just saw, I *felt* my own birth."

"What?" Embla looks shocked. "But how is that even possible? Don't you have to touch the person or something the person touched to see their memories?"

"I don't know how. Or why. I remember thinking about my mom one moment, and the next, I was in her mind sixteen years ago!" I burst into a smile. To hear my mother's first thoughts about me is invaluable. The tears come back, but this time out of happiness. And then I remember. I take hold of Embla's hand and look into her eyes. I hyperventilate for a little while until I manage to calm myself down a bit before continuing. "I have a sister!"

"Yeah, I know," Embla says, squeezing my hand twice.

"No, yes! But, no, listen. In my vision, just after I took my first breath, a voice said, 'There's another one!' Embla, don't you understand? You and I aren't just adopted-siblings; we're actually siblings!"

"But that doesn't make sense, Freija. I'm four years older than you."

"Yes, but it's like you said. Apsel may have lied on the papers. Your mother died after she gave birth to you. *My* mother died when she gave birth to me. You have powers. *I* have powers."

Embla smiles sadly.

"I am your sister, Freija, but we don't have the same mother. It's not logical. Look at us. I'm paler than Bionbyr's walls and you have rich, brown skin. I have red hair, you have amazingly thick, beautiful black hair. We're not sisters by blood but by chance and choice. I love you, but it just doesn't make sense."

I stay in my thoughts. I hate that she's right. I want it to be true so badly. But that doesn't make sense, just as Embla says. I have to stop myself before rushing off with my hopes again.

"You're right." I sigh and let go of Embla. "But, if it's not you, it means that somewhere out there I have a twin. Why did they split us up?"

Ivalde moans. I had totally forgotten that he was in the room and immediately becomes worried about what he may have just overheard.

"Okay, now it's your turn," Embla tells Ivalde. "Be honest now and tell us what happened to you."

Ivalde still seems to be in pain. He sits up and hugs his legs. He stares at the window.

"It started with being able to feel raindrops on my skin even though I was sitting indoors. It was enough for me to look at someone in the rain for the feeling to arise. At first, it was easy to ignore, but the more people were in the same room, the harder and harder it became to control. I still have trouble being able to allow myself to feel anything because everyone else's feelings are there all the time, and it drives me crazy."

"So, you mean...?" asks Embla.

"Yes, there's no point in trying to keep it secret from you anymore. I'm like you. A Tabia. Mom calls me an 'empath.' It hasn't been easy. That's why I usually keep to myself. I can handle four to five people now relatively okay, but the bigger the group, the harder it gets. Then I can hardly form whole sentences," says Ivalde. "Do you remember when we went jet skiing?"

"You mean that time Freija almost drowned because of you?"

"Embla!" I burst out.

"Sorry. It was the best day I've had here at Bionbyr. Not counting what happened to you, which I feel really bad about, but because I could get away from all the feelings here at school and just focus on the joy that was within you."

"So... You know what we're feeling right now?" I wonder.

"Unfortunately," Ivalde says, sighing. "It's not a switch I can turn on and off."

"But wait!" says Embla. "You said, 'like you.' How do you know we're Tabians?"

Ivalde raises his eyebrows and smiles.

"But if you can *feel* that we are, then shouldn't you be able to *feel* if the professors are?"

"Hm, now that you put it that way, I should be able to tell, but I haven't been able to feel anything like that from them actually."

"No, of course!" I burst out.

"Wait, huh, what did I miss?" asks Embla in confusion.

"Curadnox. The professors must take it as long as they're at the school. Esbern didn't take it – whether that was on purpose or accidentally – when we went to Ithmah, so Ivalde would have been able to feel it then, but since he wasn't there…"

"I thought that was just used to counter hallucinations and telepathy," Embla says.

"It might have more uses than that. It might inhibit powers."

"Why are they taking it at school? After all, this is supposed to be the safest place and all that blah, blah, blah," Embla snorts.

"It may have been before, but not this term. After all, they think there's at least *one* Tabia among the first-years. *You.* But they don't know what kind of power you have."

I decide to lay all the cards on the table and tell Ivalde everything that Embla and I have been talking about. What we think about the conspiracy surrounding Embla. So far, he's been part of the plan with only the knowledge that we thought Ithmah's attack was arranged by the Authority. We've left out everything about our powers and Apsel's last wish. Until now.

"This is much bigger than I thought," Ivalde says calmly and sensibly. Like he's trying to talk himself into something.

"We understand if you choose not to continue," I say.

"I know I have a lot to lose if we get caught. But it feels even more important now that we do this," Ivalde says firmly. "Thanks."

"But may I suggest that we pack a bag and hide it down in the harbor in case we need to flee the school in a hurry?" suggests Ivalde. "What we're doing is incredibly risky, and we need to be able to get away from here very quickly."

"I agree," Embla says. "Although I have nothing to pack."

"I don't mean personal stuff, but we'll need food and such. I know a perfect place that I can stash my bag tomorrow before training. I'll sneak down there before anyone else," Ivalde says, standing up. "The IPKA is probably safest with one of you right now because you don't have roommates. Even though I trust Ewind, it's probably best that we keep this to ourselves for the time being. I need some fresh air now before they lock the doors for the night. There's a lot I need to reflect on. Good night!"

We say goodnight, and the room immediately feels much emptier. I put the stolen IPKA at the bottom of the closet.

"You know, I actually think I need some time to reflect too," I say. Embla nods. She gives me a kiss on the forehead, just as Apsel always used to do.

"See you tomorrow, sister little."

"See you tomorrow, sister big."

My thoughts begin to catch up with me. *I experienced my own birth.* Not only that, but I could also hear my mother's thoughts. I've probably never been as happy as I am right now. This is the first time I've heard her "voice." The one who helped her must have been the woman who took me to the orphanage.

But what happened to my twin? Did the woman take the other baby to another place? Is my sibling alive? And if so, why did she decide to split us up? Was it because she fled and she thought it would be too dangerous for us if we were together? But who's after us? Why are we being hunted? And where is my twin?

After our morning classes, we're supposed to have self-study for the rest of the day. But Domi Amoz tells before training that the first-years will be gathering in the auditorium after we hit the showers.

Today, it's not the headmaster who welcomes us from the stage but the administrator, Yrsa. Her white hair looks as perfect as ever. Not a single strand out of place.

"Good morning, Recruits!" Yrsa's voice is loud and clear. "In about two months, you will celebrate the end of your first year at Bionbyr. But first, we have some things to get through. In the coming weeks, your schedule will be replaced by a new temporary one. If you check your IPKAs, you will see that you've been divided into new groups where the idea is that you'll create new connections and work together.

"Every week there will be a new subject. These include: 'Medical Care in the Field,' 'Surveillance and Security,' 'War and World History,' 'Military Research,' and 'Technological Equipment.'

"The new classes will start tomorrow, so be sure to check out where you need to be ahead of time. That is all. You can return to your regular schedules."

Yrsa thanks everyone and steps off the stage.

Embla turns to me and Ivalde quickly.

"What are you starting with?"

"Surveillance and Security. That sounds fun!" says Ivalde.

"I start with Medical Care in the Field. And you?"

"Technological Equipment," Embla sighs. "So we're not together in the new schedule. Wonder if it's purposeful on their part or if it's random."

"Let's not get too paranoid. It's probably just a coincidence," I say. But I can't help thinking along the same lines. And if it's not a coincidence—how much do they know?

I spent the rest of yesterday with Nói by the pool. It was nice to relax with him. A cozy bonus was the hugs and kisses, of course. I think I'm falling for him more and more. He's so kind and so good to me. I just wish I could tell him everything. But before I do that, I have to make sure I can trust him one hundred percent.

The only thing that's not going to change from our old schedule is our morning routines. In the mornings, I'll still be with Embla and Ivalde and the rest of the Gamma class. Today is the first day of Medical Care in the Field for me. It's sad not to be able to be with my friends, but we'll still see each other before and after.

The class is held by Malva in the medical bay, of course. When she sees me, she congratulates me on the excellent work Embla and I did with the Curadnox plants. Ours are apparently some of the best looking ones in the bunch.

I sit down in my usual seat and look a little sadly at the chair next to me, where Embla used to sit. I shake off the feeling of loneliness and instead look at all the students entering the room. My heart takes a leap when I see Marcell walk in. I stare at him, but he doesn't seem to have seen me— or he's become so good at ignoring me that I can't even tell when he's doing it.

"Good morning class!"

"Good morning, Domi Malimot," we all reply in unison.

"Before I get into what we're talking about today, I think it would be a good idea to give you all a little history lesson first. I promise it won't be long! I know that Domi B. Cainea is an excellent social studies teacher, but in order for you to understand what we're going over in this lesson, I have to make sure that everyone has the necessary background information. As you all know, Tabians are people born with genetic abnormalities. They have abilities and sometimes appearances that are beyond the normal variation expressed in the human genome. Their powers begin to emerge around puberty, although there are cases where they've already appeared in infancy. The first Tabia was called Anora, and some of you probably recognize her name from a fairy tale or a legend. Tabians have been around since ancient times, but it's not until the last hundred years that their population has grown. It's probably increased so extremely due to the environmental conditions caused by the Disaster. The radioactive substances from the nuclear war could also be a contributing factor—but I won't go into the nuclear war anymore for now because you'll learn more about that in one of the other special courses. Powers vary greatly between Tabians, both in terms of the kind of power and how strong it is. They're usually very difficult to control."

Marcell raises his hand, gets called on, and stands up.

"Excuse me, Domi, but it sounds like Tabians are a natural occurrence."

"In a way, that's exactly what I mean, Recruit Akula."

"Excuse me again, Domi. But how can a devastating weapon be something natural?"

"I don't think I understand quite what you mean, Recruit Akula."

"A Tabia who learns how to wield his power is just like a weapon, Domi."

Malva nods. "I understand, Recruit. This is essentially what we'll be focusing on in this class. We'll discuss what kind of powers can hurt us, how we can prevent being injured, and above all—what we can do if we are injured."

My gaze wanders away towards the cupboards. One of them contains the synthetic skin we made so long ago. I won't be able to get to them without anyone noticing, and I definitely won't be able to slip a piece into my pocket. I'm wondering if we can make new synthetic skin in the room, but I conclude that we don't have the right tools. Everything is here.

I raise my hand.

"Yes, Recruit Falinn, go ahead."

"I would like to know if it's possible to make synthetic skin in the field if, for example, we get a burn or something like that. We won't have all this equipment with us, so is there an easier way, Domi?"

"Absolutely, Recruit. We've gone over how we do it in hospitals, but there are shortcuts you can take to create temporary synthetic skin outside the hospital. There's a simple recipe in your IPKAs that you can read. You'll probably be surprised at how easy it is to produce," she says. Do I detect a small smile directed at me? "Now, back to the lesson. Your suits are made of a material that will withstand most powers, such as heat and cold, but as you've noticed in your simulation tests, there are still many that there's no good way to defend against. Yet. This is, among other things, what's being researched in the Tabian sanctuary. You'll visit the sanctuary in your third year. I myself have been there on study days."

A student asks Malva to tell us something about the sanctuary. She scrunches her face a bit and seems to be looking for the right words.

"In a way, it's reminiscent of Bionbyr. There are rules. About when you get up in the morning, when breakfast, lunch, and dinner are served, and so on. They have different activities. Training. And of course, experiments are being carried out there."

I sense a tingling sensation in the air. I think most – if not all – of us want to know what experiments are being conducted. Malva probably knows it too, because she says:

"However, you'll get to know more about that later. We need to move on with the lesson. This week, I want you to..."

Malva's voice fades out. I have trouble concentrating. The only thing I want right now is the opportunity to use our IPKAs so that I can check out the recipe Malva told us about. If it's really that simple, how did we miss it?

"You're with me," Marcell tells me, and I get confused.

"What do you mean?"

Marcell has sat down in the place Embla usually sits. I'm filled with anger and irritation at seeing him so close. I refrain from touching him.

"You and I will be reporting together at the end of the week," Marcell explains.

Typical, I think.

"I know that you're not very happy with me. But you don't understand. It was important for me to get into Bionbyr, and I was prepared to do anything for it," says Marcell. He actually looks remorseful.

"I'm listening."

"I panicked during the interview, and when they asked about the Power People, I thought of Embla, and now I know that she's not a Tabia—otherwise she wouldn't have been brought to Bionbyr, I mean, but back then...I panicked."

"You betrayed your family, Marcell."

"I know. I'm sorry. I understand that I'll probably never be forgiven, but I want you to know that I regret what I did. Sorry."

"It's not really me that you need to apologize to."

"I know. But it's easier to talk to you. She reminds too much of..."

Apsel. I know, Marcell.

"I understand what you mean. I'll talk to her."

Marcell exhales. "It was nice to get it out of the way. Thanks for listening, Freija. When Nói told me that you said you forgave me, I thought it was too good to be true."

"It's a start," I say. "Well, what injury did we get assigned to work with?"

For the rest of the lesson, Marcell and I are studying an injury that a Tabia with an electrical power has caused. The victim's skin is pale blue as if he's frozen to death, except that the skin is also burnt in several places. Every time Marcell reads aloud from his IPKA, I pretend to follow along in my own — and I'm certainly reading from my IPKA. A recipe for temporary synthetic skin that we can easily make in the room. It's the easy bit. Now we just have to try to figure out how to get a teacher's fingerprint. Maybe Ivalde or Embla have already figured it out.

Those restricted folders aren't far from reach now.

31

Ivalde and Embla get excited when I tell them the news about the skin in my room before tonight's dinner. Now, if we can just grab something – for example, a glass – with a teacher's fingerprint on it, we'll be able to construct the skin directly on the glass and then get it automatically stuck. But the only times we've seen teachers eat with students is during parties. They usually stick to their own quarters other than that. And during our classes, there aren't many occasions when they touch anything other than their own IPKAs.

"We'll come up with something," says Ivalde. "I have something else to report."

"*Report?* You don't need to report to us, but you're welcome to tell us what you've discovered," Embla snorts.

"Sorry. I'm used to... Well, we were in the control room today, and we got to look at the surveillance cameras. At least, the ones we have the clearance to check. I was curious to see if they have cameras in the storage room or not because we haven't heard anything about our little adventure. It turned out they *do* have cameras there. Not to mention, they have a perfect view of the room with the IPKAs."

"Oh, no," Embla says. I'm thinking the exact same thing.

"That was my first reaction too. So I started looking back at the recordings in the system and found the times we were there," says Ivalde, taking a dramatic pause. "Everything recorded during that time has been erased."

"What does it mean?" I ask.

"Someone actively went in and deleted the footage."

"But who?" wonders Embla.

"No clue. But I think we have to be extra careful now."

We nod.

"Especially after what I learned today," says Embla. "You know how we learned about those cameras the Guardians have that can recognize terrorists or whatever?"

"The glasses that compare faces to a database containing images of criminals in real-time? So that they can prevent crimes before they even begin? What about it?" wonders Ivalde.

"They've refined that technology. Nowadays, people who are suspected of having committed crimes get these little crystals surgically implanted under their eyelids that can project their thoughts. If someone has even the tiniest thought of committing a crime – regardless of the seriousness – a central station will find out, and they can activate the crystal, which will then drill into the person's brain. They die on the spot," Embla says.

"Are you worried that that'll happen to us? That we could have crystals implanted in our eyes?" Ivalde is skeptical.

"If they have no problem sacrificing people over a single thought, what'll happen to us when they find out what we're doing? We'll be at even greater risk, I think."

"We'll be careful," I say. "We just have to get a fingerprint that we can pick up with the synthetic skin. Then we can start gathering evidence."

"We can take our time with that so as not to draw too much attention to ourselves. Like Freija said: we'll be careful," Ivalde asserts. A warm feeling arises within me. It's almost the same feeling I get when I think of Nói. Ivalde must be picking up on my feeling because he looks at me and seems embarrassed.

How are we going to get ahold of a teacher's fingerprint? They rarely touch things that students have access to. Then it hits me. There actually is one thing.

"I think I have an idea," I say. "On how we can get a fingerprint. Although I'm not sure if it'll work now that I think about it. Ivalde, can fingerprints be left on an item if it's been in water for almost three weeks?"

"It's possible if the finger was in contact with a non-water-soluble substance such as oil, I would think. But I'm not an expert," says Ivalde, sounding *exactly* like an expert.

"In that case, I think it could work. Embla, the pump we got from Malva in Medical Arts. We had to lubricate the pots with oil. She must have been in contact with that oil too! It's worth a shot."

"There we go!" exclaims Embla. "Grab the IPKA, Ivalde!"

We hear the students talking and laughing out loud in the cafeteria across the harbor. Besides that, it's quiet, almost uncomfortably quiet. There's not much life in the medical bay either. We go straight to Malva's herb garden and where our Curadnox plants are waiting. I understand what Malva meant when she said ours were some of the best looking ones. They're both large and healthy.

While Embla and Ivalde keep an eye out, I run over to our plants, remove the pump quickly, and leave. When I'm almost to Embla, I stop. The thought comes to me like a flash. *Why make the skin in my room when we have everything we need right here?*

"Embla! Come here!" I'm half shouting. Ivalde stays put while Embla comes over to me. "Let's do this here and now. Then I can put the pump back right away."

"Okay. Tell me what to do."

At first, I wonder if we should just take some finished pieces of skin and I head over to the cabinet to check. After a quick glance, I realize it's a no-go. They're not soft enough, and someone might notice that they're missing.

"Take the cell extractor from that box," I order, as I search for the culture box myself. It's a compact mini glass variant that's programmed to speed up the growth of the synthetic skin. Out in the field, we won't have an hour to get a perfect piece, which is how long it usually takes. I unfold it to make it big enough and ask Embla to extract some of her cells to transfer them to the system along with nutrients. The effect is immediate. A gel-like mass forms, and an hour's worth of growth occurs in just a few minutes before our eyes.

I inspect the pump carefully to see where Malva may have touched it. Embla hasn't touched it, and I didn't have oily hands when I received it, so the only fingerprints on it should be Malva's.

"There!" I think I see something oily on the surface. "Quickly, the skin!"

Embla hands me the synthetic skin, and I lay it on the pump gently so I won't smudge the fingerprint and then I press it down hard. I let the heat from my hand shape the skin to fit around my own finger and lift the bit off the pump. The imprint is there. We succeeded.

"Ivalde, come here!" orders Embla.

Ivalde comes over, takes out the IPKA, and clicks his way to the confidential folders. We look around to make sure that the coast is clear. With my heart in my throat, I push against the screen to unlock it. *Nothing is happening.* I try again. Still nothing.

"Do we have the wrong fingerprint?"

"It's not possible. My fingerprints definitely dissolved in the water. Malva's would be the only ones on the pump—

unless Andor's fingerprint survived. But he should have the right clearance to access these files."

"Maybe Malva doesn't have clearance?" suggests Embla.

I feel defeated. Do we need to reach someone even higher up? Just when everything had seemed so easy. I knew it was too good to be true. I swear loudly.

"Wait. There must be something we're missing," says Ivalde. He's not giving up. "Can I look at the fingerprint?"

I hand it over. He picks up the pump and pauses to think. I'm starting to worry that we'll get caught soon. I just want to get out of here. Forget that we even tried.

Ivalde takes the IPKA and wipes off the screen. He blows a little on the fingerprint we just made and tries it again.

It works. We enter the subfolders, and I dare to give a small joyful smile. Embla and Ivalde laugh as loud as they dare and we hug. But we have to wait to celebrate until we're in the clear. We quickly make our getaway back to my room without dinner. No one has an appetite for food right now.

"Are you ready?" wonders Ivalde.

I nod. "I don't know why, but I'm actually nervous about what we're going to find."

"I know," Ivalde smiles.

"Let's do this," Embla says. All three of us are completely tense.

"Freija, do you want the honor?" Ivalde asks. "Since you figured out how to get the fingerprint."

"Okay," I say, tapping the synthetic skin on my finger again. Carefully, I push it against the IPKA when it prompts me for an imprint. We're back in, and this time we have more time to see what we have access to.

"Where should we start?" Embla asks impatiently.

A simple question, but more difficult to answer. I, and the others too probably, have so many unanswered questions: What happens to students who get expelled? Are Tabians responsible for triggering the Disaster? Can we find information about the Tabian sanctuary? About the professors? Can we find evidence that Esbern has an artificial power? Are there others at the school who have them too? The list of questions is long.

"Should we start by seeing what they've documented about us? Then maybe we get an idea of how much they know about what we're doing right now?" suggests Ivalde. That's a good idea.

"Let me see," he mutters to himself and clicks further into the files. "Okay, we can start with me since it doesn't really matter. The jet ski incident is there, of course, and the probationary period I got as a result. It says I'm an introvert, which isn't too strange considering how I am in the classrooms. They suggest that I become a weapons specialist or analyst. Interesting. There's nothing about the stolen IPKA or anything like that."

"Okay, Mr. Star student, what about me and Freija?"

"It says Freija is also a good student. However, they question your ability to follow orders because of something that happened during the Ithmah mission."

"I ran towards the explosion that hit Embla's car even though they had ordered us to stay put," I say, realizing that it's still hard to think about.

"It says that you're from the orphanage, they think it's important to point that out clearly. Let's see. You may be pleased to know that you had very good results in the Selections and that they see great potential in you."

"Nothing about them suspecting that I'm a Tabia?"

"No, nothing about that. It also says that you passed the bravery simulation test with the highest score," replies Ivalde, clicking on Embla's profile. He looks up. "It might be best to read it for yourself."

Embla takes the IPKA from Ivalde.

"Temperamental... Mediocre..." she mumbles. "They're not mincing words here. They've made notes about the crash and my miraculous survival. They have long analyses of my poor performance in the simulations. If I'm so bad, why do they insist on keeping me? Why haven't I been expelled?"

"I think you know the answer to that," I hint.

"They don't know yet," says Embla, who continues to read her profile. "They still only have suspicions. There's a note about my hospital stay. It says that I had no internal injuries, either. So why did I have to stay there? To see if I'm a Tabia? Many suggest that I am, but they have no evidence. This extends back to the orphanage. They even have the incident with the toolbox. How can they know anything about it?"

Images pop into my head of the toolbox falling on Embla, how her arm looked broken, my panic. Were they monitoring us?

"But nothing about our plans," Embla concludes, giving the IPKA back to Ivalde. He wastes no time in clicking on something else to look at.

"How can they know anything about what happened at the orphanage?" Embla repeats the question to me.

"Marcell," I point out. "He was the one who reported you. He must have told them."

"That idiot," Embla sighs.

"Hey, check this out," Ivalde interrupts. He sits between Embla and I and puts on a video. "It's from the two missions last fall."

Bionbyr's soldiers have lined people up in a long way. The people are standing with their hands tied behind their backs, and their heads are covered with black hoods.

"Are those...?"

"Rebels, most likely," replies Ivalde. The soldiers, second-years, are carrying weapons aimed at the line. I can see Nói among the soldiers. Domi Eilif Faris marches back and forth between the soldiers and the squad. She has a gun in her hand. She screams something, but I can't hear what, and within a few seconds the soldiers have shot down the people. Headshots to their hooded heads. All but one soldier. Eilif takes determined steps toward the soldier. He still has the weapon aimed at a rebel, the only one still standing. Eilif says something, but we still can't hear what she's saying. The student lowers his weapon. He turns around to leave the scene but doesn't get far. Eilif puts a bullet in his neck, and then she shoots down the rebel that the student was supposed to kill. Nói stands watching the murdered pupil without showing any emotion.

"I don't want to see any more!" gasps Embla. Ivalde turns off the video. My hands are trembling. Nobody says anything. I want to push away what I just saw. Nói. What have you done? Is this the price you pay to follow orders? Cold-blooded murder?

"I don't want to stay at this school. I don't want to be like them," says Embla. "I refuse."

"It won't happen," I say, as calmly as I can.

"How can you be so sure?"

"We won't let that happen. In addition, once we've gathered all the information, we won't be sticking around here."

"But if we fail?"

"Then we'll end up like that student," says Ivalde gloomily.

"How are we going to get out of here?" I wonder. "We can hardly swim from here."

"We have to make a plan," Ivalde notes. "I agree with Embla. I don't want to stay here either. But at the same time, I'm afraid of what they'll do to my family, to Levente, if they find out what I've done."

"If we do this, there's no going back," I point out.

"I know. But I've realized that if I don't do this, if we go back to how everything was before, that's not okay either. We can't run away from our problems, we have to face them. Even though I just want to protect them, it's not just out of love but out of fear. I can't just do what's expected of me just because it's easy. Nothing good in life is easy."

"We have to be careful," I say. "Is there anything more we can access through that IPKA?"

"Plenty. It's a gold mine of information."

"What happens to expelled students?"

Ivalde pulls up a list of the students who've been expelled from our grade. That's where Tricia is listed. I ask Ivalde to pull up her profile, and together we read about the reasons for her expulsion. No surprises. It's about her refusal to follow orders, especially regarding the use of technology. But then it says that she was mentally unstable. That she had severe mood swings. I think back and try to remember. I never thought it was strange before, but they're right that she could be extremely happy in some moments but then very bitter and sad in others. Were these strong mood swings? Ivalde scrolls down, and a report from the medical bay appears on the screen. Dated the same day she was expelled.

"Stop. Does that say what I think it says?" I gasp and read the words several times: "Death certificate."

"She's dead," Ivalde confirms.

"What?" I burst out and take the IPKA. I scroll up and down the screen and read. There's a picture of her from an autopsy. They've cut her up and sewn her back together. A large Y is formed on her chest that extends down the abdomen. I'm feeling nauseated.

"How?" Embla asks, and she gets closer to me and the screen so she can see too. My hands are shaking, but I manage to keep the IPKA still enough for me to keep reading.

"She drowned," I say. "Strange. Tricia wouldn't just leave and swim off alone." Then I see something that startles me even more. With two fingers, I zoom in on a signature.

"Malva Malimot," I whisper. "She signed this."

"She works in the med bay. Is it really that strange?" Embla shrugs. "I don't trust any of the teachers. Especially her."

"Why not? I like her," I say.

"When I was being taken care of there, after Ithmah, she asked me a lot of questions. It was almost like she was interrogating me and trying to get confirmation on whether I was a Tabia or not," says Embla.

"You didn't tell me that."

"I'm telling you now."

"Could that be why you had to stay in the med bay? Because Malva needed to interrogate you?"

Ivalde takes back the IPKA and continues reading the list of expelled students. He clicks on name after name and reads their reports. Then he stops at a name and points it out to us.

"What have you found?"

"Vera..." he says. "But wasn't she with you in Ithmah?"

"Yeah, she wasn't expelled. She died in the explosion that almost killed me..."

"Do you see any other students who died in the explosion on the list?" I wonder. Ivalde nods. "So it's true... Those who died in the crash... They're all listed as expelled... It was never an accident. It was planned."

"That's not all," Ivalde continues. "I've read about several of these expelled students. No one has been allowed to go home. With the exception of those who died in Ithmah, no one has left Bionbyr."

"Where are they then?" Embla asks skeptically.

"They're here. Dead or alive, they're still here. This student they've tested interrogation techniques on, this one they've done experiments on, she's dead, her too, but they're all here. They don't expel students, they find other ways to use us."

"I've had enough!" I burst out. "This... This... What they're doing here. It's unacceptable! I don't give a crap what they'll do to me if they find out what we're planning. I'm going to do everything I can to overthrow this horrible organization. We aren't terrorists. They are. We've seen it time and time again, but I've come up with excuses to defend their approach. But not anymore. Tricia. She wasn't mentally unstable. She tried to accept the reality she was in. As much as she could, she put on a mask of laughter and energy. So we wouldn't ask how she really was. I probably would have done the same if I'd been in her shoes. Ivalde. Surely you can save all this information somewhere? How can we get the information out to the public?"

"I don't know yet. We need to be smart about it."

"I'm not trying to pressure you. But do it. I need fresh air and a chance to sort through my thoughts a bit now," I say, leaving Embla and Ivalde in my room. Inside me, anger is boiling.

32

My thoughts were shattered that night. Are you starting to understand why? And why I have to do this? There's still so much you don't know. We've come to the conclusion that we can't do this alone. Before I tell you where I am, I have to finish what I've started. There are still secrets to reveal. There are names to expose.

When I return to the room after my walk, Ivalde is still there. He says that he and Embla talked openly about our mission.

"We stand behind you. Wholeheartedly," he assures me. I give him a hug. "We came to the conclusion that it was safest for you to have the IPKA."

He gives me the unregistered IPKA with a smile. Then he goes out into the corridor. I put it in the middle of my wardrobe. Tonight, I have no energy or desire to read more. It's been an informative evening, and if I were to take in anything more, I'd probably burst. I think of Tricia and feel the injustice within me. She was innocent.

They all were.

In the following days, we try not to behave suspiciously. We continue as usual even though it's really difficult to concentrate on what someone is saying. Our thoughts are on the IPKA and the source of information it constitutes. Every night I look at it, but I haven't found anything worth discussing with Ivalde and Embla yet. I tried to find something about Ithmah but no luck there. The only thing we have to go on is my vision where the President talked about the missiles, and since we can't export thoughts to the IPKA, we'll have to find something more concrete. We agreed to only get together when something bigger pops up.

During one of the days, it's announced that the President will return for the end of the year party. He's coming a month before graduation to supervise the work. It makes me uncomfortable to know that I'll have to be near him again.

My work with Marcell is progressing slowly. I understand now that I haven't really forgiven him after all, because I've really had to restrain myself to keep from hitting him every time we see each other. But then comes the day of our report, and I can no longer hold myself back.

"What did you say when you reported Embla?"

I understand that the question comes suddenly for Marcell because he gets a shocked facial expression.

"What do you mean? I just told them that I thought she was a Tabia," says Marcell.

"Did you give them examples of why you thought so?"

"Nothing specific, no, it was mostly just that I thought she was because I'd never seen her ill or injured. But I had no proof, of course."

"So, you didn't mention anything about the toolbox?"

"What toolbox?"

I can tell by looking at Marcell that the question is genuine. Didn't he know about it? Was he not around that day?

"I only said it to increase my chances of being admitted to the school, that's all. I've apologized."

If Marcell hadn't told them about the toolbox, the question remains as to how they found out. Did they have cameras at Sethunya after all?

"Forget it. Now let's just focus on this report. We don't need to talk about it again, okay?"

Marcell nods.

When I tell Ivalde and Embla about Marcell, they confirm my suspicions. Now we know for certain that it was no coincidence that Embla was selected. Like everything else, it was also planned.

"They really wanted to bring me here. I'm a guinea pig." Embla sits down on my bed. I sit next to her and embrace her. Her elbows are drilling into her thighs and she covers her face with her hands.

"They won't get away with this," I assure her. Empty words. There's nothing I can promise.

"I think I know how to broadcast everything," Ivalde says suddenly. "The information, I mean."

"Please give us some good news," Embla asks, turning her attention to him.

"Tarara has a radio tower. If we can get there, we can broadcast everything live. All the videos, pictures, documents. The authority won't be able to stop it."

"Is it just one tower?" I wonder.

"There are three towers," replies Ivalde.

"Okay, so where is this exactly?"

"The Edenites. They never wanted to have the tower there in the first place. I think that radio tower will be the easiest to sneak into. If we can get their help, that'll be a bonus."

"And how do we get there?"

"That's the next problem. But this is our best chance. If we can get there, anyway. I came across it when I was reading through some old articles and ran across one about the attack on the radio tower there. It's probably been about thirteen years since it happened."

"Thirteen years ago?" I just remembered that Nòi told me it was around then that his sister died in an attack. Could it have been the same event?

"Yes, terrorists had emerged from nowhere during a celebration held by the Edenites. They killed civilians and soldiers alike with the goal of reaching the radio tower. None of the rebels survived."

"Is that event included in the IPKA's database?" I wonder. Although it sounds just like Nói told me, I get a strange feeling in my stomach. Something isn't quite right. Ivalde hands me the IPKA and I get to read through a classified report from Authority.

"It's like you said," I sigh, even though the feeling in my stomach doesn't go away. "Or wait. Not really. They weren't rebels. It was the Authority that sent them there. Check this out. It says that the Authority provided these people with weapons from a company called Shiva Corp..."

"That's my dad's company," Ivalde gasps.

"So, you're saying that your dad provided these people with weapons to attack Tarara and take over the radio tower — that it was meant to look like rebels, but it was actually the Authority? Why?" Embla brings herself up to speed. "It's crazy to agree to something like that. Who would want to go on a suicide mission like that?"

"To direct suspicion and hatred towards a 'rebel' group. The Authority didn't want the tower at all, they wanted to spread fear. It's not unthinkable," I suggest. I think of Nói, who became a soldier to fight rebels. Fighting a lie. I have to tell him. But how can I do that without raising any suspicions about me?

"How do you feel about all this?" I ask Ivalde. He sits completely silent, staring at the floor. "You didn't know any of this about your dad?" Something about Ivalde's hanging head and sad look make me want to go over and give him a hug. He seems surprised at first, but then he puts his arms around me too. We sit together for a while, and I'm filled with warmth. Like we're a single entity. But then Ivalde breaks loose. He breathes violently, apologizes, and rakes his hands through his hair.

"So I've been thinking," Embla begins. "We've talked about it before, but now that we have this IPKA, is there anything to suggest that what happened at Sethunya was also planned?"

"Already checked. There's nothing about it in there," I say.

"Are you sure?" Embla presses. "Maybe Ivalde will have better luck."

I shoot her a meaningful glance.

"What? Out of all of us, he's the best with technology."

She's right. And after a few minutes, she proves to be right again.

"I found something. A report of a missile attack against Ithmah. On the orphanage," Ivalde reveals heavily.

I feel the tears welling up within me. I'm taken back to the war zone, to Nói dragging an unrecognizable child from the ashes. Who was it? Onni? My body folds, and I have to lean against the bed.

"It's my fault they're dead," Embla whispers after a while.

"Don't say that. That's what they want you to think. Don't let this break you down," I try tearfully. "We can't stop now. Do you remember what you always tell me? It's not about whether you want to or not, it's about taking action."

Embla nods firmly, but I can see that she's still sad. I can't blame her.

Suddenly my IPKA informs me that I've received a message from Nói. He wants to know if we can meet up before curfew. Actually, I'd rather stay with Embla and

Ivalde, but Embla thinks I should meet with him. That we should try to continue as usual. As if nothing's changed. As if we don't know what we know now. I know that I was the one who suggested it, but it's getting harder and harder to maintain the façade. Especially with Nói. For some reason, I find it harder to lie to him.

We leave my room, and this time Ivalde has the IPKA with him to do more research. Embla goes back to her room to be alone, and I head up to the park to meet Nói.

I'm so preoccupied with my thoughts that, at first, I don't even notice the golden bird sitting in one of the trees in the park. I react when it lets out that same scream I've heard twice before. I can feel goosebumps popping up all over my body. I stop and watch it for a while. Is it a mirage? What does it really mean? The thought is quickly forgotten along with the rest of the park when Nói comes walking towards me. I feel giddy when I see him. He straightens his blonde hair and gives me a warm hug. It feels much needed. Comfortable. We sit on the grass overlooking the sea. I look out over the water. An image flashes before me: of Tricia on the first day as she stood looking out over the sea from the balcony. Tricia, who's no longer with us.

"What is it?" asks Nói, who's obviously looking at me for something. I let out a nervous laugh.

"Nothing."

"So, there's at least one thing you're bad at."

"Oh really?"

"Lying."

"For real, it's nothing," I assure him. My heart is pounding. His hand finds mine. He caresses it with his thumb.

"End of the year exams are coming up. Only a few weeks left."

I nod. With everything that's happened lately, I haven't even thought about the test. It still feels too far away.

"Hey, Nói?"

"Mm?"

"Do you ever regret anything you've done? I mean on the job?" He's not answering. Probably because the question is sudden and no student, let alone a soldier, is expected to ask. I can see that he's wondering where the question is coming from, and above all, how to answer. I have no patience to wait, so I add: "I probably have too strong of a conscience. It would affect me too much to take a life. How do you take responsibility for something like that?"

"You can't. There's nothing you can do to take it back, no matter what. It may not be what you wanted to hear, but it's the truth."

"Are you not affected by it at all?" I have a hard time believing it.

"Yes, of course. But the only thing I can do is keep moving forward. The lives I take aren't innocent. It's a matter of life and death. Survival. They deserve it."

"You really hate Tabians and terrorists, huh?"

"Why wouldn't I? They've ruined so much for me. They've taken so much from me. My sister. My family."

"But it's not true." The words fly out of me before I have time to think about what I'm saying.

"What's not true?"

I can't lie to him. He can't keep basing his hatred on a lie. He has to know the truth.

"It wasn't rebels who attacked Tarara. It was people the Authority had sent there. It was planned."

"What are you saying? I don't believe you. Who told you that?"

I stop myself. I can't tell him about the IPKA or our plan. I've already said too much.

"After Ithmah, I did some research in the library. And then I came across an old article, so I put two and two together," I lie.

He drops my hand.

"There's something else you're not telling me."

"No, I promise," I try, and I can hear for myself how bad the lie is.

"It's okay, you can trust me. I love you."

I freeze.

"Uh, that came out wrong. Or, that's not what I mean. I do. But. Shit."

I'm confused. And *thankful*. His mistake makes him temporarily forget what I brought up. I take control of the situation.

"You love me?" I grab his hand again and hold it in both of mine.

"Is that crazy?"

I shake my head. "Not at all."

I give him a kiss. He loves me. Nói won't hurt me. Despite that, I feel like I can't really trust him. When we flee, he'll stay at Bionbyr. It's his life. A life with me is just a fantasy. But I'm not going to tell him that.

We say nothing more about the matter. Instead, we lie on our backs in the grass. I tuck myself into his arms in silence and look up at the sky. It feels strange that it's so peaceful when my mind is anything but calm. Would he still love me if he knew what we were planning? I remain in his arms until we have to get ready to go back before the curfew starts.

Just as I'm about to open the door to the common room, I feel my bladder about to burst, so I rush to the toilet quickly. As I sit there, I replay our conversation over and over again in my mind. Bionbyr has done well for *him*. I just hope that I won't regret leaving. If he loves me, would he report me to the school? Duty before love? I'm not so sure he would choose me.

I have to tell Embla tomorrow evening. About Nói's declaration of love. About my statement. And we have to come up with a plan soon on how to get out of here as soon as we've gathered enough information. Is it even possible?

I'm so caught up in my thoughts that I'm surprised when Ewind meets me at the door as soon as I enter the common room.

"Have you seen Ivalde? Like, he's not back and his stuff is gone!" she exclaims.

"What?" I burst out. "What?"

With determined steps, I march towards Ewind and Ivalde's room. The door is open, so I walk right in. Ewind is right. His stuff is gone. His wardrobe is empty. I rush to Embla's room and knock on her door.

She opens it with a jerk. "What?"

"Ivalde is gone!"

Like me, she has to see it with her own eyes. Embla dashes towards his room and also finds that his side of the room is empty. She looks at me uncertainly, and together we go to my room, where I take out my IPKA. Stressed, I look up the list for our year and feel a hole forming within me when I read Ivalde's name in red.

"He's been expelled."

Embla raises her hand to her mouth, as if to choke back a scream. I can't believe this. Is he dead? Is he being experimented on?

"We have to save him," Embla says.

"I agree. But if he's gone..." I begin, but I dare not finish the thought. Embla understands. *Ivalde had the stolen IPKA last.*

"What are we going to do now?!"

33

When I wake up the next morning, I get an unpleasant feeling. I had the most terrible dream last night. A dream where Ivalde, *our Ivalde*, had been expelled and that all the information we had found on the IPKA was gone. It would be devastating if it were true. If *they* had taken him, forced him to say things, punished him, tortured him to the point that death would be preferable.

But was it really a dream? I need to double-check to really be sure. I pick up my IPKA, where the list of first-years is already pulled up on the screen.

It was no dream. His name is still in red. I can't stop the tears. I crawl under my blanket again and pull it over my head. My body automatically forms into a ball, and I hug my pillow, feeling the dampness as it soaks up my tears.

After a long time, there's a knock on the door. I can't get up to open it. Whoever is standing there can knock forever if they want to. They've won. Bionbyr has finally managed to crack me. They take everything I love away from me. My family, my home, my friends. Why? What's the point of that?

"Freija?" I hear Embla's voice outside the door. "I know you're in there. If we don't go now, we'll be late for training."

I don't care about training. Whether it's swimming or not. I can't speak the words, but silently beg Embla to leave. Leave me alone. She'll be better off anyway; after all, they could take her too. Just to mess with me even more. If she's not with me, she's safe.

"Freija?" Embla is still stubbornly waiting. I hear a thud against the door. "Freija, if you can hear me, I just want to say… Look, I've always been your sister big, but no matter what, it's you who's always taken care of me. I'm not as good at thinking ahead as you are, I act based on my feelings, while you act according to reason. What I want to say is… I don't know. We can't give up. Okay?" Embla gives a heavy sigh. "Not yet."

My tears continued to flow. Deep down, I knew that she was right. At that moment, it was just hard for me to grasp. Why should we take on the responsibility of exposing Bionbyr? Why did everything have to fall on us? These were some of the thoughts swirling in my mind. But then there was another voice in the back of my mind. At first, it was just a whisper, and I had to really make an effort to hear it. It said that if we didn't do this – who would? We might not be able to reach everyone in the country, but reaching the right person could be crucial. Maybe we're chasing shadows, but it has to be better than not doing anything, right?

"Thank you," I whisper when I finally open the door and am met by two arms that embrace me in that familiar hug.

"We'll play according to their rules a little longer, and then we'll try to find Ivalde. It might not be too late yet, right?"

I nod.

"Do you think they took him because of…?" Embla asks.

"Yeah, I think so. I think we've started moving into deep water. We're approaching something they don't want us getting close to."

"Do you think they know?"

"I don't know how much they know, but I definitely think that Ivalde's expulsion has something to do with our snooping. We might get lucky. I know I haven't been the best example," I say shyly, "but we have to keep our heads on straight now and be extremely careful. Okay?"

"Absolutely."

"For now, we've got to keep this quiet. I know a place we can talk undisturbed later. We'll go there for lunch. Okay?"

Embla nods.

After our morning training, all of the students are directed to go down to the harbor to once again welcome the President when he arrives in the elegant amphibious car Victoria. Its silver exterior sparkles in the morning sun. Just like last time, Victoria pulls in and a gangway is pushed out of the side of the vehicle. The burgundy carpet is rolled out for the President. He smiles at us and waves a few times. All of the students give our standard greeting, and I have to force myself to join in. I remember how last time I was filled with such respect for the President, but now I'm filled with disgust.

Immediately after the welcome, we go to our new special courses. When Embla heads off to her Surveillance and Security class, I make my way to another classroom for War and World History.

Bern's blue hair looks streaky today. There are varying shades of blue and gray. In fact, even the skin on his face looks worn and blotchy. Almost to the point that it resembles the pruney texture of a raisin.

"Good morning, class," he greets us.

"Good morning, Domi," we greet him back. Next to me sits Ask. Bern wastes no time and immediately launches a hologram of our country, Ela, our world. But something feels wrong. It looks familiar but somehow not. Then I understand: it's not the present world that's displayed before us, but the old one. Just like Apsel's map in his office.

"This is how the map looked almost three hundred years ago. For many of you, this is probably the first time you're seeing this," Bern says. "In 2064, The Old Era, a worldwide war broke out. At that time, there were five great world powers. Each had access to nuclear weapons that formed the basis of the World War, which we today call the Atomic War. The same year – before the war – Eir Gersimi's powers were revealed, and an investigation was started all over the world as more and more of the Power People appeared. Several of them launched attacks against authorities and regents. They didn't want to be controlled. The first Tabian sanctuary was created in what we now call Jues. Near Calli—which, of course, wasn't there back then."

Bern swipes his hand against the hologram, and a video begins to play. It shows a large room where people stand queued in several different lines. The lines lead to desks where people in white suits and protective masks sit, stamping people's arms. A close-up of a person in the lead shows that the stamped tattoo is a number. Each person is assigned a number. A new identity.

The picture changes, and we get to see a hearing. There's a young, light-haired girl, certainly not much older than I am. She sits alone in a chair with people around her. Several of them are pointing weapons at her. She gazes directly into the camera with grave determination, but there's also exhaustion written on her face. They ask her about a crime she has committed. People have been killed. She doesn't respond, and then she's dragged away.

The picture changes again, and we get to see different images of some kind of labor camp, where the people who got numbers tattooed on their arms before are building something. A voice talks over the pictures and tells about the Power Peoples' behaviour and development. They describe the powers, dangers to society. The pictures change, and we see medical records, then the powers in action, experiments, torture, death. Bodies lying in piles.

I need to look away for a while. My gaze finds Ask again. He's sitting there like he's hypnotized, staring blankly at the video. His eyes are empty. Where have I seen eyes like that before?

"The major powers of the world couldn't agree on how they should handle the Tabia problem. Over the next three years, the attacks only increased. They caused the land to move with earthquakes, they caused great fires, floods. It was devastating. Three of the major world powers wanted to completely wipe out the Power People, while the other two wanted to research them more."

The room flickers in front of my eyes, and for a few seconds, everything is blurry. Somewhere I can still hear Bern talking, but it's getting harder and harder to concentrate on his voice.

"Instead, they wanted to use chemical weapons to anesthetize the population and capture the terrorists. The first nuclear bomb was fired by the major world power known as Korea. The others returned fire with their own weapons. The force of the attacks was too strong, and global warming increased immensely. The Disaster became inevitable," Bern says. "The Power People —"

Bern's voice fades away, and I become blind. I feel fluid running over my body. I hear something rushing. A roaring sound right in my ear. I can't breathe. There's no oxygen. I open my eyes reluctantly. I'm underwater! Fighting, I try to swim, but it's not possible. I can't move!

Suddenly, all the water disappears and I fall down on a floor. I'm in a room, and the water is splashing in every direction. I cough. My lungs are burning and I'm struggling to get air.

"I have to give him credit, brother," I hear a familiar voice say. "He can take much more than that other guy. What was his name again? Hakon? He couldn't take much."

Another voice gives a raw laugh. "Is it my turn now?"

"Very well," I hear the first person say. I quickly look up and see Bern standing in front of me. I try to get up, but I can't hold my own weight, so I fall back down to the floor with a thump.

"Are you tough now, Ask?" I hear the second voice again, and I suspect it belongs to Esbern. It comes from behind me. Suddenly, I hear myself screaming an inhuman scream. It's forced by the pain that comes from my back. It feels like I'm burning. Someone has set me on fire. The glow penetrates my skin, burning into my flesh. My eyes are watering, and my entire body feels strained. I try to writhe away, but I can't. The pain is too overwhelming.

Eventually, it becomes too much and I faint.

"She's waking up now," I hear someone say. I swallow hard and feel a throbbing headache inside my forehead. My body feels weak. My eyelids feel heavy. When I finally manage to pry them open, I can't even move my head. I sit completely still. Embla is here. Ewind too.

"What happened?" I mumble.

"You had a seizure in the middle of class and were brought here to the medical bay. How are you feeling?" says Ewind.

"I've been better," I say, trying to look at her, but I still can't. I get Embla's attention and try to make her understand that I need to talk to her. Alone. Thankfully, she catches my drift.

"Ewind, could you leave us alone for a while? Freija needs some rest," Embla apologizes and Ewind nods understandingly. As soon as she closes the door to my hospital room, Embla rushes over to me.

"What is it?"

"We were right," I say. "They have powers."

"Who?"

"Esbern. Bern. I saw. No, I got to experience Ask's punishment," I say, explaining how it felt like my body was burning. The terrible stench of burning flesh is still trapped in my nose. "It still hurts."

"Where?"

"My shoulder," I say, gently massaging it. It's actually really sore still. Instinctively, I bare my shoulder to look at it, but I can't see anything strange. I'm just pulling my shirt on again when Embla tells me to wait. She gently pulls it off and makes me lean forward a little.

"Crap," she says, patting me lightly on the back of my shoulder. I shiver with pain.

"What?" I say worriedly.

"You've got a mark there. It's big."

"How is that possible?" I ask. "I wasn't the one who was tortured. It was Ask. I was just in his consciousness."

"Maybe your power is evolving?"

"I don't want it."

Embla gently caresses me on the cheek.

"Can you listen for a moment?"

Reluctantly, I nod.

"I know where Ivalde is."

Some kind of energy comes over me. I sit up, forgetting that my whole body aches.

"Where?" I spit out.

"On the teacher's floor."

"How do you know that?"

"One of my special courses. I have what Ivalde had last week. So I saw it on the cameras. They have him in one of the rooms there."

"Are you sure?" I look into Embla's eyes.

"I don't know exactly where. All I saw was that they had him up there. In a corridor. That's all I know. But at least that's something."

"We have to go there. Immediately."

"Can you make it?"

"It's not about whether you want to or not..."

"Come on, then!"

I must have been knocked out for a long time since it's now evening. The school is uncomfortably quiet. The students are probably either in the family room or in the park. For us, it's perfect. This means that we won't have to explain anything when we sneak into the elevator that can take us up to the fifth floor.

"Dang it!" exclaims Embla. "I forgot we need a code to get there. What should we do now?"

"It's okay," I say as I press my left wrist against the dashboard. "Ivalde has already prepared me for this."

Thanks, Ivalde. We'll be there soon!

When we get off the elevator, Embla takes the lead. She asks me to follow, and we move forward carefully. She reads the signs above the doors, and I get more and more nervous that someone will find us here. If Embla could easily find this place on the surveillance cameras, it won't be long before someone comes.

"Over here!" Embla exclaims. "Do you think you can use that trick again?"

"I can try."

Carefully I press my wrist against the lock, and the door opens. We enter a dark room. I search for a way to turn on the lights, and – after some fumbling – I find a button. The room is illuminated. Although it's not really a room but more of a long corridor. Along the sides, there are additional doors, and at the far end, there's a sitting area by the balcony. We must be right above the great hall.

Embla walks over to a door and clicks on a screen next to it. She gets a name that none of us recognize.

She shrugs her shoulders. "Should we split up? He must be in one of these rooms."

I agree, and we each take a side of the corridor. Some rooms have names, others are empty. The fifth door I try has Ivalde's name, so I call out Embla. I open the door and we step inside.

It's empty.

"But he was... Where is he?" I gasp. "Embla, did we come too late?"

"I..."

I start searching the room. It goes quickly since the only thing in here is a table with two chairs on each side, a lamp hanging from the ceiling, and nothing more. No trace of Ivalde.

"Come on, let's go before someone finds us," Embla urges, and we head out.

Only to be met by Marcell.

"Marcell!" I burst out. I'm so shocked that, at first, I don't notice that he has a weapon aimed at us. Embla and I stiffen. Marcell raises a hand to his head and presses something behind his ear.

"I have them, they're in the Interrogation Corridor," Marcell reports. Shortly thereafter, Eilif arrives with Nói.

"What do we have here?" Eilif asks. "Students violating the rules? Take them to the basement."

Eilif goes ahead while Marcell and Nói both push their weapons into our backs and force us to exit the corridor. I grab Embla's hand and hold it tight. She squeezes back. Who knows what awaits us downstairs in the basement? When we stop at the elevator, she squeezes my hand twice and, just as if it was a planned signal, I surprise Marcell and she Nói by quickly moving to the side and hitting them. Although we have nowhere to go, we run back to the corridor where we were looking for Ivalde. We close the door behind us and rush over to the balcony. We have no chance. Marcell and Nói enter the corridor, and they're still armed. We have nowhere to go.

"I thought you were smart, Freija," mocks Marcell. "You're cornered."

I see Nói's weapon as he points it at me.

"Nói, are you really going to shoot me?"

He doesn't answer.

"You said you loved me. Then love who I am! I'm Freija Falinn, I'm a Tabia, I'm a rebel, and I'm just like you. Full of emotions, dreams. But if you think it'd better if I was dead, then shoot me. Shoot me!"

Nói lets out a scream. His voice is frightening.

"Come on, Nói, don't listen to her," Marcell says.

"And you, you're our family. You're our brother," I tell Marcell.

"You can stop right there because that doesn't bother me. I've found my family. It's here at Bionbyr. It's always been here," he says. His weapon is still firmly aimed at us.

"Good work, guys. If they don't want to come with us peacefully, they give us no choice. Shoot them," Eilif commands as she walks toward us.

"Nói," I cry. "Please."

There's a war of emotions in Nói's eyes. Maybe I was wrong about him after all. Maybe he can choose love over duty?

"Coward!" exclaims Marcell.

Everything goes so fast: Embla pushes me away, Marcell pulls his trigger, I hear a loud bang, and I scream. Embla flies into the balcony railing with a crash.

"Embla!" I scream and run to her.

"It's okay, I'm okay," she says weakly. She's had the wind knocked out of her. She leans over the balcony railing and gently tries to stretch herself. I look at her back and see that a bullet has barely penetrated her skin. The bullet pushes out of her and falls to the floor. "I have a plan. Do you trust me?"

I nod.

"Grab onto me and jump."

"What?"

"NOW!"

I grab onto Embla and she embraces me back. Together we jump over the balcony railing and fall. In the air, we rotate so that she's falling underneath me. I'm terrified. Her grip tightens around me.

"I love you, sister little," she whispers, closing her eyes.

Just as we hit the water below us, we're bathed in a huge white glow. We let go of each other and swim up to the surface. We're both unharmed. Not so much as a scrape. I hug Embla, but she quickly realizes that we don't have much time.

"We have to find a way to get out of here," she says.

We make our way up to the bridge.

"How?" I wonder.

"Maybe you can unlock one of these boats with your chip?"

"Maybe, I don't know."

"Let's try."

"Okay, which one?"

"Come on!" Embla calls, and we run off to the outer edge of the harbor. "One of the boats at the far end."

"Okay," I say. "How did you make that white light?"

"I wasn't the one who did it," Embla replies, looking surprised.

"No, I was," we hear a voice behind us say.

We quickly turn around to see Malva Malimot coming towards us.

34

"Malva..."

We look around desperately, but it's no use. We have nowhere to run, and even if we threw ourselves aboard one of the boats, it would still be too late. Malva marches up to us with determined steps.

"Victoria is a better choice. It's the only boat that's not connected to the school's security and alarm system. Come on."

Neither I nor Embla move from our spots. *What is going on?*

"Don't just stand there, there's no time to lose. Come on, now!" Malva commands us. Embla and I look at each other with puzzled expressions, but then we both hurry after Malva. Victoria is very close and, without any fuss, Malva is able to unlock it and let us aboard. Malva disconnects the mooring, and I'm just closing the door when something comes rushing towards me and grabs my wrist. I scream from the pain as I fall hard against the bridge.

"Ow!" I burst out when the thing that grabbed me tightens its grip. I look down at my wrist and see that some kind of metallic snake has wrapped around me. The snake extends towards the school, and the other end of the snake is attached to Eilif.

"You're not getting away that easily," Eilif screams at us and starts pulling me towards her. The snake gets shorter and shorter. Like it's receding into her body.

"Freija!" I hear Embla screaming. An engine starts. My head spins. Someone grabs my feet, and I'm lifted into the air. At one end, Eilif has me in a firm grip, and at the other end, someone else is pulling. It's Embla.

"Let her go!" Embla growls. She suddenly loses hold of me and gives out a loud groan. Eilif's other arm has also been extended and is pushing Embla away. I hit the ground hard and get dragged towards Eilif by her metal arm.

The same white light that enveloped us when we fell surrounds me once more. I don't know if it's the light or Eilif that's causing me to hover, but once again, I'm hanging in the air, unable to do anything. I feel like a twig in the wind. At any time, I could be broken. My eyes are full of tears. The air is starting to disappear from my lungs.

"Eilif, drop her!" I hear Malva shouting.

Eilif laughs. In the corner of my eye, I see her other arm projecting more metal. This time, the metal isn't tethered but acts more like gun bullets. She shoots the metal from her body towards Malva. I feel Eilif's grip loosening around me. Is it because she's distracted, or is Malva doing something? It feels like I have a warm blanket surrounding me. It's soft. I relax.

Finally, I fall to the ground again headfirst. I scream.

"Come on, Freija!" Malva shouts to me. "I don't know how long I can keep this up!"

It's not easy to get back to my feet. I feel dizzy. Suddenly, I feel a hand on me. I jerk away and try to escape.

"Freija! It's me!" I hear Embla say.

My vision finally stabilizes, and – with Embla's help – I get back on my feet. We run towards Victoria. Malva has created some kind of shield around us. Eilif's metal balls can't reach us. I dare not look back. Embla and I step aboard, and Malva rushes over to close the door. She steps toward the driver's seat and accelerates.

"How do we get out?" Embla screams and points to the bridge that's still up. It's the one that's pushed in when boats go in or out of the harbor.

Malva doesn't respond but accelerates even more. The bridge explodes into a thousand pieces. We hear thumping against the walls. Is it the bridge falling on us? No, this is something else. How could the bridge be holding us back when we just smashed through it? We're barely moving. I look out the window. It's Eilif trying to reel us in with her metal arms. Malva hits the gas, but nothing happens. A scraping sound comes from above. Eilif is on the boat and, as if someone's attached a rocket to the boat, we suddenly begin to fly over the surface of the water. Malva, Embla, and I are all knocked back by the sudden acceleration that Eilif caused when she released her grip on us, slingshotting the whole boat forward.

Malva gets back on her feet and takes control of the boat again. The threat is still above us. We can hear her heavy steps.

"I don't give up that easily," Malva mutters to herself. "Embla, do you see that box?"

Embla looks at the box Malva is pointing to and nods.

"There's a rifle that fires electrical bombs. I want you to step out on the deck and shoot Eilif. Don't miss."

Embla braces herself, walks determinedly towards the box, and picks up a weapon.

"Is this it?"

"Yes, hurry up!"

I see Embla wrestling with the idea of having to shoot someone, but in the end, she realizes that she has to.

"It won't kill her," Malva assures Embla, as if she knows exactly what Embla is thinking.

"Okay, I won't miss," Embla says decisively and goes out onto the deck. I move to follow.

"No, Freija, you must stay here!" Malva orders me. "Listen to me. Stay here."

"But she might need help!" I dash after Embla despite Malva's orders.

We've already moved a long way from Bionbyr. I can still see the school, but it's getting smaller and smaller in the distance. I don't have time to stop and enjoy the view when I see the weapon Embla took with her lying on the deck. Some distance away, Eilif stands with a chokehold on Embla, throttling her with the metallic appendages. I freeze.

"Stay there, girl," Eilif warns me. Embla's face has turned completely blue. "If you come any closer, it's goodnight for this creature. She may be bulletproof, but how long can she go without air?"

"What do you want?"

"Turn the boat around. Things look pretty bad for you now, but if we can cooperate, I can help alleviate your punishment."

"And if we refuse?"

"Then I can't do much. You won't make it out of this alive if you continue. You know it."

I act lightning fast. I throw myself at the weapon and manage to pick it up in one fluid motion. It slides perfectly into my grip.

"Let her go!" I order loudly. Eilif laughs dryly.

"You really don't learn…"

Eilif makes an effort to catch me, but I parry and throw myself on the ground behind the cockpit. The weapon is still in my grip. I lean my back against the cockpit and breathe deeply. Eilif stands still, and Embla is suffocating more and more with every second I hesitate. If I don't do it now, it'll be too late. I roll out so that I'm fully visible, stabilize myself with one leg, point the rifle at Eilif, and shoot an electric bomb that hits her straight in the chest. A wave of electricity passes through her, she vibrates, drops her grip on Embla, and falls into the water. Embla falls lifelessly onto the deck.

"Embla!"

I put my head against her chest and hear her heart beating. I can see that she's still breathing. She's alive.

"Embla?"

"Yeah... I'm... okay..." Embla whispers. I wipe away the unchecked tears that are flooding down my cheeks.

"Come on," I say, helping her back into the cabin. She can barely walk by herself and has to lean on me. I put her down in one of the sofas pushed up against a wall.

"I don't want to lose you too," I sob.

I hear a groan, but it doesn't come from Embla. I look up and glance around in confusion. I gasp loudly when I see who is lying on another sofa. His uniform is largely torn, and I can see the burn marks on his neck and arms.

"Ivalde!" I throw myself at him and give him a hug.

"Forgive me..." he whimpers. "I'm sorry..."

"What happened?"

"They found me... I don't know how. They took the IPKA."

"Who?"

"Esbern... and Bern. They took me to some room. They... I don't know what they did. They burned me... over and over. And then... I don't know. I thought I was drowning. Andor also came..."

"Take it easy now, Ivalde, everything will be fine," I try to tell him.

"No..." says Ivalde. His eyes are filled with tears as he says:

"I... I told them everything. It hurt so bad, I just wanted them to make it stop. They know everything about the IPKA, about you, everything."

"It doesn't matter. We're not there anymore."

"But how?" He asks.

"I picked you up," says Malva. "Both you and Aariel."

"Aariel?! He's here too?" I look feverishly around me and see Aariel lying on a pillow snuffling.

"Can anyone explain to me what's happening?" I scream out. My head is about to explode.

"I'll tell you everything. But first, you have to sit still," Malva tells me. She grabs my arm and reveals a knife.

"What are you going to do with that?"

"This is going to hurt," Malva tells me, making a cut in my wrist with the knife. A stinging pain causes me to bite my tongue.

"Ah! A clean removal," Malva says, plucking out the chip in my wrist. Then she turns to Embla and Ivalde. Embla starts to regain consciousness, and I rush to her side to make sure she's okay. She's alive. That's what matters.

"I have to do it to you too," Malva says, cutting out Embla and Ivalde's chips as well. Embla allows her. Then she places synthetic skin on our wrists and throws the chips into the sea.

"Can... Can you tell us now?" I ask again. "What's really going on here?"

"My name is Malva Malimot," says Malva. "But that hasn't always been my name. And this appearance," she gestures to her face, "hasn't always been my appearance. Once upon a time, I was a different person. I was the President's general practitioner."

"Even though you're a Tabia?" I ask.

"The President has other Tabians in his staff. Ones with powers he can use, you see."

"No, I really don't understand anything. Are you going to take us to him now?" Embla clenches her fists.

"I think I've done enough to prove that I'm on your side, don't you think so?"

"You could have done all that just to make us trust you. At least, I don't trust you," Embla makes clear to Malva.

"I *worked* for them," sighs Malva. "You know what, I'll tell you everything, I promise. But we're not safe yet. I'll tell you everything when we get there."

"No, tell me now," says Ivalde, who seems to have regained his strength. He's holding the weapon I used on Eilif. He's aiming at Malva. His eyes are full of rage. "Who are you?"

"They can still track this boat. We're not safe, we must—"

"WHO ARE YOU?!" screams Ivalde. Saliva flies out of his mouth. Even I'm shocked at his outburst. "NOW!"

"Okay," Malva sighs. "Okay. Let me put Victoria on autopilot, and I'll tell you. It's not a short story."

"We have time," Ivalde says.

"Okay." Malva doesn't take her eyes off Ivalde. "Lower the weapon, Ivalde."

"I don't think so," Ivalde says firmly.

"Okay." Malva goes to the driver's seat and presses a few buttons. She comes back and sits down in front of us. "Have you learned about the monitoring crystals?"

"Yes," replies Embla. "I told them. The crystals are placed under the eyelids and monitor criminal thoughts. What does that have to do with anything?"

"That'll save us some time, anyway. If I'm going to tell this story, then I have to tell it from the beginning. Is that alright?" We nod. "Good. The President's press officer is the one whose power controls the crystals."

"He's a Tabia?" I ask.

"Yes," sighs Malva. "If I'm going to tell you, I don't want you interrupting, okay? Just listen."

We nod again.

"Erikk Aalarik and his wife Gerda were the President's top employees. They chased terrorists, criminals, potential criminals, and planted the crystals in all of them. Gerda could anesthetize them with a single touch, and Erikk inserted the crystals while they were unconscious. With these crystals, he was able to reflect the person's inner thoughts, dreams, even their emotions. The host isn't aware of the crystals at all. I'm not sure if they even know if they have them or not. Gerda developed a machine that could receive transmitted information from these crystals, and that allowed Erikk to be relieved from monitoring each individual himself. She was very technical, Gerda. She was an inspirational woman," Malva takes a short break. She seems to be forcing herself to hold back tears. "Nowadays, they've also come up with a way to mass-produce these crystals, so Erikk doesn't have to do it personally. But before all that, before mass production and the machine, Gerda and Erikk used to travel with me and two men, Tamir and Fridtjov, on missions around our country to personally find the suspects. Tamir and Fridtjov were our protectors, and I was their doctor in case something were to happen. We bought peace with the crystals. That's how our President was elected. He promised soldiers, he promised peace, and he promised to put a stop to acts of terrorism. He lived off of people's fear. Back then, we didn't know that he was the one behind it all. The crystals not only have the ability to reflect the host's thoughts, but they can also control them. The machine that Gerda developed could also command people to do things they wouldn't normally do."

"That's how the Authority gets people to join in on suicide missions? Like those people in Ithmah?" I'm beginning to understand.

Malva nods. "When Gerda, now pregnant, found out how it really was – that we not only planted crystals in criminals but also innocents, that we were behind most of the criminal activity we were supposed to be preventing – she wanted to quit. She didn't want her children to grow up in such a world. But resigning from a mission given to you by the President is no simple task."

Malva stops again. There's a beep from the dashboard. She walks up to it and checks something.

"Sorry, I know I said I'd tell you everything, but we're not safe yet. They're trying to track us right now, and it won't be long until they know exactly where we are. You've seen what Bionbyr can do," she says.

"Let me have a look," says Ivalde, and he goes over to Malva. "But don't think you're off the hook just like that."

"I know."

Ivalde sits down in the driver's seat and inspects the controls.

He sighs. "I really need the bag I packed in case we had to flee suddenly. I'm guessing none of you brought it in the rush to escape?"

"It's here," Malva says and walks away towards Aariel. Behind the sugar glider, the bag is leaning against the wall. She hands it to Ivalde, who skeptically accepts it. "I've been keeping tabs on you."

Ivalde roots around in the bag for a moment and pulls out the black memory card. He puts it against the dashboard and green text appears on a screen. I don't understand what it says, but Ivalde seems to be able to read it like a picture book. While he mutters to himself, perhaps walking himself through the process, Malva goes back to the place she was sitting before. It's not long before Ivalde is back too.

"I sent out a fake GPS signal. They shouldn't be able to track us now," he says, picking up the rifle again.

"That's not necessary," says Malva. Ivalde doesn't lower it. "Well. Ela's people believe that they live in a secure society because they know that the President's elite force and EMES soldiers save the day before anything bad even happens. Of course, it can't happen every time, and therefore they make sacrifices. Just occasionally, to remind the people that the danger still exists."

"Are you saying Ithmah was a sacrifice?" Embla snaps.

"What happened in Ithmah was unfortunate, but yes. That's how they operate. With force. They want to keep people in check. In that particular case, they wanted to keep *you* in check, or push you until you were completely out of control so you would reveal yourself as a Tabia."

Embla lowers her gaze. Malva's words are harsh, but we know she's telling the truth. Is this hatred that I feel burning inside me?

"You still haven't told us who you are. You're just telling us things we already know," Ivalde says impatiently.

"I asked not to be interrupted, and I already warned you that I had to tell it from the beginning," Malva says calmly. "If I'm going to tell you everything, I need you to let me do it. Please," she looks at Ivalde, who nods. "Gerda talked to Erikk about it during a mission in Vallis. He asked her to reconsider. He also knew that it was dangerous to defy the President, and he didn't want anything to happen to the unborn child. It was due to arrive any day. So Gerda came to me. We made a plan to escape, but we couldn't manage it alone. Especially since Gerda was pregnant. We both trusted Tamir, and he promised that he would help us. Fridtjov tried to pursue us, but we managed to shake him off. In the end, we managed to get away from Vallis. But we didn't get far. A few miles outside, in a kind of forest, it became too much for Gerda. She was about to give birth. We made a fire and burned everything that could be traced back to us. Tamir and I helped Gerda give birth. But the effort took her life."

"There were two," I say half-audibly. "Right? There were two children?"

Malva nods.

"How do you know that?" asks Embla.

"Because I was one of them. Isn't that right?"

Malva nods again.

"We buried Gerda near a lake, took the twins, and continued to flee south. We knew we were being pursued. We decided to split up. It was too risky to be together. That's why we made the terrible decision to separate you and your brother."

"My brother?"

"Tamir fled northwest and I continued south. I ended up in Ithmah, and there I met Apsel. I knew who he was because I had met his mother in the Tabian sanctuary. I knew I could trust him. After that, I had to disappear. I changed my appearance and became Malva Malimot."

"And my brother?"

"Tamir took the child to Pari."

I turn to Ivalde. He has also begun to understand. His cheeks are wet with tears. His hands are shaking.

"My brother," I whisper.

35

I fall silent. All this time, he's been my brother. We've gotten to know each other, though we never knew how close we really are. Ivalde has sunk down onto the couch. The rifle is next to him. He no longer cares about targeting Malva. He's turned away from all of us.

"Before Bionbyr, I worked at the hospital in Vallis, and many, many years ago, I worked with Myra Manar—until she became a teacher in combat training. We've been in contact since then, and this summer, she came to Vallis to greet me. When I heard from her that they had found recruits from Ithmah, I was surprised. It's rare for soldiers to be selected from there. The timing seemed to match your legal age, and I was worried. I snuck into her IPKA and saw your name, Freija," Malva continues. "Myra helped me get a job at Bionbyr, but she never knew that the reason behind it was so I could keep track of you. I must say that none of you have made it particularly easy for me. I've had to delete videos from the surveillance system, edit your records, make false reports—so that nothing would be noticed by the administration. And him!" Malva points at Aariel. "What were you thinking, Freija? Don't you understand what the consequences would have been if he'd been discovered?"

"Well, he didn't get caught," I say with a distinct pout, but deep down, I know that she's right.

"No, he didn't, because I saw him before anyone else did. He has a shield all around him. He can only reveal himself to you, something I designed. That's my power: to create and manipulate protective fields. Well. I think that's enough for the moment. You're tired and need to rest. We'll be there soon."

"Where are we going?" I wonder.

"To meet up with someone I trust," replies Malva, and she goes to the driver's seat.

I sit next to Embla on the sofa and give her a hug. It's so nice to feel her reassuring touch. I become relaxed and calm. Ivalde sits by himself, staring at the wall. He hugs his knees and rocks back and forth. He's completely silent. I also have no idea what to say anymore. What to think. It feels like my whole life has been a facade. Or a lie. Embla doesn't say anything either. She looks thoughtful. There's something she doesn't quite understand.

"What is it?"

"Can we really trust her?" whispers Embla. "How can we be sure that what she's saying is true? Her name was on Vera's death certificate. And Tricia's. Something she didn't bother to mention."

I nod weakly. There are many holes in her story. But why would she come up with such a fantastically intricate cover-up? What's the point?

"Can we really be sure that Ivalde is your brother?"

"I don't know. But I feel it somehow. That it's true."

"And she hasn't told me why they wanted me, or rather, why they wanted you. Why was that so important?" Embla continues. I shrug. I look at Ivalde again. He's fallen asleep. He must've been exhausted. I'd like to check his injuries. Maybe Malva already had a chance to do that right after she picked him up? I don't know. But I don't want to wake him right now. He needs to sleep. I'll take a look at it when he wakes up later. I feel my own eyelids getting heavier and heavier...

"We're here," says Malva. She shakes me and I wake up with a jerk. She goes back to the driver's seat and clicks a few buttons, and a map pops up to show our surroundings. We're surrounded by cliffs, and it seems difficult to navigate. Malva slows down the boat.

"This place looks completely deserted. Does anyone really live here?" Embla mumbles to me.

The hologram guides the boat through the sharp cliffs. It's a maze of stone, water, algae, and moss. We seem to be entering a cave that extends deep into a mountain. The hologram shows us the right path. After a while, we arrive at a pier and everything seems to get brighter. There's a dim light coming from further into the cave, a good distance from the pier.

We stop. Malva steps out, docks the boat, and leads us ashore. Aariel is allowed to stay on the boat. My eyes adjust to the darkness, and I can see a small rowboat moored on the other side of the bridge. It bobs softly in the water. The pier is on a beach, and further up the shore, there's a small patch of garden beds. It's quite windy here, and there's no way the sun could extend all the way down here. The plants must be genetically modified.

Malva asks us to follow her. We walk towards the light further back into the cave. The light comes from a fire. The flickering flames create shifting shadows on the walls. The smoke stings my nose. Next to the fire is a table with a chair. Further back, there's something that looks like a bed space: a couple of blankets surrounded by small stones. Along the walls are shelves with jars, kitchen utensils, buckets, wooden boxes, fabrics, lanterns, and wood. There are large drawers too, some of which are open and reveal the food inside. On one wall, there are hooks bored into the rock wall where dried fish hangs.

We hear footsteps coming towards us. They echo through the cave. A shadow fills one of the walls, and the closer the steps get to it, the smaller the shadow becomes until we see a man dressed in a thick blanket that was once probably light in color but is now quite covered in brownish-grey splotches. A hole has been cut for his head, and around the waist, he's tied a thin rope.

He stops when he sees us. Then he bursts into a big smile and briskly makes his way to Malva.

"Telma!" he shouts loudly and gives Malva a hug. He lifts her up grandly and then sets her down again. I whisper "Telma?" to Embla, and she shrugs her shoulders.

"Good evening, Byrghir. I'm sorry to have to get straight to the point. But we need your help," says Malva.

Byrghir's face immediately turns serious. "Of course. Anything for you, Telma."

He asks us to sit down and points to the table. He quickly retrieves some boxes for us to sit on. I get to sit on the chair. It's rickety, and I have to be careful when I sit down. On the table stands a vase with a wilted flower.

"Are you hungry? Thirsty?" Byrghir asks and walks up to a shelf to grab a saucepan. From a can, he fills the saucepan with water, tosses in some herbs, and suspends it above the fire to cook.

"I haven't seen you since that night. How long has it been? Fifteen years now? More?"

"Seventeen. I'm still endlessly grateful for what you did," Malva responds, receiving a hunk of bread offered by Byrghir. He also offers some to us. Embla and I gratefully accept it, and Ivalde tries his utmost to smile too. I throw an understanding smile at him, but he doesn't see it. He's avoiding my gaze. We haven't eaten in a long time, and the sight of the food reminds us of how hungry we are.

"You can serve yourself," he explains, pointing to the earthen plates. He goes to the saucepan to check out the herbal tea and decides it's done. He pours tea into four cups and serves everyone except himself. "Well, what can I do for you, Telma?"

"Why does he call you Telma?" Embla bursts out sourly. "What is this? What are we doing here? Who is he?"

"That was my name when I worked for the President," Malva explains. "Telma Layna."

Malva seems to understand that we won't be able to move on until she's answered all the questions we have. She blows on her tea and takes a sip. "Fridtjov and Erikk were still looking for us. Of course, they had informed the President and his elite force. Esbern found me one night after I left Freija at the orphanage. He tortured me with his fire for information, but I gave him nothing. In the end, he left me to die on the side of the road. He didn't care that it was a busy road and that someone was bound to find my body in the morning. I remember lying there with burns all over my body, waiting for death. I didn't even feel the pain anymore, and I knew I was going to die at any moment. Then Byrghir found me. He healed me."

"So, Byrghir...?" I can't even ask the question.

Byrghir walks up to the table and moves his hands over the withered flower. Within a few seconds, he has made it bloom beautifully.

"My face was too disfigured, even for Byrghir. He managed to create a new face for me. With the new look, I adopted a new identity, a new name, and a new life. I ended up in Vallis and started working in the hospital there. With

Byrghir's help. I'm grateful for my new appearance because I haven't been able to shake the feeling that Fridtjov is still looking for me. Even after seventeen years. He always completes his assignments."

Embla continues her interrogation by questioning the information about Ivalde. "How do you know for sure that Ivalde is Freija's twin?"

"I will never forget the children I helped bring into the world. I see them as clearly in front of me as I see you right now." Malva turns to Ivalde. "The mark on your face is a birthmark. That's how I know. There's no doubt about the fact that you are Freija's brother."

"But nobody knew who I really was except you and Tamir," says Ivalde, disappointed. "When you told me, you kept saying that Gerda, our... *mom*... was pregnant with a baby. That they wanted to protect the *child*. Not the children. Didn't Erikk know about me? Didn't Gerda know about me?"

Malva shakes her head.

"That's what I thought," Ivalde sighs, lowering his head. He hasn't touched the bread or the tea.

"I'm sorry, Ivalde," Malva says. Ivalde shrugs his shoulders lightly. Indifferently. "Well, Byrghir, I've found out something I think you —"

"Wait, I'm not done," Embla interrupts. "You still haven't told us why your name was on the death certificates of our friends. Or why Bionbyr wanted me so badly."

"It's not about you at all, Embla," Malva says coldly. It's clear that her patience is beginning to run out. Embla puffs up over her tone. "They wanted Freija. They wanted to toy with her. But they made the mistake of confusing you with her. Everything goes back to an incident that happened at the Sethunya Home for Wayward Children when a toolbox broke your arm. They saw it. After that, the suspicions began to grow that they had finally found the missing child. They've looked everywhere, searched much more than your orphanage. And my name is on all of Bionbyr's autopsy reports and death certificates this past year because I was in charge of the medical bay. There's nothing more to it than that."

"Hmph," Embla snorts and crosses her arms.

"Malva? About Tricia. It said she drowned, but how is that possible?" I wonder.

"Bern can control water. They practice their powers on expelled students."

I flinch. Images from Ask's torture reappear in my mind. I got to experience their *practice* firsthand.

"It's late, and we're all tired. Byrghir, we'll have to pick this back up this tomorrow, I'm afraid. I have no energy to continue. We can sleep in Victoria," Malva says objectively.

Malva arranges the sofas for sleeping. We each get one. Embla and Ivalde start snoring immediately. Before Malva goes to sleep, she goes over to the dashboard and double-checks something. I look out the window and see Byrghir's cave. The fire is still glowing, but it's not as bright as before. He's probably gone to bed too. Who is he? Malva seems to trust him with her life. Should we do that too? I'm not so sure. Why has he stayed hidden here? He seems to have been here for many years. So he might not work for the Authority. *We'll see what they say tomorrow*, I think.

Aariel bounds up to me. He makes a pitstop at the bag Ivalde packed back when... I don't even know how long ago it was. My perception of time is completely off course. I open the bag. There are provisions and... I giggle. Some heels. I pick up one of the shoes and caress it. It's reminiscent of Freda the goat's fur. A tear falls when I think of the orphanage and how she didn't survive the attack either. I hug the shoe and look at Ivalde. *My brother.* It's a whole new chapter.

Something gleams in the bag and catches my attention. These are the bracelets I found on my birthday last year. Joy blooms warmly within me. I pick up both of them and slip one onto my wrist. I put the other one next to Embla's head so she'll see it when she wakes up.

My fatigue has become palpable, so I lie down in bed too. I fall asleep as soon as my head hits the pillow. But instead of the sweet release of sleep, a dream awaits me. A vision. I'm back at Bionbyr. The President and the headmaster are in front of me. My head is bent, and I can see my metallic appendages. I'm seeing through Eilif's eyes. *She survived.*

"...very disappointed," I hear Daegal say. We're in Andor's office.

"They had help." The voice comes from me, but it belongs to Eilif. I'm just a visitor, just like before.

"No excuses," the President says calmly. "I'm guessing they can't be tracked anymore?"

"They must have taken out the transmitters," Andor says. "We lost their signal off the coast of Eidyllion."

"How much do they know?"

"We confiscated the unregistered IPKA and were able to trace their steps. They know about The Nine Elements, but it's unclear how much. They don't know anything about Ludwig."

"Good," the President says, exhaling. "Do I need to remind you what would happen if you risked the plan?"

"No, Master."

"All the blood I've sacrificed has been for a purpose. Whatever you may think, I don't like wasting human life. Don't make me change my principles, Andor."

The President is approaching the headmaster. When he stops, their noses are almost touching each other.

"I created you. I can also annihilate you. Find the girl."

I wake up with a jerk. I instinctively pat down my body to make sure I'm me again. Ivalde is snoring on his couch. I'm back on the Victoria. I lie down again but find it hard to fall asleep. In the end, exhaustion overcomes my unease.

I was wrong about the sunlight not reaching the cave. There's a hole high up in the roof of the cave that lets in enough light to wake us up.

In the morning light, we can see Byrghir's crops better. They're bigger than I first thought. Just like the orphanage's fields, there are also beehives and some goats roaming around loosely.

Embla and I help Byrghir prepare breakfast. Goat cheese with honey and salad. He brings out the bread again and we heat some milk over the fire. After a while, Ivalde comes down from the Victoria and sits down at the table. Malva is nowhere to be seen.

I watch Ivalde. We haven't had a chance to talk since Malva broke the news about our parents. There will be time for that later. I get the feeling that he needs time to process it, and I can understand that. At least I've been prepared for the idea of having a sibling. To him, it came as a shock. I don't want to pressure him.

When we've almost finished eating, Malva comes and joins us. She's taken off everything except a light shirt and her pants. In her hand, she holds an IPKA.

"Isn't that traceable?" I wonder.

"This is an unregistered IPKA. It belonged to Tricia," explains Malva. "I took it after she was... *expelled*. She never activated it."

"But..." I say.

"But?" Malva frowns.

"Tricia sent me a message after she was expelled..." It's enough for me to see Malva's expression to understand. "Except it wasn't her. Right?"

Malva shakes her head and I sigh heavily. When Malva puts the IPKA on the table to tuck into her breakfast, I see something sparkle on her back. Curious, I lean forward to get a better look. It's a tattoo of a bird. *It's gold.*

"Malva? What's that tattoo?" I sputter.

"Huh? Oh, that, it's a tattoo of a Bird of Fate," explains Malva. When it's clear that I don't understand what she means, she adds: "It's a bird that shows up for a person when something big is about to happen."

"Surely that's an understatement?" says Byrghir. "They show when a monumental change will happen in a person's life."

"But that's just a story," Malva adds.

I nod without saying anything. I have no desire to tell them about it right now. Not when there are other things to think about.

"Telma, or *Malva*, now you must tell me what it was you wanted to tell me last night. I'm so curious," says Byrghir.

"Well, I need your help to get us to the Lynxes," Malva says hastily.

"That's not possible," Byrghir replies.

"I wouldn't ask you if it wasn't important," Malva continues. "I've found something, and I – *we* – need their help."

"Stop!" I burst out. "I'm getting tired of going on trips I didn't sign up for. Before I go anywhere. Before I find out any more secrets. Before... You have to start communicating with us. I, at least, can't keep up!"

"I agree. What are the Lynxes? I remember we came across the word in the IPKA but there was no explanation," Embla adds.

"The Lynxes as the Catfolk," explains Malva.

Embla laughs out loud. But she's the only one. Malva and Byrghir are as serious as before.

"You're joking, right? The Catfolk are just a legend. They're just fairy tales!" says Embla.

"They exist. They have their own town outside of Bergh, up in the mountains," says Byrghir. "The Authority keeps them secret. And if you want proof, you can check out the bracelet you're wearing."

"This?" I ask, picking up the bracelet. I run my thumb over the inscription "Fdokr." "Do you know what it means?"

"Of course! It's Lynx for 'strong.'"

I ask Embla to lift up her bracelet, and Byrghir says it means "Brave." All this time, I've believed that they were just made up words. So, does Byrghir mean this is a real language? Catfolk are real too? The idea tickles me.

"Why do you want to go there, Malva?" I ask.

"I can't give you a complete answer. It's just a feeling I have. It has to do with The Nine Elements," Malva answers.

"We've also read a little about that," Embla says.

"And Andor mentioned it in my dream," I reveal.

"What dream?"

"Last night. The President isn't happy about what we've done, and he's worried. Andor mentioned that we had come across information about the elements, but he didn't know how much we know. They also mentioned someone. Ludwig. Do you know who that is?"

"No idea," says Malva. Byrghir also shakes his head.

"We need to go to Bergh to talk to the chief about the elements. I suspect that at least Esbern, Bern, and Eilif have received their elements. I don't know who the other six are. And if all of them work under the President..." explains Malva.

"This is serious," Byrghir says, and immediately seems determined. "Okay, I'll help you. But it won't be easy."

"I don't really understand everything yet, Freija, but if there's any way to stop more children from losing their parents, I want to do it. For Apsel's sake."

I grab Embla's hand and squeeze it twice. She squeezes back. "I also feel like it's the right thing to do. No idea what this is about, but it feels right. What do you say Ivalde?"

Ivalde still hasn't said anything. I feel a sting of sadness when I see his hesitation. He still has his family. It wouldn't be that strange if he wanted to go back to Pari, to them.

"I'm still on board. If there's anything I can do to stop the corruption that exists in our world, I want to do it. We can go to Bergh to see if they can help us in any way. But otherwise, we have to get to Tarara and the radio tower. If we can broadcast what we know, it might help somehow, right?" says Ivalde. "And even if it doesn't do anything, it's better than not doing anything at all. If I die... If we die, then at least we'll know that we tried anyway."

I know that a lot of what you've listened to is hard to come to terms with. I've been there myself. What we now know is worse than we could have ever imagined. Our journey is far from over. The President has loyal servants everywhere. To overthrow an Authority is no easy task. We can't do it alone. To all of you hearing this, you may be our last chance.

Help us.

END OF
BOOK 1

ABOUT THE AUTHORS

Marcus Tallberg, born in 1989 in Trollhättan, Sweden, is an author, lecturer, entrepreneur, and publisher.

His debut book Bögjävel (Faggot) was published 2008.

In 2015, Marcus published the book Splittrat Glas (Shattered Glass), based on his own family history, and in 2017 came the book Att vara Alice (Being Alice), which is about the transgender Alice.

He has also published the children's book Dinosaurien Ty får en vikarie (Ty the Dinosaur and the Substitute Teacher), published in 2019.

Webpage: www.marcustallberg.se
Instagram: marcustallbergofficial

Elin Frykholm is a literary scholar that loves history in all kinds of shapes.

She loves stories about fantasy- and science fiction, as well as contemporary family relationships.

The Orphan is her debut.

Instagram: elin_frykholm

CPSIA information can be obtained
at www.ICGtesting.com
Printed in the USA
BVHW032322241120
594169BV00001B/6

9 789198 654745